Susy McPhee was born and raised in Liverpool. She studied Russian and karate at St Andrews University, harbouring vague notions of becoming a spy.

While waiting for MI5, the KGB or the FBI to come calling, she trained as a technical author with ICL in Berkshire, and set about trying to inject life into what was traditionally not the most creative of disciplines. From such inauspicious beginnings her career led her into areas that came pretty close to her spy ambitions, including training rocket scientists in the former Soviet Union. She moved to Scotland from the South of England with her husband and three small daughters sixteen years ago.

D1342477

Also by Susy McPhee:

Husbands and Lies

Susy McPhee

The Runaway Wife

EBURY
PRESS

3 5 7 9 10 8 6 4 2

Published in 2009 by Ebury Press, an imprint of Ebury Publishing
A Random House Group Company

Copyright © 2009 by Susy McPhee

Susy McPhee has asserted her right to be identified as the author of this Work
in accordance with the Copyright, Designs and Patents Act 1988

All rights reserved. No part of this publication may be reproduced, stored in a
retrieval system, or transmitted in any form or by any means, electronic,
mechanical, photocopying, recording or otherwise, without the prior
permission of the copyright owner

The Random House Group Limited Reg. No. 954009

Addresses for companies within the Random House Group can be found at
www.randomhouse.co.uk

A CIP catalogue record for this book is available from the British Library

The Random House Group Limited supports The Forest Stewardship Council
(FSC), the leading international forest certification organisation. All our titles
that are printed on Greenpeace approved FSC certified paper carry the FSC
logo. Our paper procurement policy can be found at
www.rbooks.co.uk/environment

Typeset in Adobe Caslon by Palimpsest Book Production Limited,
Grangemouth, Stirlingshire

Printed in the UK by Cox & Wyman Ltd, Reading, Berkshire

ISBN 9780091928575

To buy books by your favourite authors and register for offers visit
www.rbooks.co.uk

Writing a book is a lonely occupation. You spend vast hours ensconced in a quiet room, your only companions a bunch of characters you made up, snarling every time the door opens and a real flesh-and-blood person offers you a cup of tea, because it's broken your concentration and now it's going to take you hours to focus on the plot again. And, frankly, as Iain would testify, the plot and I were never the closest of acquaintances.

In spite of the solitary nature of writing, the end result would never have been accomplished without the help and encouragement of a whole host of behind-the-scenes people who gave of their time, their knowledge and, on at least two notable occasions, their spare rooms, whilst I did what I needed to do to bring my creations to life.

Thanks as ever to gorgeous (plural) Alice Lutyens at Curtis Brown and Gillian Green at Ebury, the best agent/editor team I could ever have hoped for. Where I would be without your guidance and support, heaven only knows. Thanks, too, to Felicity Blunt for nobly stepping into the breach while Alice went off for FIVE MONTHS on her world tour: the cupcakes in the Haymarket Hotel were legendary. Thanks to Hannah Robinson at Ebury for her tireless publicity work, and a big *danke, dank u, děkuji za pozornost* and *Köszönöm* (thank goodness for Babelfish!)

to Kate Cooper at Curtis Brown, who keeps somehow persuading people to translate my first book into lots of different languages.

Thanks to some of the best friends a girl could ask for. To Fiona Airey, Lesley Campbell, Jane Prior and my sister, Dale Hobbs, who kidnapped me the night before the publication of *Husbands and Lies* so that we could drink champagne together under the stars. To Angela and Sean O'Reilly, who have taken up new careers touting my handiwork to random people in airport bookshops. To Dr Gail Orme, for keeping me right on the best drug to use if you're planning to kill yourself, and for not having me committed when I asked you the question in the first place. To Denise and Ewan Baxter for letting Mishka and me invade your home in Tobermory, and for all the support and encouragement you've offered me as I've been trying to get a foot in the door of the literary world. Faith like yours is beyond price, and I am deeply indebted to you. Thanks to Chris and Ian Rhodes, who made Iain and me so welcome in Harrogate when I was researching Marion's stamping ground. I can't think of a nicer couple to go grave-robbing with.

Thanks to Julie Donnelly at Harrogate A&E, who took time out from saving lives to give me a guided tour and answer all my dodgy questions. Thanks to Dr Alan Wright, who shared so willingly all his memories of living in the lighthouse cottage at Rubha nan Gall, and who must make one of the finest cups of tea on the western seaboard. Thanks to my mum, Joan Harrison, who once again has been like a terrier with a rat, so fiercely has she sung my literary praises to anyone who showed the slightest interest. Never, ever cross her on this: she will tear you limb from limb. Don't say I didn't warn you. Thanks to my sister, Kerry Bussell, for taking the time to read the early chapters of Marion's saga, and emailing me her feedback from her then home in South Korea. Distance is no barrier to sibling support. And thanks to all of you, family and friends, who have sent me gleeful emails and texts whenever you've found a copy of *Husbands and Lies* in the bookshops. It's so much fun knowing you're sharing the journey with me.

A huge thank you to my family for putting up with my mood swings, my haphazard approach to timekeeping and my terrible cooking (this is where you all butt in and cry, 'No, no! You are a marvellous cook!' (Lie if you must.) To David, who learned early on in his time with us that the safest way to guarantee a safe passage through adolescence was to repeat the words, 'Would you like a cup of tea?' like a mantra. To Lauren, who learned how to make pancakes to save us all from starvation, and has never, even after nineteen years of having me for a mother, lost the ability to make me laugh. Often from hysteria, I grant you, but it still counts. To Carolyn, who lets me phone her up in the middle of seminar preparation and essay deadlines and exam revision and pick her not inconsiderable brain for guidance. To Helen, my rant-monitor, whose common sense and good-humoured equability give me strength when I'm ready to throw in the towel. To Olly, who is thinking of naming his new Malamute puppy Hector: there is no greater compliment. And of course to Iain, my first and only husband, who drives me to distraction with the way he stalks me on the Internet, but then at least has the grace to keep me company when I get there. I would dedicate every word I write to you, but you and I both know that would smack of sad loser.

And finally (Carolyn is going to kill me for this because it definitely smacks of sad loser), thanks to Mishka, who has been my staunch companion, foot-warmer and personal trainer throughout this book's gestation, and who has asked for nothing in return bar the odd tummy-rub and an occasional Bonio. You're not getting the dedication either, but only because you can't read.

To my beautiful daughters Helen, Carolyn and Lauren, whose generous laughter and ability to recite the whole of *Aladdin* word-for-word somehow reach into my crazy world and remind me why I do all of this. This book is for you, with my heartfelt gratitude and lots of love.

Chapter 1

I, Marion Bishop, being of sound mind, have decided to kill myself this evening, Thursday 24 April 2008.

That sounds like a suicide note. It isn't meant to. It's just a frank admission – to myself, mostly – of exactly how far astray my life has gone. Especially when I think of what I'm doing to Sam. Have done to Sam, I should say. Sam, who's been holding me together for months, but who, no matter how much he wants to, just can't fix me. I am beyond repair.

Twenty-fourth of April. There's nothing particularly noteworthy about the date. Except for me, of course. If things go according to plan, it will be the one that ends up on my headstone. 14 OCTOBER 1973 TO 24 APRIL 2008. Visitors to the cemetery will be able to do a quick calculation, the way I always do when I see a tombstone, and work out that I was thirty-four when I died. They might tut, like I tut if the occupant of the grave is anything under the age of forty (though the closer I get to forty, the younger it seems: if I were planning to be around beyond this evening I would have to amend my cut-off point). They'll probably say, 'Poor woman,' or something, not that that will change anything: I've been an object of pity for some time now. People have taken to crossing the road when they see me coming sooner than speak to me. People like Heather, my neighbour: I remember the times after the Thursday evening ballet class when she would come back to my house on the way home and the two of us would sit in the kitchen putting the world to rights over a glass of wine until dinner-time, while Poppy and Hope and Poppy's little brother Liam squeezed the last few moments of play out of the evening. Some days I'd need a shoehorn to winkle her out before Sam got home. She almost got herself mown down by an articulated lorry a few weeks after the accident as she scurried across Parliament Street in an attempt to dodge me. Or Martin, her husband, who disappeared back inside their house only last month rather than run the risk of having to meet me head-on. The spectre of tragedy hangs around me like a disease, and people jump through metaphorical hoops to avoid contamination. Apart from Esme McFarland from the florist's, who's maybe been through enough tragedy herself to have become convinced of her immunity: she's forever stopping me and cocking her head to one side, saying, 'Marion. You poor woman. You've been in my prayers,' or some other such platitude. Though maybe it isn't a platitude: maybe she really does pray for me. Christ, I hope not. The thought of Esme McFarland praying for me gives me the creeps.

I agree: that sounds churlish. God knows, I need the prayers, and there's no reason to suppose He's less likely to listen to Esme than to anyone else.

I was down at the cemetery this afternoon, funnily enough, after Sam had left. Well, not funnily enough at all, in fact: I am there most days now, though today was the first time I gave the place the once-over with a view to moving in permanently. I don't do much tombstone browsing any more: these days there's only one grave that draws me, and if you were to spot that one, you'd learn that its occupant never came even close to the forty cut-off point. 'HOPE BISHOP,' the epitaph reads, '27 JUNE 1998 TO 18 SEPTEMBER 2007.'

Do the maths.

I'd brought some of the overblown blossoms from the cherry tree by the front gate, and had been lying on my back in the deserted cemetery, the way I do when the place is quiet, with my head resting on the freshly tamped earth around the newly erected gravestone, looking up at a sky so blue you could have dived into it, talking to Hope. Newly erected, because you couldn't put it up until the earth had settled, apparently. The stonemason had recommended eight months, but I'd cracked at seven. A grave without a head-stone has an anonymity that's hard to stomach when it's your child who's lying beneath the soil. Beside my head the blossoms dipped and nodded in the light breeze, anchored securely in the antique silver lifetime cemetery vase I'd picked out for the grave (powder-coat finish, easy-installation, no-maintenance heavy-duty zinc: I've become surprisingly conversant in the vernacular of the dead). 'Fourteen packets!' I'd been saying to Hope. 'And I can't stand the stuff. I only got it because you like it.' Then I'd had to stop and correct myself. '*Liked* it.' I'd been grumbling to her about all the fossil fuels I'd taken to burning since the accident: the lights I left on all night because I can't bear the darkness of the house any more; the music playing constantly in her empty bedroom to give it some semblance of life. The fourteen packets referred to the buffalo mozzarella I'd bought (Hope had always had a bit of a thing about it, and I'd had a mental aberration in Waitrose the previous morning). I'd stuffed them into the salad drawer, and then forgotten to close the fridge door afterwards. I've taken to driving everywhere too – even as far as the shopping centre, which really is pathetic given that it's only three streets away – just to avoid the Esmes and the Martins and the Heathers. A catalogue of eco-sabotage, Sam would call it before he gave up trying to raise a laugh (or a smile, or even eye-to-eye contact). God knows what it's all doing to the ozone layer. I wasn't really complaining, not as such: it's just that I've developed this way of talking to her that has nothing to do with the kind of conversations we'd had when she was alive. To be honest, I've made myself so unreachable over the past seven months that Hope is the only person who still speaks to me any more.

Well, when I say speaks, I suppose it's me that does most of the talking.

All right then, all of the talking.

I'd pushed myself upright at this point, and twisted round to regard the engraving on the headstone, tracing the outline of Hope's name with my finger. Seeing it like that, cut so neatly into the white marble, the realisation that she wasn't coming back hit me like a punch in the solar plexus. I actually gasped from the shock. And then I leaned in and rested my head against the cool surface of the marble. Listening.

On a branch somewhere above my head a thrush was

noisily marking its territory, and somewhere in the distance I could just make out the subdued hum of traffic on the Wetherby Road. I squeezed my eyes tightly shut to block them out and listened even harder.

There was nothing: no whisper from the grave; no sense that somehow, stretched out in this ridiculous manner along the burial mound, I could *reconnect* in some way, reach my arms into the earth and retrieve what I'd lost.

And that was when it dawned on me that really it didn't matter how often I came here with my floral apologies, as though I were somehow responsible for what had happened, and prostrated myself at the graveside like some latter-day martyr for a cause in which nobody else believed. Who cared if I filled my fridge with food no one would eat, or kept the Sugababes playing round the clock, or chose heavy-duty zinc over plastic, white marble over polished granite, breathing over not breathing? (Though the latter example I hadn't exactly *chosen* as such: I'd just carried on because it hadn't occurred to me that I had any alternative.) My life was over. The past seven months I'd just been going through the motions.

Frankly, it was a bit of a relief.

I know that probably sounds nuts. *Of sound mind, my ass*, I can hear you thinking. But really it wasn't: quite the opposite, in fact. I felt saner this afternoon than I've been since that terrible evening when the police called round with the news. Which might not be saying much, actually, now I come to think about it. Perhaps I should revise that first sentence.

I, Marion Bishop, being of sound mind *given the circumstances*, have decided to kill myself this evening, Thursday 24 April 2008.

Happy now?

Chapter 2

I don't mention anything to Hope. I just drive back to the empty house and get stuck in to preparing it for my imminent departure, hoovering it from top to toe, all three storeys, lugging the vacuum cleaner behind me like a reluctant child, before tackling the bathrooms, laying out fresh towels and polishing the taps until they gleam. After that I get started on the kitchen, washing the floor and buffing up the Aga so that you can see your face in its shiny paintwork. I used to believe an Aga gave a house a heart but, trust me, it's only as strong as the people it serves. I throw the unopened packets of mozzarella along with the rest of the food from the fridge and anything else I can find that is perishable into the outside bin for collection the following Thursday, leaving aside a solitary bottle of just-opened vodka and a packet of minced lamb for later.

I pause then, just for a moment, standing beside the bin and thinking of that Thursday, of that point in the very near future where I will have ceased to be, waiting to discover whether there is any residual feeling of regret ready to reveal itself. But of course there is none. I've forgotten what it's like to feel regret. I've forgotten what it's like to feel most things, actually. The bereavement counsellor that Sam organised for us both tells me I'm stuck at what he

calls the 'denial stage' of mourning, refusing to acknowledge my loss by shutting down all my emotions.

I wish. An emotional shutdown would be a relief, quite
frankly, compared with the rage that courses through my
body like a fever, infecting the unwary few that come too
close. Aside from Esme, that is: like I say, she seems to be
immune.

At first it was panic: I would wake every morning in
the weeks following the accident after a fitful night, my
head throbbing, such a vicelike tightness around my heart,
I thought I was having some kind of seizure. Then I'd
remember afresh, morning after morning: the realisation
would hit me all over again that she was gone; she wasn't
coming back, and a rush of anxiety would slam into my
stomach and send me plunging into a deep pit of loneliness so profound I couldn't manage the simplest of tasks.
Even getting out of bed in the mornings was an uphill
struggle.

I was surrounded by people in those early weeks, well-
meaning friends and family who kept reaching out and
trying to pull me from the abyss, back to where they were,
safe on the shores of the unbereaved. But I couldn't reach
them. To be honest, I wasn't even sure I wanted to. And
of course eventually, inevitably, one by one I drove them
all away. Now I wonder if I did it on purpose, deliberately
isolating myself from them in order to make this afternoon's decision easier. Severing the links, if you like, one
friend after another, picking them off like ducks in a
shooting gallery. *Take things slowly,* they would say, torn
between reluctance and relief at the thought of abandoning

me to my grief. *Try to take one day at a time*. Even that was beyond me: I was already stalled, pinioned by misery, incapable of moving slowly, one day at a time, one *minute* at a time, whatever. I would watch them leave, and something inside me wanted to beg them to come back, to stand and scream and kick and punch and cry with me, to grieve as I was grieving, but it was impossible. None of them were inside my skin, walking in my shoes.

Lucky them.

These days I do a pretty good job of keeping a lid on the rage, though in spite of my best efforts sometimes it just spills over. Those closest to me get the largest helping; Sam most of all. His helping was so huge, in the end it was just too much for him to swallow. We've become best pals, the anger and me. It's no wonder that Hope's the only person who can bear my company these days.

Although, of course, it might be that she just has no obvious means of escape.

I go back inside the house and survey the results of my handiwork. It's far from perfect. The towels in the bathrooms are bothering me: who are they for? I re-fold them and put them back in the linen cupboard, and immediately change my mind and hang them back out again. Then, standing back and checking them over for a second time, I change my mind *again* and replace them in the cupboard, silently chastising myself for vacillating. I swear to God, deciding to kill myself was easier. The sheets on the bed are a problem as well. If I change them, that will mean leaving a pile of unwashed laundry behind. But if I don't, that will mean dying on dirty sheets. Do I want to do that? Die on dirty sheets, I mean. The sheets being the moot point. As opposed to the dying.

In the end I change them, not that it really matters. Whoever finds me – Sam, I expect – will probably have the whole house cleared anyway. A final dismantling of a life already in pieces.

Still, at least the place is clean. Back in the kitchen, I call Hector and stick him in the scullery, and then I take the minced lamb and cook it up on the Aga, stirring it carefully to make sure none of the bits stick together. Once it's cooked off I tip it into his bowl and raid the dog food, adding a good handful of biscuits to the mixture to bulk it up a bit. Normally I regulate his diet with the iron discipline of an old-fashioned hospital matron – he can put on weight just by watching you eat a slice of toast – but I can't be entirely sure how long this meal will have to last him. Sam is due round tomorrow to collect some of his things, but he might not come until after Hector's mealtime and it hardly seems fair that the dog should suffer just because I've decided to put an end to it. I stamp firmly on the unsettling thought that Sam might not show up for one reason or another: if the worst comes to the worst, Hector is quite capable of howling down the neighbourhood for his dinner.

He gives me a quizzical look as I set the food down in front of him, and retreats back into a corner of the scullery, ignoring the carefully prepared meal as though he suspects me of foul play. Does doing yourself in constitute foul play? Or is it something you can only do to someone else? I steel myself not to look back at his reproachful face as he watches me walk out of his life.

It's close on nine-thirty by now. Back in the kitchen, I retrieve the vodka and get myself a glass. Then I dig out the tin that doubles as a medicine cabinet from the cupboard above the bread maker and upend it, rooting around among the bandages and the Winnie-the-Pooh plasters for the antidepressants I'd been prescribed in the aftermath of the accident, when it had become obvious that I wasn't coping very well. Sam had gone nuts when he'd seen the prescription – they were the drug of choice for those in the know when it came to topping yourself – but I'd barely started the course before lethargy kicked in and I couldn't be bothered to take them. I'd gone along to my two-week check-up with my GP and lied, telling him I thought perhaps they were making a difference, and he'd duly written a prescription for another fortnight's worth. After that I'd gone regularly, accumulating another couple of prescriptions before beginning the weaning-off process from a drug I'd hardly started in the first place.

My memory must be a bit foggy, even so, because when I eventually run the packet to earth there are only nine tablets in it. Will that be enough to do the trick? I try to recall what Sam had said when he'd been losing the plot about them in the first place – had he been specific about dosage? The nine tablets look so innocuous in their foil bubbles: it's hard to imagine they'd be capable of the kind of devastation he'd ranted about.

I could always go for a cocktail of drugs, I suppose. Aside from the antidepressants, there are a couple of packets of paracetamol ratting around in the tin, but on further investigation I discover that one of the packets contains a solitary tablet, the other, two. The only other painkiller I can locate is an opened bottle of Calpol Six-Plus, but I draw the line at that. There's something – I don't know – tasteless about using the medicine you used to use to alleviate your dead daughter's pain in an effort to put an end to your own. But then the other options – the wrist-slashing, the car-crashing, the cliff-jumping – terrify me. Not the dying: I'd got my head around that part. I was even looking forward to it. But the suddenness of it – the idea of that one moment when decisive action is required – that was the bit I couldn't handle. The prospect that I might not pull it off. I guess I am just your overdose kind of girl.

I rummage a bit further in the addict's nightmare that is our first-aid kit and find a full packet of out-of-date indigestion tablets and some antibiotic capsules from a course prescribed for Sam that he never completed. I contemplate the haphazard assortment of drugs with a sigh. Really, antidepressants aside, between them and the vodka I've taken more during a good night's partying.

I fret over the problem of my lack of medication, and then inspiration strikes. I'm pretty sure I still have the prescriptions lying around somewhere: if I'm quick, I'll just make the late-night chemist in Station Parade. I scrabble around and find the prescriptions underneath a bag of rubber bands and a takeaway menu in the junk drawer in the kitchen, and pick out the most recent of them. Then I collect my keys from the hook beside the front door, snatch up my handbag and leave the house.

I park just along from the bus depot and make my way across the road and then stop in bewilderment. The chemist shop has gone. In its place is a glossy Sony outlet with an array of televisions and hi-fi equipment displayed in the window. When did that happen? I could swear I was here just a couple of weeks ago picking up vitamin pills for Hope. But then time plays tricks on you when you've lost something precious (the plot, for instance, or a child). You find yourself marching to a tune that no one else can hear.

I am heading back for the car, muttering to myself, wondering whether I should postpone the whole thing until I can get the prescription made up or whether I should just go for it with the nine pills I have, when someone steps out in front of me.

I don't see him at first. Then, when I realise he's standing there, I just put my head down and pretend I haven't noticed him. I've become quite good at that lately, and frankly most people are happy to be ignored. But as I try to pass him, he steps right into my path and mutters something I can't quite catch.

I give an exasperated tut. 'What?' I squint in the street light, trying to make out a face beneath the hood.

He steps in closer and I can feel the fetid warmth of his breath on my neck. Then suddenly he reaches over and seizes a handful of my hair in a not-too-clean fist, causing me to gasp in pain. But only at the point where I can feel the cold metal of something sharp against my neck does it dawn on me that this isn't a concerned friend or neighbour about to enquire after my emotional well-being. As my head struggles to make sense of what's happening, my heart sets off at a gallop and I realise with a gasp that I haven't forgotten all those other feelings after all. After the

months of condolences and counselling and people tripping over themselves around me while the rage bubbled
and simmered away inside, it takes the stench of the boy's
casual viciousness and the hard unyielding knife at my
throat for me to realise – a tad late, perhaps – that maybe
I'm not quite so ready to die as I'd thought. Not like this,
anyway. Not on his terms.

The boy presses harder on the knife. 'Ah said, gimme
your money.'

'What?' I am repeating myself: probably not the best
strategy for defusing the situation.

'Swear down, ah'm not kiddin'.' He leans his scrawny body
against mine, pressing my back painfully against the wall
behind me, and then abruptly releases my hair and starts
fumbling around in my handbag, wrenching out my purse
and causing the prescription I am clutching in my hand to
flutter to the ground.

'Hey!' I am more concerned with the loss of the prescription than anything else.

He shoves the purse under my nose. 'Your money. Get
it out.'

I regard him in astonishment and then the irony of the
situation hits me and – I can't help myself – I give a short
shocked laugh. 'Are you – *mugging* me?'

He looks at me as though I am deranged. 'Nah, ah'm
askin' for a fuckin' date.' Which, given the circumstances,
I actually think is quite witty. Then, without releasing the
pressure of the knife on my neck, he shakes open my purse
and peers inside. The look of contempt he shoots me would
curdle milk.

'Is that it?' He upends the purse, and one five-pound note and an assortment of small change rain down upon the pavement.

'Yes, well.' I feel absurdly defensive. 'I only came out for a couple of things.'

'Fuck's sake.' He spits disgustedly right at my feet and increases the pressure on the knife at my neck. 'Right, then,' he breathes, leaning in close once again. Someone really ought to tell him about his breath. 'Get your card out, an' we'll go to t' cashpoint together. And don't go trying owt daft.'

'What?' I stare at him in consternation. 'No – I can't go to the cashpoint. I have plans for the evening.' A sudden recollection of my lovely clean house, waiting for me to come home and do myself in, flashes into my head. 'I've changed the sheets and everything.'

'What?' His jaw drops, and I capitalise on his hesitation to push him away from me and snatch back my purse from his hand.

'I said no.' I fasten the purse irritatedly, noting with satisfaction a surge of anger beginning to build inside me: I am back on familiar territory. It's one thing to have taken the decision myself to end my life, quite another for some spotty kid with bad teeth and bitten nails to presume to threaten it. 'Who do you think you are?'

The boy's brow darkens, and suddenly I notice, not without a twinge of alarm (another feeling! My whole being is suddenly alive with them!) something I'd failed to spot earlier – a gleam of lust behind his eyes. I open my mouth to say something, but before I can speak the boy

– youth – steps in close once again, and passes his tongue lasciviously across his lips, testing the tip of the knife against his forefinger with a cold smile.

'I'll tell you who I am, luv.' He runs the blade almost seductively down the side of my face, leaning in closely, and for one absurd moment I think he's going to kiss me. I almost brace myself to respond. Then he breathes his next sentence right into my mouth.

'I'm your worst fuckin' nightmare.'

Chapter 3

Actually, that's a bit presumptuous of him. I can remember my worst nightmare, leaving aside the nightmare that my life has become over these last months, and he certainly isn't it. But I'll come to that. As he stands there brandishing his knife at my throat, I wait for my life to pass before my eyes. But what flashes into my head as he breathes his putrid intentions into my mouth is a single snapshot. A memory, as clear as a photograph, of Hope and Sam and me one winter's afternoon, coming back home from somewhere or other – the supermarket, probably – and me standing at the front door surrounded by bags, grumbling at the two of them as they ducked and dived up the path, throwing hastily gathered handfuls of snow at each other, telling them to hurry up because it was freezing. They turned in unison and stuck out their tongues at me before dissolving in a heap of complicit laughter and more snowballs. And that's where the picture froze, with the two of them laughing and cavorting together as I stood there tutting and complaining and trying to pull them back into line. They'd done a lot of laughing, I realise now, partners-in-crime who would gleefully sabotage any efforts on my part for us all to take ourselves more seriously.

It used to drive me mad. Why was it always me that had to be the grown-up in the family? Sometimes it was hard to tell who was the bigger kid: Sam or Hope. I would find myself constantly on the fringes whenever they got into one of their games, half of me wanting to throw myself into the fray while the other half looked on, frowning and disapproving. On a good day I could smile indulgently and hide my discomfort under a blanket of what-are-they-like shakes of the head. 'It's lovely to see the relationship Sam has with Hope,' Heather had commented one time when Sam had arrived home before the winkling-out process had been completely played out. She'd stood at the kitchen sink, a wistful expression on her face, watching him through the window, romping around the garden with Hope and Poppy and Liam, lost in some game they'd invented. 'By the time Martin gets home at night he's too exhausted to be bothered with the kids. And at the weekend, when he could be spending time with them, he's usually disappeared to the golf course.' I'd silently scolded myself and tried to feel grateful for a husband who enjoyed his daughter's company so much, while all the time a small worm of something I could never quite put my finger on but that I had a horrible feeling might prove to be jealousy or some other such unpalatable emotion would be squirming around inside me.

I'd brought it up one time in an all-too-rare conversation with my sister Charlie, who lectures in psychology at a college in a far-flung corner of Michigan, and she had laughed and said, 'Oh, Marion, of course you're jealous, but you're supposed to be. It's pure Freud: a classic example of the Electra complex. Hope is angry with you for not providing her with a penis, and has transferred her affections on to Sam because he possesses the very thing she wants.'

'Don't psychobabble me, Charlie,' I'd said in some consternation. I wasn't sure which part of her comment had rattled me more: her confirming of my fears about my own jealousy or her suggestion that Hope was harbouring a secret desire for a male member. 'Everybody knows Freud was an idiot. Of course Hope doesn't want a penis.'

'Of course she *does*!' Charlie had been unrepentant. 'Don't we all? Not on a conscious level, naturally.'

'Speak for yourself,' I'd retorted. 'I certainly don't want one.' Did I? The sudden idea of what it might be like flashed across my mind, and a hot bolt of something I'd like to think was revulsion shot through my body.

Charlie gave another laugh. 'Say what you like, Marion, but I remember you being positively green with envy when Christopher Greenwood peed clean across the climbing frame in primary school, and you were only six. Same syndrome, different generation. In fact, I cite you to my students when we're studying the psychoanalysts.'

I felt myself flush. 'I was not green with envy!' I had been, actually – I could remember watching with yearning as he arched his pee right over the head of the highest kid on the climbing frame – but I was blowed if I was going to admit that to my overanalytical big sister.

She'd given a snort of laughter. 'Poor old Christopher – you spent the whole of the following week trailing around after him in the playground like some sort of mini-pervert demanding that he pee over ever-higher obstacles. You were a right little Hitler. You only stopped when one of his efforts went right through the open window of the staffroom and he got suspended. Anyway.' She swept on before I could make any further denials about my early career as a sexual deviant. 'I shouldn't worry about Hope. She'll eventually realise that she can't have what Sam has, and be happy with who she is.'

That night I'd woken in a cold sweat after dreaming of Hope taking part in the end-of-term production with the rest of her ballet class, flitting across the stage in a pink tutu with a very pronounced and bulging jockstrap underneath. The shout of fright I'd let out had roused Sam, who'd roared with laughter when I told him what had been troubling me, and who had laughed all the harder when I tried out Charlie's theory on him. 'I tell you what,' he'd said when he'd eventually composed himself enough to speak, 'if you've really been harbouring a secret hankering for a penis all this time, I could probably be persuaded into giving you a shot of mine . . .' He'd wiped the tears of laughter from his eyes, and then applied himself enthusiastically to the business of my left breast, and the two of us had abandoned any further speculation about Hope's hidden desires to fulfil a few of our own, though not without the odd muffled snort of residual laughter erupting from my shameless husband from time to time.

Maybe my whole life *is* flashing before my eyes, because the rosy memory of Sam and me laughing in bed together fades, and all of a sudden I am jerked painfully forward to this morning, when the rage that had been bubbling away inside me since the accident had finally erupted in a flush of recrimination while the two of us were eating breakfast together, keeping up the pretence that we were a normal happily married couple (well, married, at any rate) and not two people who couldn't stand the sight of each other any more.

Sam had done his best, God knows, to keep me together in the months after Hope had died, but every effort he made, every smile he attempted to produce, had only served to stoke the fire under my fury. I'd tried every weapon I could lay my tongue to in an effort to provoke some similar feelings of anger in him, so that we could at least meet on common ground, and found myself increasingly incensed by his ability to act normally, smile, speak, eat, sleep, *move on* from what had happened before the headstone had even been erected. He just seemed so *accepting*. I couldn't bear it.

And then finally, inevitably, he cracked.

'This coffee's cold,' I'd complained as I picked up the mug he'd just set down in front of me.

'Then put it in the microwave and heat it up,' he'd said mildly, lifting Hector's biscuits from the cupboard and tipping half a dozen into his bowl. Hector's tail thumped against the tiled floor hopefully.

I'd pushed myself irritatedly to my slippered feet with a sigh. 'I wouldn't have thought it was too much effort to make a hot cup of coffee,' I'd muttered, loud enough for him to hear me. He'd ignored that comment. 'But then everything's too much effort for you, isn't it?' (Rich, I know, coming from someone who hadn't lifted a domestic finger for months.) He'd ignored that one, too. I'd crossed to the microwave. 'Let's face it, if it hadn't been too much effort for you to check that Brownies was actually on when you dropped off Hope, she'd still be alive instead of lying under a bloody marble headstone feeding the worms.'

The air in the kitchen grew suddenly still, and in that instant I knew he wasn't going to ignore my last comment.

For a moment neither of us moved, though I could still taste the bitterness of what I'd said on my tongue. And then Sam had very quietly placed the dog bowl in front of Hector and turned to face me. If I'd been hoping to find common ground for a fight, I was in for a disappointment: there was no fight in him. The look he gave me was defeated, not angry. His shoulders slumped suddenly and he lowered his eyes to the floor. Then he gave a sigh and dropped a bombshell that, frankly, I'd had coming for some time.

'I can't live with you any more.'

He raised his eyes to look at me again – searching for some kind of reaction, probably, though I offered him none – and then crossed the kitchen and disappeared upstairs, returning a few moments later with the holdall he normally used for his squash gear. He stood in the kitchen doorway for a few moments just looking at me, waiting, I suppose, to see whether I was going to retract what I'd said. Once he opened his mouth to speak, but then he changed his mind and clamped it shut again. Finally he gave me a slow, disappointed shake of the head.

'I'm sorry, Marion. I can't hang around to be your emotional punchbag any more. You're not the only one who's grieving.'

I stared at the holdall, like its sudden appearance made it complicit in the breakdown of my marriage. 'You had this planned, didn't you?'

He faltered, and looked as though he were about to contradict me, but then he shook his head again and said something about coming back tomorrow evening after work to collect some more of his stuff. To be honest, I wasn't really paying attention: my mind was too full of what he'd just told me. He stood there for a moment, still apparently waiting for some sort of reaction from me. Eventually, getting none, he turned and left, and I, bitch that I was, never lifted a finger to stop him.

That comment he'd made returns to me now, as I stand shivering in the street while some hygienically challenged yob holds a knife to my throat.

I can't live with you any more.

Well, it looks as if we've found our common ground, after all. I can't live with me either.

Chapter 4

Anyway: back to the boy with the knife. I know: I keep jumping around. Mind like a grasshopper. But you can hardly expect rational thought from a would-be suicide, and after all, I'm just telling it like it was. There I am, with some bits of my life – edited highlights, I suppose, interspersed with a pretty major lowlight – flashing into my head, and it feels as though we've been standing there together for hours, the boy and me, locked together in our uncomfortable embrace, though in reality it's probably only a few seconds (I mean, I don't imagine a man up a dark street with a knife is going to be endowed with much in the way of patience), and suddenly I am *overwhelmed* by this terrible sense of hopelessness as I remember the look on Sam's face when he left, and it hits me that I really *can't* live with me any more.

Luckily, I wasn't planning to. And what does it matter, after all, whether it's a knife in the street or a few pills at home on my nice clean sheets? It's like all those other choices I've been making over the months since the funeral – nobody really gives a shit. I have a nanosecond of regret about the bottle of chilled vodka waiting for me in the kitchen – one way or another, it was a far more *civilised* way to end it all – and then I shake my head. Either I'm ready to die or I'm not. I look hard into the boy's dark eyes.

'Go on, then.' I give him a brief nod of acquiescence and then brace myself, waiting for the end.

His face clouds. 'What?'

'Do it.' I squirm a little against him. 'And hurry up. The wall's digging into my back.'

I can feel his grasp on the knife slacken and then tighten again. God, I wish he'd just get on with it. The suspense is killing me. (Not literally, obviously. Wouldn't that be ironic?)

'What the fuck – I'm not messing, you know.' He scowls at me over the knife, then licks his lips nervously.

'Look, would it help if I put up a fight or something?' I give him a bit of a shove, and I must catch him off-guard or something, because he staggers backwards and almost falls. 'Oops – sorry.' I hold out a hand to steady him.

'Look, bitch –'

'Don't call me that.'

'You what?'

'Bitch. Don't call me that. I mean, I *am* one, I know. I just don't want that to be the last thing I hear before you kill me.'

I swear I can see sweat beginning to glow on his forehead. He glances up and down the deserted street nervously, as if looking for someone to come to his aid. Then he looks back at the knife in his hand, and steps in close once again, actually nicking the skin on my neck this time, before leaping away from me as though he's been scalded.

'Fuck! Fuck! What is fucking *wrong* with you? Con!' he suddenly shouts, looking around him wildly, though whoever Con is doesn't respond. He steps towards me again, and then paces out a complete circle in front of me. He's so jumpy by now, you can smell it.

'Look, if you're going to do this, would you mind getting a move on?' I gesture at the empty road. 'Only, someone could come along at any minute and call for help or something, and we'll never get it finished.'

He sweeps in towards me again, but this time his hand has replaced the knife at my throat. I am oddly disappointed. 'You know what? You're fucking weird, you are.'

I sigh patiently. 'Are you going to kill me, or aren't you?'

He looks at me as if I am insane, and then snatches the handbag off my shoulder, wagging it under my nose menacingly several times without speaking, while his facial muscles perform a contortion act Houdini would have been proud of. Then he shoves me, hard, against the wall again, and the force of his anger knocks all the wind out of me.

I am still gasping and clutching my stomach and trying to catch my breath when I realise that he has disappeared, and I am alone on the deserted street. Alone, with no handbag, no keys and no money. No cut throat, either. Looks like the whole suicide ball is right back in my court. He even has my mobile phone, tucked away in one of the inside pockets of the handbag. And my driver's licence. With my address on it.

So he has the keys to my house. And he knows where it is.

I chew over this last piece of information as I gather up the small bits of change off the pavement – evidently too small a sum for any self-respecting mugger to bother bending down for. There's no sign of the five-pound note or the prescription: they must have blown away somewhere while the two of us were locked in combat. It looks like nine tablets are going to have to be enough to do the job after all.

I pause for a moment, reflecting on what has just happened, trying to work out if it has affected my plans for the evening, if I'm still of a mind to end it all; or if, somewhere in the midst of having someone else threaten my life (even if he was too much of a wimp to carry through the threat), I've discovered a new zest for living. Has the evening suddenly become clearer, the stars brighter, the buildings around me more lovely than they were when I first arrived in the street such a short while earlier?

They may have: it's hard to say. But whether or not the world has become a more beautiful place, it's still a world without Hope. Literally, now that Sam has left me as well. And as the grief settles afresh on my shoulders, I am overwhelmed by tiredness and an urge to lie down somewhere and sleep for a very long time.

Which, let's face it, is kind of what I'd been planning all along.

And so I pick my way along the still-quiet street towards home, musing as I go about whether the boy will follow up on this evening's encounter and come looking for me once he's got back his nerve. That look on his face when I told him to hurry up! He's probably going to have to come back if only to retrieve his pride, which is no doubt lying somewhere in the gutter along with my prescription and the five-pound note. Wouldn't it be a riot if he were the one to discover me? The experience would probably scar him for life.

There is an odd air of expectancy in the house when I finally let myself in using the spare key that we keep – sorry: *I* keep: I was forgetting for a moment that there is no *we* any more – under a loose stone beside the kitchen window. You'd almost think there was a bunch of people hiding in the living room, waiting to leap out and shout, 'Surprise!' as soon as I open the door. There isn't, of course. The only sign of life is the answerphone light, which is flashing steadily in the corner. Sam, I think to myself, but as I press the 'Play' button it's my sister's voice that spills out. 'Marion,' she says, 'I have news. Call me!'

Her voice echoes hollowly around the living room, accentuating its emptiness. Apart from that, there's no sign that anybody actually lives here at all. Yet there's something about the place – it's like a film crew holding its breath at the start of a take, waiting for the director to give them their cues.

Better not disappoint then. I retrieve my stash of drugs and booze, such as it is, from the kitchen and take it up to the bedroom, wavering indecisively for a moment before making myself a little nest among the pillows and the duvet on Sam's side of the bed. That way I can at least pretend I'm dying in his arms. God, I'm pathetic. Still, isn't that what we all want, at the end of the day – to die in the arms of a loved one? Is it my fault they're so thin on the ground these days?

That, by the way, was a rhetorical question.

I leave the bedroom door open so that I can hear the music playing away quietly in Hope's bedroom, and I open the curtains so that the street lamp outside the front garden can spill its soft amber glow into the bedroom.

Lights.

After that I climb into the nest I've made of the bed, pour myself a generous glassful of vodka and pop all the tablets out of their little plastic bubbles. Then I lift the glass high and salute the photograph of the four of us that hangs on the wall above the dressing table opposite the bed.

Camera.

Reaching down amongst the pillows and the duvet, I grab a couple of the tablets and toss them into my mouth, washing them down with a generous swig of the vodka. They stick a bit, making me gag, but another mouthful of vodka and they are away.

Action.

I lean back into the pillows, and close my eyes.

Chapter 5

Once upon a time when I had a life, I had a proper job as a play therapist. I'd done a teaching degree at Manchester University, but after I'd qualified and completed my probationary year I found myself increasingly drawn to the kids in my class who were struggling to get along with their classmates and couldn't engage in whatever activity was on the go. The rest of them – the smart ones, the popular ones – were just too easy: I'd draw up detailed lesson plans and then leave them in the hands of my very capable classroom assistant, freeing myself up to spend hour after hour with the small group of misfits who just didn't seem able to cope. I rubbed along like this for a couple of years before finally deciding to do something about my obsession with the oddball kids, and then in the space of a fortnight I resigned from my teaching job, much to the dismay of my parents (how could I *waste* all that studying?), took a six-month lease on a flat in a crumbling Victorian tenement in one of the dodgier parts of York and applied for a place on a two-year diploma in Non-directive Play Therapy at the university there. The non-directive part particularly appealed: its premise was that a child's behaviour was always the result of them trying to fulfil their own potential, and as such it made no effort to control or change them. I found that concept exciting: the idea that the child might at some fundamental level know what was best for them better than the adults who surrounded them. It was a far cry from the classroom, where the emphasis was increasingly focused on keeping order and getting the kids through their SATs. There was a practical element to the course, which I'd completed through a placement with a behaviour and education support team at a centre near the hospital. They helped kids whose needs were impacting on their ability to cope in school. It was right at the coalface of child development, and I loved it. With a passion.

And that was how I met Sam. I'd been at the centre one morning, working with a kid called Annie who had been excluded from school because of her unpredictable behaviour in the classroom. We'd been having a great time with a collage she was making, cutting out pictures of people from magazines and gluing them onto an oversized piece of pink sugar paper, when out of nowhere she'd picked up a freshly sharpened green colouring pencil and stuck it right through my jeans and into the top of my thigh. Then she'd calmly taken up the scissors again (plastic-encased, blunt-ended, thank God – heaven alone knows the damage she might have done with a sharper pair) and gone on cutting out the next person from the magazine, while I rolled around on the floor, clutching at my leg and trying not to cry from the pain. One of the team had run me up to the hospital, where I'd been treated by a disturbingly young and good-looking Doctor Bishop, who had sat in a chair pulled up beside the examination bed, his face about an inch away from my knickers, and scowled in concentration as he carefully extracted the broken point of the pencil from my inner thigh. For someone who hadn't seen much action in that department since I'd graduated (the demands of probationary teaching didn't leave a lot of time for a personal life), the sudden intimacy was more than a little bit disconcerting.

'There,' he'd said after a few minutes' probing. He wiped the blade of the scalpel he'd been using on a piece of paper towel and stood up. 'I'm just going to clean it up and put a dressing on it. How did you say it had happened?'

'One of the kids at the centre where I work.' I winced a bit as the antiseptic bit into my flesh. 'She has trouble keeping inside the lines when she's colouring.'

He'd looked at me properly then, his mouth pursed appraisingly, before ducking his head back down between my legs and focusing on drying off the area around the wound and applying a lint dressing. 'I'll need to see you again,' he said without looking up.

'Right,' I replied to the top of his head. His hair was the colour of dark chocolate. The 85 per cent cocoa sort. I had to resist a sudden urge to lean over and lick it. 'Um – when?'

'Tomorrow.' He pressed down the edges of the dressing with his thumb, and to my shock I felt a tingling sensation shoot from my stomach in a general southerly direction. 'I want to make sure the wound doesn't become infected.'

'OK.' I realised I was blushing furiously. For God's sake, Marion, I told myself. Get a grip.

'Good.' He put his hands on the bed either side of my thigh and pushed himself up, and I swear both my legs turned to water. What the hell was wrong with me? 'Make an appointment at the reception desk before you leave.'

When I came back the following afternoon, he was busy with another patient and it was a nurse who removed the dressing and examined the rapidly healing puncture mark. 'Well, that seems to be nice and clean,' she'd said. 'No sign of any infection. I don't expect you'll need to come back.'

I felt sick with disappointment. 'Oh – OK. Well, that's . . . good news.' I gave her a bright smile to hide my frustration.

'I'll just get Doctor Bishop to take a quick look,' she went on. 'He's the one who will have to discharge you.'

I could have kissed her.

He was brisk and businesslike when he came into the cubicle, his eyes sweeping across my naked legs like a farmer eyeing up a particularly unsatisfactory cow at the market. He set to work straight away, probing around about a millimetre from my crotch. 'How does that feel?' he'd asked. *Bloody fantastic*, I'd stopped myself from saying just in time. 'Um – a bit tender,' I'd eventually gulped.

'Hmm.' He was frowning at my thigh. 'Can you get the discharge papers organised?' he said to the nurse, who nodded and disappeared off somewhere beyond the curtain.

He crossed to the small sink in the corner and began washing his hands. 'I'd like to see you again.'

'Oh.' Hadn't he just told the nurse to get the discharge papers sorted? 'But I thought –' I broke off, confused. 'Should I make another appointment with the reception desk?'

'Only if you're planning for them to join us.'

My mouth opened but no words came out. Did he just say what I thought he'd said?

He shook his hands over the sink and then dried them on a paper towel. 'You can put your clothes back on now,' he commented without looking at me.

No, of course he didn't, you dozy moo, I chastised myself. You've been so long without a man, you're hallucinating.

I slid off the bed and pulled my jeans gingerly over the newly changed dressing. 'So – when d'you want to see me next?'

He looked up then and glowered at me for a moment before suddenly pulling the curtain abruptly apart and stalking off without answering. I stared open-mouthed at the space he'd just been occupying. Obviously the lowly patients weren't supposed to ask the great doctors anything quite so menial. Did they teach that kind of arrogance at medical school? The idea that I'd found him even remotely attractive suddenly seemed laughable. The man was a pig. I could feel a bubble of anger mixed with a large dose of humiliation rising inside me. No doubt he was off fetching one of his minions to handle all the boring bits of my next appointment.

The curtain swung aside again and he was back. 'Here,' he said, handing me an envelope. 'Drop that in at your GP surgery next time you're passing.'

'What is it?'

'Your discharge letter. You're now officially no longer my patient.'

'Oh – right.' Boy, was he in a hurry to be shot of me. He was brusque to the point of offensiveness. I snatched the envelope out of his hand to demonstrate that I could be just as rude if I set my mind to it.

'And – um – here.' He handed me another piece of paper. 'I don't think we need to go through the reception desk, do you? Frankly, I'd prefer it to be just the two of us.'

My heart gave a little skip as I looked at what he'd written on the paper. It was an address. My address, in fact, apart from the street number. My face puckered in puzzlement.

'I hate restaurants,' he was telling me now. 'But I'm not a bad cook myself.' He nodded at the piece of paper. 'That's my address. I could come and pick you up.' For a brief second he looked like an awkward teenager, and then his face rearranged itself into its more usual expression of someone who was far too busy and important to be hassled with the social minutiae of life.

'Well.' I looked at the address again. He must live along the road a bit. I made my voice deliberately casual and shrugged. 'Sure, why not?'

'Really?' His whole face lit up. Maybe he wasn't quite so hideous after all. He waggled a pen under my nose. 'Can you write your address on the other side?'

I did so without meeting his eye, and then handed him back the paper. His eyes widened as the coincidence registered.

'OK, then.' He nodded his head at me solemnly. 'Friday, eight o' clock.' It wasn't a question. He gave me a considering look for a moment, as though daring me to contradict him. I folded my arms across my chest and returned the look.

He cleared his throat. 'I don't normally ask patients out on dates. The GMC would have apoplexy. Though, of course, strictly speaking you're not my patient any more. But I promise you I'm entirely respectable.'

'Well, in that case –' I gathered up my coat from the end of the bed and raised my eyebrows at him '– I'm not coming.'

Charlie went nuts when I told her on the phone later that evening. After our parents were killed in a road traffic accident when they were holidaying in the West Country, she had appointed herself *in loco parentis* from her Michigan apartment, in spite of the fact that I was twenty-three by this stage and scarcely in need of any hand-holding. She took my moral development far more personally than they ever had. 'Marion, you can't go. You barely know the man. He could be a trainspotter or a kiddy fiddler or heaven alone knows what else. I'll bet he does this sort of thing all the time.'

'What sort of thing?'

'Picking up desperate women in hospital cubicles.'

'*Desperate?* Me! This from the woman who buggered off to Michigan because somebody told her the ratio of men to women was forty to one.'

'It was three to one, actually, and it turns out I was wrong about that. But at least I've never gone back to some random guy's flat on a first date. I mean, really! What in God's name were you thinking? You could at least have arranged to meet him somewhere public. But no, you had to fall for that ridiculous line about him not being a bad cook.'

'It's fate,' I told her smugly. 'He lives just down the road from me. We were destined to meet. In fact, it's a wonder we haven't run into each other already.'

'Hmmph.' Charlie was unimpressed. 'If you ask me, it's quite obvious he's only got one thing planned for dessert. You.'

'God, Charlie.' I grinned into the telephone. 'I bloody well hope so.'

'Take condoms!' she'd shrieked at me as I'd hung up the phone.

I hadn't needed any, as it turned out. It had taken another three months and several more dates for Sam to prove to me he wasn't quite as respectable as he'd claimed. By then I'd lost myself to him completely. When he asked me before the end of the year if I'd marry him, I never hesitated. And when, four years after the wedding, I gave birth to a baby daughter in the maternity unit a few buildings along from where we'd met, I think I really believed that the gods had marked us out for a charmed life together.

In spite of our best efforts, there were no more children after Hope, though medical checks gave us both a clean bill of health. Sometimes that was just the way of things, Sam told me, calling upon his early training: there wasn't always a clear reason behind an apparent problem. We briefly discussed IVF, but to be honest our lives were so full and Hope such a bubbly, irrepressible little girl, neither of us was terribly keen to rock the domestic boat by embarking upon such an unpredictable and emotionally fraught journey. We moved to a village just outside Harrogate when Hope was five, after an old colleague asked me if I'd consider getting involved in setting up a therapeutic resource centre with her in the town centre. That was when Hector had arrived into our lives, an acquisition I'd strenuously resisted but eventually been forced to capitulate on following a combined offensive from both Hope and Sam, who finally clinched things by telling me that Hope needed some company other than the two boring old people bringing her up. I suppose somewhere in the back of my mind the idea of a dog assuaged some of the guilt I was feeling for failing to come up with a brother or sister for her.

The following four years were the happiest I'd ever known, doing a job I loved and looking after Sam and Hope, who were everything to me. Even the dog, in spite of managing to chew his way through the legs of every kitchen chair we owned, managed to wheedle his way into my affections. Then Sam was offered a consultancy in emergency medicine with Harrogate and District NHS Trust and we'd moved again, right into the middle of town this time, to a beautiful old Victorian town house with an enclosed walled garden that was perfect for Hector and was within walking distance of our respective work places. Life, it seemed to me, just couldn't get any better.

And then barely six months later Hope died, and what was left of Sam and me I managed to kill off in the seven months that followed.

I haven't been back to the centre since the accident. The counsellor mooted the idea of me returning to work about a month after the funeral – he suggested it might help me to 'move on' from what had happened. But I just couldn't do it. A lot of the kids I saw were close in age to Hope, and the thought of seeing them every day, holding their hands, talking to them, helping them with whatever project we had on the go, was too excruciating to bear. I was terrified of discovering I hated them all for being alive when Hope wasn't.

One way or another, it seems to me that things are easier when it's just myself I hate.

Chapter 6

Anyway, sorry for the distraction. You want to know what happens, don't you, after I've taken all those pills? I just wanted to tell you that stuff about Sam and me. To let you know I was once normal. As normal as the next person, anyway. You certainly couldn't tell from the outside that one day I'd just up and kill myself. But, quite honestly, dying didn't strike me as any kind of a big deal. Once the worst thing in the world has already happened to you, it kind of loses its sting.

I wasn't always this blasé about my own mortality. When Charlie and I were small, I went through a stage – maybe all kids do – where I was terrified at the prospect of death. The thought of ceasing to exist filled me with terror, a fact that Charlie would capitalise on by cheerfully describing in detail – usually at night when it was dark and we were supposed to be asleep – every stage of the body's decomposition that she'd managed to pick up from a variety of sources: teachers who thought her thirst for knowledge was a sign of high intelligence; our unsuspecting parents who mistook her obsession for a deep-rooted fear of her own mortality rather than ammunition for torturing a sibling; and classmates who really didn't care whether there was any truth in their wildly colourful interpretations of death as long as it struck fear in the hearts of the unenlightened (me). Heaven, she told me gleefully, didn't exist. After you died there was only the cold earth, a hard box with the lid nailed shut (oh, God – the thought of those nails really used to freak me out) and silence. Your eyeballs fell out of your head, and your fingers and toes dropped off one by one. Eventually, when you had rotted into sufficiently small bits, the worms moved in and finished you off. It wasn't so bad if you were really dead, but of course she had a whole catalogue of real-life cases where people had been buried alive, and had woken up once the soil had been piled on top of their coffins and left to scream and scrape off their fingernails, clawing at the wooden lid just inches from their noses with their eyeballs rolling around somewhere by their feet and an army of hungry worms lurking just out of sight, gleefully sharpening their cutlery and tying napkins around their necks. Eventually you expired, after days of torment, naturally, through lack of oxygen. I would lie wide-eyed and terrified in bed at night, planning ways I might manage to escape from my nailed-shut, soil-laden tomb: maybe if I pushed really hard with my knees, the lid might give a bit, and if I could just get a finger out, I might just possibly be able to poke out an air hole, and if I hadn't expired by then I could press my lips to the air hole and shout for help . . . the effort of trying to work out a plan of action wrung me out, and the worst part about it was that I knew in my heart it was hopeless. The nails (those awful nails!) wouldn't give, or my finger would get crushed by the weight of all that soil, or my voice would be barely audible on account of there being too much ground for it to work its way through on its way to the sweet, fresh air, or even if it did make it up to the light of day, there would be nobody passing by at that exact moment to hear my muffled cries. By the time I was eight I had written my first will, leaving everything to my hamster and stipulating that I wanted to be cremated. Being burned alive seemed like a marginally better option than clawing blindly at the nailed-shut lid of my own coffin, though frankly there wasn't a great deal to choose between the two.

The reality of being dead, I am vaguely relieved to note, is nothing like the terror-filled tales Charlie had fed to me when we were little. Firstly it isn't cold: I can feel the warmth of the sun on my face as I open my eyes. Secondly there is nothing hard about the box I am in. It's so soft it could be my own bed. Which, on closer examination, it proves to be. Nor is it silent. Somewhere inside my head I can hear soft music playing. Harps, maybe?

It doesn't sound like harps.

In fact, it sounds distinctly like the Sugababes singing 'Angels with Dirty Faces', which isn't what I'd been expecting at all. And someone – a girl's voice – is singing along.

I swear my heart misses a beat.

I push myself upright and haul myself gingerly to my feet. My head spinning dizzily, I make my way quietly across the carpet to the bedroom door. Down the landing, I make out a shadow flitting across the floor.

There is someone in Hope's bedroom.

'You don't know that we're going down low,' she is singing, 'you don't know that we listen to the morning.'

Right down to the messed-up lyrics, it sounds just like Hope.

Holding my breath, I push the door open so that I can see the figure inside. And, miraculously, there she is, sitting at the dressing table, her fair hair tumbling messily down her shoulders, playing with the bits and pieces of jewellery in front of her.

I clutch a hand to my heart, which is now thumping away so hard I can hardly bear it. How can I be dead, with such a vigorous heartbeat? I stretch out an arm towards her and then, unsteadily, my mouth dry, I croak out her name.

'Hope?'

She leaps to her feet, overturning the dressing-table stool, and the necklaces and hair clasps and bracelets scatter in a sparkling cascade onto the carpet. 'Jesus fucking Christ,' she hurls at me, her eyes wide with panic. 'Don't go sneaking up on people like that. Ah nearly died o' fright.'

Of course it isn't her. My expectations crumble to dust about my feet.

Face on, she is a few years older than Hope. Somewhere around fourteen, I would say, though it's hard to tell − I haven't been around many teenage girls, and it's a while since I was one myself. Now that she's standing up I can see that she's taller than Hope, too, though not by much. Her eyes, still wide with fright, are the same blue, though: that vivid, clear blue that makes you think they're looking right into your soul. She's no angel herself, that's for sure − the grubby trainers and torn jeans are a dead giveaway. Plus there isn't a hint of a halo.

'Didn't think you was ever going to wake up,' she says cheerfully, as my heart continues to gallop away in my chest.

'Wha– I mean, who –?' I feel totally bewildered, and horribly aware all of a sudden that my insides are performing some kind of digestive can-can and my legs have lost the capacity to support me. I clutch at the end of Hope's bed before sinking shakily onto the mattress. When I gather enough courage to look back at the girl, she is watching me appraisingly, waiting for me to say something.

'You're not an angel, are you?' I give my head a shake, an action that sends the room spinning dizzily around me. I groan and clutch at my stomach. 'Ugh. No, of course you're not. Whoever saw an angel with a pierced eyebrow?' God, I had to get a grip.

'Charmin', that is.' She drops onto the mattress beside me, causing the bed to lurch sickeningly. 'First good deed ah've done in years, and ah don't even get a thank you.'

Good deed? My brain is reeling. Maybe she *is* an angel, sent to fetch me and take me to join my daughter, who is waiting behind a bright light somewhere. But then – the first good deed in years? I suppose she could be a fallen angel, back in the field for the first time in a while. Probably after a spot of retraining. I squeeze my eyes shut for a moment, then turn to regard her once more. The eyebrow ring is really putting me off. Try to be more broadminded, Marion, I chastise myself sternly. Have a little faith.

I take a deep breath, then offer her a wobbly smile. 'Have you come to take me to Hope?'

'Hope?' she queries, pronouncing it *Horpe*. She looks at me blankly. 'In't that what you called me just now, when you come in t' room?' She shakes her head. 'Ah've never heard of no one called Hope.'

My stomach gives another growl, and suddenly something I remember hearing at the funeral of an elderly great-uncle years ago, about there being no more sickness in Heaven, pops into my head and I am forced to acknowledge the unlikelihood of my being dead after all. All the same, though, I would have expected nine Amitriptylene and however much of the vodka I'd managed to get down me before passing out to produce a bit more than a dodgy tummy. A wave of nausea sweeps over me and my mouth fills with an acrid bitterness.

'Would you mind −?' I hold up a hand to the girl and push myself to my feet. 'I just have to −'

I barely make the bathroom before throwing up copiously into the toilet. When I am done, the girl is standing behind me in the doorway.

'D'you want a towel or summat?' She glances around the gleaming bathroom. 'Have you not got no towels?'

I incline my head gingerly. 'Airing cupboard. Next door along.'

She's back in a moment with a towel and a face cloth, which she wrings out in the hand basin before passing it across to me, and I sink my face into it gratefully.

'Must be a bit of a pain, that,' she observes wryly. 'Having to fetch a towel from t' cupboard. You know, some people leave them out in t' bathroom. It's a good idea is that: saves you messing around every time you go to t' toilet.'

She perches herself on the edge of the bath and regards me with that appraising look of hers. 'Ah were there last night, you know,' she offers after a moment.

'There?'

'In t' street. Wi' Ryan. Ah'm supposed to be t' lookout.'

'Ah.' I nod slowly as comprehension dawns. 'You're Con, I suppose.' I weigh up this new information. 'Short for Connie?' I hazard.

She pulls a face. 'Constance. Only everybody calls me Con. Just as well, really. Ah don't look like a Constance, do I? I don't think so, any road. What d'you think?'

'I don't know.' I am suddenly exhausted again. 'What does a Constance look like?'

'Oh – I dunno. Posh, ah suppose.' She digs the toe of her grubby trainer against the skirting board, then gives me a bright smile that lights up her eyes. 'That'd be t' day.' Her expression changes suddenly. 'You look like shit, if you don't mind me saying. Maybe you should go back to bed.'

'What are you doing in my house?' I finally get around to asking. Now that the question's out, I can't for the life of me think why I never asked it earlier.

'Brought your bag back, didn't ah? Trust me, you don't want Ryan coming round here. He were in a right mood last night after what happened. Ah've never seen owt like it. Telling him to get a shift on.' She gives a snort of laughter. 'You must be barmy.' A pause: I'm not going to argue with her. 'Any road, it's on t' table in t' kitchen. Come on.' She pushes herself off the edge of the bath and makes to take my arm. 'You get back to bed, and ah'll go and make us a brew, yeah? Nothing like a cup of tea when you're feeling a bit ropey.'

The thought of a hot drink is suddenly so wonderful I almost swoon. What with being mugged, and then failing to kill myself, I am beyond arguing with her, and so I capitulate with relatively good grace. At least if she goes off to make some tea, it will give me a chance to try to straighten out my spiralling thoughts without her constant chatter buzzing like a persistent mosquito in my ears. 'Do you know where to find everything?'

She grins at me impudently. "Course ah do. Had a good snoop round while you were out for t' count. You've no milk, mind. Bugger all in t' fridge, actually.' There's that look again, weighing me up.

'There's some long-life in one of the cupboards.' I return the look. 'Evidently your snooping wasn't as thorough as it might have been.'

I can hear her clattering around in the kitchen as I grope my way back to bed. Before climbing in, I draw the curtains to take the edge off the dazzling sunshine that is still streaming through the window and doing nothing for the headache that is just beginning to announce itself around the corners of my eyes. Then I fall gratefully back onto the mattress, where I discover the empty vodka glass lolling in the middle of the duvet, resting drunkenly on a similarly empty packet of antibiotic tablets. There is not a trace of the Amitriptylene, pills or packaging, anywhere to be seen.

I must nod off again, because when I wake for the second time the room is growing dark. There's something different about the house too, a stillness it takes me a moment or two to comprehend. And then it dawns on me: someone – Con, presumably, unless there have been other uninvited guests while I was asleep – has turned off the music in

Hope's bedroom. Oddly, the silence isn't oppressive, the way it had been in the months after her death. It's almost a relief, in fact. A mug of tea is standing forlornly on the bedside cabinet. I reach out and touch the side of the mug with the back of my hand. It's stone cold.

'Con?' I call out into the quiet house, straining to hear if she's still around. There's no answer. After a few moments I push back the duvet and cross to the landing. 'Con?' I try again. Nothing. I cross to Hope's room, where the necklaces and hair clasps have all been carefully retrieved and placed neatly back on the dressing table, and then pad downstairs to the kitchen, which is empty as well. I find myself feeling both relieved and – bizarrely – disappointed. My handbag is standing in the middle of the table, alongside the tumbled contents of the first-aid kit (the unfinished box of Amitriptylene foremost among the rest of the bits and pieces) and a quick glance inside it seems to suggest that its contents are all intact. There's nothing out of place in the rest of the kitchen either: no soggy tea bags in the sink, no second mug standing on the draining board. In fact, if it weren't for the quietness of the house and the cold drink sitting beside my bed upstairs, there's no sign, none at all, that I didn't dream the events of last night and that no one has been here at all.

Chapter 7

By the time Sam turns up for his things a little after eight o'clock, I've removed the evidence of my abortive attempt to do myself in from the bedroom and put what's left of the vodka back in the fridge. The antidepressants have been returned to the medicine tin, which in turn is back in its usual place in the cupboard above the bread-maker and, apart from being spectacularly clean and tidy, the place looks pretty much like normal – nothing to arouse anybody's suspicions, anyway. Granted, I could look better – my clothes are crumpled from being slept in and I can't be sure there isn't a faint smell of vomit hovering around me – but he's so used to me not paying any attention to my appearance, I can't imagine he'll notice anything out of the ordinary.

It's weird having to open the door for him. I don't know what to say at first: he's standing on the doorstep looking uneasy, like a nervous teenager come to pick up his date for the school dance. For a moment the pair of us just stand there, tongue-tied, trying to figure out the protocol for a situation like this.

'Um – come in,' I eventually manage. I want to ask him why he didn't use his key, why he's suddenly behaving like a stranger, but I don't. I already know the answer. I throw him a sidelong glance as he steps across the threshold to see if he can spot anything of yesterday's intentions in my face.

He can't – he doesn't actually meet my eye, in fact: doesn't wrap his arms around me and burrow his nose into my hair and inhale me to get rid of the smell of hospital, the way he usually would when he got back from work in the evening. He doesn't notice the uncharacteristically immaculate state of the house nor the even-worse-than-usual state of me. He doesn't notice anything at all, apparently. He dives straight past me as though he's late for an appointment and then stops at the bottom of the stairs, glancing around him nervously as though he hasn't lived here for the past year. 'I won't be long,' he says, shuffling nervously from foot to foot in the hall. 'I just need a few more clothes for now.' The words hang in the air between us, and I wonder how long he envisages 'for now' as being, whether he's planning a reconciliation or a more permanent separation. Not that I've any room for complaint, given the permanent separation I tried to pull off last night. He throws himself at the stairs, taking them two at a time in his desperation to get away from me. I can hear him clattering around upstairs while I go through to the kitchen and sit uncomfortably at the table, feeling as awkward as him. The depth of our unease with one another is staggering.

I follow his progress as he moves about upstairs. There's the creak of the loose floorboard in front of the wardrobe door: he must be packing up some more shirts for work. Then the rattle of a drawer: underwear, maybe, or a jumper. After that it goes quiet for a bit, and then I hear the clomping sound of his shoes on the tiled floor of the en-suite: shaving gear, maybe? No: he would already have taken that with him yesterday, surely. His shower gel, then. My eyes drift to a scratch along the surface of the table as I try to distract myself from the unwelcome thought that upstairs my husband really is giving up on us and moving out of my life.

A short while afterwards he comes hurrying down the stairs and appears in the kitchen doorway. 'Right,' he says awkwardly. 'That's me.' Behind him in the hall is one of the suitcases we use for summer holidays. I try to gauge from its size how seriously he's taking this break-up, and then chastise myself silently: I'm hardly in a position to criticise. I pushed him to this in the first place – in some respects, I've been crying out for it. I want to throw myself on his neck and beg him to give me another chance to prove to him that I'm not the vile person I've been pretending to be all these months, because without him around I'm not sure I'll exist any more, but something stops me. Something keeps me pinned in my seat. I think it might be the knowledge that I really am that vile person.

I glance at him nervously. 'Is this it, then?'

His shoulders slump. 'I don't know. I just – I need some space.'

I clear my throat. 'How much space?'

He doesn't answer me, but retreats into the hall and picks up the suitcase. 'How much space?' I ask him again, following him into the hall, and he turns on me with an exasperated sigh.

'I don't know! Just – leave it, will you? Christ. I can't breathe around you at the moment.'

I can't breathe, either, in the ragged space left by his words. What comes out of my mouth next does nothing to alleviate the panic that is filling every pore of my body as it hits me that he really is leaving, that I'm going to have to start coping without him.

'Can you take the dog?'

'What?' He is looking at me as though I am insane.

'Hector.' I am struggling to retain some semblance of composure. 'Can you take him with you? I don't think I can manage him on my own.'

I've momentarily stunned him into speechlessness. 'Wh– No, of course I can't take the dog! I'm staying in the doctors' accommodation. Where on earth do you suppose I would keep him? In one of the triage rooms, maybe?' He regards me incredulously for a moment, and then looks around suspiciously. 'Where is he, anyway?'

'In the scullery. No – leave him!' I say as Sam drops the suitcase and makes for the scullery door. 'I told you, I can't cope with him. He's too much for me.'

He ignores me, flinging the door open and stepping into the scullery in a rush of cold air. 'Hector!' he calls out. 'Good boy. Come here.'

He stays there on the threshold to the scullery, squatting in front of Hector, making soft crooning noises and caressing his ears. A sharp stab of jealousy shoots through my body. Then he turns back around to face me and his expression hardens.

'I don't know what's happened to you.' He says the words lifelessly, as though something inside him has died. 'Where you went, why you won't come back from it.' He shakes his head in despair and lets out a deep sigh. 'I don't know who you are any more. But I'll tell you something. If you can't rouse yourself enough to look after this poor bloody creature, I will never forgive you. Ever.'

The expression in his eyes is so bleak I can hardly bear to meet his gaze. Then, abruptly, he pushes himself to his feet and strides back across the kitchen to the hall. Almost without breaking his step, he picks up the suitcase once again. And then he hesitates at the foot of the stairs and drops his gaze to the carpet. Now, I think to myself. Now he's going to turn around and tell me it's all been a terrible mistake and he's changed his mind.

He doesn't. He keeps his eyes firmly on the carpet. 'I'm going away the week after next,' he says stonily.

'Away? Where?' I can feel panic rising in my breast.

'Nakuru.'

I think my heart actually stops for a moment. The medical team at the hospital have links with a health-care project based at a rural Kenyan village, and they've been fundraising for months to help finance a few of them going out there as part of an exchange programme. Before Hope died, Sam had talked about going, torn between a real passion for the project and a reluctance to abandon Hope and me for the duration of the six-week visit. After the accident, he just stopped talking about it completely. And now, it seemed, he'd come full circle and resolved any feelings of guilt he had once harboured about who or what he might be abandoning.

My throat has gone dry. 'I thought Frank was going,' I eventually manage to croak. *Not you. You can't just leave me.*

Frank Billington was one of the other ER consultants who often worked back-to-back shifts with Sam.

'We swapped.' That's it: no further explanation as to why Frank, single and footloose, should suddenly give up his much-coveted place on the programme in order to make room for Sam, who had a whole host of reasons to be staying at home.

'You – swapped?' I can hardly keep the incredulity out of my voice. 'Why?'

A pause. 'His father's not well. He doesn't think now's a good time for him to disappear off for a month and a half.'

'But it is a good time for you,' I say, bitterness making my mouth twist.

He looks at me now. 'Given the circumstances, yes, I think it probably is a good thing.' He puts the suitcase down again and crosses to where I'm sitting, then kneels in front of me and takes hold of my hands, looking me in the eye at last. 'We both need some space, Marion. Proper space, away from each other, to work things out. Neither of us is very good for the other one at the moment.'

I give a half-laugh to mask my desperation, shrugging him off. 'Well, it sounds to me as though you've got it all worked out already, haven't you, Sam? Your timing couldn't have been any better. You get to run away to Africa and I get to stay here, drowning in this – this *mess* we've become, on my own. I don't get to run anywhere at all.'

He gives a heavy sigh and pushes himself back to his feet, hesitating for a moment as though he's about to say something else. Then he gives a sad little laugh and shakes his head at me. 'Is that really what you think?' He gives that laugh again, the one that's more despairing than any cry of anguish. 'You've been running away for months, Marion. You might have stayed put, holed up in this house, turning it into a prison for the pair of us, but you've still run away. You've run so far, I don't recognise you any more.'

There is such an air of forlornness in his voice, I can't think of anything to say. As he makes his way back out into the hall and picks up his things once again I just go on sitting there frozen in my seat, trapped by the accusation he's just levelled at me about turning the house into some sort of a prison, trying to work out whether there's any truth in it, not wanting to face it if there is. And before I can reach any conclusions, before I can cry out, 'You're right, I have run away, but I want to come back,' he's gone, closing the front door heavily behind him.

I look around at the kitchen, at the Aga and all I once thought it represented sitting stolidly against the far wall, and all of a sudden I can see what he means. There is no heart in our house any more. It's just walls, doors, windows and a whole heap of . . . of *stuff* that used to represent a family. I try to get up, but then I remember the look of despair in his eyes as it finally dawned on him just what a vile person he was married to.

I am so steeped in foulness, it's sticking me to my seat.

And then I feel a warm chin resting itself tentatively on my knee, and a diffident paw comes up apologetically onto the seat beside me. I let my hand fall onto the dog's broad back and run my fingers through the coarse fur, feeling its heat stealing through the numbness that has taken hold of me. When I lower my eyes to his, he is regarding me contritely, as though trying to apologise for all the trouble he's caused. I drop to my knees on the floor and wrap my arms around his warm body in a hug, and a warm, fat tear squeezes from my eye and plops onto the floor beside us.

'I'm sorry, Hector,' I tell him, and he turns his head and licks at my face to show that there are no hard feelings.

If only I could forgive myself as easily, I think as I clutch onto him and bury my tear-streaked face in his downy coat, we wouldn't be in this mess in the first place.

Chapter 8

I am in uncharted territory.

Over the thirteen years that Sam and I have been together, our arguments have been swift, sharp flashes of discord followed by easy contrition and sheepish, giggling reconciliation. After Hope was born, during the early months when each day rolled into the next in a sea of nappies and night feeding and my eyes grew gritty with tiredness, we fell into small, bickering quarrels for a time, petty disagreements fuelled by hormone-induced sense of humour failures on my part and exasperation and exhaustion on Sam's. There has never, ever been anything even remotely approaching a separation. Somehow, in the midst of our heated tempers, we've always managed to see the funny side of the situation and, sooner or later, have a good laugh at ourselves.

The bickering when Hope was a baby came to an abrupt end after a typical contretemps one evening after I'd taken her upstairs for a last feed before settling her down for the night. *Attempting* to settle her, I should say: Hope's early months were plagued with colic and fretfulness, and at six months old she still hadn't managed anything approaching a full night's sleep. Needless to say, Sam and I hadn't either. Anyway, this particular evening around eleven-thirty I was sitting up in bed, almost comatose with fatigue, nursing her while Sam moved around softly downstairs, putting the house back into some sort of order. He did this every evening, quietly righting the devastation Hope and I managed to wreak during the day, restoring our home to some semblance of normality so that we could get up in the morning while he was out at work and mess it up all over again. It had become a kind of ritual between us.

It was as I heard the creak of his footstep on the bottom stair that I remembered I'd left a mountain of washing hanging out to dry in the garden. 'Sam,' I'd called down to him, 'can you bring the washing in from the whirligig before you come up?'

He gave a laborious sigh, and then tutted, a censorious tut heavy with *why-can't-you-manage-a-single-thing-around-here* condemnation. Not that he ever suggested anything of the sort, you understand. Not in so many words. Sam's criticisms of my domestic prowess were always shrouded in ambiguity, making them difficult to fend off. (Though they might have been the feverish imaginings of my overwrought state of mind, which made them even harder to parry.) 'Can't you get it?' he called up to me. 'I need a bath before I turn in.'

A bath! I surged with resentment: I couldn't remember the last time I'd managed a bath uninterrupted by the wail of a hungry baby demanding instant gratification. 'No I bloody well can't get it,' I'd snapped, sense of humour failure ready and raring to go. 'I have a small child latched to my breast draining the last few remaining dregs of energy from me after bleeding me dry all day.' I was nothing if not colourful in my irritation. 'Of course, if you'd like to swap places with me and breastfeed your own daughter for a change while I bring it in, I'll be delighted to nip downstairs.' Irrational? Of course I was irrational. I was a breastfeeding mother. Cut me some slack, can't you?

He gave another sigh. 'Can't it wait until morning? I'm all in.'

'Oh, for God's sake.' I threw a sigh of my own back at him. 'Yes, it can wait until morning. And then I'll have to wash it all over again, because rain is forecast overnight. But don't let that worry you. My life is one long grind of getting nowhere nowadays, punctuated by shitty nappies and screaming babies.' (Suddenly there was more than one to contend with − a girl has to grab what she can from the armoury of domestic strife if she's to stand any chance at all of scoring a hit.) 'Some of us don't get to swan off to hospital and spend the day being waited on hand and foot by that gaggle of fawning nursing staff, all running around mopping our brows and bringing us cups of tea every half-hour. Some of us are stuck indoors with no chance of an adult conversation and no hope of escape and no sign of ever having a career again and a load of wet bloody clothes that they've *already washed* to do all over again, because their husbands wanted a nice hot relaxing bath before they came to bed at night. Yes, you just leave the washing. Don't you give it another thought.'

I shut up then, knowing I was being ridiculous, refusing to admit it to Sam. At my breast, Hope had nodded off, still firmly latched on and suckling occasionally, in spite of the exchange (mostly one way, admittedly) of slings and arrows that had just taken place above her downy head. She did this just to fool me, I'd learned: try to prise her off early, before she was completely out for the count, and she'd rally suddenly with an indignant wail and demand another fifteen minutes' nursing, finally releasing me for an all-too-short couple of hours' exhausted oblivion before beginning the whole circus all over again. It was like being shackled to a large and very vocal leech.

Downstairs, an ominous silence hung in the air for a moment, and then I heard the creak of the bottom stair again. I leaned forwards in the bed, straining to follow Sam's movements, but I couldn't work out from the furtive rustling that followed precisely what he was doing. Twenty minutes passed – what on earth was he up to? – before finally he appeared in the bedroom and lifted the sleeping baby out of my arms.

'Nappy?' he enquired.

'Already done.' It was quite amazing, the way I managed to inject a tone of injured smugness into those two little words.

He nodded and took Hope through to her cot next door, and then returned to our bedroom, peeling himself out of his clothes and dropping onto the mattress on his side of the bed.

'Did you bring the washing in?' I demanded.

'Mm-hmm.' He rolled onto his side with his back to me, a solid wall of keeping-me-at-arm's-length husband who wasn't going to allow me the satisfaction of victory, and I sighed, remembering the times before Hope when sleep had been the last thing on his mind when we retired for the night. These days our sex life seemed to have given up the ghost along with my sense of humour.

I regarded the back of his head in silence for a moment, a wave of guilt washing over me. 'I thought you were going for a bath.' I fought to keep my voice from sounding too conciliatory.

There was no answer. Beside me in the bed, having put in a twelve-hour stint at the hospital before coming home and cooking dinner and then spending the past hour tidying the house and bringing the washing in, my exhausted husband was already asleep.

I woke to an unusually silent house the following morning, and a wave of panic washed over me as I struggled to figure out what was wrong. The light in the bedroom was brighter than it normally was when the five-thirty Hope alarm clock clamoured its way into my subconsciousness. I blinked at the clock beside the bed and real panic set in when I saw that it was gone eight. There was no sign of Sam: evidently he'd not forgiven me for the washing and had left for work without saying goodbye. I threw back the covers and hurried through to Hope's bedroom, my heart lurching at the thought that something must have happened for the night not to have been punctuated by her shrill cries.

She was lying on her back in her cot, waving her arms and legs in the air and cooing quietly to herself. I bent over her suspiciously. 'What have you done with the real Hope Bishop?' I asked, scooping her up in my arms and glowering at her dubiously. She gave a great gurgle of delight and reached out a chubby hand to pull on my nose.

I carried her through to my bed and spent the next half-hour feeding her and playing Pat-a-cake with her, giddy with the hitherto unknown luxury of waking to a happy baby after a full night's sleep. If it hadn't been for the fact that Sam and I had gone to sleep under a cloud, I'd have been walking on air.

Eventually, as Hope's eyes were starting to droop after the novelty of using all those unaccustomed smile muscles and I could put off the chore of getting up no longer, I slid my feet into my slippers and padded downstairs, Hope balanced on my hip, to make some coffee and try a last feed before seeing if she could be fooled into taking a mid-morning nap. 'Your daddy,' I told her, setting her down in her bouncy chair so that I could pour the hot water onto the coffee grounds, 'is very, very cross with your mummy.' She regarded me solemnly from the chair, and then yawned extravagantly.

As I busied myself fetching a mug and warming some milk, I tried to gauge how annoyed Sam must be to have left for work without a word to me. The fighting might have increased over the past few months, but we'd never parted from one another without one of us (usually Sam, I grant you) making some attempt at conciliation. It hadn't even been that serious a row, I thought: just me being irrational and crabby and hoping he would jolly me out of it.

Once the coffee was brewed, I scooped Hope up to carry her through to the living room, pushed the door open with my hip and stopped dead. Before me, carefully erected on the carpet in the middle of the floor, the whirligig stood in outsized glory, its arms reaching out and almost touching opposite walls, the washing still gaily hanging from it like bunting at a carnival.

I gasped. And then I started to laugh. I couldn't help it: the whole thing looked so ridiculous standing there in all its incongruous splendour, filling the room with a kind of irreverent grace. Part of me wanted to be cross – it would take hours for me to get it back out into the garden (well, maybe not hours, but you have to bear in mind that I was still trying to underpin the moral high ground here). But I just couldn't do it. Tears of laughter streamed down my face. Six months of exhaustion and secret fear that I was doing the whole motherhood thing wrong were swept away in a heartbeat. I thought of Sam, already worn out after a gruelling day in A&E, going to all the bother of wrestling the thing in through the French doors – he'd have had to collapse it: there was no way it would have fitted in its erected state – and in an instant I'd forgiven him his apparent lack of co-operation the previous evening. Wiping the tears from my cheeks, I fastened Hope back into her bouncy chair and went straight to the phone and dialled his mobile – the one he kept on him especially so that I could reach him in an emergency and that I was forbidden from using except in times of dire crisis. He answered almost immediately.

'Get home now,' I told him.

'Why? What's the matter?'

'I need to show you how cross I am with you.'

I could feel him grinning into the telephone. 'I was only doing as I was told.'

'Now,' I repeated sternly.

He hesitated. 'I can't. What if there's an emergency?'

'There already is an emergency,' I told him. 'I'm in urgent need of immediate medical attention. Besides, you live five minutes away from the hospital. You'll beat the ambulance.'

I could almost feel him wrestling with the thought of breaking hospital protocol in the interests of getting home to me. 'Look, I really shouldn't,' he said after a moment. 'But let me see if Frank's still around. If he can cover, I'll see what I can do. But I'm making no promises.'

He was still wearing his stethoscope snaked around his neck as he came through the front door twenty-nine minutes later (I timed him, in between settling Hope back in her cot with some cuddly toys for company). 'Well now,' he said, uncoiling the stethoscope and giving me a stern look. 'What seems to be the trouble?'

God, he was sexy. My stomach did a little backflip. 'Um,' I told him, 'there is a large erection in my sitting room that shouldn't be there. It just seems to have sprung up overnight.'

He nodded gravely. 'Nasty,' he said. 'But don't worry, there's a very effective treatment for that.'

'There is?'

'Oh, yes.' He stepped in closer and slid his hand inside the waist of my dressing gown, pulling me hard up against him. 'Immediate bed rest. After a full examination, naturally.'

'Oh, naturally,' I agreed breathlessly, and took him happily off upstairs.

Remembering this now, in the aftermath of his having left me, I am overcome by a yearning for those early days when arguments were part of the ebb and flow of our lives, and making up afterwards just another step in the journey we were making together. Seen from my new perspective as an abandoned wife, they were untroubled days where everything was there on a platter, just waiting to be taken for granted. I want them back so that I can live them all over again in the hope that I might manage to get things right second time round.

Chapter 9

Over the past few days I have turned into a batty old woman.

I'm not sure how it happened. One minute I was your average grief-stricken, suicide fuck-up whose husband had just walked out on her, and the next I'd become a hygiene-deficient hermit wandering round the house talking to myself and jumping out of my skin every time the phone rings before hurling abuse at it when the answerphone cuts in and I realise it isn't Sam who's calling. It's usually Charlie, actually – she keeps doing a repeat of her previous message telling me to call her without telling me what her news is. Between that and the fact that for reasons of lethargy rather than sentimentality I'm still in the same knickers I was wearing when Sam left, I feel like Bill Murray in *Groundhog Day* with none of the life-enhancing skills he manages to accumulate while his life is stuck on rewind. Wake up. Stick feet into slippers. Go downstairs. Put kettle on. Let Hector out into back garden. Brew tea. Let Hector in from back garden. Take tea through to sitting room. Sit on sofa. Stare at fireplace. Jump when phone rings. Stare at fireplace some more, etc, etc.

There has to be more to life than this, surely. I seem to recall old Bill becomes a virtuoso on the piano during his incarceration in no-man's-land. The only thing I seem to be getting better at is poop-scooping the garden. Well, maybe *better* is putting it a bit grandly. Faster, anyway. Marion Bishop, shit-shoveller extraordinaire. Thunderous applause, please. All I need is a dozen or so cats to complete the metamorphosis from a once-rational thirty-something to an eccentric old bat who never opens her front door except to let the cats in and out and spit at passing children.

Heather called round on Tuesday afternoon. I nearly had a heart attack when the doorbell rang. I did a bit of curtain tweaking and spotted her from the upstairs landing window, and I panicked and hid in the bathroom for forty minutes until I was sure she was gone. I only came out because the cats were pestering me for their tea.

The fictitious cats, that is. The ones that only exist in my mad old-biddy fantasy.

I need to get out more.

I'm mulling over this idea (I seem to be doing an awful lot of mulling these days) when the ritual daily jangling of the telephone cuts into my thoughts. 'Number withheld' the caller display reads. I imagine myself reaching down and picking up the receiver, speaking into the mouthpiece, greeting the caller. The prospect makes me light-headed.

The phone continues to ring a couple more times, and then the answerphone cuts in. 'You've reached the Bishops,' I hear myself say. 'We can't come to the phone at the moment. Leave a message and we'll call you back.'

There's a beep, a sigh and then the hum of the dialling tone.

I wait until the 'New Message' light comes on, and then

I play back the non-message, wondering whether Charlie has finally given up leaving her daily messages instructing me to call her, and then playing with the idea that it might not have been her this time: it might actually have been that long-anticipated call from Sam. I listen to the sigh afresh to see if there's anything about it that I recognise, any sign of him weakening. I mean I know I can't be sure it really is him, but frankly I can't think of anyone else who would ring up and just sigh down the receiver at me. And while I'm still standing there wondering about the identity of my mystery caller, the telephone rings again and this time the caller does leave a message.

'Marion, it's me.' My heart somersaults in my chest. Almost a week of silence, and then I get two phone calls one after another, even if one of them is just a sigh. I stretch out my hand, vacillating about answering, and then he gives that same sigh again, and I let my hand drop back to my side. 'Look, I know you're there – where else would you be? It's not like you have this hectic social life at the moment.'

'The cheek!' I say aloud to Hector. 'For all he knows, I could have been out whooping it up every evening since he left.'

'Anyway – the thing is, I'm leaving for Nakuru on Sunday, and there's some stuff I need before I go.' A wave of panic washes over me, and then I remind myself that I've been on my own for the past six days anyway – much longer than that, actually, if you count the months I've spent shutting everyone out – and I've somehow survived the experience. I focus back on the message again. '. . . my briefcase. And my passport.' There's a pause, and I can imagine him racking his brains trying to figure out how he can get the things he needs without running into me. 'So I thought I'd come round on Saturday evening and pick it up. About seven. You don't need to be there if you'd rather not be: I've got a key.' Another pause. 'Right, then. See you later. Or not, as the case may be. Um . . . bye.'

I sigh myself after hearing his message. No sign of weakening, that's for sure. If anything, his tone is irritated, verging on sarcastic. *It's not like you have this hectic social life.* Who does he think he is? A surge of resentment sweeps over me, along with that fluttering feeling in my stomach that I've just decided can't be panic about being left on my own. Maybe it's nerves at the prospect of seeing him: it's been almost a week, after all – the longest period we've spent apart since we met.

I wander through to the study and stand in the doorway, surveying the cluttered jumble of Sam's home office. Maybe if I get all the bits and pieces together for him he'll not need to hang around for so long. I take a deep breath as the fluttering feeling sweeps across me once again, and lift out his briefcase from beside the desk. Then I go to retrieve his passport, which is in the top drawer of the desk along with Hope's and mine.

My stomach gives another lurch as I lift out all three and flick through them until I find Hope's. The picture is almost three years out of date, taken shortly after her sixth birthday when we were planning a trip to Michigan to visit Charlie. In it she is studiously serious, having taken to heart the warnings I'd been issuing for days about not smiling for her passport photograph. 'But you're supposed to smile,' she'd argued with me. 'It's what you do, Mummy. The man who came to take our pictures at school told us funny stories to make us smile.' I'd told her she wouldn't be allowed to go and stay with Auntie Charlie if she smiled, a directive she'd taken so seriously that she spent the first two days of the trip frowning at everyone we met. Neither Sam nor I cottoned on until the second evening when Sam had been putting her to bed and had come through to say she was in floods of tears and wouldn't tell him why. It turned out that she'd inadvertently smiled at the waitress in the diner where we'd had supper, and was convinced she'd be sent home on the next flight out. The recollection ought to have me smiling, but doesn't – another casualty of the hit-and-run catastrophe. Nobody tells you about that part, about the fact that when you lose a child the way we lost Hope, you lose all the happy memories you've spent their lifetime accumulating. Looking back over them is just too hard to bear.

I tread down on these unwelcome ruminations, and am stuffing the passports back where I found them when something in the drawer catches my eye – a small piece of dark-blue velvet that is nestling incongruously in beside some highlighter pens and a memo pad. I lift it out to examine it, and discover it's actually a little pouch, complete with a silk drawstring around the top. I pull at the drawstring to loosen it and give the material a shake, and a tiny silver house, hinged on one side, falls into my palm.

The roof is crooked, the tiles scratched unevenly into the silver, and the door hangs lopsidedly ajar. There's a small catch on the opposite side to the hinge, underneath a rickety-looking chimney. If I fit my nail underneath it and prise it open, the whole roof swings backwards to reveal the interior of the house, empty aside from the solitary presence, hanging from one of the rafters, of a miniature silver ghost.

A haunted house. I stare at it, aghast, because I know, with sickening certainty, why there is a silver haunted house in Sam's drawer, and why finding it there has set my heart off at a gallop and the old familiar feeling of panic sweeping over me. It's the latest in a series of charms Sam has been collecting for Hope over the past few years, to add to a bracelet his grandmother bought her as a christening gift. Made of silver links threaded with pink ribbons and beads, it had been about as unsuitable for a six-month-old baby as it was possible to get. 'It's for when she's older,' she had defended herself when Sam had pulled her leg about it. 'Look: there are extra links you can add in as her wrist gets bigger. I'm going to get charms for each of her birthdays. You'll see: by the time she's eight she'll love it.'

She'd loved it long before then. When she was five we'd allowed her to wear it the day she started school, a distraction from the first-day nerves that had worked a treat, not least because of the attention it had attracted from the other girls in her class. At that point it had boasted five charms, three of which had been chosen by Sam's grandmother, and the remaining two picked out by Sam himself after she'd become too infirm to do her own shopping. 'They have to begin with the letter H,' his grandmother had instructed him upon transferring the responsibility for charm purchasing onto her clueless grandson. 'H for Hope, you know – that way everyone will always know it's her bracelet.' An instruction Sam had stretched to the limit with the purchase of the fourth charm by procuring a tiny dog charm and strenuously asserting that it was a hyena. It took its place alongside the heart, the hat and the horse his grandmother had already procured, and the following year, when Hope started school, a miniature crab ('A hermit crab, if you must know,' Sam had asserted) joined the motley collection. After that he had honed his acquisition skills, and in the four years that followed the bracelet had boasted a hockey stick, a tiny helicopter whose blades and wheels rotated, a handbag that opened and a hedgehog.

He had been dismissive when I'd warned him that the task would become more difficult as the years progressed: 'Not a bit of it. There are plenty of things still to go.'

'Like what? You've already cheated with the crab.'

'Hermit crab. That conforms to the criteria.'

'Only just. And you were stretching it with the dog, too. Hyena, my backside.'

'It's a husky,' he told me brazenly. 'I changed it from a hyena after we got Hector.'

'You can't just change it like that!' I said indignantly, but laughing at the same time. 'And anyway, Hector isn't a husky. He's a malamute. That's an M, Sam. M for malamute.'

'Well, then, it's just Hector. H for Hector. That counts.'

'You're really clutching at straws, aren't you?' I shook my head, pretending to chastise him. 'Anyway, I still can't think of anything else you can add, even with your loose interpretation of the rules.'

He'd started to count on his fingers. 'Harp. Horn. Hummingbird –'

'Where on earth are you going to find a hummingbird charm?'

He'd swept on, ignoring the interruption. 'Hen. Hippopotamus. Heffalump –'

'Heffalump? As in Winnie-the-Pooh-speak for an elephant?'

'It still counts. Hare. Hamster. Hylaeosaurus –'

'*What?* You made that up.'

'No, I didn't. It's a type of dinosaur. Flat head. Spikes. Looks a lot like your sister. Hyena. Hornet. Haunted house –'

'Sam.' I'd managed to stem the flow. 'I defy even you to procure a haunted house charm for your daughter's bracelet. Let alone a Hylewhatsit dinosaur.'

He'd waggled his eyebrows at me comically. 'The trouble with you, Marion, is that you have no faith. By her next birthday, Hope will have a haunted house for her bracelet. With ghost,' he'd added for good measure.

I'd forgotten about it, until now. Forgotten completely about the bracelet, too – the bracelet Hope had loved so much she'd had to be persuaded to take it off for a bath when she was small. She had worn constantly for the past four-and-a-half years – a habit that, amongst all the fear and anger and devastation that had followed her death, I had somehow managed to lose sight of completely. As it comes back to me now I find myself overwhelmed by the panic that has been lurking just behind my consciousness for so long now. Because there had been no sign of it afterwards – no trace of the hermit crab or the Hector-hyena or any of the other charms, no sign of the pink ribbon that threaded its way through the silver links. Nothing. The only evidence that it had ever existed lies in the tiny silver house I am gripping tightly in my hand. And suddenly I am overwhelmed with the feeling that I have to find the bracelet, that if I can lay my hands on it again it will somehow bring Hope back to me.

I tear out of the study and up the stairs to her room, throwing myself at the dressing table to rake through the collection of jewellery and hair clasps that lie on its surface. Of course it isn't there: I'd always known at some level that it wouldn't be. Hadn't I dusted the place a hundred times over the past months – sat in here at this very seat, picking over the assorted treasures she had loved so much? It had never been here. I drop to my knees in front of the bookshelves, pulling off each of the books in turn and shaking them, even though I know the likelihood of a reasonably chunky charm bracelet having insinuated itself between the pages of a book is slim to non-existent. I open up her toy cupboard and empty the boxes of toys she'd accumulated over the nine years of her short life, raking amongst the Sylvanian barge and the Lego and the plastic pony collection, hoping to catch a glint of silver among the clutter. I even strip the bed, throwing the pillows onto the floor and tipping the mattress up in case the bracelet has somehow found its way underneath it. There's nothing – of course there isn't. I find myself reeling all of a sudden, the room spinning giddily around me so that I have to grasp the edge of the dressing table to prevent myself from falling down.

Because if it isn't here, and it hadn't been with Hope when she was found, then where on earth has it gone?

Chapter 10

Before I realise what I'm doing, I am running down the road through the town. I'm not even sure where I'm going, but as I'm heading down Station Parade I find myself turning into York Place and on into Knaresborough Road, heading for the hospital and Sam. Ten minutes later, out of breath and sweating profusely, I fall through the double doors into the Accident and Emergency department. A security guard I don't recognise is manning the reception desk, his eyes fixed on a computer monitor in front of him. I bypass the desk and head for the doors that lead to the triage areas, rousing him from whatever is claiming his attention. 'Oi!' I hear him call as I push through the doors. 'You have to register before you go through there!' I ignore him and hurry on along the corridor, scouring each of the treatment bays for any sign of Sam.

The first bay is empty: afternoons are rarely the busiest time in a hospital's A&E department. The calm before the storm, Sam calls it. In a few hours the place will be crawling with the battle-scarred survivors of a night on the town. The waiting area I've just left is plastered with posters urging patients to refrain from assaulting medical staff, testimony to livelier times. The next treatment area contains a man lying apparently asleep on the examination bed, his thick-soled black boots sticking out incongruously from underneath a white hospital blanket. I hurry on, scanning each treatment bay in turn until finally I spot my husband in the last bay, head to head with one of the young nurses, poring over a computer monitor, while beside them an elderly woman is cradling her arm to her chest, her face crumpled in pain. '– quite a nasty distal radius fracture,' he's saying as I appear in the doorway. 'Intra-articular from the look of it. Look, here.' He points at the X-ray on the screen in front of him. 'You can see how the fracture extends right into the joint.' The nurse is hanging on to his every word: you'd think he was foretelling her future. 'I think we'd better get Bob to take a look.' Bob McGee, I happen to know, is one of the hospital's two orthopaedic surgeons: we used to see him and his wife Sally for dinner fairly regularly in the days before the accident.

'Excuse me!' A voice, heavy with authority, fills the corridor, causing all four of us to look around. 'You can't just come in here, you know.' The security guard, bursting with self-importance, is hurrying along the corridor towards us. Well, me, specifically. 'You have to wait in the reception area.' He draws to a halt next to me. 'You come along quietly with me.' I am half-expecting him to produce a pair of handcuffs.

'It's all right, Malcolm.' Sam's voice is quietly authoritative. He grimaces apologetically. 'She's with me.'

'Oh.' The guard gives me a disgruntled look. 'Right.' His face drops in disappointment: evidently he'd been hoping for a bit of action to brighten up his afternoon. In a smooth, conciliatory movement Sam dismisses him and ushers me out of the triage area. 'Give Bob a call,' he tells the nurse as we leave. 'Ask if he can swing by to take a look at Mrs –' He gestures vaguely before leading me into a small side room, closing the door on us both before turning to face me.

'Marion.' His tone is unreadable.

Oh, God. It's awful, seeing him like this. I want to throw myself into his arms and cling onto him and ask him to make everything all right again, put it back to the way it was before our lives fell apart. I want him to somehow make us into the kind of people who don't need a polished marble headstone and who don't know how much a burial plot in the local cemetery costs. I want him to perform miracles: not the ordinary kind he performs every day on broken bones and cut heads, but real ones, Lazarus ones, that raise the dead seven-and-a-half months on and take the survivors travelling backwards through time so that they can leave behind all the cataclysmic emotional devastation they've accumulated since disaster struck. It hits me then that this is what I've been after from him all along. I've been so caught up in trying to get him somehow to *fix* what happened, to make it *not* have happened at all, I haven't given him room to be what he is: a grieving husband mourning the loss of his child. I've been after a messiah.

And the truly awful thing is, even now that I've recognised his pain, I'd still take the miracle-worker over the grieving husband if it meant I could have my daughter back.

We stand for a moment regarding one another, and then he makes a movement. 'Here.' He pulls out a chair from beside the treatment bed and gestures for me to sit down, then perches on the edge of the bed. 'What's happened?' he asks.

I can't answer straight away. My head is still reeling with the realisation of what I must have put him through over the past seven-and-a-half months.

'Marion,' he says again after a moment. 'Tell me what's wrong.' His tone is still carefully guarded. 'Come on. I'm sure this —' he gestures with a hand '— visit can't be just because I said I'd be calling round on Saturday. And if it is, we can work something out. I just need to pick up a few things —'

'Hope's bracelet is missing,' I blurt out, interrupting him.

'What?' His face puckers in a confused frown. 'What bracelet? Marion, are you all right?' Sam crouches in front of me and reaches out, covering my clenched fists with his hands. 'You're shaking.' He tries to take hold of my hand, and as he does so the little silver house I'm still clutching drops to the floor, where it lies accusingly between us.

I see him focus on it, watch his forehead pucker as he tries to make sense of what he's seeing.

'The haunted house.' His face clouds briefly, and he swallows. And eventually, after a few moments' reckoning, he reaches down and picks it up, turning it over in his fingers so that he can examine it more closely.

I shiver, cold all of a sudden. 'I found it in your desk. I was looking for your passport. For your trip,' I add after a moment, as though I needed a reason to be rummaging in his drawers.

He isn't really listening to me. 'Two Hs,' he says musingly, almost to himself. 'I thought it would make up for the crab.' He is a million miles away, his face unreadable.

'Sam.' This time it's me who reaches out to touch his hand. 'Sam. Did you hear what I said?'

He takes a moment to focus on me. 'What?'

'I said I can't find her bracelet. It's disappeared.'

'What?' he says again. 'I don't understand what you're saying, Marion.'

I try to keep my voice level. 'She hardly ever had it off, Sam. She would have slept in it if we'd let her. That night when you took her to Brownies, she must have been wearing it.' He still looks mystified, dazed, almost. 'But it wasn't with any of her things –' I break off for a moment, the old feeling of panic rising in my throat. That afternoon when the police had returned her possessions to us – her little red purse with the kitten on the front, her Brownie subs still intact inside; her shoes; the red coat she'd been wearing over her Brownie uniform, which went with the purse; the bits and pieces of her life, which they'd gone over with a vengeance looking for forensic clues – had been one of the worst points in the whole sorry episode. That, and the awful day we had to choose an outfit for her to be buried in. So many memories tied up in a few clothes. I give my head a shake to try to clear away the old anguishes. 'It wasn't with any of her things,' I repeat.

Sam is shaking his head as well. 'Well, maybe she wasn't wearing it that night.' *That night* hangs between us like an accusation.

'Then it would still be in the house,' I assert. 'And it isn't. I've been through all her stuff. It's not there.'

'Well,' Sam tries again. 'Maybe she lost it. Maybe it fell off when –' He falters.

'The police went over that whole area with a microscope. They would have found it. They *would* have, Sam,' I insist, as though he has contradicted me. 'They could even tell what kind of trainers the driver was wearing, just from a couple of smudged footprints in the verge. They'd surely have spotted a silver bracelet with a pink ribbon lying on the ground. They couldn't have missed it –'

There is a soft knock on the door to the treatment room, and Sam looks up, distracted. 'Yes?'

The nurse he was with earlier sticks her head into the room. Her expression is a study: I can't work out if it's compassion or curiosity, though I can't help thinking it's curiosity that's brought her back to see what's going on. My bursting in like this will be the talk of the department for weeks. 'I thought some tea might be a good idea,' she says, pushing the door fully open and depositing a couple of steaming mugs in front of us. Then she retreats without waiting for a response from either of us, closing the door behind her, and I am forced to revise my judgment.

'She seems nice,' I comment irrelevantly.

'Marion –'

'Are you sleeping with her?' Now why did I ask that? *Why?* What is wrong with me?

He doesn't dignify the question with an answer, but continues to regard me askance. 'You're in shock,' he decides after a moment.

'Is that a professional diagnosis, or another cop-out?' Please, somebody, staple my tongue to the roof of my mouth. I didn't come here for a fight. I drop my face into my hands with a groan.

'Marion.' He tries again. 'Look –' He leans over and pulls my hands away from my face. 'Maybe Hope just lost the bracelet. Before the accident, I mean. Maybe it fell off when she was out playing one day –'

'It had a safety chain,' I counter stubbornly.

'Well, maybe the safety chain broke as well,' he ploughed on. 'You know what kids are like – the scrapes they get into. Maybe she got it caught on a tree or the handlebars of her bike or something and it fell off, and she didn't want to tell us she'd lost it.'

I look at him askance. 'Is that really what you think happened?'

He gives an exasperated sigh. 'I don't know! I'm just offering suggestions. Because if it really isn't in the house, and it didn't come back with any of the rest of her things, what else could have happened to it? Marion? What other explanation is there?'

My shoulders slump in despair. He is right, of course. There is no other explanation. 'It's just –' I break off. 'Well, it seemed so *important* before. I can't explain why. Like – well, like if I could find it, I'd be able to figure out what happened that night, fix it somehow –'

'We already know what happened.' He covers my hands with his once again. 'And it can't be fixed. You know it can't.'

I glance into his eyes, just for a second, and they are full of anguish. I can't bear to look at them. A tear spills down my cheek. 'But I want you to fix it.'

He cups a hand around my cheek and tries to draw me into his arms, but I push him away, holding my palms out against him. 'Stop it!' I tell him. 'Stop trying to make me accept what's happened. I can't accept it, Sam. I *won't* accept it.'

His shoulders slump, and he gives a sigh. 'I know you won't. And that's the problem, Marion. You won't accept it, and you want me to fix it.' There is a look of absolute defeat on his face, and I hate him for it. 'And I can't do anything about either one of those things.'

I turn my back on him. 'I'd better go.' I gesture round the empty treatment room. 'You must have a stack of work to do if you want to leave everything straight before you go to Africa.' I am shutting him out, and both of us know it.

'Marion –'

I turn back to look at him, a bright, false, angry smile plastered to my face. 'Doesn't matter. I'm fine.' My eyes are glittering dangerously.

He continues to regard me for a moment, and then drops his hands to his sides in defeat. 'Fine.'

'Right. Well, I'll see you on Saturday, then.' Mustering up as much dignity as it's possible to muster given the circumstances, I turn my back on Sam and leave, retracing my earlier sprint with dragging heels and a heavy heart, burning with frustration and wondering how on earth I'm going cope when my husband, whom I've alienated more or less completely by now, comes home to collect a few more of the bits and pieces that will allow him to get on with his life without me.

Chapter 11

On Thursday morning I'm sitting in my usual spot in front of the fireplace staring into space, and trying to motivate myself to actually get on and *do* something, and finally I decide that I could perhaps walk to the bus depot to retrieve my car. I chew this idea over for a few minutes, trying it out, gauging whether I actually have the energy to see it through and probing around to see whether there's a good reason not to do it. I might be really brave, in fact, and nip around to Asda while I'm out: what's left of the long-life is started to taste funny and I'm not sure how much longer I can keep going on my current diet of cold baked beans. I don't need to be out long. Hell, I don't even need to talk to anyone, if I keep my head down and pull my collar up around my ears.

Of course I realise now that I must have imagined all the events of a week ago. (Apart from the bit where Sam left me, I mean. I wish to God I *had* imagined that part, but no: it appears to be burned in gory Technicolor into my memory.) Here's what I think happened: I went out to get the prescription made up – I can remember rooting it out and, besides, my car is definitely not sitting in its usual place outside the house and so is presumably still parked up beside the bus depot. Then when I discovered the chemist shop had at some point changed into a Sony Centre I must have had some kind of mental blackout and walked straight home. I let myself into the house, dumped my bag on the kitchen table and took myself off to bed with the bottle of vodka and the pills, switching off Hope's music myself before I turned in, because . . . because this was the end of it, after all, and leaving electrical equipment playing indefinitely like that was a fire hazard, and I didn't want the whole house turning into some kind of funeral pyre after I was gone. Apart from anything else, Sam might want to come back eventually, and I'd already played things pretty badly with him. I couldn't imagine that burning his house down would soften his memory of me.

So now I've managed to talk myself through to the point where I'm in bed on the Thursday night with everything I need to finish myself off, and when I eventually come round after making such a pig's ear of my suicide, I am sick in the bathroom (the towel and facecloth were still there to prove it, not to mention some not very nice marks around the rim of the toilet). I made myself a cup of tea after throwing up, took it back upstairs to bed and fell asleep before I could drink it. The rest of it – the boy with the knife, the girl called Con in Hope's bedroom – was nothing more than the drunken mean-derings of a vodka-soused mind. Then Sam came home for the rest of his things, which just tipped me over the edge so that I was beyond logical thought for a few days. And there you have it. A perfectly logical explanation that seems far more likely than the idea of me telling some would-be mugger in a dark street to hurry up and slit my throat.

Of course there are one or two discrepancies – a small clot of dried blood on my neck, for instance, and the absence of my used tea bag in the kitchen. The blood I explained away to myself relatively easily: I had caught my neck with a fingernail or something when I was rummaging around under the counter for the first-aid kit. The tea bag was trickier, though, and eventually I decide that, unlikely as it seems, I must have had a moment of uncharacteristic meticulousness and put it straight in the outside bin in order not to sully my immaculate kitchen.

The only piece that doesn't fit in the puzzle is the bathroom. How come I ended up in there, throwing up my overdose of antibiotic tablets, instead of in the much nearer en-suite? For the life of me I can't explain that one.

I can ignore it, though. It's the tiniest detail, after all.

A flutter of something that might just be excitement flits across my stomach as I'm getting ready to go out: I feel like an explorer about to make some momentous discovery after months of traipsing through the wilderness. I shrug myself into my coat and leave the house quickly, before I can change my mind, gathering up my handbag and keys before cowardice can set in, and swing by the cashpoint in Station Parade – the one that had featured in my dream about being mugged – so that I can withdraw a couple of hundred quid for my milk and provisions. It's more than I need, but at least it'll save me having to come back for more any time soon. Now I really am worth mugging, but I manage to get to the car without running into anyone, and as I turn down Bower Road towards Asda I am beginning to feel positively proud of myself for finally conquering my qualms and managing a humdrum trip to the shops.

My confidence wobbles as I approach the doors to the supermarket, which is heaving with shoppers. A cacophony of noise hits me along with a blast of overheated air as I walk through the doors, pushing my trolley ahead of me. I grip the handle of the trolley tightly and physically resist the urge to turn tail and flee back to the sanctuary of my house and my non-existent cats. I take a few deep breaths and force myself on deeper into the store. Once I've committed myself it gets easier, and before I know it I've managed to accumulate a packet of crumpets, half a pound of butter, a carton of milk and a ready-prepared shepherd's pie for one in the bottom of my trolley. I feel inordinately proud of them: given my state of mind recently, these few bits and pieces strike me as a pretty major accomplishment.

I am just beginning to think about doing battle at the checkout when I become aware of a disturbance behind me. One of the store security guards is striding down the aisle, a uniformed police officer at his side. Between them, struggling and kicking, a tousle-haired youngster is vigorously but silently protesting about the stronghold each of them has on her shoulder. I draw my trolley to one side to let them pass, and as they do so the girl tosses her head backwards and our eyes meet.

It's Con.

For a moment the world spins. And then they are past, making their way towards the exit, where I can make out the blue and yellow strip of a police vehicle waiting for them.

'Just a minute!' someone shouts (me, actually, though I don't realise it until the three of them stop and turn around to stare at me). 'What's going on?' I demand. I am surprised at the truculence in my tone and, from the expression on her face, so is Con.

'D'you know this girl, madam?' the police officer wants to know.

'Yes.' I catch Con's eye, and that appraising look I remember from last Friday, the one I didn't dream up after all, is back. 'She's my – niece,' I finish.

The security guard purses his mouth sceptically. 'Your ... niece.' The way he imitates my hesitant tone really gets my goat.

'That's right.' I catch Con's eye, muttering a silent prayer that she doesn't contradict me.

'Well, your – niece –' he puffs out his chest importantly, using that same derisive tone: he might as well go the whole hog and call me a liar, which I am, of course, but he can't know that '– 'as jus' been caught nickin' a CD.' He pronounces the 'a' to rhyme with 'hay', which is the final nail in his outsized coffin as far as I'm concerned.

'No, she hasn't.'

'What d'you mean, no she 'asn't? We've got the 'ole thing on our in-store camera. Took it right of t' shelf, she did, an' stuffed it inside 'er jacket.'

'Oh, dear.' I turn my attention to the police officer, who is looking from the security guard to me and back again, clearly dithering about where to take things from here. I decide to take advantage of his hesitancy with a full-scale charm offensive, and offer him my most dazzling respectable-thirty-four-year-old-woman smile, praying it doesn't come out like a scary old biddy manic grin. 'I'm afraid there's been a misunderstanding.'

'Ow d'you mean, madam?'

I turn back to the security guard. 'I'll bet it was the *Brits Hits* CD, wasn't it?' The dozy bugger is still holding it in his hand, actually, but he doesn't twig: he just looks completely gormless and nods. 'Aye, it were, but –'

I bestow another beatific smile on the police officer. 'Constance knows I want it for my birthday. I expect she stuck it inside her jacket so that I wouldn't see it when she caught up with me.'

'Well, she shoulda said so,' the security guard counters. 'She ant said a word since ah collared 'er.'

'No, she . . . um . . . she can't speak.' I improvise wildly. 'English, I mean. Obviously she can speak, ha ha ha. She can't speak English. She's . . . erm . . . French.' I smile brightly at the pair of them.

Con has stayed studiously silent throughout this exchange, but I notice her mouth twitch at this point. Fortunately both the police officer and the security guard are transfixed by my tale and don't notice.

'French?'

'That's right. On her father's side. She's from the south. Near . . .' My mind at this point helpfully obliterates the names of every southern French town I've ever heard of from its memory banks. 'Near the coast,' I finally manage. 'She's come over to learn the language. Can't speak a word at the moment, but hopefully she will by the end of her trip.' I'm aware that I'm babbling, but I don't seem able to stop myself. '*N'est-ce pas*, Constance?' I say, nodding at her encouragingly. She bites her bottom lip by way of a response. Her eyes are sparkling with suppressed laughter.

'Anyway, I'm terribly sorry you've been troubled, officer,' I say to the policeman. 'But we really mustn't waste any more of your time.' I reach out and pull Con towards me and, amazingly, both men let her go. 'I mean, it's not as if she left the store with the CD, is it? She was just trying to get it to the checkout without me spotting it. I'll have a word with her and make sure she understands not to do it again.'

The security guard is eyeing me suspiciously. 'Go on, then,' he says. "Ave a word.' He folds his arms across his chest and glowers at me defiantly.

'What – now?' I can feel sweat breaking out under my arms.

'Might be a good idea, madam,' the officer agrees. 'Kind of like a warning. I can't just let her go wi'out sayin' summat.'

The three of them are looking at me expectantly. Con, needless to say, is giving me that considering look of hers, though I swear I can see laughter behind her eyes.

'Erm . . .' I smile nervously. 'Constance.' I stop and clear my throat, and the police officer nods at me encouragingly. '*Comment allez-vous?*' I glance nervously at the two men, and they are watching me, transfixed. The security guard's mouth is hanging half-open. I plough on doggedly with the only French I know, which apart from the most rudimentary grammar left over from my school days unfortunately happens to be a couple of nursery rhymes I learned from watching a children's French DVD with

Hope years ago. I try to inject a note of authority into my voice. '*Sur le pont d'Avignon, l'on y dance tous en rond.*' I swallow nervously. '*Au clair de la lune mon ami Pierrot.*' I am finding it hard to remember the words without humming the tune in my head, which is doing nothing for my fluency. '*Prête-moi ta plume pour écrire un mot.*' I nod wisely and wag my finger at her. '*Ma chandelle est morte, je n'ai plus de feu.*' I am beginning to find my stride. '*Ouvre-moi ta porte, pour l'amour de Dieu!*' I throw my hands in the air at this last bit, which I happen to know means 'For the love of God' and hence is possibly the only relevant bit of my little speech, then turn triumphantly to the police officer. Hopefully he won't have noticed the fact that every second line rhymed with the one before it. 'Well, I think that should have got the message across.'

There is a wry look on the officer's face, but he nods sagely. 'Oh, ah'm sure it has.' I can't be sure, but there's something in his eyes that I don't think I like the look of very much. 'If ah could just take a note of your name and address, in case we've any further questions?'

'Oh, of course!' I gush, writing down a few creative details in his little notepad. I can't believe we've got away with it. I feel light-headed with relief.

The security guard has a confused frown on his face. 'Ah've seen 'er in 'ere before,' he mutters. 'Ah could swear—'

I grab Con's arm and head for the checkouts before either of them changes their mind about letting us go. Then, just as I think we're safe, I hear the police officer striding after us. 'Excuse me!' he calls out, and I stop reluctantly, my heart thumping.

He comes to a halt beside us and holds something out. '*Votre* CD,' he says, pronouncing it *say day* and handing the box to Constance. '*Ce serait dommage de l'oublier, après tous les efforts de votre –*' he hesitates and catches my eye '*– tante.*'

Oh. My. God. He rolls his 'r's and everything.

I am frozen to the spot, waiting for him to produce a pair of handcuffs and arrest the pair of us, when suddenly he smiles at Constance, nods at me and turns to go, leaving me open-mouthed and gaping at his back as he disappears out into the bright afternoon.

Chapter 12

We don't even make eye contact until we are sitting in my car. The security guard watches us suspiciously the whole time we are queuing up to pay for my precious supplies (not to mention a CD I've never heard of until five minutes earlier, but which I can hardly send Con to put back), and then follows us to the door of the shop, still muttering to himself and scowling at us. 'I'm parked right there: straight on and then left a bit,' I murmur to Con through the corner of my mouth, keeping my eyes fixed forwards. 'The dark-blue Passat. Act as if you know exactly where you're going.' The guard is still standing there, frowning away, as Con diligently takes the trolley back to the collection point and returns to the car. Only when she's climbed into the passenger seat and shut the door behind her does he give up, pushing himself off the window he's been leaning against and slouching off like a disgruntled bear back into the store. And then, finally, I exhale deeply, blowing out my cheeks, and turn to regard Con sitting meekly in the seat beside me. She looks at me sheepishly from under her fringe, trying to gauge my mood.

'Oh, my God.' I finally manage to articulate what's spinning through my head. My hands are trembling on the steering wheel. 'I can't believe I just did that. And he *knew* – that policeman knew I was talking shit. I nearly *died* when he came out with that . . . that *stuff* at the checkout just now.'

'What were he on about?' Con wants to know. 'I couldn't understand a word.'

'I haven't the foggiest idea.' The sheer lunacy of what just happened sweeps across me in a rush, and I am suddenly overcome by an urge to laugh. It's been so long since I've experienced anything as being funny, it takes me a moment to recognise the feeling. And then when I do, the utter unexpectedness of it forces a snort down my nose, making me giggle all the harder. Before I know it I am convulsed, as much with delight at the experience of laughing again as at the idiocy of our narrow escape in the supermarket just now. Con's face is a picture of confusion – a fact that makes me positively howl. Tears are streaming down my cheeks. 'Oh dear,' I gasp, trying to control myself. '"Have a word," that guard said, and I – I – well, I mean, really. *Sur le pont d'Avignon.* I can't think what came over me.'

'Sounded all right to me,' Con says admiringly, setting me off once again. 'What's it mean, any road?'

'He he he,' I wheeze. 'On the bridge in Avignon –' I give another gasp '– we all dance.' I clutch at Con's arm. 'In a circle.' I can barely get the words out, I am laughing so much. My stomach is beginning to hurt with the effort.

Con purses her lips at me and shakes her head pityingly. 'You're mad, you are,' she says eventually. '*Auntie* Marion.' An appellation that sets me off again, but that after a moment brings my snorting abruptly to a halt.

'How d'you know my name?'

She grins at me, that familiar grin I am beginning to recognise. 'Saw it on your driving licence, didn't I? When I were trying to find out where you lived, so's I could bring your bag back.'

Maybe it's the recollection of the events of that Thursday evening, but the pair of us sober up suddenly and contemplate one another in silence.

'You know, I thought I'd made you up,' I tell her after a moment.

'How d'you mean, made me up?'

'After I woke up. There was no sign of you. I decided you must have been a figment of my imagination. And then there you were just now in the supermarket, large as life, and being manhandled by a couple of gorillas. You looked like you might need a bit of help.' I smile at her. 'And I suppose you could say I owed you that.'

Con clears her throat. 'I'll pay you back,' she promises. 'For t' CD, like.'

I shake my head at her. 'Consider it paid in advance.' I smile ruefully. 'If it hadn't been for you, I wouldn't even have had a card for getting money out of my account. Which would mean I couldn't have gone shopping. I'd have been forced to exist on the few tins of beans I have left in my cupboards, after which point I would have expired through starvation or, worse, gas inhalation from all the beans.' I give a mock-shudder. 'Doesn't bear thinking about.'

She manages another grin, and I turn on the ignition. 'Come on.'

'Where we going?'

'Well, I don't know about you, but I could murder a cup

of tea.' I raise my eyebrows enquiringly. 'Unless there's somewhere you need to be? I could drop you off.'

'Nah.' She shrugs, and I get the feeling she is being deliberately nonchalant. 'Cup of tea sounds all right.'

It's odd having company in the car. I've become so used to being on my own, talking to myself, muttering away in my mad old biddy persona, I have to physically restrain myself from doing it now. I don't want Con thinking I'm completely deranged. And so we drive in silence – I'd call it comfortable, but if the truth be told I'm squirming a bit, wondering what the hell I'm getting myself into. Con, on the other hand, is the picture of relaxation, humming quietly under her breath and every now and then giving me that considering look that I find so unsettling.

We're halfway home when I suddenly realise I feel a bit uneasy taking Con back to the house. She's already been through all my kitchen cupboards and seen me sleeping (well, passed out, anyway) and watched me throw up in the bathroom: the prospect of taking her back to the one place where she's held all the cards whilst I've gone to pieces makes me feel I'm putting myself at a further disadvantage, and I'm not sure I'm ready to allow her any more intimacy than she's already managed to help herself to. But then again, the alternative – going some-where public – doesn't exactly fill me with joy either. And then inspiration strikes, and I turn the car and head down Commercial Street towards Valley Gardens, parking up on the corner of Crescent Road. 'Come on,' I tell Con, nodding towards the entrance to the park. 'Let's hit the park.'

'Bit nippy for a picnic, in't it?'

'Not a bit of it. There's a great little tearoom: we can sit inside if you're cold.' I'm not in the mood for a long explanation of why I can't face anywhere more public. Or more private. 'And there's a fleece on the back seat you can borrow.'

The fleece – an old one of Sam's – drowns her, but she puts it on anyway. The sleeves hang over her hands, making her appear even more waiflike than before. She stands beside me at the counter in the tearoom, blowing into the cuffs and giving me sharp, sidelong glances as though she's trying to work out what she's doing in the park with a woman she barely knows.

'What would you like?'

She bites the inside of her cheek, considering the menu on the wall in front of her behind the server's head. 'Hot chocolate,' she says. 'If that's all right,' she adds diffidently.

I pay for the chocolate, and for a tea for myself, and we carry our drinks over to a vacant table on the veranda, settling ourselves like a pair of old dowagers out enjoying the morning air. It occurs to me, sitting there with Con watching me appraisingly from over the rim of her mug, that inviting her for a drink constitutes the first effort I've made since the accident to engage with another person rather than pushing them away. In front of us on the grass, a couple of young boys are throwing a Frisbee back and forth while a small black terrier races between them trying to intercept its flight. I think absently of Hector, stuck at home in the scullery, and wonder whether we'll ever manage a proper walk again.

'What's up?' Con is giving me that considering look once again.

'I'm sorry?'

'You were miles away just then. You were looking at them kids, but you were miles away.'

'Oh –' I give my head a shake. 'Just daydreaming. You know. Anyway.' I manage a bright smile. 'Tell me about you. How come you ended up being a lookout for my mugger friend – Ryan, did you say he was called?'

At the mention of his name her face clouds over infinitesimally, making me wonder just how voluntary her role that night had been, and how much she'd had it foisted upon her.

'Yeah, Ryan.' She gives a shrug and looks up at me from under her untidy fringe. 'We don't go out looking for trouble, you know. Leastways, *I* don't. We were supposed to be meeting a mate of his that night, but he never showed up. And that put Ryan in a right mood. Then he saw you stomping along t' road, and he just –' She shrugs again. 'Ah told him not to, to just leave it, but he weren't in t' mood to listen. He can get like that sometimes.' She smiles nervously, lifting a hand to her neck, and I notice for the first time some rather angry bruising on the delicate skin underneath her ear. Then she catches me looking and drops her hand again, letting her long fair hair tumble over the bruises, hiding them. 'He wouldn't really have hurt you, you know. He's full of shit, is Ryan.' I can tell from the edge in her voice that she wants to believe what she's telling me, though the thought goes through my head that if he's responsible for those bruises, he's probably quite capable of following through on the threats he was uttering the other evening when he had a knife at my throat.

'So why d'you hang out with him, then?' I keep my voice light, hoping the question won't back her into any kind of a corner.

'Well, he looks after me, doesn't he?' She bites her lip, looking vulnerable and all of about thirteen, and then takes a large swallow of the hot chocolate. While she's occupied licking the chocolate from her lips and adjusting the lid to the cup, I take the opportunity for a closer look at her.

I'd already noted the familiar features: the blonde hair, the clear blue eyes, that way she had at looking up at me through her too-long fringe. She's like an older, more unkempt version of Hope, the way she might have turned out given a couple more years, though I'd have drawn the line at the eyebrow piercing. I'd have seen to it that she'd had nicer clothes to wear as well – I'm not so out of touch with things that I can't tell the difference between jeans that are fashionably torn and jeans that are just plain worn out and filthy. I'd have done something about her grooming, too – or tried to, at any rate – kept the hair regularly cut to avoid that straggly, neglected look, and made sure she was getting enough sleep and a proper diet to combat the slightly worn-out greyness that seemed to hover around the edges of her eyes, in spite of the carefully applied make-up that just makes her look even younger. It occurs to me that, given the opportunity, I could do a much better job of looking after her than Ryan.

She can feel my eyes upon her. 'What?' she challenges, an edge of truculence creeping into her voice.

'Oh, I was just wondering.' I give her an appraising look. 'How old are you, Con?'

She sucks her teeth consideringly, as though she's trying to work out why I'm interested in her age all of a sudden. 'Eighteen,' she says with that same air of defiance. Then she slumps her shoulders. 'Sixteen,' she amends. 'Why?'

Sixteen! I wouldn't have put her past fourteen, and that was stretching things. 'Well, it's just –' I give my head a little shake. Sixteen? Not in a million years. 'You seem awfully young to be hanging around with someone like Ryan.'

She gives a sudden laugh, which lights up her face and shaves another couple of years off, taking her down to around eleven. She's morphing into Hope before my very eyes. 'Suppose ah can't blame you for not liking him. I mean, he did have a knife at your throat. Sometimes ah don't like him much myself, and I'm his girlfriend.'

I return the smile, keeping things light. 'Yeah?'

'Yeah.' She leans towards me conspiratorially. 'Men can be right arseholes sometimes.'

Well, I wasn't going to argue with that.

'Still, though.' She sits upright again. 'He's all ah've got. Beggars can't be choosers, eh?' She gives another self-deprecating laugh.

'Really?' As my mind has now reduced her to somewhere around the age of ten, I can't compute that the only person she's got in the world is a low-life bottom-feeding scumbag like Ryan (she's right; I don't like him much). 'What about your parents?'

She makes a snorting noise, then decides to enlighten

me. 'Me mam lives out Bradford way. Never knew me dad. Ah'm not even sure she knew who he were. Ah moved out when ah were fourteen. Haven't seen her in over a year.'

Which would put her somewhere around fifteen. My face creases in a frown. 'How come?'

She wrinkles her nose, which I notice has a light dusting of freckles across it. The sight of them makes me swallow, hard. 'It were just easier that way.'

'How d'you mean?' I'm trying to tear my eyes away from the freckles, trying to concentrate on what might be easy about leaving home at fourteen.

She hesitates, trying to decide whether to go into detail, and then shrugs. 'Let's just say there weren't room for me no more.' She takes a mouthful of hot chocolate and gives me a sidelong look. 'She had this new boyfriend, yeah?'

'Yeah?' I can't keep the bafflement out of my voice.

She grimaces. 'He had some funny ideas about what he could do with her belongings. Thought I were one of her belongings.' She hesitates. 'Ah weren't. So ah left.'

'You mean –?' I am looking at her in horror.

She raises her eyebrows at me and takes another mouthful of her drink.

I'm doing my best not to look shocked, and failing.

'Oh.' Con's tone is cheerfully dismissive. 'Weren't first time ah'd had to bugger off. Ah were in care off and on when ah were younger. Me mam got six months for neglect when ah were four. Social services reckoned ah were a bit young to cope on my own. Ah couldn't reach the knobs on t' cooker unless ah stood on a chair.'

'*On the cooker!*' I look at her askance: is she joking with me, or was she really trying to feed herself before she'd even reached school age? 'So where did you go then?'

'Into a residential unit for a bit, then into a foster placement. Didn't work out, though.'

'Why not?' In my head I'm seeing Con at four. She's the image of Hope at the same age: all wide eyes and tousled curls and a wicked smile, and a small, clammy hand wanting to hold mine whenever we were out in public. I can't imagine anyone not wanting to keep her.

'Wet the bed, didn't ah? Every night. The woman used to tell me ah were doing it on purpose. She made me sleep in t' wet sheets to see if that would stop me. And then in the end she just cracked up – lost the plot. Battered me so hard she cracked a rib.' She gives a short laugh, as though a broken rib on a four-year-old were nothing to get upset about. 'Wound up back in t' unit.' She gives me a light smile. 'That were better, really. They had the machines there to cope with all the washing. And ah weren't the only one doing it. You never feel as bad when you're not the only one.'

My head is spinning with what she's just told me. 'So how long did you stay there after that?'

'Till me mam got out.'

'You mean –' I can't keep the incredulity out of my voice. 'They let her have you back? After the way she'd neglected you?'

She gives a light shrug. 'Cheaper, innit? For t' social services, like. Costs them a fortune to put a kid in care. Besides, she told them she'd turned over a new leaf, didn't she? And her mam were going to be helping out, she said.

So yeah, ah went back for a bit, but it were always up and down. She liked a drink, you know? Still does. You never knew what sort of mood she'd be in when you come in from school. Then when ah were nine, she rang social services up and said she couldn't cope with me any more – ah were still wetting the bed, yeah? So ah wound up back in another unit for a bit. They couldn't find me a placement that time. Nobody wants a nine-year-old who wets the bed every night.' She shrugs. 'It were all right. Nice staff. No funny business. Not like some of those places.'

My mind is boggling: she's nine years old – Hope's age – and living in a *unit* – God, what an awful word – instead of a proper home with proper parents to take care of her. I refuse to allow my brain to compute what funny business she's talking about. I would have taken care of her if I'd known her then. I would have. Proper care. I wouldn't have minded the bed-wetting. I'd have coped with it: I wouldn't have made her sleep in wet sheets for a week. I wouldn't have broken a rib. The thought of that small, vulnerable bone cracking sends a wave of panic creeping up towards my throat from somewhere around my heart, and I force myself to breathe, reminding myself that she is already beyond nine – already beyond saving. 'So how come you ended up going back home after that?'

'Oh, well –' She gives another short laugh. 'Ah just thought – ah kept hoping she'd changed, she'd be able to cope. Ah mean, she's me mam, in't she? You go on hoping. And ah'd stopped the bed-wetting by then, yeah?' She hesitates, and then comes out with something that makes me want to take her home right this instant. 'Ah wanted us just to be a family.'

She takes another swig from her drink, wiping the back of her hand across her mouth when she's through. 'Any road, then Brian moved in when ah were thirteen. Took me a while to realise he weren't one of her one-night stands; he weren't going anywhere. Then when he started his shenanigans ah tried telling her about it, but she wouldn't believe me, said ah were trying to split them up.' Her face is a study of impassivity as she's telling me this. 'So ah moved out. Slept rough for a few months, and then ah hooked up with Ryan. Proper knight on a white horse, he were.'

'With a bit of a predilection for crime,' I chip in. I can't help myself: the idea of Ryan as some kind of a hero seems laughable.

'Aye, well, Robin Hood weren't no saint, neither, not to t' folk he went nicking off.' There's the slightest edge to her tone, a sharpness that wasn't there before, warning me to back off. 'You do what you have to do to get by. We haven't all got fancy houses and posh cars.' She drains her drink, and I sip thoughtfully at my tea and try to digest what she's just told me.

'Any road –' she puts down the empty cup and regards me thoughtfully '– ah'd best be off. Thanks for t' drink.'

'Oh!' I'm taken aback: I can't just let her leave like this, can I? Not after what she's just told me?

'Right – well . . .' She stands, looking at me awkwardly for a moment. 'You look after yourself, yeah? No running into dodgy blokes in dark streets. Ah mean, ah might not be there next time.' She shakes her head at me, and for a moment I feel as though our roles are reversed and she's become the protector, I'm the vulnerable kid in need of a hero. Before I can reflect on this sudden switch, she's swinging herself off the veranda and down the steps.

'See you around,' she says, lifting a hand in farewell. Then she turns and walks quickly away, across the grass, skirting the boys with the Frisbee and the dog, through the gates to the park and disappears out of my life, leaving me alone on the bench with a couple of empty drink containers and the bitter realisation that, drawn to her as I am, the chances are I'll never see her again.

Chapter 13

She's back the following day.

I'm lying in bed trying to summon up the energy to get up when the doorbell rings downstairs, sending my stomach into a little backflip. My first thought is that it must be Sam: he's woken up this morning and realised he can't live without me, and he's come back to claim me. The prospect of opening the door and seeing him standing there on the other side sends a shiver of nervous excitement through my insides as I throw on my dressing gown and hurry downstairs, almost tripping over myself in my anxiety to get there quickly so that he won't think I'm out and give up and go away. So convinced am I that it's him, I almost fall over my own feet trying to put the brakes on when I see that in fact it's Con who's standing there.

She must spot the way my face drops, because she backs immediately down the steps, holding up a hand in a gesture of submission. 'Sorry,' she's saying as she withdraws. 'Never realised you'd still be in bed. Ah'll come back –'

'No, no, it's fine.' I pull the dressing gown more tightly around myself and step backwards into the hall. 'Come in. Really,' I add as I see the doubt on her face. 'Really,' I say again. 'It's nice to see you.'

It's true: it *is* nice. She might not be the person I was

hoping to find, but nevertheless it's given me a lift, seeing her there on the doorstep, a look of – well, *eagerness* on her face. I can't remember the last time anyone looked pleased to see me.

I don't know what it is about her that's got under my skin so much – why I felt that sudden urge to interfere in the supermarket when I saw her being hauled off like that yesterday – but I can't deny that I'm drawn to her somehow. The rational part of my brain knows that she's nothing to do with me – if our lives hadn't collided that night in the street with Ryan, we'd never give one another more than a passing glance under normal circumstances. But there's a niggling undercurrent somewhere in there that won't let go of the idea that there's a link between us, a connection that goes beyond the superficial physical likeness she bears to Hope.

Maybe it's just because she brought back my bag. Somewhere in that gesture was a motivation that didn't seem to fit with the life she's living. That's probably what it is. I've seen something in her, something I used to pick up on in those misfit kids I used to work with – a redeeming quality that I want to explore further. I want to help her, the way I used to want to help the kids at the centre. I want to reach into her and help her find that uniqueness that makes her different from everybody else.

It's got nothing to do with Hope.

'Sorry,' she says again as she steps into the hall. She holds out something she's carrying. 'Ah brought your fleece back.' She hands it to me like a bribe, still unsure about whether she's welcome or not.

I give her the warmest smile I can muster. 'Cup of tea? I'm only just up: having a lazy start to the day.'

She hesitates, giving the dressing gown another once-over. 'Only if it's not holding you back.'

I purse my lips thoughtfully. 'Well, I did have some fireplace-staring planned, but I guess I can put that on hold until later.' The look of bafflement on her face makes me laugh. 'No, I'm just kidding. Of course you're not holding me back. I should probably put some clothes on, though. Why don't you go through and stick the kettle on, and I'll just nip upstairs.'

She looks pleased, as though the idea of being entrusted with the run of the kitchen has compensated in some degree for my obvious disappointment when I found her on the doorstep instead of Sam. 'OK, then.' She shrugs herself out of the thin denim jacket she's wearing and hangs it on the end of the banister.

By the time I come back down, she's almost finished brewing the tea, and is moving around the kitchen like she's lived in it all her life. I watch with a wry smile as she disposes of the used tea bags into the outside bin, swinging the back door shut behind her as she returns to the kitchen. She smiles tentatively at me as she sits down on the opposite side of the table.

'Thanks again for yesterday,' she says, breaking the silence between us.

'That's all right.'

She casts a look around the kitchen. 'It's like a show house, this,' she says after a moment. 'Ah've never seen owt so clean. Ah'm almost scared to put me feet on t' floor in case ah dirty it. You'd never think anyone lived here.'

I give her a rueful look from over the top of my tea mug. 'No one does.'

She frowns at me. 'How d'you mean?'

'No one's lived here for months,' I tell her. 'Sam and I – well, we've *existed*. You couldn't call it living. Even the dog's been on his best behaviour.'

Her face brightens. 'You've got a dog?'

I stand and cross to the door to the scullery. 'Hector!' I call, and after a moment he comes lumbering across, stopping on the threshold to stretch himself luxuriantly before trotting inside looking for his morning biscuits.

Con is ecstatic. 'Cool!' she exclaims as he pads across the floor to greet her. 'Big, in't he? Like a wolf. Ah never realised you had a dog. Where were he when ah brought your bag round?' She is tickling behind his ears, and Hector is responding by placing his great hairy head in her lap, a look of rapture on his face. This is more attention than he's seen all week.

'In the scullery.' I don't venture anything further by way of an explanation.

She doesn't seem to find anything odd in my answer. 'What kind of dog is he?'

'A malamute. The HGV of the sled dogs.'

'Ah've never seen a dog like it before.'

'They aren't very common in the UK. They're descended from dogs bred by a tribe called the Mahlemuits in Western Alaska.'

'He must be rubbish as a guard dog. Never made no

noise that night. What were he doing in t' scullery? Is that where he sleeps?'

'Um – he does sometimes. And he doesn't bark, really,' I add, steering the subject away from why Hector was incarcerated in the scullery that Thursday evening. Hearing my voice, Hector lifts his head for a second and treats me to one of his accusing looks before settling his chin back in Con's lap with a sigh. I swear he understands every word he hears. He does sometimes. I can see he's thinking. Oh, sure. Why don't you tell her why I've been banished to the scullery? I ignore the guilt trip he's bent on initiating and address myself to Con again. 'He's very gentle-natured. The Mahlemuit women used to use them to babysit their kids when they went out hunting. He howls sometimes. When he's really happy. Or when he wants his tea.' A stab of guilt hits me in the stomach as I realise I can't remember the last time I actually heard him howl for happiness. He must have been picking up on the vibes between Sam and me. He has collapsed at Con's feet now and rolled onto his back so that she can tickle his chest.

'So who's Sam, then?'

'My husband.'

'Right.' She looks around my spotless kitchen and nods at a photograph of Sam and Hope, a favourite of mine that I'd taken when Hope was little, that stands on the sideboard behind the table. 'Is that him?' She picks it up and studies it for a moment. 'He looks nice.'

'Yes.' I pause. 'He is.'

'Who's the little girl?' She nods at the photograph again, and I reach over and take it from her hand.

'My daughter.' I study the picture for a moment, running a finger along the side of Hope's face.

'How old?'

I clear my throat. 'She was about four in that picture.'

'She's cute,' is Con's judgment on the photograph. There's an infinitesimal pause while I wait for the next inevitable question. 'So how old is she now, then?'

It's odd, sitting in my kitchen with someone who *doesn't know*: I've become so used to people tiptoeing around me, her bluntness is a bit of a shock.

'She would have been ten in June.' The thought of her birthday fast approaching makes my hand tremble and I put the picture down on the table. I am aware of Con's eyes upon me. 'Would of?' she queries.

'She was killed by a hit-and-run driver in November last year.' I can't believe how matter of fact I sound.

There's a sudden shift in the air, as though someone has taken a knife and sliced right through it. For a moment the ragged shards hang between us, threatening to rip us apart if we make any sudden moves. Then Con nods slowly, awkwardly. 'Right.' She licks her lips and glances around her nervously, and I think to myself, she's too young to know how to handle other people's grief.

I look at the photograph again, touching Hope's face as though I might be able to reach her through the image in the frame. 'Sam left me last week, because he can't cope with the person I've become since then.' The bitterness of that second admission makes my mouth twist.

I give her a covert glance, bracing myself, waiting for her face to arrange itself into the usual expression of pity

I've been dealing with for months. In fact, I'm half-expecting a double dose of compassion: after all, she's the first person who knew about both Hope *and* Sam. But it doesn't come: she just went on sitting there looking at me uneasily.

'Actually, that's not strictly true,' I admit after a moment. 'Sam left me because I accused him of being responsible for Hope's death.'

Still she doesn't speak, and I feel an obligation to fill the silence with explanations. I clear my throat, setting the picture carefully back down on the sideboard. 'Hope used to go to Brownies. Every Tuesday night. Not here: she didn't want to change packs when we moved house, so we said she could carry on at the old place. It's not that far – just a few miles out towards Beckwithshaw. D'you know it?'

She shrugs, and I launch back into my explanation. 'She had a lot of friends there. I suppose she would have made new friends if she'd gone to a local pack, but we thought it might make the move easier. We should have insisted.' I wait for her to agree with me, which she doesn't do. 'It's always easy to be wise after the event. That's what everyone says, isn't it?' I break off to give Con another chance to vouch an opinion on the matter – people are usually full of opinions at this point in the story – but she's still regarding me warily, chewing the inside of her cheek as though she's weighing up what I'm telling her before coming to some momentous conclusion.

'The night of the accident, Sam dropped her off. Only Brownies wasn't on that night: the hall was being used by a mobile blood unit. The trouble was, he didn't wait to check: he just dropped her at the door and drove away. *I* would have checked, you see, if it had been me that dropped her off. I would have noticed that there weren't any other Brownies around. Mothers notice that sort of thing. But Sam – he just didn't. It probably never occurred to him. We think – the police reckon – she must have gone inside, realised she shouldn't be there, and come back out looking for Sam. We can't be sure. Nobody from the blood unit remembered even seeing her.'

She is still sitting there saying nothing, a response that I'm so unused to, I find myself ploughing on to be sure she's getting the point.

'The police reckoned the car that hit her was doing at least seventy. They could tell from the marks on the road, and from where they found her – how far the car had knocked her. Who drives like that on a winding country road?' Still nothing: just that enigmatic look. 'There were no witnesses, though: there never are, are there? Nobody saw or heard a thing. All those people inside the hall, and none of them –' I break off and take another deep breath. Con is still sitting there not saying anything. I am starting to find it disconcerting.

'The impact didn't kill her.' I give her a twisted smile. 'She bled to death. Ironic, isn't it? All those blood donors in the hall, all those nurses, and Hope is lying on her own in a ditch just yards away.' I swallow to try to suppress the lump that has formed in my throat. 'And the bit I can't really get my head around, the bit that makes me so *insane*, is that whoever was driving the car got out and looked at her: they actually stood over her while she was –' I break off and take a breath. 'They could tell that from the marks as well: footprints and stuff.' I falter again. 'I have this rage inside me. All the time. I'm so angry. I just want to find the bastard that did this and – oh, I don't know.' I try a weak smile. 'I expect you think I'm quite mad.'

For a minute she remains frozen in her seat. And then she stands up abruptly. 'Ah've got to go.'

'Sorry?'

She's out in the hall and grabbing her jacket from the end of the banister before I've quite taken in what's happening. 'Con?' I follow her out. 'Look – I'm sorry,' I say, holding out a conciliatory hand. 'I shouldn't have dumped all that on you. I forgot – I've lived with it for so long now, I forget what a shock it can be to other people.'

'No, it's not that: it's just –' She thrusts an arm ineffectually at one of the sleeves. 'Fuck's sake –'

'Con, please –'

She turns on me angrily. 'That why you done it, then?'

The sudden shift in the atmosphere takes me completely by surprise. 'What?' I say.

'Come off it, Marion.' She's glaring at me now. 'Ah saw the stuff. The pills and the vodka and that. And you were out cold. Ah couldn't wake you up. That's why ah hung around for so long. I only meant to dump the bag and go. Ryan were proper mad when ah got back on Friday afternoon. Especially when he couldn't find your bag anywhere. 'Course, ah never told him ah'd brought it back, like. Said he must've dropped it somewhere. He didn't believe me.'

I draw my breath in sharply, remembering yesterday's

glimpse of the bruising around her neck. 'Is that why he hit you?' I ask.

Now it's her turn to be wrong-footed. 'What?'

'The bruises on your neck.' She puts a hand up to them self-consciously. 'I noticed them yesterday in the park.' I lean over for a closer look and she shies away from me like a dog that's used to having a hand raised against it.

'Did he do that to you?' I nod at her neck, which she's keeping defiantly hidden behind her hand.

'We're not talking about me.' She glares at me. 'We're talking about you.'

'Did he?' I ask obdurately.

'Yes!' She hurls the word at me angrily. 'Did you try to kill yourself?'

I don't answer, which is enough of an answer for her.

'Stupid cow.' Her tone is still angry: bitter, almost, which shocks me. Nobody's raised their voice around me in months.

'What did you call me?'

'I thought you had more guts than that.'

Her truculence is beginning to bug me. 'What the hell would you know about it? You're not me, you're not in my shoes.' I am shouting now: how dare she judge me like this? I can't believe that what started out as a perfectly pleasant cup of tea has deteriorated into a slanging match in my hall. Con is beside herself with anger, heading for the door. 'What's it to you, anyway?'

She swings around at the last moment. 'Ah fucking *care*, don't ah?' she yells at me.

I look at her in utter bewilderment.

'But – why?'

She is still yelling. 'Ah just do, all right?'

I am astonished.

'Look.' She takes a step back towards me. She is visibly trying to rein herself in. 'Ryan's all ah've got, right? He might not be Prince Charming, but he looks after me.'

I nod at the bruises around her neck. 'I don't call that looking after you.'

'Well, he were mad, weren't he? He in't always like that. And ah'd be stuffed without him – back in that halfway house or living in a cardboard box, probably. Wouldn't be t' first time. But that's my point. You stuck up for yourself. You put him in his place. It's what he needs, is that. I haven't been able to get it out my head. And then what you did yesterday, in t' supermarket.' A smile flickers briefly across her face and for a moment she looks all of about twelve. She hesitates. 'Ah just like you,' she finishes defiantly.

Her admission, delivered so truculently, blows me away. 'Oh, Con.' I can feel tears stinging at the back of my eyes. 'Look – come back and sit down. Please. We can have another cup of tea. Don't disappear off like this.'

She hesitates for a moment, and eventually allows me to lead her back through to the kitchen, though she keeps her jacket with her this time. I put the kettle back on and cross to sit beside her again, contemplating her for a moment before speaking. *Ah just like you.* Honestly, you'd think with the general mess I seem to be making of my life, I might be able to show a modicum of gratitude. I wrinkle my face at her.

'I'm not really a very nice person, you know.'

'No?'

I nod earnestly. 'Just wait till you get to know me better. I can be a class A bitch, especially to the people closest to me.'

'Right.' She weighs up what I've just told her. 'Why's that, then?'

'Why's what?'

'Why are you not nice to the people closest to you?'

I draw a sigh. Honestly, she's more intrusive than the bloody bereavement counsellor. 'I don't know – I suppose it's easiest to hit out at the people closest to you. Don't you find that?'

She sniffs indifferently. 'Wouldn't know, would ah? Never been that close to no one. Me mam were never the touchy-feely sort. And the staff in t' unit – well. They were nice enough. But it's a bit hard really, getting close to someone when their shift finishes at six and they bugger off home.'

I think about that one for a moment, and the same feeling of outrage I had yesterday at the thought of Con being stuck in a residential home all those years sweeps across me. 'What about Ryan?' I ask her eventually, offering a crumb of comfort, realising as I do so that I'm scraping the barrel here. 'You said he was a knight on a white horse yesterday. Aren't you close to him?'

'S'ppose so.' She hesitates. 'But he's usually the one does the hitting out.' She grins at me briefly to lighten her words. 'Just kidding,' she adds, defying me to challenge her again about the bruises.

I let it go.

'So, what you going to do with yourself now, then?' She casts another glance around my immaculate kitchen. 'Are you going to try and get your husband back, or what?'

Am I? I don't even know where I would start. In the past when Sam and I have argued, I've had ample reserves of emotional energy I could call upon to stoke my indignation at whatever apparent misdemeanour had provoked the fight. So we'd yell at each other for a bit (well, I would yell, and Sam would stay obdurately reasonable and rational, which used to drive me *nuts*), and then eventually I would say something so outrageous even I couldn't keep a straight face any more, and would either burst into tears, in which case Sam would stop taunting me and just hug me and apologise, or burst out laughing and *then* get upset, in which case it was usually me who did the apologising.

But this time it was different. This time, when I accused Sam of being responsible for Hope's death, there were no reserves left. No funny side to see. We just kind of . . . fizzled out. When he told me he was off to Africa, that was the full stop at the end of our marriage. We flatlined. That's how I knew it was over.

Because if there's one thing I have learned over the past seven-and-a-half months, it's that there's no resurrecting the dead.

I lift my eyes to Con. She's still sitting with a look of expectation on her face, waiting for me to answer her question. I give a light shrug by way of an answer.

'What's that supposed to mean?'

'Well –' I hesitate. 'It's not that easy.'

'Why not?' She's looking at me intently now.

I lift my shoulders again. 'It's just not. It's . . . compli-
cated.' Then, when she doesn't say anything, I add, 'I
suppose I just pushed things too far with Sam, and now
I'm having to deal with the consequences.'

Her face crumples in a frown, and then she shakes her
head at me. 'I just don't get you.'

'What d'you mean?'

She's watching me consideringly, and after a moment
she gives another slow shake of the head.

'What?' I say again.

'See when ah first met you? In 't street, wi' Ryan?'

'Mm-hm.' Where's she going with this?

'You were mad as hell when he tried to mug you, yeah?
You didn't just . . . roll over and take it.'

A small frown creases my forehead. 'No, I didn't, but I
don't see –'

'You stood up to him, right? Didn't let him – you
know – call t' shots.'

'Well, he had a knife at my throat!'

'Aye, ah know. Ah were there, remember. It's not the
first time I've seen him do summat like that. And, trust
me, most people do just roll over. They don't stand up to
him the way you did.'

I think about what she's saying, and somewhere inside
me I feel the beginnings of a warm glow uncurling in my
stomach. 'Really?'

'And in t' supermarket yesterday, you went for that
security guard all guns blazing. "What's going on?" you
went, like you owned the place. You never rolled over
then neither.'

I am smiling now, feeling vaguely proud of myself. The unexpected appreciation is doing wonders for my self-esteem. 'Well, you needed –'

'Ah mean, ah know you still took them pills, right? Ah know you must've been feeling pretty crap to do that. But you never actually did it, did you? And you don't look like you're about to do it now.'

'Well, I'm not, of course. I mean –'

'No, 'cause you don't just roll over, do you?' she says, interrupting me. 'You fight for what you want.'

I am practically beaming at her now. It feels like she's the first person who's understood me in months.

'So how come,' she says, narrowing her eyes at me, 'you've rolled over now?'

The smile freezes on my face. 'What?'

'You want him back, yeah?'

'Well, of course I do! But he doesn't want to come back. And I can't make him do something he's determined not to do.'

She raises her eyebrows at me. Then all at once she straightens in her chair and changes the subject so abruptly it takes my breath away. 'Can I take t' dog for a walk?'

'What? Erm, well, I suppose so.'

I shoot her a quizzical look as I'm fetching his lead from the scullery, but she's moved on from our earlier conversation and is looking nothing but eager at the prospect of taking Hector out. It takes him a minute to realise his luck's turned when I return with the lead, and then he emits a low howl, lifting his head almost apologetically, as though he's scared I might change my mind. I fire instructions at

Con as I'm sliding the lead over his neck. 'Um – don't let him pull you: he's very strong. And keep him on the lead, otherwise he might run off, because he doesn't really know you yet. Plus it's easier to pull him away if he starts trying to jump up at people. He likes people, but they can be a bit intimidated by him, especially when he jumps up. He thinks he's giving them cuddles, but they don't see it that way. Not all of them, anyway. Some of them quite like it, but you can't take the chance. Don't let him near any foot-balls. Or Frisbees,' I add, remembering our trip to the park yesterday. 'He's OK with other dogs, but if they're aggressive towards him he will probably eat them. And you need to watch out for –'

'Marion,' she interrupts me.

'What?'

'Nothing. Come on, Hector.' She shoots me a look of exasperation as they leave. 'Don't go telling me how to walk a dog when you haven't even got the courage to sort your own life out. You don't have to fix everything, you know.' She raises her eyebrows at me to make sure I'm getting the point.

I stand staring at the back of her head as the pair of them set off together, hearing her words hanging in the air long after the flurry of their departure has settled.

You don't have to fix everything.

Why, in God's name, didn't someone tell me that earlier?

Chapter 14

I'm exhausted for the rest of the day. The session with Con has left me utterly drained, and the bugger of it is, no matter how hard I try, I can't get what she said out of my head. In fact, the more I try to forget them, the more her words keep coming back to haunt me. *You fight for what you want.* It's true: I do. Did, anyway. I remember my mother saying something along the same lines the day I told her I was giving up teaching to pursue a new career in play therapy. 'I suppose there's no point in your father or me trying to change your mind,' she'd said, her shoulders slumping in disappointment at yet another sign of my lack of compliance. 'You were always very single-minded about getting what you want.' She hadn't made it sound like a compliment.

Con did, though. Con made it sound like there was hope for me, even if she did then accuse me of not having the courage to sort my own life out. And that, of course, is completely ridiculous. Anyone would think I was afraid of trying to patch things up with Sam, in case he turns me down. Which, by the way, he would never do. I mean, it's not as if he wanted to leave in the first place. He only went because I made it impossible for him to stay. All he'd need would be one sign – one tiny *crumb* – and he'd be back like a shot.

I mean it. He would.

I told Con as much as she was leaving after her walk with Hector, when she'd studiously avoided making any more provocative comments as she took off his lead and hung it up in the scullery and I followed her around giving her all the arguments I could think of for being so sure of my husband. I hung over her neck as she was wiping his paws with the towel I gave her, driving home the point I was making. The less she protested, the more I did. And eventually, as she was about to leave, as she was actually stepping out of the front door onto the path, she turned to look me in the eye.

'Marion, I believe you.'

'You do?'

'Mm-hm. I believe that if you gave Sam a way back, he'd take it.'

'Oh. Right. Well, good.'

She gave me a considering look, and then shook her head and laughed.

'What?' I caught hold of her arm. 'What's the laugh for? I thought you said you believed me.'

She shrugged indifferently. 'Ah do. 'Course, it's not me that needs to believe it, is it?' She stepped into the garden, and turned one last time as she reached the gate. 'See you around.' Then, with one final challenging nod in my direction, she was gone.

Well, what was that supposed to mean? *I* believed it; of course I did. I could just pick up the phone and – oh, I don't know – invite him to stay for supper tomorrow evening, when he comes back for his stuff. Forget about offering tiny crumbs: I'll have a veritable feast waiting for him, with me as the pièce de résistance. I could seduce him over the soufflé.

This last thought makes me laugh and cringe at the same time, and I toy with it over the course of the afternoon, plotting strategies in my head. Somewhere at the back of my mind is the unwelcome thought that Sam might be so shocked if I do set out to seduce him, he won't take me seriously. I mean, I can't actually remember the last time we had anything approaching intimacy, to put it delicately. Certainly not since Hope was killed. Jesus. Seven months. How did we – I – allow that to happen? There were a couple of abortive occasions when Sam tried to initiate something – the memory of the way I rejected him makes me wince – but eventually he just seemed to accept that I was a no-go area as far as any physical comfort was concerned. And actually, truth to tell, I was a no-go area as far as pretty much anything was concerned.

Not now, though. Not any more. Since Con came crashing back into my life, I'm starting to remember who I am and, frankly, I think the time to claim back what's dear to me is long overdue.

By the time evening falls, a plan is starting to form in my head. I'll have something tasty simmering on the stove when he arrives for his things, and I'll invite him to stay for a bite to eat. It will smell so utterly irresistible he won't be able to say no, and by the time he's finished licking the last traces of sauce from his lips he'll be so relaxed he won't want to go anywhere except upstairs, and I'll make it quite clear that that's fine by me. Before we know where we are, he'll have forgotten all about Africa and be all set to explore other territories much closer to home. In fact – brain-wave! – I'll reproduce that meal he cooked for the two of us on our first date together all those years ago back in York. Beef stroganoff, he'd made, the sauce melt-in-the-mouth light and the meat still pink in the middle. To someone on a student budget who'd secretly been expecting spaghetti Bolognese despite his assertions at the hospital that he wasn't a bad cook, I'd been seriously impressed. The very fact of my remembering, let alone cooking up the same meal, is bound to work wonders.

I barely sleep, I'm so excited with my plan, and the next morning I'm back round at Asda first thing, trying to track down the ingredients for my stroganoff after looking up a recipe on the Internet. The basic bits and pieces – the butter and the sour cream and the shallots – are straightforward enough, and I'm pretty sure we'll have the seasonings at home in the cupboard. The meat I'll pick up from the butcher's in Beulah Street on the way home. I come unstuck on the mushrooms, though, which according to the recipe have to be a particular type that I've never heard of. Eventually I give in and brave one of the assistants, who points me at some unprepossessing brown specimens that I heap into a brown paper bag.

After I've paid an arm and a leg for some sirloin at the Meat Company, I make a final stop-off at Oddbins and pick up a couple of bottles of Stonewell Shiraz that the guy behind the counter insists will set off the beef to a tee. Frankly, at almost thirty quid a pop, I would expect it to do the washing-up as well, but I stump up the money with relatively good grace. It's worth it, after all. Sam was always a sucker for a full-bodied Australian. He won't be able to resist.

By the time I get back home it's almost eleven. I'm already exhausted, and so when Con arrives unexpectedly and offers to take Hector out for another walk, I accept with gratitude and take myself off for a small nap so that I can be sure of being fresh when Sam arrives. I don't mention my plans for the evening to her when she returns about an hour later with Hector panting happily at her side, but she can tell straight away that something's up: I can feel her eyes upon me as I'm filling the kettle and setting out a couple of mugs for the two of us. I take my time brewing the tea, setting it down carefully in front of her before pulling up a chair for myself, and only after she's taken an initial sip and replaced her mug carefully on the table does she sit back and fold her arms across her chest with an accusing, 'Well?'

I lift my chin and return the look. 'Well, what?'

She continues to outstare me, and eventually my bravado crumbles. 'Well, OK. Sam is coming round tonight.'

'Aha.'

'No – not "aha": he's just coming over to collect some of his things.'

'Mmmm.' She nods thoughtfully, narrowing her eyes at me. 'I suppose that's why you've got that look in your eyes.'

'What look?'

'Like a cat,' she elaborates, 'with its eye on a mouse.'

'Oh, don't be ridiculous.' For someone who's only known me five minutes, she's disconcertingly frank. It's as if some of the niceties of social behaviour – the occasional bit of well-placed hypocrisy, for example – have completely passed her by. I wave a hand at her to dismiss such an outlandish suggestion. 'If you must know, I'm not even sure I'm going to be here when he comes. I thought I might – you know. Go out. Leave him to it. Much less awkward that way. I mean, the last thing he wants is me hanging around like some needy little cling-on.'

'True.' She gives another slow nod. 'Right enough, that purple dress *is* a bit desperate.'

I can feel my colour rising. 'What purple dress?'

She inclines her head towards the hall. 'The one you've got hanging up in t' hall.'

I give a high-pitched laugh. 'Oh, that old thing! I just – I'm having a bit of a clear-out.' The dress in question – a shot silk purple wraparound – is hanging from the banister in the hall because I brought it down to run the iron over it: it's been so long since it came out of my wardrobe, it's got hang-creases running down the length of it. I'd chosen it because – I'm embarrassed to say – the tie is very easy to undo. I hesitate. 'D'you really think it's desperate?'

She takes another sip of tea. 'Mm-hmm.'

'Oh.' I feel unaccountably crestfallen.

'Still, eh. Don't matter, does it, if it's just going to t' charity shop.'

'No.' I give her a discomforted smile. 'No, it doesn't matter a bit.' I pick up my own mug and take a nervous swallow.

'Mind you,' she continues, 'you want to make sure you're wearing *something* good, all t' same. Just in case you run into him, yeah? On your way out.' Her eyes are sparkling wickedly in a manner I'm beginning to recognise.

I hesitate, and finally capitulate. 'What sort of thing?'

'Depends . . . I mean, you really want to look amazing, without looking like you've made any effort, yeah?'

I nod slowly. What she's saying makes a lot of sense. The last thing I want to come across as is desperate. Plus, if I go for understated sexiness, it will make things much less embarrassing if he turns me down.

Which, of course, he won't.

'Right. So, go for something like jeans, say. And a T-shirt.'

My face drops. '*Jeans!*'

'Tight ones,' she amends. 'With heels. And lose the ponytail. Makes you look about twelve.'

'Well, I'll do that, of course, but – a T-shirt? Are you sure? Only, I've got this really pretty blouse –'

She tuts in irritation. 'Well, in that case, wear your pretty blouse. And, while you're at it, don't forget to stick a big notice on your chest with GAGGING FOR IT written all over it.'

I blow my cheeks out in frustration. All of a sudden, I feel like a complete novice in the art of seduction. 'Maybe it wouldn't be such a bad idea if I *did* go out for the evening.'

'Nah. Where's the fun in that? Tell you what.' She glances at the clock on the wall. 'What time's he coming round?'

'Seven.' I narrow my eyes at her. 'Why?'

'Oh, nothing. I were going to say I could come back later on and help you get ready, do your make-up and that.'

'Really?' I stare at her in astonishment, torn between the idea of getting ready with a fellow conspirer, which sounds like it could be fun, and the uncomfortable prospect of lowering defences I've spent seven months erecting and letting someone get close to me, with all the potential for getting hurt that that entails.

She shrugs, withdrawing from me. 'It were just a suggestion, like.'

Her face has closed over, like she's already preparing herself for a knock-back, and all of a sudden it occurs to me that, for someone who's had the kind of start in life she's had, this rather oddball friendship is probably just as daunting a prospect for her as it is for me. The thought makes me feel a bit ashamed of my initial reaction, and I chide myself inwardly. If I'm going to start re-engaging with life, Con's as good a place to start as any, surely.

'You know what?' I lean towards her, and she gives me a wary look. 'I think that's a great idea.'

'Yeah?' When she realises I'm serious, her face lights up. 'OK, then.'

'OK,' I say back to her. 'About half-five?'

'Right, then.' She pushes herself to her feet. 'Best be off now, then, else Ryan'll be asking questions. See you later, yeah?'

I can't help it: a broad grin of excitement has spread across my face. 'See you later.'

Chapter 15

I spend the rest of the afternoon getting ready for the evening. The house is first: I set a fire in the sitting room so that all it will need later is a match, and root out a CD of classical music that's a particular favourite of Sam's. I prepare the stroganoff ingredients and lay them out on the worktop like a science experiment waiting for his arrival. The fancy but nondescript mushrooms I tip into an unremarkable heap in a dish alongside the onions, and the spices — the salt, the pepper, the tarragon and the nutmeg — I set out like foot soldiers alongside the Aga. I slice the sirloin thinly, as the recipe instructs, and store it in the fridge with cling film over the plate to keep it fresh. Then I open one of the bottles of Shiraz in anticipation and leave it on the worktop to breathe. After that I focus on myself, spending so long buffing and exfoliating and shaving in the shower, I swear I shed a full skin. For the first time in months, I use conditioner on my hair, and after it's dried I get busy with the straighteners, working on it until it is sleek and ramrod straight. I plan to be standing at the Aga when he comes in, stirring the sauce with my back to him, so that he gets the full effect of the aroma of the frying shallots and the sizzling beef. In my head I have a picture of him crossing the kitchen and nuzzling in to the nape of my neck, and then getting completely carried away by the smell of my perfume mixed with all those mouth-watering cooking smells and taking me right there on the kitchen floor. I even hoover, just in case.

True to her word, Con's back later in the afternoon, pink-cheeked and breathless as I open the door to her a little after twenty to six. 'All right?' she wants to know, sliding her hand inside her jacket and producing a half-bottle of vodka. 'Doctor's orders,' she says, plonking it down on the table and fetching a couple of glasses from the cupboard. I swear, she knows her way around my kitchen better than I do. She must have had a jolly good snoop that night when I was out cold. 'Got any orange juice?'

'I don't think so. But honestly, I'm not sure I should –'

'Don't worry, we're only having the one,' she assures me. 'Ryan'll go mental if he finds out.' She delves in the freezer and fishes out a tray of ice cubes. 'Tonic?'

'There might be a bottle in the scullery. Don't let the dog out!' I call after her as she disappears off in search of the mixer.

'Blimey,' she says a couple of minutes later, spotting the already-open wine as she's handing me the drink she's concocted. 'You started early. Shouldn't have bothered with the vodka.'

'I haven't started it,' I protest. 'I just opened it so it could breathe.'

She looks at me askance. 'You what?'

'It's what you do with red wine,' I clarify. 'You open it an hour or so before you want to drink it so it can – you know – breathe,' I finish lamely.

'Right.' She gives me a sideways look. 'Are you sure you've not been on t' juice already?'

We abandon the kitchen and take our drinks off upstairs, where Con makes short work of dismissing the trousers I've selected, along with most of the tops I've spread out on the bed. 'Naff,' she says, plucking a fluffy short-sleeved sweater from the mattress, and, 'Christ Almighty,' when she spots the lace top I'd thought earlier about wearing. 'Haven't you got nothing sexy?'

'That fluffy top's sexy,' I protest. 'Sam likes me in it.'

'No, it's not,' she counters. 'It's naff. There's a difference.'

In the end she selects a pair of stonewashed bootleg jeans I haven't worn since before I had Hope, which she teams with a disappointingly plain black T-shirt. It's only as I'm taking them from her that I realise the jeans are the same pair I was wearing the day that Annie stuck the crayon in my leg. The first item of clothing I ever removed for my husband, I realise as Con hands them across to me. Maybe it's an omen.

'I haven't worn these in years,' I tell her. 'They probably won't fit.'

'Just try them. They're the hottest thing in your entire wardrobe.'

Amazingly, they slide easily over my hips. The past months have obviously taken their toll on my waistline. I run my hands down over my thighs and locate the small puncture hole where the crayon went through, and a whole host of memories comes flooding back. Suddenly there's a rightness about Con's choice, and I'm filled with a giddy excitement I'd been lacking up until now.

'Right.' I turn to her with an excited smile. 'What else?'

She teams the jeans and T-shirt with a pair of high black boots that also haven't seen the light of day in I don't know how long. I feel ridiculous putting them on, but Con is brooking no arguments. 'But why would I have boots on in the house?' I want to know, tugging the zip up reluctantly over my calves. 'I thought I was supposed to look like I hadn't made any effort.'

'What – you want to win him back in your slippers?'

'Well, I just think that would look more . . . natural.'

She shakes her head at me in disgust. 'You haven't got a clue, have you?'

Once she's satisfied with my outfit, she sits me down with my back to the dressing table and comes at me with a pair of tweezers, ignoring my cries of pain as she swoops in at my forehead like a frenzied blackbird, plucking out rogue eyebrow hairs I didn't know I had. After that she gets busy with the few paltry items in my make-up bag, supplementing them with a few extra bits she seems to have secreted about her person. She huffs and puffs a bit during the transformation, but eventually finishes with a muttered, 'Right, that'll have to do,' at which point she scrabbles around in my chest of drawers, eventually emerging triumphantly with a pair of curling tongs I'd forgotten I owned.

'I already did my hair,' I tell her, running a hand over it protectively.

'Yeah, ah can see that.' I can tell from her tone that she's less than impressed. She plugs in the curling tongs underneath the dressing table.

'Oh, Con. I'm not sure about curls. Aren't they a bit – eighties?'

'Not the way you'll be wearing them, no,' she says, disappearing abruptly off downstairs and returning a moment later with a chopstick from the cutlery drawer. By now the tongs are hot enough to satisfy her, and she spends a good twenty minutes undoing all my careful efforts with the straighteners until my head is a mass of tumbling curls. Then, just as I'm about to object again, she gathers them all up in her hand and skewers them to the back of my head with the chopstick.

'Right,' she says, straightening. 'You're done.'

I teeter apprehensively across to the wardrobe and swing open the door with the full-length mirror on the back of it so that I can admire Con's handiwork, and a woman I don't recognise materialises before me. She's a good bit taller than me, with long, long legs and a cleavage I'd kill for, framed quite magnificently by the innocuous-looking black T-shirt. Her eyes – I don't know what Con's done with the makeup, but the eyes are smoky and mysterious. Mine seem to have been pink-rimmed and tired for so long, I'd no idea they could look this good. And the cheeks: I suppose I'd expected overkill on the cheeks, but somehow she's managed that same smoky sensuality without my being able to discern just what she's done to achieve it. I reach a hand up and touch my face. 'How –?' I manage, and she grins.

'Eye shadow. Thought the blusher would look too obvious.'

'And my hair –' I break off again, tilting my head so that I can see the way she's scooped it up, the way the odd rogue curl has escaped artfully around the nape of my neck. 'I look like a model.'

'A low-key model,' Con amends. 'One that's just naturally gorgeous.'

'Con.' I turn to look at her. 'You're a genius.'

'I am, aren't I?' She's grinning with false modesty. 'Who'd have thought an old bag like you would scrub up so well?' She ducks out of the way before I can thump her. 'Any road, ah'd best be off. It's ten to.'

'It never is!' A glance at the bedside clock confirms what Con's said, and all at once I'm galvanised into action. 'I have to get the beef on!'

The two of us make our way downstairs and Con stands awkwardly in the hall for a moment. 'Right – well. Good luck.'

'You'll be around tomorrow?' Suddenly I'm loath for her to leave.

She looks down at her feet. 'Well –'

'Hector will be upset if he doesn't see you. He'll be expecting his walk.'

'Well, that's true, he will.'

'Around eleven, then?' I'm itching to give her a hug, but something tells me she'll run a mile if I attempt it.

She shrugs in that way she has, affecting nonchalance. 'OK, then.' And then before I can change my mind and do anything foolish like kiss her she's away, ducking off down the front path and through the gate, where she pauses long enough to grant me a final nod. 'See you tomorrow,' she says, swinging the gate shut behind her and disappearing off down the road without looking back.

After she's gone I hurry through to the kitchen to put a knob of butter into the pan and set it on the hot plate, and while it's heating up I pour myself a half-glass of the Shiraz, not to drink it so much as to *look* like I'm drinking it: I don't want it to seem like I've been waiting for Sam to arrive before I have a drink. The temperature has to be high enough to cook the beef quickly, the recipe says, but not so high that the butter burns. I leave the pan on the Aga and nip through to the sitting room, where I light the fire I laid earlier and a couple of candles that are sitting out on the coffee table. I press the play button on the CD player, and some hauntingly beautiful music spills out, filling the room. Standing back, I can see that the whole thing has a trying-too-hard look about it, so I blow out the candles again and mess up the cushions on the sofa a bit. Then as a finishing touch I rummage out an old magazine, which I open up at random and drop onto the coffee table. I turn the music down a notch or two as well. It's still not quite right – still too staged, somehow – but there's no time for me to do more: I can already smell the butter starting to catch.

Back through in the kitchen, I tip the sliced beef into the butter, making it sizzle alarmingly. The stress of getting it right is making me panic, and I can feel beads of sweat breaking out on my forehead. Unlike Sam, I've never been an instinctive cook: to be honest, a couple of chopped chicken breasts and a jar of cook-in sauce are usually about as adventurous as I get. A cloud of black smoke billows from the butter and I snatch the pan quickly off the plate, wishing I'd gone for something less risky.

Beef stroganoff, for crying out loud. Who do I think I'm kidding?

I've just about got things back under control when I hear the sound of a key in the front door, and I know he's arrived. The back of my neck tingles in anticipation; I can almost feel his lips against my skin. I shift restlessly and try to arrange myself so that it looks like the most natural thing in the world for me to be standing at the Aga pushing sliced sirloin around a pan in three-inch heels.

The front door closes and I sense him moving across the hall towards the kitchen. Then he freezes. 'Marion?' I can hear the incredulity in his voice, and – I can't help it – a slow, smug smile spreads across my face. I keep my back to him and try my hand at emulating Con's nonchalance.

'Oh, hi. Sorry, be with you in a mo. I don't want my dinner to burn.' I manage a half-turn then: a half-turn and a quick smile. The expression on his face is priceless – hardly surprising, really, when you consider that over the past seven months the closest I've come to making an effort has been putting on clean pyjamas.

'You're cooking?' He can't keep the disbelief out of his voice. 'Smells amazing.' He crosses the kitchen to join me at the stove and picks up one of the mushrooms sitting on the worktop, lifting it to his nose to smell it. 'Cremini mushrooms?' His face folds in confusion.

I keep my face deliberately nonchalant. 'Mm-hmm.'

He peers at the beef in the pan. 'Beef stroganoff?'

I give him a bright smile, tipping the nicely browned

(even if I do say so myself) beef onto a waiting plate and then adding the sliced shallots to the pan. 'Yup.'

He looks at me properly now, staring so hard into my smoky, come-to-bed eyes, my knees turn to water. Then he runs his eyes over the innocuously sexy T-shirt, the tight, figure-hugging jeans, and I can feel myself growing crimson under the intensity of his gaze. Inside my stomach a whole swarm of butterflies sets off at once.

'Um.' It emerges as a croak. 'You can stay for some if you like,' I tell him, and he raises his eyebrows at me. 'Supper,' I clarify, flushing again. 'You can stay for supper. I think there'll be enough. If I add extra mushrooms.' For God's sake, Marion, I chide myself. What on earth d'you suppose he thought you were offering?

'I didn't bring any wine,' he counters, not taking his eyes off me, as though the oversight amounts to some terrible social gaff that nullifies the offer of supper.

'I have wine!' I say, a bit over-hastily, and I make a huge effort to rein myself in, Con's words about not appearing desperate loud in my head. I turn my back on him and busy myself with the shallots to allow myself time to recover. 'There's a bottle on the worktop,' I tell him without looking round.

I manage to sneak a look at him under the pretext of needing more butter for the shallots. He's picked up the bottle of Shiraz and is studying the label. 'Stonewall,' he observes, pursing his lips and raising his eyebrows approvingly, and immediately I wish I'd chosen something a bit less obvious, a bit less over the top.

'Well, I wanted something with a bit of body to set off

the beef,' I tell him, but I can tell he isn't really listening. Instead he's looking at me again, a wry smile on his face.

'What?' A note of truculence has crept into my voice, thank God: it makes me seem less desperate.

'Oh, nothing. It's just –'

'Just what?' Crap. He knows – of course he does – that I've deliberately set out to seduce him with all this fancy food and fine wine and these stupid three-inch heels. Unreasonably, I suppose, I feel angry all of a sudden. 'Look, I expect you're in a hurry to get your stuff. I'll just –' I gesture ineptly at the shallots, filled with sudden loathing for the way they're lying so smugly sizzling away in the butter, and thanking God I took Con's advice and stuck to jeans and a T-shirt. I can just imagine the humiliation if I'd been standing there in my easy-access wraparound silk dress. I turn my back on him and lift the pan off the plate, my eyes smarting with unexpected tears.

'Actually, I was thinking about how much your tastes have changed. Remember the first time we ate stroganoff together, that time in my flat?'

'Not really.' I keep my frustratingly brimming eyes fixed on the stove.

He crosses to where I'm standing and takes the pan of shallots from my hand, setting it down gently to the side of the hot plate. 'Sure you do. You brought round a bottle of Lambrusco.'

He's so close to me now, I can feel the heat of his body through my T-shirt. I blink a couple of times. 'Bloody shallots,' I say, wiping the back of my hand across my cheek and probably wrecking Con's handiwork in the process.

'Marion,' he says, reaching out and taking both of my hands in his. 'Look, I'm not really all that hungry.'

If it weren't for the fact that his eyes are telling a different story, I'd probably have launched into another kamikaze you-must-be-in-a-terrible-hurry speech. Instead I swallow. 'Aren't you?' It's working, then. The butterflies have set off afresh in my stomach.

He doesn't speak: he just leans over and kisses me, tentatively at first, and then, when I don't slap his face or tell him not now or say how could he or any of the other things I've spent the past seven months using to keep him away from me, he grows bolder, pushing my head back so that the chopstick falls from my hair just as Con had no doubt known it would and the curls come tumbling down my neck. 'Christ,' I hear him breathe, and the next thing I know he's scooped me up in his arms, which is just as well as I'm not sure my legs would have supported me much longer, and is carrying me through to the living room, where the soft strains of Beethoven's Fifth are playing away quietly in the background and the fire is just getting going, and he sets me down gently on the rug and I think, staged or not, this couldn't be more perfect. After that I don't remember much, just the feel of his hands against my body, urgent and insistent, as though he's afraid he hasn't much time, the two of us fumbling with the fastener to my jeans, gasping in our hurry to be shot of them. And then his body hard against mine, locked together, skin against skin, his half-discarded jeans rough against my thighs, and the sound of somebody crying out, though I don't know which of us it is. And afterwards the feel of his head heavy against my shoulder, where I remember it being a lifetime ago, and somewhere deep inside me a small voice saying, *Oh, yes: Marion Bishop. I remember her.*

All of which probably sounds ridiculously corny. What can I say? It beat the hell out of stroganoff.

And then afterwards . . . Are you up to hearing about afterwards? Because it's kind of important, what happens next, in the grand scheme of things. If the earth had just moved, what happens afterwards is it cracks wide open and I fall right down into the gap. And it's the last thing I'm expecting, you see. The very last thing. Just when I'm starting to feel him stir, and I'm wondering whether we could go for it a second time – we've got seven months to make up for, after all – he lifts his head from my shoulder and pushes himself to a sitting position, rubbing blearily at his eyes, and he says,

'I've got to go.'

I must have misheard him. What he probably said was, 'I've got to have another go.' Of course he did. That first time it was over so fast: we can afford to take things much more slowly this time. I reach up and pull at his shoulder, and he leans down and kisses me again. I shift my body against his, accommodating him.

And then he pulls away from me and he says, 'No, really, I've got to go.'

I look at him stupidly. 'Go where?'

He's pulled himself upright now, and is shrugging his jeans back over his hips, and I'm thinking to myself that this is all wrong, that he should be shrugging himself *out* of them. He's shed so few of his clothes he's dressed again in a matter of seconds. By contrast, my carefully selected outfit is scattered across the floor like litter and I'm feeling more than a bit exposed, lying there on the rug, naked aside from a pair of three-inch-heeled boots. Suddenly I feel like a wham-bam-thank-you-ma'am hooker from an Amsterdam knocking shop.

'Our flight leaves at half-six. We have to be at Manchester by five.'

'What flight?'

He doesn't look at me now. Instead he crosses to the door. 'You put my stuff in my briefcase, yeah?' he says, disappearing into the hall.

I can't believe it – can't believe he would do what he's just done and then go calmly ahead with his plans to bugger off to Nakuru after what just happened. 'Marion?' he says, sticking his head around the door.

'What?'

'My passport. Did you put it in my briefcase?'

'It's on the desk in the study.' He doesn't seem to notice anything odd in my tone.

I'm still sitting there in shock, hugging my knees to my chest to cover my nakedness and feeling like a prize idiot, when he reappears again. He crouches beside me and tries to wrap his arms around me, but I shrug him away.

'Marion –' His shoulders slump. 'Look, people are expecting me. Depending on me.'

I can't bring myself to speak. I press my lips together tightly and nod my head. *Men can be right arseholes.* Con had it right on the nail.

He pushes himself upright again, regarding me for a

moment before crossing once again to the door, where he pauses, and I think, Of course he's going to realise he can't just go. Not now. Not after that. I turn my face towards him hopefully, and he gives me a sheepish half-smile.

'It was good to see you,' he says.

Bastard. Fucking, lousy bastard. 'You can leave the money on the table in the hall,' I say, and his face folds in confusion.

'Money?' Then comprehension dawns, and his jaw drops. 'Oh, for God's sake, Marion –'

'Go,' I tell him tiredly, turning back to face the fire. 'Just get out.'

And that's that. When I next look around, he's gone.

Chapter 16

I know. I couldn't really believe it, either. But that's what happened.

I was dreading telling Con about it when she came in the next morning to take Hector for a walk. But she must have taken one look at my face and realised that something was far from right, because she never mentioned anything about it. She just stepped into the hall with her customary 'All right?' before ducking off to fetch the dog. Then when the two of them returned from their walk and we were sitting with our mugs of tea at the kitchen table, she said, 'Want me to come in tomorrow, then?' like we were continuing an earlier conversation. I gave her a bit of a lopsided smile. 'That would be great.'

Over the next couple of weeks she continues to drop in around the same time every morning, and after a couple of visits I start augmenting our tea with the odd bit of toast. Before we realise it we've fallen into a habit of sharing a late breakfast together.

Hector's like a different dog: the slightly worried look I've seen hovering around his eyes since Sam moved out has disappeared. As for me – well, God knows where I'm up to. Certainly I'm grateful for the companionship: if it weren't for her, there would be some days when I never saw another living soul. I still cringe when I think about that evening, about sitting there on the rug wearing nothing but those ridiculous boots while Sam blundered around looking for his passport. The memory makes me want to curl up in a ball, but Con's daily visits mean I can't, which is probably just as well really.

The phone rings periodically every day, but I can't face answering it. The thought of hearing Sam's voice all the way from Nakuru is too much to be borne. And so I let it ring until the answerphone kicks in, and whoever is calling doesn't leave a message, making it easy for me to retreat back into my narrow existence. It's like we've built a fortress around ourselves, Con and Hector and me, and when we're together we can hide away from the bits of our lives we don't like all that much.

We could have carried on like that indefinitely, I suppose. But after she's brought Hector back one morning, and I've managed to persuade her to stay for a spot of lunch, the whole edifice comes crumbling down around my ears.

The weather this particular morning is blisteringly hot – the sort of sun that you associate with holidays abroad and that makes you wonder why you would ever want to be anywhere other than home. We are sitting on a rug in the garden, the remains of a rudimentary picnic scattered on around our knees, while Hector loiters on the fringes of the rug hoping for a lapse in vigilance so that he can home in on the pâté that is growing soft in the afternoon sun. Con's face is tilted towards the sky, her eyes closed, a small smile hovering at the corners of her mouth. 'Mmm,' she says without opening her eyes. 'This is bliss.'

She's not the same girl I rescued from the supermarket what feels like a lifetime ago. Maybe it's all the walking with Hector, but her skin has lost its sallow look, and there's a sparkle around her eyes that wasn't there before. Her hair looks less lacklustre as well, and the bruising on her neck has faded to a sickly yellowish-green and dirty-brown stain that is slowly bleeding its way downwards towards her collarbone. Seeing it like that, remembering the ugly black and purple colours it had been when I first spotted it, a sudden wave of anger towards Ryan for what he did to her washes over me. Watching the change in her over the past couple of weeks has been like watching a butterfly emerge from a chrysalis. I find myself wondering just how big a transformation might be possible if she didn't keep running back to him every afternoon.

'You're looking at me.' She is still sitting with her eyes closed, her head tilted to the sun.

'Sorry?' Her comment drags me back from my speculating with a stab of guilt, as though I've been caught out doing something I shouldn't.

'I can feel you looking at me.'

'Well, yes, I was looking at you, as it happens.' I pause. 'I was just thinking how well you're looking.'

'Yeah?' She opens one eye and squints at me from across the rug.

'Yeah.'

'What's different, then?' She sits up properly now, enjoying herself, wanting to hear more.

'Hmm.' I pretend to be considering for a moment. 'Well, your skin, for example.'

She runs a hand self-consciously across her cheek. 'What about it?'

'I don't know: it's just . . . clearer, somehow. Fresher. It looks like happy skin instead of sad skin.'

She shakes her head at me. 'You're mad, you are. I knew it when I first saw you. *Happy skin!*' She gives a small snort, then grins at me again. 'What else?'

'Well . . .' I draw it out a bit. 'Your eyes are brighter. And your hair is shinier.'

She plucks at one of the long locks and scrutinises it, wrinkling her nose as if she doesn't like what she's seeing. 'You reckon?'

'Absolutely.' I lean over and take another lock between my fingers. 'You have beautiful hair, Con.'

'Oh, I don't!' Her tone is pleased. 'It's just long, that's all.'

'No, it's not just long. You should see how it's shining in the sunlight. It's full of natural highlights.' Like Hope's, I remember, the thought reaching up and squeezing at my heart in a way I can't quite define.

'Full of split ends, you mean.' She's doing her best to sound self-deprecating, but her cheeks are pink with delight.

'Well, that's easily sorted.' I hesitate for a moment. 'I could trim them out for you if you like.'

'Yeah?'

'Sure.' I catch my breath, then chastise myself inwardly. You've only offered to cut her hair, I tell myself sternly. You haven't asked her to move in and start wearing your dead daughter's clothes. I'm shocked at the direction my subconscious seems to be pushing me down, and turn my back resolutely on the thought. I manage a bright smile. 'You did my hair the other week. It's only fair that I should do yours. And I'm quite good at cutting hair.'

'Yeah?' She's looking at me doubtfully.

'Really, I am. Besides, we're only talking about a trim.' She thinks about this for a moment. 'OK, then.'

'You'll have to wash it first. I need it wet to cut it properly.' I can see her vacillating, torn between wanting the haircut and not wanting to be a nuisance. 'There's some shampoo in the bathroom upstairs. Special stuff for blonde hair.' Hope's shampoo, in fact, that I still haven't managed to throw away. It has sat congealing on the edge of the bath for months now. 'You can use that if you like.' I keep my tone light to show that it's no big deal whether we do this or not.

'OK.' She's on her feet in a flash, all eagerness and excitement.

While she's away washing her hair, I pack up the bits and pieces of the picnic, much to Hector's disappointment, and take it through to the kitchen. Then I set a chair out in the middle of the floor, and fetch the hairdressing scissors and a comb from one of the drawers and the hairdryer from my wardrobe. My hands are shaking slightly as I lay them out on the table.

By the time she comes back downstairs, her hair swathed in a towel, I've composed myself a bit. She's managed, in her attempts to wash her hair over the edge of the bath, to soak the collar of the top she's wearing, and so I fetch her one of mine, a pink-and-navy rugby shirt Sam brought back for me from a trip to Dublin a couple of years ago. I hang her damp top over the back of one of the chairs, positioning it where a pool of sunlight is spilling into the kitchen so that the collar will dry quickly.

'This is so cool.' Con is skittish, like a little kid, as she takes her seat in the chair I've prepared for her. She shrugs the towel from her head, rubbing perfunctorily at the long hair before draping it across her shoulders. 'Like playing at hairdressers. I've not had my hair cut in years. Don't take too much off, mind. Ryan likes it long.'

The trembling kicks off afresh in my hands as I pick up the comb to run through her hair, teasing out the tangles and smoothing it against her back. 'I think it would suit you a bit shorter,' I say. 'Shoulder-length, say.' The way I'm feeling towards men generally right now, and a couple of them in particular, the prospect of pissing Ryan off by taking more off the length than he might like gives me a guilty thrill.

'Yeah?' Con's tone is doubtful. 'Maybe not shoulder-length. Sort of – here.' She indicates with the side of her hand. 'Ryan'll go nuts.' She grins conspiratorially, as though this is about more than just a haircut.

Which, of course, it is.

Her hair is thicker than Hope's. I have to pin it up in layers in order to get through it properly. By the time I've reached the final layer, almost half an hour has passed, during which I've worked mostly in silence, lost in the task of snipping away at all the different sections of hair, while Con has kept up a stream of chatter I barely register. Fortunately she doesn't seem to need my input and lets me work away quietly. There's a line of soft downy hair that runs from the nape of her neck towards her back. I trace it with my eyes as I'm drying the hair, noticing the stark contrast of the delicate skin with the ugly bruising around her throat, realising too late that there'll be no concealing the remains of the assault behind this new length of hair.

My eyes keep sliding back to the bruises; I can't help feeling that there's something not quite right about them. I snip away for a bit longer, half an eye still on the bruises, and then it dawns on me what it is about them that's troubling me.

They should have faded long ago.

Shouldn't they? I rack my brain, trying to remember how long a bruise lasts, taking another sidelong look at the dark purple marks on her neck, and give a barely concealed gasp as I realise that these aren't the same bruises she was sporting a fortnight ago.

These are fresh.

'You all right?' She's picked up on the gasp.

'Fine.' I give her a bright smile. 'Almost done.'

She's right, I realise with a lurch that's half-pleasure, half-panic: Ryan *will* go nuts.

'There,' I say finally. 'That's us. You can go and admire yourself; there's a mirror in the hall.'

She jumps up and hurries through to the hall and I follow a few steps behind, leaning on the door frame and watching with pleasure as she twists and preens in front of the mirror, admiring the swing in the hair, enjoying the way it catches the light as it falls softly against her jawline, framing her face. Then she frowns slightly and leans in towards the mirror, scowling at the now-obvious bruises, touching them lightly with her fingertips, pulling at the hair to try to conceal them and failing. After a moment she gives up.

'It's lovely,' she says, generously ignoring the fact that I've taken off far more than either of us had anticipated, and it is. Apart from the issue of the bruises, that is, which stick out now like a sore thumb against her collarbone. I cross to where she's standing in front of the mirror and regard her reflection over her shoulder.

'You look really beautiful,' I tell her, and she blushes, pleased. I gather up the hair in my hands, sweeping it back off her neck. 'You could wear it up if you wanted to; it's still long enough.'

The bruises sit between us like an accusation.

'Con –'

'No, don't,' she tells me, ducking her head away from me. She lopes back into the kitchen, and after a moment I follow her. She's crouching on the floor making a fuss of Hector, and doesn't look up as I come in. I stand in the doorway for a moment regarding her, not knowing how to quiet the tumult of feelings coursing through me.

'You shouldn't have to put up with it,' I tell her eventually. Neither of us is in any doubt about what the 'it' refers to.

'Ah said, leave it!' She pushes herself angrily to her feet. 'Don't go spoiling things. I never said nothing about Sam, did I? Never stuck my nose in where it wasn't wanted.'

'There's a bit of a difference between the way Sam has

treated me and the way Ryan treats you,' I tell her tartly. I want to bite out my tongue, so hell-bent is it on voicing the venom I feel towards this boy who's had the audacity to bruise that delicate skin.

'Yeah?' She is looking at me in disgust. 'So where is he, then? At least Ryan's there for me when I need him.'

'There for you?' I give a harsh laugh. 'Oh, sure, he's there for you. There with his fists at the ready.'

'Shut up!' She spits this through clenched teeth. 'Just shut up!'

'You know, you're worth more than this,' I tell her. 'No man with an ounce of decency in him would raise a hand against a woman.'

She is beginning to tremble with anger. 'Stop it! You're spoiling everything.'

I can't help myself: I plough on regardless of the rage I'm inducing in her. 'You should kick him into touch, get rid of him. Move out.'

'Yeah?' Her eyes are bulging. 'And go where? Move in here, with you? You think just because you cut my hair and lent me your clothes, you get to tell me what to do? Is that what you think?' She gives a harsh laugh, then leans across to me. 'Ah know what you're trying to do. But ah'm not your daughter. It weren't my fault she died, right? It were an accident. I don't have to take her place.' She clamps her lips together suddenly, and then shakes her head as if she's trying to clear it of the awful vision that the idea of taking Hope's place has conjured up inside it. 'Ah'm scum. Get it? *Scum.* Ah'm not like you. It'd take more than a shower and a haircut to wash the dirt off of me. And Ryan loves me, right? He loves me in spite of that, and I love him. So don't you dare try and tell me what ah'm worth, or talk to me about decency.' Spittle has formed on the edges of her mouth. 'Don't you dare. I know what I am, right? You don't get to come along and save me.'

'Somebody needs to!' I am shouting now, desperation making my voice crack.

'Oh, don't make me laugh!' She is tearing at the top I lent her now, pulling it over her head, messing up the just-styled hair, grabbing her own top from the back of the chair. 'You can't save me, Marion.' She thrusts her hands angrily into the sleeves of the top and wrenches it over her head. 'You can't even save yourself.' Her words stab at me like a knife. 'You think you own me, just because ah've been coming round to walk the dog. Ah were only doing you a favour.' *Stab, stab, stab.* I can hardly breathe in the viciousness of her attack. 'You don't get it, do you? Fixing me isn't going to fix what happened to Hope. Sometimes shit just happens, and you have to get on with it. I should know: shit's been happening to me all my life. Only the difference between you and me is, ah'm dealing with my shit, ah'm getting on with my life, even if you don't like the way I'm doing it. You don't get to tell me what to do. And you don't get to take it off me either, just because you don't like Ryan.'

'He doesn't love you,' I say in quiet despair.

She freezes, and then she crosses quietly to where I'm standing by the door to the hall, stopping beside me and looking me hard in the eye as though she's trying to work out where I'm coming from. Then she shakes her head at me. 'Fuck this,' she says. 'I don't need it.' She shoulders past me into the hall, no longer an older version of Hope but an angry stranger whose life has somehow collided with my own. A moment later she's gone, swallowed up in what's left of the afternoon sun, slamming the front door furiously behind her.

Chapter 17

I spend the best part of a week looking for her. I can't explain why: I just feel . . . unanchored, somehow, as though my very sanity depends on getting her back. I know I shouldn't; after the things she said, I should leave well alone. But I just can't. I've grown dependent on our friendship. It's almost as if she holds some secret truth about where I am in my life, some obscure kind of link to Hope that's got more to it than the fact that they have the same colour of hair. And if she *is* the link, and I can't find her, how am I going to get back to Hope? How am I going to avoid losing her all over again?

Hector has been sulking since her hasty departure; the afternoon walks scouring the streets are scant compensation for the sudden disappearance of his new friend. I try all the places I can think of in the hope of running into her. I even make several trips to the supermarket in the hope that she might turn up with another CD stuffed inside her jacket. When there's no sign of her anywhere, I turn my attention to tracking down Ryan. If I can find him, maybe he will lead me to Con. I loiter outside one or two shady-looking bars at throwing-out time like a misguided hooker, buttoned up to the neck in my very come-hither Laura Ashley coat. No joy. One night I try leaving Hector behind in case he's proving to be too much of a deterrent, and go back down Station Parade with my handbag dangling from my shoulder like bait, hoping to lure Ryan out into the open. I offer myself up to the seedy underworld of Harrogate, but to no avail; it seems the harder I try to find a mugger worthy of the name, the safer the streets become. It's as if neither of them ever existed.

It hasn't even entered my head to worry about who I might run into while I'm out scouring the streets. And so I'm caught on the back foot on Tuesday night, when I come back home from another please-mug-me wander down by the shopping centre and run smack into my neighbour Martin, Heather's husband, the one who's been so strenuously avoiding me since the accident. He's just pulled up outside his house as I'm coming down the road, and he must catch sight of me in his rear-view mirror or something, because he stays sitting in the car and watches me covertly like one of those dodgy private detectives on a low-budget TV programme. I think about letting him off the hook and going in the front gate, but frustration at my lack of success in finding Con has made me bolshie. I charge right up to the car and knock on the passenger window. He does this great golly-fancy-seeing-you-here jump, and lowers the window a few inches, his face flicking through a variety of emotions while he tries to decide which one is appropriate for a neighbour whose daughter died just over eight months ago. Happily he doesn't know about Sam leaving, so there's no need for him to factor that into the decision-making, which is lucky, really: we'd be here all night.

'Martin!' I put on my breeziest smile, though I know my tone is brittle. 'Haven't seen you in ages.'

'Yes, yes, um –' His face runs through another few expressions and finally settles on concern. 'How *are* you?'

I hate that – the way people drop their tone on the 'are', like the answer is bound to be that I am suicidal or something. I am so sick of being treated like an invalid.

'Great!' (I don't say, 'I've gone round the twist and am spending my days trying to hunt down a mugger's lookout because I think she might lead me back to my dead daughter.' I am making a great show of being normal.) 'Listen, we really must get you and Heather in for supper one evening.' I've momentarily lost sight at this point of the tiny problem I might have conjuring up a husband if he accepts.

He squirms a bit in his seat. I'm obviously making him uncomfortable.

'It's all right, you know.' I make my tone deliberately reassuring, the kind of tone I used to use on Hope when she'd hurt herself. 'We're not contagious.'

He has the grace to look discomfited. Good, I think to myself. And then all of a sudden he gives me this odd look and swings himself out of the car, picking up a takeaway from the back seat and then crossing to stand beside me on the pavement.

'Look, Marion, it's just –' God, he is still squirming. How hard can it be to be civil to a grieving neighbour? 'I'm not sure we'd be very good company. The thing is . . . well, Heather's having a bit of a tough time at the moment.'

'Oh.' I am momentarily taken aback on realising that the look of wretchedness on his face isn't anything to do with me. My self-centredness makes me squirm. 'I hope it's nothing serious.'

He makes a wry face. 'It's not brilliant. She just found out she's got breast cancer.'

Shit. A thought occurs to me, and I swallow. 'When?' He frowns at me quizzically. 'When did she find out, I mean?'

'She got the lab results about three weeks ago.'

'What day?' Even to myself, the question sounds bizarre.

He looks at me as though I've taken leave of my senses. 'Um, I'm not sure. It was midweek, anyway – I was out at work.'

'Was it a Tuesday?' Why am I tormenting myself like this?

He is frowning distractedly. 'Erm, it might have been.' He gives me an apologetic smile and gestures with the takeaway bags in his hands. 'Look, I'd better take these in. Nothing worse than cold takeaway, is there?' He hesitates by the gate. 'I'll ask her, anyway. Might do her good to get out.' He tries an experimental smile, but misery is etched into every line of his face. Then he turns and walks up the path to the front door, his shoulders slumped and his head down. I stand on the pavement for a few more moments, following his shadow, which is silhouetted against the blind in the front room; seeing a second shadow stand up to greet him; watching him fold the second shadow in his arms, pulling his wife in close without even pausing to put down the takeaway he is still holding.

You're not the only one shit's happened to.

Con is right, I realise with a sinking heart. I *am* selfish.

I sat and hid in the bathroom upstairs while my friend stood outside ringing my doorbell because she needed me. I am selfish and self-absorbed and so wrapped up in me, me, me; I think I'm the only one on the planet with the right to feel sorry for myself.

No wonder Sam has left me.

I go back to my own empty house, where nobody is waiting to fold me into their arms, fetch a very surprised Hector and drag him upstairs with me and force him onto the bed, where he lies apologetically, trying to disguise his great hulking bulk as one of the pillows, because he knows perfectly well that under normal circumstances he isn't even allowed upstairs, let alone on the furniture. Then I clamber in alongside him, wrap my arms around him, bury my face in his fur and cry myself to sleep.

Chapter 18

I wake early on Wednesday morning, feeling unaccountably worried about something I can't put my finger on. You'd think I'd have grown used to these early-morning slumps; in the days and weeks after the accident, when I managed to snatch a couple of hours' oblivion, there was always an inevitable trade-off upon waking and being brought back to a reality I didn't want to face. But today is different. Today – I don't know – it's as if there's something niggling at the back of my mind that I've forgotten to do.

The thought slips elusively further out of reach, and I give up and burrow a bit deeper under the duvet, reluctant to abandon my sleep at such a hideous hour. It's then that I become aware of the unaccustomed weight on the mattress, and I prise my eyes back open and lift my head off the pillow long enough to take in Hector's recumbent form down at the bottom of the bed. I can't figure out what he's doing there at first, and then it comes back to me in a rush: the late-evening encounter with Martin; the news about Heather; the picture of the two of them silhouetted against the window of their house, trying to come to terms with what life had just thrown at them.

I was right, I realise now: I *had* forgotten to do something. I cast my mind back to that afternoon when

I hid in the bathroom while Heather was ringing my front doorbell, and I wince. I've been so wrapped up in my friendship with Con I've forgotten to be a friend to Heather. Actually, now I think about it, I've forgotten to be anything at all, other than a mother without a child to love, which is probably why it was so easy to latch on to Con the way I did.

I chew that over for a little while, lying there in my too-big bed while Hector snores on quietly at my feet, and eventually, after I've thought myself into a fine old funk, I push back the covers and go downstairs to put the kettle on, trying as I do so to find some crumb of an identity for myself in this post-apocalyptic life I seem to be stuck with. Everything I used to use to define myself – mother, colleague, wife, friend – it's all been stripped away in the fallout.

I sigh as I'm pouring the hot water onto a tea bag. Maybe I should just barricade the house and wind chicken wire along the front fence to keep people away from me. I'd be doing them a favour, really. Disaster seems to be following me around these days.

I carry my mug of tea out in to the hall and pause beside the front door for a moment, imagining how it would look nailed shut and, as I'm standing there, the bell rings and I leap out of my skin, spilling hot tea over my hand and onto the carpet.

'Ow! Jesus, bollocks, shit.' I shake my hand off and crank the door open a couple of inches to reveal Martin on the other side, wild-haired and looking hassled. I pull the door open wider and he makes an attempt at a smile.

'Bad time?'

I stare at him blankly, trying to figure out what he's doing turning up on my doorstep at a quarter to eight in the morning. Then I collect myself. 'No, you're fine. I just slopped tea everywhere.' I hold the mug up as evidence. 'Want one? The kettle's still hot.'

He shakes his head. 'I don't have time.'

'Oh. Right. Well, um, come in.'

He follows me into the kitchen. 'Look, this is a bit of a cheek, I know. It's not as if you haven't got your own problems, especially with Sam buggering off and everything.'

I do a double take. 'How d'you know about that?'

'The woman with the florist shop – what's her name again? Edna or something. I was in the other evening getting a bunch of flowers to cheer Heather up. She was saying he's gone out to volunteer at some mission in darkest Africa.'

I tut under my breath. 'That woman must have a finger on the pulse of every line of gossip in North Yorkshire.'

He looks embarrassed. 'We weren't gossiping. She was just saying that she hadn't seen much of you lately, and she was wondering if you were OK. She said she hoped we were keeping an eye on you while Sam was away. Which we have been,' he says earnestly. 'Albeit from a distance.' He squirms awkwardly.

I don't know whether to feel angry at the fact that Sam's going off to Africa appears to be common knowledge or relieved that people don't seem to know he's left me as well. Martin's so ill at ease, I take pity on him and decide to help him out. 'Martin, was there something you wanted?'

He sighs. 'Like I said, it's a bit of a cheek, really. But

it's about Heather.' He pulls a face. 'She's due at the hospital to get the results of her CT scan at nine.'

Oh, God, I think, he's going to ask me to take her. The prospect of having to go up to the hospital makes me feel faint.

'I've booked the morning off work so I can go with her.' (Oh, thank Christ, I think, and then immediately feel like a complete heel.) 'And I can't now, because my mum was supposed to be coming across to look after the kids while we're out – there's a strike on at the school this week. Bloody typical, just when you don't need it. But she's just rung and told us she can't make it – her car won't start.' He runs a hand through his hair distractedly, making it stick up crazily. 'I *said* she should have come over last night, but she wasn't having any of it – likes to sleep in her own bed. You know how some people are. There's no arguing with her sometimes.'

I smile non-committally, wondering what all of this has to do with me.

'So I was wondering – could you do it?'

My heart sinks, and then I think, for God's sake, Marion, it's not as if Sam's going to be there. Besides, it's an early appointment: with a bit of luck you'll be done and dusted by half past. And after all, isn't this exactly the opportunity you've been waiting for: a chance to be a better friend to Heather?

'I suppose so,' I tell the voice in my head, not realising I've spoken aloud.

'Really?' Martin looks at me in undisguised relief. 'God, Marion, you're a saint.' He grabs both my arms and kisses me enthusiastically on the cheek. 'We shouldn't be more than an hour, I don't think.'

'What?' I frown at him, not understanding, and then realisation dawns. He doesn't want me to take Heather to the hospital at all. He wants me to look after the kids. I stare at him in undisguised horror. 'But —' my mouth has gone dry '— I thought you meant . . . I mean, I thought you wanted me to go with Heather.'

He's already halfway out of the front door. 'God, no,' he says, apparently oblivious to the panic that's coursing through my body. 'I wouldn't inflict that on you, though bless you for offering. Besides, I think Heather wants me there with her when she gets the results.'

'Martin, I can't!' I cry after him. 'I —' He's stopped, and is regarding me quizzically. 'I can't leave the house. I just remembered. I'm expecting a delivery,' I improvise lamely.

'Oh. Right.' He looks crestfallen, and I feel like a total rat. And then suddenly his face brightens. 'Well, not to worry, I can drop the kids round to you if that's easier.'

Oh, yes, that's much easier. Bring them round here, where no child has been in months. Leaving aside Con, of course, and look what a disaster that turned out to be. My heart is thumping so loudly now, I'm surprised Martin can't hear it. 'Just stick 'em in front of the telly,' he's saying. 'Poppy's been watching some helicopter rescue programme all week: she's hooked. We'll be back before the credits, I swear.'

He's gone before I can think up any more excuses and, as I'm closing the door on him, I sink to the floor with a groan. I can't believe he's asked me to do it. Taking Heather to the hospital would have been hard enough, but this! A sudden urge to vomit sweeps over me, and I push myself upright and run into the downstairs toilet, secretly rejoicing that I may have stumbled on the perfect excuse. *Just thrown up my breakfast. A tummy bug, I expect. Don't want the children catching it. Another time, maybe . . .*

I crouch in front of the toilet hopefully for a few minutes but, typically now I could actually do with chucking up, nothing is forthcoming. I even spit a few times, hoping to hurry things along, but eventually I give up and push myself upright. I splash some water onto my face and pause for a moment to regard my reflection in the mirror above the washbasin. The woman looking back at me is a million miles away from the smoky seductress I'd encountered on that fateful evening a few weeks ago. This face – the pink-rimmed eyes, the pallid skin – is much more familiar. This is the face of the woman who just spent half the morning bemoaning the fact that she'd nothing to anchor her sorry little half-life any more.

I pull a face at my reflection. 'Fine, then,' I tell it. 'I'll do it. Only don't say I didn't warn you.'

I've got to stop talking to myself like this.

I spend the remainder of the time before the children arrive sorting Hector out with some breakfast and letting him out into the garden before showering and getting dressed, panicking about what to wear in order not to look like a grieving mother. In the end I select the same jeans I wore for my evening in with Sam, and couple it with the fluffy top Con had dismissed as naff. As I'm fastening the buttons a fluttering of nerves sets up in my stomach, and I tell myself that I'm being ridiculous, that this is just a favour I'm doing for a friend. And then there's a soft knock at the front door, and my heart gives another leap.

Poppy's shot up in the months since I last saw her. Her features have lost some of their plumpness and she looks grown-up and serious. Beside her, five-year-old Liam still carries traces of his babyhood in the soft curls that frame his face and the two fingers clamped firmly inside his mouth. Seeing them standing there on the doorstep makes my breath catch in my throat. I feel insubstantial, unreal.

They step across the threshold and stand regarding me solemnly in the hall. Poppy is holding firmly on to Liam's other hand, the one that isn't busy acting as a surrogate dummy, evidently taking her big sister duties very seriously. I'm trying to think of something to say to them, and wondering when exactly I lost the ability to talk to small children, and then Liam pulls his fingers out of his mouth and breaks the silence.

'Can I have a drink?' he wants to know.

'Liam!' Poppy pulls sharply on his hand. 'Mummy said not to ask for things.'

'Did she?' I give the pair of them a smile, feeling better now that the ice has been broken. 'Well, I'm sure we can manage a drink of water. Would that be OK?'

'Can I watch TV?' Poppy demands, conveniently forgetting Mummy's instructions.

'Of course you can. Go through to the sitting room. I'll get Liam a drink.'

Liam trots after me into the kitchen. 'Do you have apple

juice?' he enquires, and his face falls when I explain I'm all out of juice. And then he rallies and says in that case he'll have water, and he pulls out a chair from the table and clambers onto it. I half fill a glass and bring it across to him, and he wraps his chubby fingers around it and takes a large swallow before setting the glass down in front of him and wiping the back of his hand across his mouth.

'Aren't you allowed apple juice any more?' he asks, regarding me with a troubled frown on his face.

'Of course I am, sweetheart,' I tell him. 'Why wouldn't I be allowed it?'

'Because it's for children,' he explains. 'And you haven't got any children now.'

My heart catches in my throat. 'No, I —' I clear my throat. 'Apple juice isn't just for children, Liam. Adults can drink it too. I just forgot to buy any, that's all. I'll try and remember to get some next time I go to the shops, OK?'

'OK.' He reaches out and takes another swallow of water, wiping his mouth with his hand again when he's done. From the living room, the soft strains of the television come drifting through to the kitchen. 'Can I go and watch TV now?' Liam demands, pushing himself down from the chair.

I manage a nod. 'Yes. Of course you can.'

I take my time washing up the glass he's used, wiping it slowly with the tea towel and returning it to the cupboard. From the living room I can hear the soft murmur of the children's voices mixed in with the babble of noise from the television, and I take myself off out of earshot, into the garden, where I throw one of Hector's toys half-heartedly for a bit. He must pick up on my agitation, because he's about as enthusiastic at the prospect of a game as I am, and eventually the pair of us abandon the idea and retire back to the house.

In the living room, Poppy's eyes are glued to the TV screen. 'Good programme?' I ask her, then, looking around, 'Where's Liam?'

She shrugs without taking her eyes from the television. 'Poppy!' I say sharply. 'Where's your brother?'

She tuts. 'I don't know! On the toilet, probably.' I chastise myself inwardly: it's not Poppy's job to watch her brother, it's mine. I take myself off to find him. He's not in the downstairs loo, so I head upstairs and, as I'm passing the door to Hope's bedroom, I hear a noise coming from the inside, so I stop and push the door open wide.

Liam is sitting in the middle of the floor, amidst all the heaped-up mess of toys and books I created when I was looking for Hope's bracelet, engrossed in some kind of game. As I step into the room I can see that he's dug out her Sylvanian barge from among the clutter of toys. He's lined up some of the animals – the badger and the frog and a couple of baby ducks – and is talking to them in turn, lost in the game he's created. He carries on like this for a few minutes, and then he must realise I'm there, because he looks around suddenly and bites his lower lip, as though he's afraid I'm about to tell him off for coming in here.

'It's all right, Liam.' I manage a smile. 'Hope wouldn't mind you playing with her toys.'

He considers me gravely for a moment. 'Hope's dead, isn't she?' he says suddenly.

I swallow. I can't bring myself to answer him.

'Did you kill her?'

I draw my breath in sharply. 'What?'

'Poppy's always saying Mummy will kill me if I don't tidy my room.' He looks back around at the toys lying strewn across the carpet. 'And this room is very messy.'

'It is, isn't it?' I sit down beside him in the middle of the mess. 'But Hope didn't make it messy, Liam. I did.'

He gasps at the idea of a grown-up doing anything so irresponsible. 'Why?'

'I was looking for something.'

'What?'

'A bracelet.'

He considers that for a moment. 'Did you find it?'

I shake my head. 'No.'

He scrambles to his feet suddenly and comes and plonks himself in my lap. It's so spontaneous, so unexpected, I don't have a chance to stop him. 'I drew Hope a picture,' he tells me. He links his fingers in mine. 'It was a picture of her and Poppy and me, playing in the garden. I put it on the wall at school.'

I clear my throat. 'Did you?'

'Lots of people drew her pictures. Miss Egerton's class wrote her letters saying they missed her. And Poppy wrote a poem about going to ballet with her. They're all on the wall at school, next to the quiet garden. My picture is near the top, and it's got my name on the bottom of it.' He leans in and touches a finger to my face. 'Are you crying?'

I manage a watery smile. 'A bit.'

He leans his cheek against the soft wool of my jumper. 'My mummy's got a lump,' he tells me unexpectedly.

I look down at the top of his fair head, wondering what's going on in there to help him make sense of the world.

'Is she going to die as well?' He lifts his head up and looks at me again, his eyes wide and wondering, and I don't know what to tell him. And suddenly, as we're both sitting there looking at each other, I become aware of another presence, and I glance around. Behind us, Poppy has materialised in the doorway and is listening intently.

'I don't know, Liam.' I tuck a rogue curl behind his ear. 'The hospital will try to make her better.'

'If she dies, I'll draw her a picture too. I'll draw a picture of her like an angel, and I'll give her wings, so that she can fly.' He sighs suddenly. 'I wish I could fly.' Then he pushes himself out of my lap as abruptly as he'd sat down in it a moment ago and busies himself with the barge once more, and when I look around again Poppy has disappeared.

She's back in front of the TV when I come downstairs a few minutes later, and gives no sign of noticing me when I go to join her on the sofa. Her eyes are firmly fixed on the helicopter programme, though she doesn't seem to be registering what's happening before her on the screen. After a few moments she inches along the sofa towards me and leans her head against my arm, and I lift it up so that she can move in closer. My head is buzzing with things I want to say to her, assurances I want to offer but can't, because I know, at the end of the day, that I can give her no guarantees about anything. So I content myself with holding her, and she allows herself to be held, and we stay like that, the two of us, each of us somehow taking comfort from the other, until Martin arrives back from the hospital and takes his children home.

Chapter 19

On Thursday evening I have an appointment to see my counsellor. Colin, his name is. I never mentioned that before, did I? It's our three-month check-up appointment, made reluctantly some time after the last session we had with him back in March, when I realised the faster Sam and I committed to a date, the sooner we'd escape. At the time, I hadn't planned on actually turning up for it. I even called yesterday evening, in fact, to cancel, using Sam's absence as an excuse — the appointment had been for both of us, after all. It had even been scheduled for the evening to make it easier for Sam to attend. But when I got up this morning I found a message from Colin saying he'd like to see me anyway.

His office is in the centre of Leeds — not the most convenient of places to get to, but at least we're well beyond peak hour when I turn up shortly before 8 pm. He greets me like I've made his day just by showing up. We're supposed to have established a rapport during those early meetings following Hope's death, some kind of bond that means I can trust him enough to pour out my innermost thoughts to him.

'I'm talking to myself,' I tell him as soon as the pleasantries (I'm using the term loosely) are out of the way. He nods thoughtfully and balances his chin on the tips of his prayer-clasped hands.

'Actually, it might not be myself. I just presumed it was, because there's never anyone else around when I'm having these conversations. Maybe I'm going mad. Mad with grief.' I roll my eyes to show what a ridiculous suggestion this is.

He nods again, like he knows the answer to why I am behaving like this, though past experience has already taught me that actually he knows diddly squat; he's just waiting for me to say something else until finally I stumble upon a reason I can live with and he can take all the credit for it. I don't really know why I bothered coming to him.

'Who else d'you suppose it might be, Marion?' He is looking at me enquiringly, as though I hold the secret to eternal life rather than something as underwhelming as the identity of the phantom person dominating my conversations.

I shrug. 'I don't know.' I shift in my seat. 'I suppose you want me to tell you it's Hope or something.'

'I want you to tell me whatever you feel comfortable telling me. Do you think it's Hope?'

Christ, this is worse than going to the dentist. 'No, of course it isn't Hope. I know she's dead. I know she isn't coming back.' The words tumble angrily from my mouth, and then I shock myself by bursting into tears.

Wordlessly, Colin hands me a tissue from a box standing between us on a low coffee table. Throughout my sobbing and heaving he doesn't speak, he just keeps furnishing me with tissues and taking the used ones away and dropping them in a bin underneath the desk behind him. If I weren't so wrapped up in my own misery, I'd feel sorry for him.

Counsellor. Dealer in snotty tissues. Someone has to do it, I suppose.

'You were saying that Sam has moved out.' (This was one of the pleasantries, dropped lightly into the hello-how-are-you-Sam-has-left-me bit of the conversation.)

I nod wordlessly, still gulping into my latest tissue.

'How did it make you feel when he left?'

'How d'you suppose it made me feel?' His simplistic probing is making me angry, which is a step up from snivelling, I suppose. 'I threw a party, got the neighbours in. Shagged half a dozen of the best-looking blokes at the end of the night.'

He raises his eyebrows at me.

'Sorry,' I mumble after a moment. 'It's just – I don't know what to do with myself any more. I don't know who I am. One minute I was a mummy and a wife and I had a good job and friends and a *life*, and now I've lost it all and I don't know how to get it back, but I can't get it back anyway because Hope is dead and I've chased Sam away, and instead of the lovely, wonderful life I had before, I'm a sad, lonely old cow who talks to non-existent cats.'

'Mmm,' he says after a moment in that infuriatingly non-committal tone he has. 'What I'm picking up on is that you feel your main problem is your deep sense of loneliness.'

'It isn't just that.' I can feel frustration clawing at the inside of my skin at this habit he has of waiting for me to say something and then repeating it back to me. Maybe that's all they do, counsellors. Maybe they don't actually dole out any counsel. Colin certainly doesn't – heaven forbid. He just gets you talking, and then he dresses it up a bit and says exactly the same thing, but in a really thoughtful way, nodding sagely as though it was him that had the idea in the first place. I ought to think about counselling as a new career direction. I've got all the jargon. 'I'm angry. Almost all the time. And when I'm not angry, I'm scared. But I'm mostly angry. Not just annoyed, but livid. Furious, even. Really, completely, filled with rage. Even my fingernails are angry. I've been like this since the accident. That time when you said I'd shut down emotionally, it wasn't true: I'd just put this iron cover on my feelings because I was afraid of what I would do if the anger escaped. And now it has, and I've lost everything. I've become a great festering pit of anger. I'm angry right now, because actually I thought I was doing OK this past couple of weeks and that I was actually starting to get my act together – yesterday, for instance, I even did a favour for my neighbour – and you asked me one question about who I thought I was talking to and bang! I was a snivelling heap all over again. I think coming here is making me regress, in fact, rather than helping me. All this probing around my feelings is like picking the scab off a wound. And if you dare say now that what you are picking up on is that my main problem is that I feel angry all the time, I will add you to the list of people I hate.' I sit back in my chair and glower at him, bitter tears stinging behind my eyes.

He doesn't answer me for a moment, but purses his lips at me as though he's actually thinking about what I've said for once. And then all of a sudden he stands up and crosses to the desk behind him, where he picks up a pad and a pen and tosses them down on the coffee table in front of me. The unexpected movement takes me aback; he's never done anything before other than sit opposite Sam and me nodding and repeating everything we said. 'I want you to do something,' he tells me now, sitting back down and leaning his arms on his knees, clasping his hands together again as though in supplication. 'I want you to write down your judgments about Hope's death – everything about it that makes you feel angry or frightened or confused. I'm not looking for a literary masterpiece: just write down your thoughts, the way they are in your head. Put your mind onto the paper in short, simple sentences. You can be as harsh and as petty and as vindictive as you like in whatever you write, but you are not allowed to judge yourself. You are off the hook, just for today. Do you think you can you do that?'

I glare suspiciously at the piece of paper, as though this might turn out to be some kind of trap. 'I don't know. Why d'you want me to write it down? You've never asked me to write anything down before.'

He ignores the question. 'I'm going for a glass of water,' he says, standing and heading for the door.

After the door has closed behind him I throw myself back in the chair and fold my arms across my chest. Of all the stupid, ridiculous things! *Be as petty and vindictive as you like.* What kind of a halfwit nincompoop does he think I am? It smacks of the sort of thing I used to have to deal with in the playground. *Kirsten pulled my hair. I hate her. She's not coming to my party.*

I stay like that for a few minutes waiting for Colin to reappear, my arms still folded huffily, and when he doesn't I lean over and pull the pad towards me. Picking up the pen, I write, *Counsellors are stupid. They think just because you write something down you can make it go away.* There. I toss the pen down on top of the pad, and fold my arms again.

The door to the consulting room remains resolutely closed. My eyes keep straying back to what I've written on the pad, and I can't help but smile a bit. So childish. I pick up the pen again and suck the end of it thoughtfully.

And then I start to write.

It's not fair. I stare at the words for a moment, and then I think, what the hell, it bloody well isn't fair, and why shouldn't I write that down if I want to? Didn't Colin just say I could be as petty as I liked? *It's not fair that this has happened to me. I feel angry all the time, towards everyone that ever mattered to me. I'm angry at Sam for leaving like that, just after he'd had his fun. I feel used and discarded. I'm angry at Charlie because she went back to Michigan after the funeral and I needed her to stay. I'm angry at Heather and Martin for still having their two beautiful children when I've lost my only child. I'm angry at Con because she came barging into my life and wouldn't be organised into improving her lot in life when she could improve it so easily, while there's NOTHING I can do about the shit in my life. And I'm also angry with her because she buggered off out of it just when I thought that between us we might be able to make some sense of everything. I'm angry at everyone, and it's all because Hope died. It's like her death has polluted my life. I'm angry about that, too – angry at her for dying. I hate that all this has happened. I HATE MY DAUGHTER FOR DYING.*

I stop suddenly, shocked by the words I've just written down. Seeing them there on the paper, I realise just how warped my thinking has become. I am so full of anger and hatred, it's a miracle people don't fall down dead just by meeting my eye. I want to scrub the words out, bury all those awful feelings again, write something nice so that nobody ever gets to learn about what a truly vile person I am for hating my dead daughter, but I remember what Colin said about not judging myself and so I plough on.

I write for about ten more minutes. Half the stuff that comes into my head as I'm doing this doesn't make much sense, even to me, but I write it down anyway. At one point, I dig the point of the pen into the paper and scribble, hard, across its white surface. It's so addictive, watching all the poison I've written disappearing under the flood of ink, I keep going, moving the nib in short, sharp jerks, until there is nothing left of the words and the paper is covered in deep black scores. It's not about scribbling over the awful words any more: it's more to do with wanting to blank out the whole sorry episode so that I can't tell it ever existed.

After I've finished I am overcome by a mixture of exhilaration and shame. I'd had no idea I was capable of such vicious, bitter thoughts. By the time Colin returns carrying a couple of glasses of water I am almost dreading his reaction when he sees the state of my work. I feel like a naughty schoolchild who's been sent to the head for defacing her own homework.

Oddly, he doesn't appear to be put out at all. He picks up the pad and studies it for a moment. 'Good,' he says briefly. *Good?* How can a page full of scribble be good? He gives me an approving nod, and I can feel the exhilaration draining away though, typically, the shame lingers stubbornly on. It's hard to hold off judgment on myself when I know what a truly awful person I am, even if I have made efforts to conceal the fact (though maybe that makes me worse). He sits down opposite me again.

'Don't you want to know what I wrote?' I demand.

'Not particularly,' he replies in that frustratingly calm voice of his. 'You weren't really writing it for my benefit, though from the way you've obliterated everything, I'd say you're having a tough time facing up to your feelings.'

I don't know what to say to that, so I keep quiet.

'When you were writing,' he continues, 'was there anything that stood out from the rest, anything that came as a surprise to you?'

I glance at him sharply; the thought goes through my head that he must have been spying on me. Either that or he's somehow managed to read between the lines of scribble on the pad.

'Would you like to share with me what that was?' he asks in response to my look.

I hesitate. 'I didn't expect some of it. Like, I realised that I'm even angry with Hope.' I can't articulate the word *hate*. I give a short bitter laugh. 'You see? Even dying is no guarantee you'll escape my wrath.'

'So you feel anger towards Hope.' He nods again, and I think, Here we go with the repeating again; he would make a great parrot, and then suddenly he surprises me by asking, 'How would you like to feel towards her?'

'What?'

'Imagine you had a magic wand. How would you change things?'

'Oh, don't be ridiculous, Colin.' I can't believe he's asking such a moronic question. His look doesn't waver. 'Well, I . . . Well, I mean, I would bring her back! I would make that night never have happened. I wouldn't feel angry because she wouldn't have died! I would turn back time and make her not dead, because she isn't supposed to be dead. She's supposed to be alive and safe at home playing with Hector in the garden, and she isn't. She's in the ground in a grave and I want to climb in alongside her and make the world go away because without her I have turned into this vile creature who doesn't know how to be happy any more.'

He purses his lips for a moment, considering what I've just said. And then suddenly he leans across the coffee table towards me and takes hold of one of my hands in his own. 'Marion,' he says intently, looking me hard in the eye, 'is that true?'

'What?' He's not supposed to say that. He's supposed to say, *What I am sensing is that you feel you can't be happy without Hope.* He's not supposed to challenge me like this.

'Is it true that you don't know how to be happy without Hope?'

I pull my hand away sharply. 'Of course it is.'

'Mmm.' What does that mean? How on earth am I meant to make any sense of 'Mmm'? He is still staring at me intently. It's very disconcerting. 'Can you absolutely know that it's true? One hundred per cent?'

'Yes. One hundred per cent. Why are you asking me this?' I don't like this new cards-on-the-table Colin. I want the old waffly one back.

'Because I think you're ready to face the question. So, in the three months since you and Sam last came to see me, you have never felt a flicker of happiness. Not once.'

'I –' I hesitate and, as I do so, a picture comes into my head. Con and me, sitting in the car after I'd snatched her out of the supermarket, tears of laughter coursing down my cheeks. 'But –' Watching the look of delight on her face after I'd cut her hair. Waking up in the morning knowing that in a couple of hours she'd be turning up on the doorstep and we'd be sharing breakfast together. They're not much, I know, but they're crumbs. Crumbs of happiness. 'No,' I say quietly after a moment. I don't look at Colin. 'No. I have felt a flicker of happiness. Sometimes.' A stab of guilt as I realise the truth of this hits me in the chest: how can I have felt happiness after what happened to Hope? 'So I can't absolutely know that it's true.'

'Right,' he says. 'So tell me, Marion, how does it make you feel when you believe you don't know how to be happy without Hope?'

A ghostly tendril of the dread I felt after Hope died flickers across my heart. 'Scared,' I tell him. 'Panicky. Out of control. Empty.' I take a deep, juddering breath. 'I feel as though I'll never be normal again.'

'Anything else?' he prompts.

'I feel like I'm not worth being around any more. Like

this poison inside me will kill off everything left that's good in my life, sooner or later. Like the world would be better off without me.' I swallow, remembering the pills. 'Even when I think about those times when I've actually felt happy, I feel like a bad person because I'm betraying Hope in some way.' This time I do lift my eyes to his. I know they're full of despair and pleading with him to make it go away, and I hate myself for it, but there's nothing I can do to stop them.

'Marion,' he tells me, 'you're doing really well. Just stay with this a bit longer, OK?'

I manage a nod.

'Here's another question for you,' he says. 'Who would you be without the thought?'

I think about that one for a moment. Who would I be if my head weren't full of the thought that I can't be happy without Hope, and Hope isn't coming back? If I could lay down this burden of despair and walk away from it? 'Free,' I say suddenly. I don't know where the word comes from. 'I'd be free.'

'But you already told me you can't absolutely know it's true,' he reminds me. 'And if it isn't true, then there's only one other thing it can be, isn't there?'

'It's untrue.' I stare at him in astonishment. 'In order for me to be happy, I don't need Hope not to have died.' The panic is back. 'But I can't just let go of it like that. I can't. I've believed it for so long. Who will I be without it?'

He smiles at me. 'You already answered that question, Marion. Free, I think you said.'

'No – stop!' I jump up and start pacing the carpet. 'I

feel like you're stripping me of my identity. Such as it is,' I add after a moment.

He nods at me understandingly, immediately arousing my suspicions. 'Mm-hmm. And yet, you told me a short while ago that a few months ago you had a completely different identity. You were a mother and a wife, you said, with a life.'

'And that's true,' I insist. 'I was all of those things. And now I'm the mother of a little girl who died and the wife of a husband who can't stand to be around her any more.'

'So tell me, Marion.' He's got that look in his eyes again – that challenging look that I'm starting to realise means I'm wriggling on a hook and he's not about to let me off. 'What's changed?'

I stare at him, aghast. 'Hope DIED!' I yell the word at him. 'She died. And I became the mother of a dead child instead of a little girl who went to school and loved mozzarella cheese and never picked up her clothes. I was a mother, and I never protected my child. That's what changed. I failed her, and she died.'

'So you're angry with Hope because she's shown what a lousy mother you were?'

'Yes!'

'But you were a good mother before the accident.'

'Yes.' Where is he going with this? 'I was a good mother,' I say in a small voice.

'Right.' He nods solemnly. 'And then an accident happened that was nothing to do with you – you weren't there; you weren't supposed to be there – and in that instant you became a bad mother.'

'Well, yes, because – look at the consequences!'

He gives another nod as though agreeing with me. 'In whose opinion?'

'What d'you mean, in whose opinion?'

'Well, who told you that you'd become a bad mother? Sam, perhaps?'

'No, of course he didn't. He didn't need to. I knew it myself.'

'Aha!' He is smiling at me now. 'So now we're getting to the root of things.'

'What d'you mean?'

'Well, don't you see? It's not what happens to us that makes us who we are. It's what we believe about what happens to us.' I am frowning at him in confusion. 'Let's see if I can give you an example.' He pauses for a moment, concentrating. 'OK,' he says. 'Come and sit back down again.'

I take my seat reluctantly.

'Good.' He smiles at me as though I've done something clever. 'Now, when you were a little kid, were you scared of the dark?'

'I suppose so. I can't remember.'

'Come on, Marion.' His tone is cajoling. 'Humour me.'

'All right, then. Yes, I was scared of the dark.'

'OK. Can you close your eyes for me?'

The man is a certifiable fruitcake. 'What for?'

'Just –' He gestures with his hand, and I shut my eyes reluctantly with a sigh.

'Great. Now, I want you to think back to being small and being scared of the dark. Can you do that?'

'Mm-hmm.' I'm beginning to realise if I don't humour him we'll never get finished.

'Imagine it's late at night and you're in bed trying to get to sleep, and the room is very dark. Some kids have nightlights that they have to have left on all night. Did you have anything like that?'

'No.' There is still a trace of truculence in my tone, and I make a massive effort to soften it. 'But I used to make my mum leave the landing light on so that I could see the crack of light at the bottom of the bedroom door.'

'Right. And was there ever a time when the landing light got switched off by mistake?'

'Sometimes. Not often.' I give a half-smile without opening my eyes. 'I used to make such a fuss, my parents became pretty good at leaving it on.'

'How did you feel when the light got switched off by mistake?'

I cast my mind back. 'I was terrified. Especially if my sister hadn't come to bed yet. I used to think there were monsters hiding in the bedroom – under the bed, inside the wardrobe, behind the curtains – and they would come out and get me if it was dark.'

'So what did you do when you realised the light had gone off?'

My smile broadens a little. 'Screamed the house down.'

'And then what happened?'

'Oh, someone – my dad, usually – would come running upstairs to calm me down.'

'What did he do to calm you down?'

I think back. Vividly, the picture of the hysterical little girl in brushed cotton pyjamas comes flooding back. From my position twenty-eight-odd years into her future I smile at her indulgently. 'He put the light on! That was the biggest thing. And then he would check everywhere – behind the curtains and everywhere else I told him to look – and prove to me that there weren't any monsters.' I smile again at the memory, my father blundering around the bedroom shouting at non-existent monsters to come out from their hiding places and then affecting astonishment when he wasn't able to find any.

'And then you could go back to sleep again, because you knew there were no monsters lurking anywhere.'

'Yes. But I still made him leave the landing light on,' I add.

'So. From the time when the light got switched off to when it got switched on again, what changed?'

'Well, when it got switched off I thought the monsters were going to come and get me. And when it got switched on again I could see that there weren't any monsters.'

'Right. When the light was off, you thought there were monsters and that frightened you, yes?'

'Mm-hmm.'

'And once the light was switched on again you no longer believed that thought.'

'No. I mean yes. That's it exactly.'

'Let's be quite clear about this. Between thinking there were monsters and thinking there weren't, aside from not being frightened any more, would you agree that you were the same person after the light went back on as you were when it got switched off?'

'Well, aside from the being frightened part – yes.'

'Can we agree, then, that it was your thoughts that were frightening you?'

'Well, yes, of course we can.'

'And that when you changed your thoughts, you felt a lot happier?'

I don't answer straight away. Suddenly I can see where he's going with this.

'What's real, Marion?'

I snap my eyes open. 'What?'

'The monsters in the wardrobe. Were they real?'

'Of course they weren't.'

'But your fear of them was.'

I acknowledge what he's saying with a nod.

'And when you stopped believing in them, your fear went away. You changed what was real for you by changing what you thought. So you were able to control your reality by changing your thoughts.'

'Yes, but, Hope's dying is real,' I say. 'There's no escape from that. I don't have a magic wand, and I can't bring her back.'

'I know you can't.' He leans towards me again and nods slowly. 'I know you can't,' he repeats gently, 'but you can change what you choose to believe about her dying.'

'I never –' I stare at him. 'I never realised I was choosing.'

'Nobody else blamed you for the accident, did they? The police never took you in for questioning. And I'm willing to bet Sam's said to you a thousand times that it wasn't your fault, that there was nothing you could have done to prevent it from happening.'

I don't answer him. My head is reeling from what he's

saying, not to mention the uncomfortable thought that that's exactly what I did to Sam – accuse him of being responsible for Hope's dying. Even if it was so that I could convince myself I wasn't to blame.

'So who was it that made you feel responsible?'

I swallow. 'Me,' I say in a small voice.

'You know,' he says, sitting back in his chair, 'I'd say it was about time you got yourself some new thoughts. Seems to me the old ones aren't serving you very well. You know that Hope isn't coming back. You can't change that. But you can change your thoughts about it. After all, if you're going to construct your own reality, you might as well make it one worth living in.' He glances up at the wall behind me and leans back in his seat. 'Time's up, I'm afraid.'

I start to gather myself slowly; I feel as though I'm waking up from a bad dream. 'How do I go about doing that?'

'Well, that's something you're going to have to work on. But as a general rule of thumb, I think each time you experience one of those negative thoughts about yourself, you should just ask, "Does this thought serve me?" If the answer's no, then ditch it and think up another one that does.'

I give him a rueful smile. 'You make it sound so easy. I don't know if I can do it.'

He returns the smile. 'That's just it. It's as easy as you choose to make it. Whether you think that you can or that you can't, you're probably right. Henry Ford,' he adds after a moment.

'Really?' I purse my lips. 'I'm not sure I like the sentiment.'

Colin gives me a knowing smile. 'That's because it takes away your ability to see yourself as a victim.'

I open my mouth to protest, and then close it again, wishing that Colin hadn't turned out to be so spot on for once.

'He also said, "Failure is the opportunity to begin again, more intelligently."' He gives me a look that has a challenge caught up in it somewhere. 'Clever chap, old Henry, seeing the bright side like that.'

I'm brooding over what he's told me as I weave my way out of the city centre towards the ring road, playing with different variations of it while admitting to myself that perhaps Colin is not quite such a waste of space as I'd had him down as being. *Whether you think you're happy or sad, you're probably right. Whether you think you're loved or hated, you're probably right. Beautiful or hideous. Smart or stupid. Guilty of failing your daughter, or not.*

It's such a revelation, I pull over in a quiet side street to take stock for a moment, lowering the window so that I can feel the warm night air on my face. I look back at all the crazy situations I've found myself in over the past few weeks – the night when I decided to do myself in, the scene in the supermarket when I lied to a police officer, that cringingly awful night with Sam before he left for Nakuru – and I think, yes, I've made a bit of a cock-up of things recently, but maybe all that means is that it's time for me to begin over, only more intelligently this time. Focus on the things that are important to me. Stop chasing after ghosts and start engaging with the real world once again. And if I can't find Con, if I can't put right that awful row we had, then that's something I'll just have to live with.

I can do that. Can't I? All it will take, according to Colin, is a bit of self-belief. Somewhere inside me, a small kernel of hope takes root.

I'm just about to pull away when a movement further down the street catches my eye and I spot a lone figure – a woman, I think it is – walking through the darkness towards the car. She pauses to cross the road about fifteen feet from me and, as I'm sitting there idly watching her, a second figure materialises from the shadows and comes quickly up behind her. And then a voice I know only too well carries across on the night air.

'Your purse, luv. Get it out, there's a good girl.'

Chapter 20

I'm out of the car and creeping up the street towards them before I have a chance to think, sliding like a wraith from shadow to shadow until they are only a few feet away, ignoring the voice inside my head that is chastising me, telling me to get back in the car and drive home and leave Con and Ryan to get on with their own lives and to start living my new normal intelligent life as quickly as possible. So caught up are they in their respective victim/mugger roles, neither shows any sign of noticing me lurking in the darkness behind them. Only when I'm almost upon them both do I become aware of the fire extinguisher I'm clutching, the portable one that normally spends its days rolling around under one of the seats of the Passat in case of an emergency. I clutch it tightly to my chest and imagine myself using it to whack Ryan across the back of the head.

I'm so close now I can see the whites of the woman's eyes, wide with horror as Ryan stands there intimidating the hell out of her.

He's enjoying himself, I can tell, the bastard. Evidently the fright he got when he tried the same stunt on me has worn off. The woman is rigid with fear, words tumbling from her mouth in an attempt at conciliation. 'Here,' she's saying, fumbling at her handbag, struggling with the shoulder strap. 'Have it . . . I'll just . . . Only don't hurt me. I've got a little girl.'

It's this last comment that does it. 'Honestly, Ryan,' I say to him, making him spin round in alarm. 'You just don't learn, do you?' Then, before he has a chance to gather his wits, I pull the pin from the extinguisher and aim the nozzle straight at his eyes.

The knife he's brandishing clatters to the ground and, almost without realising it, I kick it into the gutter and out of reach. He is wheeling around wildly, clutching at his eyes and screaming. 'Aaargh! Aaargh! My eyes!' Out of the corner of my eye I see the woman take to her heels, evidently too relieved at her sudden escape to hang around getting acquainted with her rescuer. That's fine by me; I was only ever really interested in Ryan.

Now that I've incapacitated him, though, I don't know what to do with him. He's collapsed onto his knees on the pavement, arched in on himself, his fists balled and the heels of his hands pushed hard into his eye sockets. 'Jesus, fuck,' he's moaning, 'my eyes, my eyes!' I have a momentary qualm when I wonder whether I've actually blinded him – I've no clue what they put into these fire extinguishers – and then the picture comes back to me of those bruises on Con's neck, and suddenly I wish I'd battered him over the head with the can after I'd finished emptying its contents into his face. I never realised I had such a thirst for violence.

I'm standing there trying to figure out my next move, picturing myself hauling him to his feet and demanding that he take me to Con, imagining the kind of response

I'm likely to get if I do, when suddenly he starts fumbling in the pocket of his jacket and pulls out a mobile phone. He holds it briefly in front of his face, cursing when he realises he can't make out the keys, and punches a number in blind. 'Yeah,' he says after a moment. 'Oh, fuck, man, get here, will you? I've been attacked. I dunno – fucking mace or something. Bitch must've had it on her. Can't see a fucking thing. Fucking eyes feel like they're on fire. No, I don't fucking know which road. On t' way to t' chippy. Just come and look. What?' He gives a strangled cry. 'What d'you mean, how will you find me? I'm the one rolling round on t' fucking pavement.'

As it appears he can't actually see me, I shrink back into the shadow of a stone gatepost while he's rubbing at his eyes again and cursing roundly. 'Fucking bitch,' he spits, making me start guiltily until I realise it's a general expletive rather than a personal insult aimed specifically at me. He folds in on himself once more, letting out a strangled sob, and I think, God, I actually made him cry. The thought gives me a nervous thrill. After another few groan-filled minutes he clambers gingerly to his feet, feeling his way up the low wall that borders a row of terraced buildings behind him, then leans against it for support and finally eases himself onto it. He wipes the palms of his hands on the front of his jacket, still moaning and swearing under his breath. Then he tilts his head back and swears again. The hood of his jacket falls backwards and the light from the street lamp catches his features, his eyes squeezed tightly shut, crumpled in pain.

I'm still vacillating about my next move when I hear

footsteps making their way down the road towards us. Evidently Ryan catches them too, because he tilts his head in their direction. I'm half-expecting Con, but it's a male who appears, a youth who looks to be about the same age as Ryan, dressed from head to toe in black, his pale skin glowing translucently out of the darkness. 'Matt?' Ryan ventures tentatively, squinting upwards and blinking painfully. 'That you?'

'Fuck's sake, Ryan.' The newcomer perches on the wall beside him. 'You're not safe to be out on your own. I thought you were just going for a fish supper.'

Ryan lashes out ineffectually.

'Hey, whoa, mate,' Matt says in a more conciliatory tone. 'Weren't me that maced you.'

'Fucking bitch.' Ryan is repeating himself. 'Come out of nowhere. I think she's blinded me.'

'Yeah, t'streets just aren't safe any more.' Matt's tone is lugubrious: if he's being deliberately ironic, he hides it well. He drops a sigh into the night. 'Come on, let's get back to t' flat and wash your eyes out.' He helps Ryan, still cursing, to his feet, and takes his elbow, then steers the two of them off slowly down the street to the corner, where they take a sharp left and disappear.

I don't hesitate. Slipping from the protection of the stone gateway, I duck my head down low and follow them.

At the next junction they take a left again and cross over, ducking into another quiet side street. They are walking (hobbling might be a better description for Ryan's clumsy gait) quite quickly, given that one of them can't see a thing, but Matt is clearly impatient to be off the streets and is half-supporting, half-dragging Ryan behind him. I'm not used to this kind of cloak-and-dagger stealth, but the pair of them appear oblivious to the possibility that they're being pursued. Matt looks behind him once, briefly, at a point when I am fortunately tucked in behind some oversized refuse bins, and then shrugs the pair of them into another side street, trying to urge Ryan to greater speed.

We carry on in this manner for a couple more minutes, ducking and weaving through half-lit streets, burrowing deeper and deeper into some of the seedier areas of the city, and then all of a sudden they stop in front of a narrow terraced building lit by the unsteady light of a flickering street lamp. I wait until they've disappeared inside and then give it a few seconds before sidling up to the door myself. It's slightly ajar; in fact, when I look closely I can see that the lock is broken and hanging lopsidedly on a single screw. Tentatively I ease it open a couple of centimetres, just in time to catch their shadows on the first-floor landing before they're swallowed up into what I presume is a flat, the door slamming noisily behind them. A moment later a key turns.

The hall itself if strewn with litter, and a bad smell assaults my nostrils as I withdraw back out onto the pavement, where I see their shadows appear briefly against a window on the first floor. I smile to myself in grim satisfaction; I reckon I have tracked Ryan to his lair. My heart is thumping in my chest: a mixture of adrenalin and nerves. I steal a look through the ground-floor window of the building. The room appears to be empty, although it's difficult to identify much through the grimy glass. I cup my hands around my eyes to try to help me focus, and then, while I'm straining to make out whether there's anything in the room at all, I suddenly become aware of a face staring back out at me – a pale-skinned, wild-eyed woman leering at me from her side of the glass every bit as intently as I'm looking in from my own. I drop back with a barely stifled shriek, fear coursing through me like an electric current, and as I do so the face at the window vanishes.

I don't stop to find out whether I've been rumbled, but take to my heels, racing back the way I've just come without a backwards glance. If anybody follows me I manage to outrun them, in spite of colliding with the wheelie bins as I round the corner and winding myself so badly I have to run the rest of the way bent double. By the time I reach my car, my lungs burning and the blood coursing loudly in my head, I find I am alone on the dark street with not another soul in sight. I am sick with disappointment at myself: having managed an undercover stalking operation without a hitch, I go and lose it at the last minute and run away at the sight of some wild-looking tramp who was probably just bedding down for the night in the abandoned building. Still, I console myself, at least I've found what I was looking for. I slide the key into the lock with trembling hands and throw myself into the car, where I spend a few terror-filled minutes hunched over the steering wheel, the door locked behind me, willing my legs to stop shaking so that I can drive myself home. It takes me three attempts before I manage to turn the key in the ignition, and I drive off with a squeal of tyres into the night, still scanning the roads anxiously for any sign that the creature I disturbed has given chase.

It's only when I'm safely home, leaning weakly against the front door after I've locked it behind me with the taste of my own fear still burning at the back of my throat, that the identity of the wild-eyed tramp I disturbed finally dawns on me.

I think it was the way her eyes widened in horror when she caught sight of me, the way her mouth opened in a gasp of fright, at the exact moment when I was doing precisely the same thing from my position out on the pavement. I've just spent the past half-hour running in terror from my own crazy-woman reflection in the murky glow of a flickering street light.

Which, in the whole beginning-again-more-intelligently scenario, I think sheepishly to myself as I'm kicking off my shoes, really doesn't bode well.

Chapter 21

On Sunday morning I am woken up by Hector licking enthusiastically at my face and demanding to be taken out. My body is still stiff and sore from its unaccustomed sprint through the streets of Leeds on Thursday evening, not to mention the collision with the wheelie bins, which left my stomach feeling tender and bruised. I ease myself into an old jogging suit and running shoes, pull my hair into a ponytail and make my way with difficulty down the stairs, holding on to the banister like an arthritic old woman. In the kitchen I retrieve Hector's lead from the cupboard beside the back door, and the two of us slip out of the house into the hushed morning of the still-sleeping town, Hector bouncing exuberantly at the end of his lead while I limp painfully alongside him. It's hard to tell who's walking whom.

When we reach the entrance to the park I do a quick check to make sure there are no other early-morning walkers around before unclipping the lead from his harness. You're supposed to keep your dog on a lead in the park – there's a sign saying so just inside the entrance – but most dog owners pay it no attention. I'm always cautious about letting Hector off: between his size and wolflike appearance he cuts a pretty intimidating figure to the uninitiated. But this early in the morning there are few people around, which has a double bonus in that we're less likely to meet anyone I don't particularly want to talk to.

Hector is delighted to be free, and makes a beeline for the stream that runs parallel to the path. He is indifferent to the water, but not to the ducks that congregate along its banks, hurling himself after them with reckless abandon and returning every few minutes to where I've settled myself on a nearby bench to pant and drool into my lap before giving chase once again. I watch him with half an eye, my mind taken up by what I found out on Thursday, and the implications it might have for my finding Con and setting things right with her.

If there were only some way of getting her away from Ryan. What she could really do with would be a job. I toy with the idea of appointing her Hector's official dog walker, but in my heart I know she'd never accept something she regarded as charity. *You don't get to save me.* No, it would have to be something a bit less obvious than that. I sigh, wondering why I'm finding it so difficult to let sleeping dogs lie as far as she's concerned.

I don't know how long I sit there, watching as Hector cavorts with the ducks, but he suddenly catches sight of something and his ears prick up. I follow his gaze and spot another lone figure walking across the park, a small dog (though frankly anything is small beside Hector) at their heels. I call him over and slip him back onto his lead, making him sit quietly beside me. The figure advances, until eventually it is close enough for me to recognise who it is.

Esme McFarland.

Bloody buggering hell.

There is no hope of escape. Even if I made a run for it, Hector is so keen to say hello to every other dog he meets, and so much stronger than me, he would drag me bodily through the boating pond if he had to. I sigh resignedly and arrange my face into something vaguely identifiable as friendly. Not openly hostile, at any rate. 'Of all the parks . . .' I say as she draws level with me, but she doesn't seem to get the jibe. Hector's welcome is warmer; he almost turns himself inside out in his efforts not to jump all over Esme's spaniel. 'Let him off if you like,' she says, taking a seat beside me on the bench. 'Amelia can take care of herself.'

'Amelia?' I purse my lips: the woman is completely gaga.

'Amelia Jane, if we're going to use her Sunday name,' Esme clarifies.

'That's . . . um, quite a mouthful.' I slip Hector dubiously back off his lead, and he and Amelia Jane bound off back towards the ducks together, biting at one another's ears enthusiastically and falling over their paws in their efforts to outrun one another.

Esme leans in towards me confidentially, though as far as I can see there's not another soul in the park at this early hour. 'To tell you the truth,' she says in a low voice, as though she's afraid the dog might take offence, 'I didnae really like her when I first got her. So I gave her a really fancy name, in the hope that it might endear her to me a wee bit.'

'Oh, um, right.' Yep: totally bonkers. 'And did it?'

She looks at me as though I'm the fruit loop. 'No, of course it didn't. But the bloody creature won't answer to anything else now. I'm sure she does it just to spite me.'

I laugh in spite of myself, and feel a sudden unexpected rush of warmth towards this oddball woman who seems to have been stalking me with condolences since Hope died. There it is again, that stab of happiness that insists on breaking out even in the middle of my bereavement. I remember what Colin said, and set my shoulders resolutely, going with the feeling, refusing to feel guilty about it.

'So,' Esme says, as though picking up on a previous conversation we'd been having. 'Haven't seen you around in a while.' Her eyes are on the two dogs as she speaks. Amelia Jane has taken to the water and is paddling furiously after one of the ducks, while Hector watches from the banks, bouncing up and down with his front paws in the water, clearly torn between fear and delight at the prospect of immersing himself further.

'No: I've been . . . a bit tied up,' I say lamely.

She turns and regards me properly for a moment. 'Is that right?'

Out of the blue I find myself recalling the conversation I had with Martin when he called round to ask me about looking after the kids while he took Heather to hospital. Esme had asked him to keep an eye on me. I feel churlish all of a sudden.

'Esme?'

She turns and looks at me again.

'Oh –' I shake my head at her. 'Nothing.'

She looks at me keenly for a moment, and then returns mutely to her dog watching.

I clear my throat. 'I just wanted to say thanks. For your

support, I mean. I know I haven't been exactly . . . approachable.'

She nods, acknowledging the comment. 'Aye, well, you lost your little girl. It's not everyone who knows how to approach something like that.'

I think about that for a moment. 'You did, though. Even though I wasn't very nice to you. You asked my neighbours to keep an eye on me.'

'Well, somebody had to. Especially once your husband left like that. One of the reception staff at the hospital told me,' she said by way of an explanation. 'Awful woman: loves a bit of gossip. She knows I know you a bit; couldn't wait to come in to the shop and crow. Said your husband had moved in to staff accommodation. I sent her off with a flea in her ear. Told her she didn't have a clue what she was talking about: that you'd gone to see your sister that lives abroad while Sam was away in Africa and you had the decorators in while you were away.'

'Really?' I give a bitter laugh. 'Nice try, but I expect I'll be the talk of the hospital by now.'

'Och, today's news, tomorrow's chip wrappings,' Esme says consolingly. 'I happen to know that receptionist is sleeping with one of the consultants up there; she was bragging about that the other week. I could let that slip to one o' the women at church, if you like. Be round the town in a flash.'

We laugh companionably together, and then lapse into silence again, watching our irrepressible hounds making the most of our attention being caught up by each other to cavort all the more outrageously together. By now

Amelia Jane has returned to the banks and is shaking herself extravagantly all over Hector, who leaps away from her in alarm before bouncing back in and biting at her nose affectionately.

'Esme?' I say again after a moment.

She turns and looks at me again.

'How come you could cope with approaching me? In all those weeks and months, how come you always came up and spoke to me? I mean, most people round here think I've become stark staring mad.'

She doesn't answer straight away. A small, fragile smile hovers around the corners of her mouth for a moment, and she looks up at the cloudless early-morning sky. 'Och,' she says after a moment, 'grief can do strange things to a person.'

Her eyes have taken on a faraway look, and I am suddenly pierced by the realisation that it's not me she's talking about. Esme McFarland, the woman I had down for a frustrated spinster, had a life and a family once upon a time. Much as I want to, I don't press her for details; I suppose I'm scared of trampling on old wounds that haven't healed. But the realisation makes me aware all of a sudden that there are other people besides me carrying their own anguishes into a different kind of future from the one they'd envisaged for themselves.

She says, as if she's read my thoughts, 'Life moves you on, whether you want it to or not. Things happen, people come into your life, you suddenly find that people still need you even though you thought you were no use to anyone, that they have expectations for you, that you've maybe even got one or two expectations for yourself. 'Course, it's up to you what you do with those expectations. It was buying that wee florist business did it for me. I couldn't tell a thistle from a nettle before I came down here, but I learned fast. These days I hardly have time to spit, the shop's that busy.'

'Really?'

'Run off my feet, I am. I could do with taking someone on.'

'Really?' I say again. Stop it, the voice inside my head says, but I shush it up. 'Well, maybe you should.'

She gives a little defeated sigh. 'I've thought about it, believe me. More than once, if you must know. I thought it would be great – an extra pair of hands, a bit of company, someone who could learn the business, maybe. There's enough money for it, anyway.'

'Well, I think it's a great idea!' I can see it in my mind already: Con and Esme working away together side by side. Esme would overlook the eyebrow ring, I'm sure she would, once she'd had the chance to meet Con and got to know her a bit.

She wrinkles her nose. 'Nah, wouldn't work.'

'But why not?' The vision pops like a bubble.

She shakes her head at me. 'Tried it already.'

'Oh.' She must have had a really awful experience.

She shrugs resignedly. 'I put an advert in the job centre. You'd want to see the replies I got. Two, that was all. One was a lass in her teens with a laddie of about eighteen months in tow. Told me she'd need to bring him with her to work, as she couldn't afford childcare. Bonny wee thing, he was, too. Ate his way through half a bucket of daffodils while I was interviewing her, and all she said when she realised was, "Are them things poison?" Never mind that he'd just polished off a good tenner's worth of stock.' She's grinning as she talks. 'Between you and me, I'm not sure she even knew what a daffodil was.'

We're both laughing now. 'What about the other one?'

'What other one? Oh – the other applicant!' She gives me a mischievous look. 'He was quite nice, actually.'

'*He!*' I raise my eyebrows at her.

'Aye. He was that handsome – looked a lot like that laddie off of the films. Name's something to do with flowers.'

I look at her blankly. 'Flowers?'

'Aye. Och, you'll know him. He was in that pirate film. Copped off with that girl – the one with no meat on her. Oh, you know – always pouting, she is. Pretty wee thing, if she didn't look so much like a trout. Kiara Whatsherface.'

Realisation dawns. 'Oh, you mean Orlando Bloom!'

'Aye, that's him. Knew it was something to do with flowers. Anyway, he looked just like him. "Ding dong, Esme," I said to myself when he walked in. "That'll bring in the customers." But he didn't work out either.'

'Why not?'

'Well, I gave him a two-week trial. Even let him stay in the flat upstairs.' Oh, my God, I think to myself, there's a flat as well. The image of Con and Esme working together intensifies suddenly now I know there's somewhere Con could stay. 'He was good, too. A real light touch, he had. Made the most beautiful bridal bouquet out of sweet peas. I wouldn't have even tried it myself – they're all very well as a table decoration, but they don't last any time out of water. But no: the bride was set on them. I think it was her pet name for her man or something. Or his for her, maybe. Aye, that'd be more likely, eh?' I blink in an effort to keep up with the direction the conversation has taken. 'Anyway, he says to me, "Esme," he says, "we'll leave the stems uncovered, and she can pop them in a vase every now and then." Och, she was that happy: came in the week after the wedding with a bottle of champagne and two bits of cake – nice cake, it was, too: we had it with a cup of tea – and said he was a miracle-worker. She wasn't far wrong, either.'

'So what happened to him?' I give secret thanks that the mysterious flower-whisperer hadn't worked out. If he had, there wouldn't be any room for Con.

'Wait till I tell you.' She lays a conspiratorial hand on my arm. 'I was out in the back one day, looking for the beading wire, and I heard the door of the shop go. And then I heard Josh say, "What do you want?" in this really shocked voice. For a minute I thought we were being robbed, not that there's ever that much cash in the till, and you don't tend to hear of many smash and grabs for a bunch of flowers. Anyway, I sneaked up to the door and listened, to see if I could get to the phone to call the police, and then whoever it was said, "You're being ridiculous, Josh," so I figured it wasn't a burglar, anyway. And then Josh said, "Look, Simon, I think you made your feelings plain the other week." I'm behind the door there, thinking, aye, aye, what feelings? And then the other bloke, Simon, says, "OK, OK: we'll do it, if you're sure it's what you want.

I don't want you turning round in six months' time and telling me I trapped you into it. And you know that means moving to London." I'm thinking to myself, the two o' them must be plotting a bank raid or something. And then Josh says, "Who cares where it is, as long as we're together?" which doesn't sound very much like they're planning a heist to me. So then I decide to go through and find out what's going on. And Josh gets all embarrassed and introduces me to his friend Simon, who to tell you the truth is very nearly as good-looking as him. Such a waste,' she says inconsequentially. 'I offer them both a cup of tea, and Simon says he'll do it, although I know he's only offering so that Josh can tell me he's moving to London.' She gives a little sigh. 'He was gone before the end of the day. The pair of them were like a couple of love-struck teenagers.' She sighs again. 'He phones me every now and then. Got taken on by a place in Covent Garden. His pal Simon's a dancer. Been given the lead in some West End show. After Josh went I kind of lost heart. There's an art to flowers, you know? Josh reminded me of that when I saw what he did with the sweet peas. You can't just stick a carnation in front of someone and tell them to make up a buttonhole. Most of the folk round here couldn't tell a thistle from a dandelion, so they couldn't, and they don't want to learn, either.' She gives me a quick, conspiratorial smile. 'I'm supposed to be going down to see them next month; they're having one of those civil ceremony thingies. But it'll mean shutting the shop, and I can't do that. I'm booked solid with weddings. Nightmare month, July.'

I hold a hand up. 'Listen, Esme.' I'm starting to feel

excited all of a sudden. There's a rightness to this – a feeling that this chance meeting in the park has somehow been orchestrated for higher reasons. 'I think I might know someone who might be just what you're looking for. Someone who could really benefit from what you've got to offer. The flat, the chance to learn a new skill.'

'Och, that flat. It's in a bit of a state, to tell you the truth.'

'She wouldn't mind! She'd probably enjoy fixing it up. And you could train her up for an hour or so at the end of each day, after you've done all your deliveries. Then if she works out, she could look after the shop for you when you go down to London.'

'Aye?' She is looking at me warily.

'It's someone I only met recently. But I think she'd be great. Perfect, even.' Wouldn't she?

Esme is giving me a considering look. 'Perfect, you say?'

'Perfect,' I repeat firmly. 'She makes a great cup of tea,' I offer, hoping to seal the deal here and now.

A half-smile is hovering around her mouth. 'So, how d'you know this paragon of virtue?'

I hesitate, torn between not wanting to blow Con's chances before we've even started and not wanting to lie to Esme. She is looking at me brightly like a little sparrow, her head tilted to one side.

'Um . . .'

I take my courage in both hands.

'She broke into my house about a month ago.'

Esme's eyebrows shoot up, and then she purses her lips and looks at me appraisingly. 'Well.' She shakes her head at me like I've given her proof positive I really have lost the plot, which I probably have. 'She sounds just perfect, like you say.' She pauses for a moment, weighing things up, and then she seems to make up her mind about something. 'Why don't we pop across to the shop and stick the kettle on? Something tells me this might take some time.'

Chapter 22

I can't find the house at first. The route I trawled on foot after dark, stealing in Ryan and Matt's limping wake, has taken on a whole different personality in the bright sunlight of a Sunday afternoon. Streets that on Thursday night had seemed to offer a multitude of shadowy opportunities for a host of nefarious deeds have become ordinary, mundane, almost attractive, their houses no longer sinister frontages harbouring who knows what behind their darkened windows. A windowbox here, a set of cheerful curtains there, and I am a lifetime away from the nightmarish world through which I fled in terror that evening with an imagined she-devil hot on my heels. I refuse to give up, though. Now that I've somehow managed to talk Esme into at least meeting Con, the task of finding her has suddenly become rather more urgent.

After driving around for several minutes, searching in vain for a familiar landmark, I eventually manage to locate a set of bins clustered importantly on the pavement and, hoping they're the same bins I hid behind when Matt looked back towards me on Thursday evening, I pull in and park the car alongside the kerb. It's not the street I'd stopped on the last time, but I'm confident-ish that I might be able to complete my journey on foot now that I've (hopefully) got my bearings.

It's still difficult. On a doorstep near the corner of the street a couple of sari-clad women are standing chatting together while a small child wraps itself around the legs of one of them. Through the open doorway an alchemy of cooking aromas spills out into the street, making my mouth water unexpectedly. The women look up as I approach. 'All right, luv?' one of them says with a friendly nod before resuming her conversation with her friend. Was it here that we crossed over to the other side, or farther along? There's a postbox set into the wall of the end building that I don't remember noticing before. Would I have missed that? Its bright paint gleams mockingly in the midday sun, and I sigh. What I could really do with is another bungled mugging, just to point me in the right direction.

I stop midway along the street I'm in to take stock, looking up and down the road for a landmark I recognise. It feels as though I've been walking far longer than I did on Thursday: maybe I overshot the house and I'm somewhere we never even got close to. And then I turn around to continue on my way, and discover I am actually standing right outside the house where Ryan and Matt disappeared.

Even in broad daylight it's unmistakable, having managed somehow to hang on to its seedy frontage among its more respectable neighbours. Not even the indefatigable optimism of a bright June morning can redeem it. The lock still hangs drunkenly on its solitary screw, and what's left of the colour on the front door is parting company with the wood and has scattered little flakes of dark-blue paint apologetically onto the pavement at my feet. I hesitate for a moment, trying to decide upon the best way forwards, dithering between sneaking in through the broken entrance and retreating to the corner and waiting to see if anyone appears either coming in or going out of the building. I peer in at the window again, the one that housed the old tramp that turned out to be me, cupping my hands around my face to shut out the sunlight. It's empty – looks unfit for habitation, in fact.

Suddenly bold, I ball my hand into a fist and deliver three sharp hammering knocks to the door, which swings lazily inwards and back as each blow makes impact with the wood. There's no answer. I knock again, for longer this time, and wait, stepping from one foot to the other in impatience, or nervousness – I can't be sure which. And then I get tired of just standing there like a lemon, and I push the door boldly open like I own the place and step inside.

The smell hits me like a blow to the face, making me recoil: a heady mixture of stale food overlaid with the pungent aroma of urine and something else I can't identify – a mustiness that makes me think of a large dead rodent. Which it could well be. I have to force myself forwards, stepping delicately over the discarded takeaway packaging that litters the narrow hallway, trying to avoid the broken glass scattered among the food-smeared wrappings. At the end of the hall there's a door to the left leading into my non-existent madwoman room, hanging brokenly ajar, and a narrow staircase leading up. A glance inside the doorway confirms that nobody's lived here in a very long time. 'Hello?' I call out anyway, stopping myself just in time from adding, 'I come in peace.' I'm not sure that'd be true anyway. There's no response from anywhere inside the building, and so I take my courage in both feet and start climbing gingerly to the first floor, doing my best to avoid the discarded syringe on the fourth step and something long and rubbery that I deliberately choose not to investigate too closely on the ninth. On the landing there's another solitary door, with another staircase opposite, promising who knows what manner of delights to anyone still of a mind to investigate the place further.

I try the handle of the door on this first floor, the one through which Ryan and his pal Matt had presumably disappeared yesterday evening. Unsurprisingly, though perhaps a bit incongruously considering the lackadaisical approach to security I've witnessed so far in my explorations, it's locked. A sudden thrill of adrenalin rushes through me as the thought spills into my mind that perhaps Ryan is keeping Con prisoner here. I can't believe anyone would stay in this shit-hole voluntarily. I press an ear to the wood, listening for any sign of life beyond the door. There's nothing: no voices, no sound of anyone moving about, no sign of life at all, in fact. 'Hello?' I call again, more boldly than downstairs now that I am becoming convinced the place is deserted. I hammer recklessly on the door. 'Anybody home?' After I stop the noise of my knocking continues to ring around in the mote-filled air before coming to rest quietly at my feet on the dirty floor.

Nothing breaks the silence: no hasty shuffling on the other side of the door; no irritated stomping across the room to find out who's banging around on the landing outside. My body sags in disappointment, and I am turning to leave, have actually descended two of the stairs, in fact, when suddenly I hear a fumbling noise behind me, and I spin around. The door has been cranked open a couple of inches, and the gap that this has created is filled with a long sliver of humanity, pale-skinned and with a shock of wild black hair. If that complexion is anything to go by, it's Matt, just up from the look of him, and not looking too pleased to see me. 'Yeah?' he demands truculently.

'Oh!' I am taken aback; in spite of having followed the pair of them back here the other night, I'd given up hope of finding anyone in this dump of a building. Close up, he has the blackest eyes and the whitest skin I've ever seen on anyone outside of a horror movie − skin that looks almost translucent, as though it hasn't seen daylight any time this century. I wouldn't have been surprised, had he managed anything remotely resembling a smile, to discover his mouth was graced with a pair of blood-dripping fangs. Not only that, but from the angle I'm standing at he also looks to be stark naked. He raises an eyebrow at me expectantly.

'I'm looking for Ryan.' I try to tear my eyes from his whiter-than-white, completely hair-free chest and inject into my voice some of the same truculence I've heard in his.

He opens the door a bit wider and leans towards me, sniffing the air in front of me like a werewolf seeking out its prey. I find myself wondering if he sleeps in a box. 'An' 'oo shall I say is calling?'

Crap. I can't give my name; aside from anything else, it won't mean anything to Ryan. And I can hardly introduce myself to Matt the Dracula lookalike as the woman

Ryan mugged in Harrogate, the one who mugged him back on Thursday night. 'Police,' I say after a moment, blurting the word out and wanting to bite my tongue off the minute it's spoken. 'Special Branch,' I add when he looks me up and down, taking in my non-official state of dress and generally dishevelled appearance in utter disbelief.

The door opens another couple of centimetres and a pale arm snakes around its edge, holding out an expectant hand. 'Got some ID, 'ave yer?'

'Erm, no. I'm off duty,' I say lamely.

He gives me a caustic smile with his lips pressed together tightly, so I still can't rule out the fangs. 'I'll bet you are,' he says in that same insolent tone. The he adds after a moment, ''E in't here.'

I try to look beyond him into the room to check and he tsks, though without any heat. He swings the door fully open – I'm relieved to discover his privates are actually concealed by a pair of grubby boxers – and sweeps an arm backwards invitingly. 'Come in an' check if you want.'

I crane my neck again, reluctant to step over the threshold into what must be the most squalid flat I've ever seen – and this from a woman who's partied in some of the least salubrious student flats Manchester had to offer. The floor is almost completely hidden beneath piles of clothing and unmarked cardboard boxes while, pushed against the wall opposite the door, a sagging mattress on top of which a tangled heap of dirty blankets shows evidence of recent vacation. My eyes are drawn to a bluebottle, angrily head-banging against the grimy glass in the narrow window, seeking escape. I can't say I blame it. Matt watches my careful scrutiny of his living quarters with an amused smile hovering around the corners of his mouth. 'Cup o' tea?' he asks sardonically, turning and disappearing back into the filthy mess. From somewhere amongst the tangled heap of clothing on the floor he plucks a pair of crumpled jeans and steps into them, shrugging them over his narrow hips and turning provocatively to face me before buttoning them.

'Do you know where I can find him?' I take a tentative step inside the room to show willing.

'Who? Ryan?' He shrugs and pulls a face. 'I dunno, do I? I in't his mum.'

'He was here the other night, though.'

He raises his eyebrows at me. I can see him reassessing his initial decision to dismiss my claim that I'm with Special Branch. As he does so his eyes flicker nervously towards the bed and he runs a hand across his mouth and chin. I realise with something of a thrill that I'm making him edgy.

I take a purposeful step towards the mattress and purse my lips suspiciously as though I am about to come to some great deduction, and he leaps to intercept me. We are so close now I can feel his sleep-stale breath on my face.

'Look –' He holds his hands up. 'I said he in't here, didn't I? I've co-operated with you, been nice to you.'

'Oh yes, Matthew.' My casual use of his name really unnerves him; I can almost smell his increasing nervousness. 'You've been very nice to me.' A faint line of perspiration has appeared on his upper lip, and his ears and neck are flushed an ugly puce, in stark contrast to the whiteness of the rest of his complexion. I turn away from the mattress towards the door, and I feel his body slump in relief at the prospect of me leaving. Then I turn back to him unexpectedly and he immediately tenses again. 'Now, Matthew.' I speak his name briskly, enjoying the way it makes him squirm, bestowing a bright smile upon him. Being a police officer is bloody good fun. 'Where can I find Ryan?' I raise my eyebrows at him enquiringly, and he falters.

'I dunno.' He throws his response at me, so keen is he to have me gone. 'He moves around a lot, right? Only comes here every so often.' His eyes flicker to the mattress again and then back to me.

'What – just when he needs to score a line?' Is that the right terminology, or do I mean get a fix? I bluff it out by glowering at him assertively. 'How often is that then, Matthew?'

He is really starting to sweat now. 'I dunno what you're talking about! Swear down –'

'Listen.' I cut him off. 'I don't want to have to come back here any more than you want me to. So don't make me. Because next time, Matthew, I won't be on my own. Next time I'll have a search warrant and half a dozen of my colleagues with me.' My God, the lies that are spilling from my mouth! This is more fun than the supermarket. I scowl at him meaningfully and wait.

His face contorts a bit, but finally he capitulates. 'Sod it,' he says, 'I don't need this crap.' He shrugs. "You know t' paper mill out Pool way?' I nod, though I haven't a clue where he's talking about. 'There's an old worker's cottage 'bout half a mile on towards Otley, down a farm track.' He wrinkles his nose, as though expressing disgust at the prospect of living in an old cottage out in the sticks rather than the little jewel of a flat in the city centre that he calls home. 'Ryan hangs out there sometimes.'

'Only sometimes? Where is he the rest of the time?'

'Look, that's all I know, OK? What's he done, any road?'

I give him what I hope is an enigmatic look. 'We just have a few questions we need to ask him.'

'Bad, is it? I've bin telling 'im for months you lot'd catch up with him sooner or later.'

'Have you, now?' I am alert all of a sudden. 'Quite the Boy Scout, aren't we, Matthew?' I scowl at him in what I hope is a menacing way. 'You know, I hope for your sake that's just a shot in the dark, because withholding evidence is a very serious matter.' I'm getting so good at this I'm beginning to wonder why I ever went into play therapy as a career.

It goes to show that I must have instilled some doubt in his mind as to my identity, because he doesn't tell me to fuck off like I'm expecting him to. Instead he stands watching me in silence, his thin, pale body taut with tension, willing me to leave. I cross back to the door and hesitate on the threshold, casting a last look around the nasty little flat. 'You want to get tidied up a bit, Matthew. Throw away some of those empty food cartons. Pick up your clothes. This place is a health hazard.'

I leave before he can collect himself sufficiently to think up an appropriate riposte, picking my way delicately through the minefield of rubbish that litters the narrow staircase and back out onto the street, where I gasp in the sweet smell of urine-free air like a drowning swimmer who's been thrown a lifebuoy. An elderly man in a turban is making his way slowly along the pavement as I emerge, and he stops and looks me up and down in surprise. 'You from t' council?' he asks. 'I've bin on to t' environmental health about that place. Wants boarding up, it does. All sorts going on. Drugs and whatnot. Disgusting, it is. Used to be a good area, this.'

'Yes, I heard,' I tell him absently. 'The streets just aren't safe any more.'

He shuffles off down the road, shaking his head sadly and lamenting the drop in standards under his breath. 'No sense o' community,' I hear him mutter as he stops a couple of doors further down and begins trying to fit a key into the lock with a shaky hand. As he steps across the threshold he shoots me a dark, disappointed look, as though I am personally responsible for the decline in the neighbourhood. I take a note of the number above the door, jotting it down in a small notebook I keep in my handbag. What with my newfound talents as a police impersonator, there's no saying when it might come in handy.

Chapter 23

'This it, then?' Standing under the canopy outside the little florist's shop amid the clutter of buckets, Con's expression is unreadable.

'Yes, this is it. Isn't it lovely? All the flowers. Beautiful.' I wince as I hear myself: my tone rings with forced effort as I try to squash the qualms of doubt I've been having ever since I tracked her down at the cottage the previous afternoon. 'Aren't those peonies fabulous?'

Con pulls a face. 'They're all right.' If there's any glimmer of excitement inside her at the prospect of working for Esme, she's doing a great job of keeping it under wraps. 'We going in, or what?'

I nod resignedly and smother a sigh. I am beginning to question how on earth I could ever have considered this to be a good idea.

Finding her had, in the end, been easier than I'd anticipated. The disused paper mill Matthew had talked about provided a very obvious landmark, and the cottage was less than half a mile down a rutted dirt track that played havoc with the suspension on the Passat. From a distance it seemed almost quaint, a tiny farm worker's cottage nestling among the trees at the edge of the road. Close up, it was a disappointment, barely qualifying as a cottage. Single-storeyed and built of a featureless red brick that matched the brick of the old mill at the end of the road, it squatted at the edge of the muddy track like a beggar in need of a good bath, glowering back at me as I loitered inside the car, as though resenting the scrutiny. It looked at first to be deserted; the only sound as I cut the engine was the relentless drum of the rain that had swept in during the afternoon on the bonnet of the car.

I sat for a moment taking stock, sizing up the place. Behind its curtainless windows, I was sure I could feel eyes upon me, waiting for my next move. I hadn't stopped to consider quite how I would tackle things if Ryan were around, but I was sure I'd be able to improvise.

There was no response when I hammered on the door, and so I resorted to a bit of quiet snooping, seeing as I was here anyway. Around the side of the house, a beat-up Corsa with rusting green bodywork caused a sudden lurch of panic in my stomach; I half-expected Ryan's glowering face to appear behind the steering wheel bent on mowing me down. I pushed through the overgrown wilderness that might once have been a tended garden to the back of the house, and was in the process of clambering past an abandoned oil drum to peer in at one of the windows when the back door opened with heart-stopping swiftness and Con appeared on the step. We stood regarding one another in silence for a moment, and then she gave a sniff.

'Auntie Marion.' Her tone was rich with irony. She shook her head in disbelief. 'What you doing here?'

I tried to muster some dignity – no mean achievement when you're wearing half the garden as a hair accessory.

'I came to see you,' I said as casually as I could manage. 'Aren't you going to invite me in?'

She gave a slight shrug and pursed her lips. 'Please yourself,' she said after a moment, then turned and retreated back into the cottage, leaving me feeling wrong-footed and more than a bit foolish standing in the garden. After a moment I followed her into the gloomy interior.

'Is . . . um . . . is Ryan around?' I asked tentatively as I stepped into the squalid little kitchen.

'No, he isn't, luckily for you.' She gave me that considering look of hers. 'What you up to any road?'

'Oh, I just –' I waved an arm around airily '– wondered how you were doing, you know.'

'Right.' She sucked in her lips and folded her arms across her chest defensively. 'Just passing, were you?'

I felt a wave of irritation surge across me all of a sudden. I'd spent a good hour or so earlier trying to persuade a reluctant Esme to give Con a chance at the assistant florist role while inside my head that bloody voice nagged and scolded and told me to stop interfering; the least I might have hoped for was a sliver of gratitude. Granted, she didn't actually know any of this yet, but her churlish sarcasm was getting on my nerves. 'Look, Con, obviously I wasn't just passing. It's taken me weeks to find you.' She looked a bit taken aback at that, but I ploughed on before she could say anything. 'I just couldn't help thinking that we'd parted under a bit of a cloud after our quarrel, and I wanted to sort it out with you. That's all,' I finished lamely. *Yeah right*, the voice said. *Shut up*, I told it.

I can't say there was an instant softening, but she

unfolded her arms resignedly and gave a sigh. 'Oh, Marion.' She shook her head at me again. 'What am I going to do with you?' Once again I felt as though we'd switched roles all of a sudden: she was the adult; I'd become the hapless child.

I took another hesitant step further into the kitchen. The soles of my shoes clung stickily to the floor as I walked. 'I know I upset you when you were at my house, and I didn't mean to, and I'm sorry.'

She leaned against the wall at the far end of the kitchen and shrugged. 'Well, it weren't your fault, really. I've always had a bit of a temper on me. Ryan says I can be a right moody cow sometimes. Oh, don't worry –' I'd stiffened at the mention of his name '– he'll be gone ages. Sunday afternoon, in't it? Pub day. Sometimes he don't come home till t' morning.' She said this without any heat, as though Ryan's unpredictability were all in a day's work for her. Which, I suppose, it probably is.

'Oh.' I inclined my head towards the back door. 'I thought that was his car outside.'

'Aye. Can't use it, though, can he? Can't see to drive.' Was it my imagination, or was she looking at me suspiciously?

I cleared my throat nervously. 'Can't he?'

'Nah. Got something in his eyes, didn't he? One of his mates came to pick him up.'

Not Matthew, I hoped. I didn't want Ryan getting wind of my snooping quite so quickly.

'What –' I keep my voice casual. 'What did he get in his eye?'

She shrugged dismissively. 'Didn't say. He were in a right state, though. He could hardly see at all yesterday. He were in agony.' A vicious thrill of pleasure shot across my stomach as she told me; the thought of having made Ryan suffer gave me a real kick. 'I'd make you a cup of tea, only we've no milk.' She managed a half-smile. 'And no long-life in t' cupboard, neither.'

I returned the smile. 'Not to worry. I've drunk enough tea to sink a battleship already this morning.'

'So . . .' she hesitated, as though searching for something to talk about. 'How's that dog of yours, any road?'

'Good!' I nodded to emphasise the point, glad to be on safe ground. 'Missing you,' I added, smiling to show there was no malice in my words. 'He's with a friend of mine at the moment.' At Esme's insistence, I'd left Hector to spend the afternoon with Amelia while I came out to see if I could track down Con. 'On a play date with her dog.'

'Cool.' She mirrored my nodding and the smile broadened.

'Actually, Con, that's sort of why I've come.' The words spilled from my mouth before I could stop them, tripping over themselves in their eagerness to be out.

'Yeah?' She was instantly wary, and I realised I would have to tread carefully if I wanted to avoid patronising her, or scaring her off, or offending her by making her feel I'd turned up like some interfering do-gooder wanting to turn her life around.

Which I was. And I did.

'It's about this friend of mine.' That considering look was back on her face. 'She's in a bit of a pickle, and – look, could we sit down or something?' I felt unaccountably nervous all of a sudden.

She pushed herself off the wall and led me through to a dingy sitting room. Someone had made an attempt at tidying it, but no amount of straightening or cleaning would be enough to hide the torn and moulding paper on the walls, or shift the grime from the threadbare carpet, which felt almost as sticky underfoot as the kitchen floor had been. She gestured diffidently at the sofa. 'It's a bit lumpy,' she apologised, 'but it's that or t' chair, and the back falls off of that if you don't sit on it right.'

'You should speak to the landlord – get him to fix it.' I lowered myself gingerly into the sofa and tried not to allow any of the revulsion I felt at the state of the place show on my face. Honestly, Esme's flat might need a bit of work, but I was willing to bet that compared with this it would be a palace.

She gave a snort of laughter and shook her head at me again. 'Sometimes I wonder about you, I really do. There in't no landlord, is there?'

'But –' I looked around me in bafflement. 'Surely you don't *own* the place?'

This time she threw back her head and laughed out loud. 'Oh, God, Marion, you're a riot, you really are. Yeah, me and Ryan own it. His granny left it to him after she died.'

'Really?'

She looked at me as though I were a couple of sand-wiches short of a picnic and gave an exasperated tut. 'No, 'course not really. It were empty, weren't it? Ryan broke a window round t' back to get in.'

'You mean —' I tried hard to suppress the middle-aged fuddy-duddy shock in my voice '— you're squatting?'

'So what if we are?' The truculence was back in her tone. 'Look, I thought you wanted to talk about your friend, not give me t' third degree about where ah live.'

'I did, you're right.' I held my hands up in a conciliatory gesture. 'Sorry. Yes, my friend. She runs a small florist business in Station Parade. That's where —' I stopped myself just in time: it hardly seemed helpful to mention the mugging at this point '— you know,' I finished lamely. 'Near the house. Close by, anyway. Flowers, you know.'

'Aye, ah know what a florist is, thanks very much. I'm not stupid.'

'No, sorry. I didn't mean —' Oh, God, this was turning out to be a lot harder than I'd anticipated it being when the scheme first came into my head in the park. I licked my lips and ploughed on. 'The thing is, the business is very busy, and she's looking to take someone on to help her. Someone young and enthusiastic, who can learn about — well, becoming a florist themselves, perhaps. Working with the flowers. She even has a flat above the shop, and whoever took the job would be able to use that — to live in it, you know. Make it their home,' I finished lamely with another surreptitious look at our shabby surroundings.

'Right.' She gave a slow nod. 'And you thought of me, right?'

I nodded.

'Because —?'

'Well, honestly, Con! Isn't it obvious?' I realised as soon as I'd said it that this was possibly not the most tactful thing I'd ever come out with. 'What I mean is, it's an opportunity for you to do something for yourself. Something new. Who knows what it might lead to?'

'Yeah, because I'd been on t' lookout for a new career.' Her tone was heavy with sarcasm.

'Well, it has to be better than being a lookout for Ryan's criminal activities, surely!' Her expression hardened on the mention of Ryan's name. 'I mean, come on, Con! What kind of a way is this to live?' I gestured around me at the shabby interior of the cottage.

As a method of persuasion I have to admit that it failed miserably. She jumped angrily from the chair, which clattered noisily to the floor behind her in a tangle of broken limbs. 'Don't you dare come round here and start criticising the way I live! We haven't all got pots of money and fancy big houses. You did all this last time, remember? Telling me Ryan were no good for me. We've already had this row.' She stood over me for a moment, seething with indignation and looking as though she might just punch me.

After a moment I gave a defeated little sigh. I must have been mad coming here. Con wasn't some obscure link to Hope: she didn't hold any secrets about what happened to her, and I didn't owe her anything. Nobody asked her to save my life. She was just a screwed-up kid who'd dropped off the edge, somehow, and taking her on like a lost cause was never going to bring my daughter back. Colin had been right, I realised: I *had* been stuck since Hope died. My emotions mightn't have shut down, but I'd been trapped in a place where I couldn't cope with reality and so had created a little fantasy world for myself where I thought that if I could fix every broken person who crossed my path, I might manage to mend myself somehow. 'You're right,' I said to Con. I shook my head at my own folly and eased my way out of the lumpy sofa. 'I shouldn't have come. It's just that Esme needs someone trustworthy, someone she can rely on who will look after the business when she has to go away.' I turned my eyes upon her. 'I thought you would have fitted the bill rather well.'

It was this last piece of information that flummoxed her. Before then, she'd been getting ready to throw me out – I could see it in her body language. Instead, her shoulders slumped suddenly as though all the fight had gone out of her, and she looked at me, astonished.

'What?' I gave a half-laugh at her expression. 'I know you're honest, Con, whatever low-down, dirty business Ryan's got you doing for him. Why else would you have brought my bag back?'

I began picking my way across the sticky carpet to the kitchen, feeling suddenly exhausted. 'You know,' I said, turning to face her one last time, 'you're worth more than this, Con.'

She never said anything straight away, but pressed her lips together as though unsure what might emerge if she didn't take care. I could see her mulling over the revelation that someone thought her trustworthy, that maybe she could do something about where she was going with her life. Then suddenly her expression hardened again and she scowled at me. 'So what's in it for you, then?'

'What?' I was already halfway through the door when she spoke.

'What do you get out of it? How come you're playing Lady Bountiful all of a sudden?'

I shook my head in disbelief. 'I don't get anything out of it! I just –' I threw her own words back at her. 'I just like you, that's all. And I thought that I could help out a couple of friends.' That, I had to acknowledge silently to myself, wasn't strictly true: there was a whole host of other reasons I'd been drawn to Con, none of which made any sense now that I was standing here confronting her truculence.

'That what we are, then?' She raised her head to me. 'Friends?'

I gave a sigh. 'I thought so. Evidently I've overstepped the mark.' I gave a resigned shrug. 'I'd better go.'

I'd almost reached the back door when she spoke again. 'Ah wouldn't need t' flat.' I turned around to face her. 'Me an' Ryan – we're fine here.'

I considered her for a moment, and then shook my head. 'No – look, Con. Forget it. Forget I even came here. You and Ryan – well, you've got your own stuff going on. I can't see him being thrilled if you told him about any of this. To be honest, I hadn't anticipated him being part of it at all. It was just you I was thinking of.' Now that we'd reached this point, the sheer impracticality of what I'd done hit me with horrible clarity.

She weighed this up for a moment. 'He wouldn't have to know.' She gave an imperceptible shrug. 'Not yet, any road. I could come and talk to your friend in t' morning if you like.'

She looked vulnerable all of a sudden, and I realised

with a pang of bitter irony that I hadn't the heart to walk away from her now that I'd got her hopes up.

'All right. Come over about eleven, and I'll take you round to meet her.'

I'd driven away full of mixed feelings along the muddy track, which was quickly turning into more of a bog, thanks to the relentless rain. A few more hours of this and it would be impassable. And now, outside the shop the following morning, standing on the glistening pavement as the clouds above us start to thin and clear, I can't say I feel any better about all of this: what had struck me as such a perfect solution in the park yesterday morning suddenly seems ridiculous and naïve.

Neither of us looks overly confident as we hover in front of the door, and in the end it's Esme who comes out to greet us, inviting us in, brewing tea for us all so that we can make the introductions and talk about whether this mad scheme of mine stands any chance of success.

Which is a bit of a joke, really, considering it was hatched by a woman who keeps fictitious cats and is only of sound mind if you consider all the circumstances that have sent her round the bend in the first place.

You'd think I would have learned by now, wouldn't you?

Wouldn't you?

Hello?

Is there anybody there?

Chapter 24

The week slides by in a murk of more rain, and it's not until Friday that the first offering of sun manages to break through the clouds. I am woken by its warmth on my face as it spills into the bedroom and, as I push myself upright, I can see it through the window, sparkling on the rain-laden leaves of the cherry tree in a shower of tiny glistening crystals. Beside me on the bed Hector is already awake and watching me with a look of expectation on his face, as though he, too, is picking up on the general climate of guarded optimism. A flutter of something I don't quite recognise flits across my stomach, and I prod at Hector through the duvet. 'Get this,' I tell him. 'I think I'm glad to be alive.'

The meeting between Con and Esme had gone far better than I might have hoped, and by the time we'd finished a second cup of tea they were working out some terms and conditions together. I began to dare hope that maybe suggesting Con as a trainee might not turn out to be such a daft idea after all. Not wanting to appear like I was trying to micro-manage either of them, I'd stayed away for the rest of the week, but today, given that the sun is back out at last and I still haven't managed a trip to the cemetery in I can't remember how long, I decide that as soon as breakfast is out of the way, I'll take myself across to the shop to see both of them and pick up some sunflowers to take down to Hope.

She'd always loved sunflowers; ever since a nursery school project where all the children planted seeds and watched them grow from tiny green shoots into ridiculously high cartoon flowers that towered above them, their extravagant looks had never failed to make her laugh in delight. The year we took her over to the Ardèche on holiday, she'd been ecstatic to discover there were whole fields full of them, their heavy heads nodding and turning in the heat of the afternoon as they followed the sun's slow progress across the landscape. I'd found fabric on a stall in one of the markets – a deep, olive-green background of leaves clustered with the bright golden heads of the sunflowers – and, digging deep into my secondary school needlework skills, fashioned her a simple pinafore from it. She'd lived in it for weeks after the holiday, until the weather turned suddenly cold and forced her back into dungarees.

My heart hurts as I remember that holiday – the three of us together, Sam and Hope fooling around in the pool of the villa we'd rented while I tossed oversized tomatoes and lettuce leaves into simple lunchtime salads washed down with local wine on the shady veranda, the alcohol and the heat combining to turn the whole thing into something unreal, like we'd fallen into someone else's dream. I sit with the pain for a moment, acknowledging it, and then I wrap my arms around my shoulders and give myself a tight squeeze, the way Sam might have tried to do if he'd been here right now. 'Come on,' I tell myself sternly. 'You're lucky to have all those memories to hang on to. Plenty of people don't. Now stop moping and get your backside in gear.' At the end of the bed, Hector lifts his head and regards me quizzically. 'I wasn't talking to you,' I say sternly. 'I was talking to myself.' I acknowledge ruefully that my visit to see Colin hasn't broken me of that particular habit. On a plus note, though, at least the conversations seem to have taken a more positive turn.

Con is sitting alongside Esme behind the counter when I turn up on the threshold of the shop, her head bent over a cluster of flowers and greenery and her brow furrowed in concentration as she winds them together with green plastic tape. The two of them lift their heads as they hear the door to the shop open, and I notice that the eyebrow ring has disappeared. 'Marion!' they say in unison, and a warm flush spreads across my face at the enthusiasm in their voices.

'Look!' Con holds up the flowers for me to inspect. 'My first corsage. First decent one, ah should say. The others looked like a right dog's dinner. No offence, Hector.' She bends and tickles Hector behind the ears.

'Constance, why don't you take Hector out the back to see Amelia?' Esme asks her. 'And pop the kettle on while you're through, will you, dear? I'm sure Marion has time for a cup of tea.' She waits until Con has disappeared through the door and then turns back to me.

'Marion, that girl is a magician. Look at this!' She picks up the corsage Con is in the middle of completing. 'Good enough for any wedding guest. Not even Josh picked things up this quickly.'

I smile in relief. 'I'm so glad. I would have felt terrible if she hadn't worked out.'

'Och, wouldn't have been your fault, now, would it? You were only making the suggestion. It was me took her on.'

'I know, and she looks as though she's loving it. You don't know what a difference it might make to her,' I confide. 'Honestly, nobody's ever given her an opportunity like this in her life.'

'Aye, I've been picking up bits and pieces from her during the week,' Esme tells me. 'What a start in life, and her so young. So cheerful, she is, too. A breath o' fresh air. And the customers love her. She's even got Fiona from the hotel eatin' out her hand, and she can be a toffee-nosed bitch at the best of times.' She shakes her head and sighs. 'Makes you realise how easy the rest of us have it, by and large.'

'I see the eyebrow ring has disappeared.'

Esme gives a sly laugh. 'I told her the pollen from the lilies might make it flare up. She had it out so fast you'd think her skin had really started to itch.' She looks at me sharply suddenly. 'There's something different about you today. Have you changed your hair?' She frowns and shakes her head. 'No, it's not that. You look –' Her face softens suddenly. 'Oh,' she says, and then she comes round from the far side of the counter. 'You're getting better. I'm so glad.' She gives me a short, fierce hug, and I nod wordlessly, tears smarting unexpectedly at my eyes.

'Still determined she doesn't want the flat?' I nod towards the back of the shop, wiping the back of my hand across my eyes.

'Och –' Esme passes me a tissue from somewhere below the counter and lowers her voice. 'At first she was really defensive about it. Remember when you brought her round on Monday, she wouldnae even go up and look at the place? Well.' She leans conspiratorially closer. 'The other morning – Wednesday, ah think it was – she said to me, "So that flat upstairs is just sitting there empty, is it?" "Aye," I said. Then I didn't say anything else and neither did she, but I could see her mulling it over. And then yesterday afternoon, just after we'd finished tidying up and were about to lock up for the day, she says, "So what's it like, then, the flat?" And I says, "Och, it's just a wee place. No room to swing a cat, really. I'm thinking I might rent it out, though. Might as well earn its keep."'

'Oh. I didn't realise you were thinking of renting it out.' I am oddly disappointed.

'Och, Marion! Of course I'm not thinking of renting it out! I was just saying that to tempt the lassie.'

'Oh!' I smile at Esme's cunning, feeling I've underestimated her yet again. 'So what did she say then?'

'Well, her face wasn't a million miles away from yours just now when you thought I was serious about getting a lodger in. I just carried on as normal, got the order book out to check today's workload while she was giving the place a wee sweep, still brooding away, like, and then when she was finished I said to her, "Constance, just nip upstairs to the flat, will you, lassie. I mind Josh left some floral wire up there before he left, and we're running a bit low for tomorrow's orders."'

'Oh, Esme! Brilliant. So did she say anything when she came down?'

'She didn't come down – that's what I'm away to tell you. I had tae go upstairs looking for her. And there she was, sitting in the window seat in the bedroom, just staring out at the view. So I said to her, "Are you all right, lassie?" and she didn't even move, she just carried on staring out the window, and then she said, "It's lovely up here. You can see right out over all those houses to the church." And I said, "Och aye, the view's all very well, but the place needs a good sorting before I can rent it. I don't know how I'm going to manage it all on my own, what with my arthritis and everything. I can't go climbing ladders at my age."'

'I didn't know you had arthritis.'

She looks at me as though I'm simple. 'Did you take a stupid pill or something this morning? My arthritis is about as real as that lodger I'm thinking of getting. Anyway, she says to me, "I could give you a hand with it if you like – help you with the painting and that, after work, before I get off in the evenings." And I said, "Och, Constance, d'you mean it?" And she said aye, she'd love to. So that's what we're going to do,' she finished. 'We're going to close up a bit early this evening and hit B & Q together. If that lassie isn't begging me to move in by the end of next week, I'll eat that bucket of lilies, stems and all.'

I stare at her in admiration. 'Esme, you really are a witch.' The door to the back swings open and Con reappears balancing three mugs in her hands. 'Ow!' she says, setting them down on the counter between us. 'Hot.' She gives us a bright look. 'Finished talking about me?'

'Oh, Con, we weren't –'

'Aye, we were,' Esme admits. 'I was telling Marion about how you've offered to help me fix up the flat upstairs, get it ready for renting out.'

'Oh. Right.' Con buries her face in one of the mugs, and Esme gives me a sly wink.

Over our tea Esme and I chat about inconsequentials while Con sips thoughtfully at her tea, and then I pick out a bunch of the ridiculous sunflowers to take down to the cemetery. 'They're lovely, aren't they?' Esme says as she's wrapping them in cellophane. 'Such happy flowers, I always think.' She hands them to me with a nod, waving away the money I'm proffering. 'On me. Seeing as we're celebrating.'

Con looks curiously from Esme to me and back. 'What are we celebrating?'

Esme regards me seriously for a moment. 'Marion's return from the brink,' she says ambiguously to Con. Then she smiles at me, a warm, approving smile that tells me she understands just how big a step it is and that she's as pleased with the change in me as I am. 'Mind and put your head in next week.' She gives me another sly wink as I call Hector in from the back and the two of us begin to take our leave. 'You can see how we're getting on with the flat.'

Chapter 25

The cemetery is Friday morning quiet. It has its busy times, I've observed over the past few months. Sundays, typically, the number of visitors increases, and there's usually a surge during the religious holidays as well – Easter and so on. You couldn't move here at Christmas for mourners. Really and truly. Boxing Day was a nightmare. I resented them at the time – resented the lack of solitude, the garishness of the normally sombre graves suddenly bright with fresh flowers. It was an intrusion on my own grief. I couldn't concentrate with all those other people around; couldn't lie on the ground and talk to Hope the way I'd become used to doing when I had the place to myself. Instead I'd been forced to stand at the bottom of the mound and stare at the spot where the headstone now rested, simmering with rage at the sudden intrusion, at the apparent insensitivity of other mourners who'd had the audacity to infringe upon my precious time with Hope.

Today there are no such distractions. I don't pass a single person as I make my way through the gate into the cemetery. Along the edges of the path, the leaves on the shrubs and trees are scattered with diamonds of raindrops that sparkle in the morning sun, and the air is washed with birdsong. As I reach the grave, I can see that what's left of the cherry blossoms I brought with me last time I was here has truly given up the ghost: the limp branches lean forlornly against the headstone, any trace of the pink flowers long since washed away in the downpour of the past week. I crouch down and lift them out, then lay them on the ground beside me and empty the old water out onto the grass, taking a moment to trace the letters on the headstone and realising with a lurch that Hope's birthday is just three weeks from now. Then I unwrap the sunflowers from the cellophane Esme wrapped them in and try to arrange them in the vase. It's not easy; with their thick stems and their heavy heads they refuse to sit properly, instead they loll and tip every which way. I try arranging them individually, but just as I manage to get one or two of them into a position I like, they topple forwards before I can add any more flowers to the vase. I try breaking off a couple of inches from their stems, but it's like trying to snap through a particularly tough branch. So then I use the cellophane to support them, tucking it in around them in the vase so that they are wedged in position.

I step back to survey my handiwork, dissatisfaction at the way the sunflowers refuse to co-operate making me tut and shake my head at them in frustration; they're like recalcitrant children refusing to do as they're told. And as I do so a realisation sweeps across me that is so unsettling I have to put my hand out to steady myself on the sycamore tree behind me. Since arriving here – what? – some fifteen minutes or so ago, I haven't said a single word to Hope. Not one. Not even a hello. And it's not as if there's anyone around to inhibit our usual conversations. The place is quiet. Quiet as the grave. The thought springs unbidden into my head.

I stand for a moment, still steadying myself against the tree, trying to make sense of this new revelation. Then I step forwards and sink to my knees at the bottom of the burial mound, resting my hands upon the still-damp grass at the foot of the grave. The words from a poem by Mary Frye that Charlie had read aloud at the funeral come back to me. Something about the person who had died not being where they were laid to rest. *Do not stand at my grave and weep. I am not there; I do not sleep.*

That same silence I remember from my previous visit comes rushing up to meet me, and in the space that accompanies it I make no attempt to cover it up with inconsequential chit-chat like I always have in the past.

I am a thousand winds that blow. Charlie's voice comes to me across the months since she read the poem, clear as a song on the morning air.

I let the silence fill my head, soaking its way into my veins the way the damp grass is soaking through the knees of my jeans, while around me the same sunlight that is warming the back of my neck continues to sparkle on the blades of grass around my hands and to dance off the rain-heavy branches above my head.

I am the diamond glints on snow.

Nothing has changed. The realisation sweeps over me in a rush. Hope was never here. We might have buried her body in the earth, but that was all it ever was. It was always only ever silence. The only difference between the last visit and this one is inside me. For the first time since she died, I've been able to accept the silence.

Do not stand at my grave and cry. I am not there; I did not die.

But you did die, I think. You aren't here, but you did die. I just haven't been sure until now that I could carry on without you.

Gingerly I push myself to my feet and move around the side of the grave to the vase of flowers at its head, where I remove the still-protesting sunflowers from their lopsided confinement. I contemplate them for a moment, recalling the look of wonder on Hope's face when she first set eyes on a field full of them, the way her face lit up in exultation at such bounty. Suddenly, I can see her clearly in the sunflower pinafore I made her, running across the garden at home after Hector while I watched from an upstairs window, her laughter flying up into the air to meet me, and I realise that I'm holding the essence of what's left of her in my hands, captured in a bunch of sunflowers, and that while I'd have chosen a different path for all of us if I'd had any say in the matter, these memories, exquisitely painful as they are, are mine for the cherishing. All of them. The thirteen years Sam and I had together, nine of which we shared with our daughter. 'Enough,' I say aloud to myself – the first word I've spoken since I got here. Enough what? Enough grief? No, it can't be that. Somewhere inside I know I'll go on grieving for my daughter for as long as I draw breath. But I've also recognised that I *will* go on drawing breath, that in spite of everything that's happened, there is still some solace to be found in what life has left behind for me.

I take another look at the headstone. Hope Bishop. 27 June 1998 to 18 September 2007. That's all. No flowery words. No sentimental epitaph. At the time it didn't seem that words had anything to offer.

I take a single sunflower from the bunch I'm holding and lay it carefully across the burial mound. It's all I can spare. I want the rest of them at home with me, where I can soak up their beauty and relish whatever memories of Hope they hold every day when I wake up.

At the car Hector is waiting impatiently for my return, his tongue lolling from his mouth comically. 'Come on,' I tell him as I climb inside. 'Let's go home.' I turn the key in the ignition and drive away without looking back, leaving behind an empty grave marked by a solitary bright sunflower that is already starting to wilt in the heat of the sun as it climbs high into the cloudless sky.

Chapter 26

During the afternoon I take Hector out for a proper walk, the first I've attempted in months. We drive out to Lindley Wood reservoir and park at the bridge, then take ourselves off, heading north-west and following the river upstream along Norword Bottom towards Folly Hall Wood. The going is tricky underfoot after all the recent rain, but the walk is heart-stoppingly beautiful. The afternoon sun is scattering sparkling crystals across the surface of the river, and a heron, raising a curious head as we approach, takes off from the riverbank and circles the trees before coming to rest on the far side. Once upon a happier time this had been a favourite outing for the four of us. Stepping gingerly along the muddy path with Hector hard on my heels, I feel as though the two of us are reclaiming it.

We stop intermittently along the way, once so that I can soak up the views over the Washburn Valley, and shortly afterwards so that Hector can circumnavigate a field of sheep whose noisy bleating is unsettling him. He has the grace to look sheepish himself at his sudden onset of bashfulness, like he knows he's supposed to be the one doing the intimidating. 'Hector,' I tell him as the two of us struggle to negotiate a stile (never easy at the best of times; nigh-on impossible with a nervous dog on a long lead), 'you are nothing but a sheep in wolf's clothing.' He manages a quick, panting grin once we are over the stile and the killer sheep are safely behind us.

By the time we reach the car after a good four hours' hard walking, my legs are aching gratifyingly and my whole body feels as though I've wrung it out. As I'm rubbing the worst of the mud from Hector's legs with the doggy towel that lives in the boot of the car, I'm starting to fantasise about the hot bath I'll be running for myself as soon as we get back home. I might even take a glass of wine up with me. A glass of wine and a good book. I can't remember the last time I actually picked up a book and lost myself between its covers.

I am humming quietly to myself as I close the gate to the back garden and let myself in through the back door to fetch a fresh towel to finish drying Hector's paws. We should get out and about more often, the two of us. My heart feels lighter than it's felt in months.

I'm just kicking off my muddy boots and stepping into the kitchen when a voice I recognise cuts across my thoughts, and all those warm fuzzy feelings I was having curl up and die.

'Well, if it in't PC Nosey Knickers.' Ryan is leaning with his back against the Aga, watching me with an expression I don't like very much on his face. 'I heard you was looking for me.'

I almost have a heart attack on the spot. I swear this boy will be the death of me one way or another. I cover up my shock by busying myself with my boots, keeping my back to him while I line them up next to the step.

Then when I've composed myself a bit I turn and look him in the face.

'What are you doing in my house?'

Fear has lent my voice a confrontational edge, for which I'm grateful: the last thing I want is for him to suss out just how much he's shaken me. How the hell did he know I'd been asking questions about him? It's not like I left a calling card with his low-life drug-dealing mate Matthew. More to the point, how did he find out where I live?

He pushes himself off the Aga and comes over to the table. 'Thought I'd save you the bother of coming to find me,' he says, pulling out a chair and settling himself into it, swinging his feet up on the table as though he owns the place.

'How did you get in?' I sweep the kitchen with my eyes, looking for any telltale signs of a break-in. He ignores the question and gives me a nasty smile instead. 'You want to be careful whose business you go poking your nose in, you do.'

He sniffs disparagingly. 'I knew it were you, mind, the minute Matt said about you telling him you were Special Branch. Bit of a feature with you, isn't it, lying? Oh, aye,' he goes on, though I haven't said anything back to him, 'I know about that stunt you pulled in t' supermarket with Con, and all. Tells me everything, she does. Everything,' he adds, to be sure I'm getting the point.

So it was Con, then. She must have told him where I live, given him directions. Matthew must have got straight on to Ryan after I left and given him a full description, and the two of them – him and Con – must have put two and two together and figured out the rest. And yet there hadn't been a hint of it when I'd seen her in the shop earlier. My heart sinks with what I can't help but acknowledge is a ridiculous sense of betrayal. Hadn't I known all along that Con's loyalty to Ryan went beyond anything she might feel towards me?

'I'm calling the police.' I make to cross to the hall, and he moves quickly to intercept me, a familiar flash of steel glinting in his hand.

'Now, I don't think that's a very good idea, luv.' He gives a harsh laugh at the look of shock on my face. 'It's against the law, you know, making out you're a police officer. You could find yourself in a load of bother. Any road, I just want a little chat.' His eyes still bear residual traces of redness from the fire extinguisher, making him look even more dissolute than usual. He gestures with the blade of the knife. 'No need for either one of us to go getting excited.' He nods towards the table and I acquiesce reluctantly, pulling out a chair and dropping into it, any residual feeling of well-being from the afternoon killed off by the sick knot of fear in the pit of my stomach. There is something manic about him; he seems to be hanging on to his equilibrium by a thread. He returns to the seat he just vacated and starts cleaning out his nails with the tip of the knife, sucking air through his top teeth as though trying to make up his mind which bit of me he's going to cut first. I wait for him to say something, all the time weighing up the chances of my being able to reach the phone and dial for help before finding myself with my throat slit, and not liking the odds. And then, once he's quite sure I'm feeling thoroughly undermined, he stops messing with the knife and looks at me appraisingly.

'See, Marion –' He grins as my eyes widen at his casual use of my name. 'Oh aye, like I say, she tells me everything, does Con.' He pauses again to allow the full implications of what he's saying to sink in. 'Any road, thing is, I don't like people snooping around asking questions about me, poking their noses in my business. Makes me nervous, right? An' you don't want me getting nervous, Marion. Bad things happen when I get nervous.'

He sounds like a ham actor in a third-rate film. Any minute now I can just tell he's going to come out with something like, *Go ahead, punk, make my day*. I fold my arms across my chest defiantly. 'I don't really give a shit whether you like it or not.'

His eyes flash suddenly and his knuckles tighten on the handle of the knife, and I get that same sense that he's a ticking bomb set to go off any minute. 'Right cocky bitch, in't you? You know, one o' these days, that mouth o' yours is going to get you into a lot of trouble, Marion.' He draws out my name slowly, 'Ma-ri-on', gritting his teeth slightly, as though trying to suppress some uncontrollable rage that is bubbling away inside him. Then all of a sudden he laughs, and his shoulders relax. 'You weren't frightened last time either, were you? Fucking nightmare, you were.' I'm kind of hoping that as far as he's concerned, last time was when he was mugging me, rather than when I was spraying hazardous chemicals into his face.

'What d'you want, Ryan?' I allow a degree of impatience to spill into my voice.

'Now, in't this nice?' He smiles at me, a sickly sort of smile that is somehow full of menace. 'You and me, just like old friends.' He sucks his teeth again and gives me a considering look. 'Shouldn't it be me asking you what you want? You're the one came looking for me. Not come back for a bit more action, have you? Fancy a bit o' rough, do you? 'Cause, you know, Marion, that can always be arranged.' He leers at me in a way that turns my stomach.

'What d'you want?' I stick doggedly to my question. I won't give him the satisfaction of seeing I'm afraid.

'Turning me down, are you?' He licks his lips at me lasciviously. 'That's harsh, is that.' He studies the blade of the knife closely, sucking his teeth again, and his next words send a chill down my spine. 'You cut me deep, Marion.'

'What –' I articulate the words slowly and deliberately through gritted teeth '– do you want?'

Abruptly his face hardens again: he's up and down like a whore's knickers, as Charlie would say. 'I'll tell you what I want, Marion. I want you –' he gestures at me with the point of the knife '– to stay away from me and my business. Stop asking questions about me. Keep your nose out.'

I shrug, affecting a nonchalance I don't feel. 'Or what? It's a free country. I'll do as I please.'

He leaps up suddenly and sweeps a hand out, scattering everything from the sideboard behind him to the floor – papers, a lamp, the photograph of Sam and Hope, which smashes noisily into a shower of broken glass against the edge of the table. I keep my face studiously neutral whilst he has his outburst. He's not to know that underneath my calm exterior my heart is galloping along like the leading horse in the Grand National with the bit between its teeth.

'Look, you –' He leans in close all of a sudden, holding up a threatening finger which, oddly, I find more intimidating than the knife. Maybe it's because I think he's more likely to use it. 'I've had just about enough of your lip. You want to watch yourself, lady.'

I see in a sudden flash the recollection of a bruised neck, a hand raised to cover the marks and a cold blanket of fear washes over me. 'Con didn't tell you where I live, did she?'

The sudden change of subject throws him. ''Course she did. Like I say, she tells me everything.'

'Really?' In spite of the fear, I give him a look of disgust. 'And just how many times did you have to hit her before she told you?'

It's the last straw as far as Ryan's concerned. I see something snap behind his eyes, and his arm flies backwards. And then my vision dissolves in an explosion of stars as he brings his fist down upon me, knocking me from my chair and sending me sprawling onto the kitchen floor, where I land awkwardly with a sharp cry of pain. The next few moments are an eruption of confusion, noise and screaming. Somewhere in the chaos another chair goes flying, and this time I know somewhere deep inside me that I've pushed him too far. And I'm raging: raging that this yob has broken into my house just when I've finally decided that I want to live, and seems hell-bent on preventing me from doing so. The screaming continues, though I'm not sure which of us is actually making the noise. I see him coming towards me with the knife held aloft, yelling words at me I can't make any sense of, and I fill my lungs with the sweet need to live and hurl words back in his face. If he's going to kill me, as he keeps threatening to do, I'll be damned if I'm going to go quietly. On and on I scream, yelling words at him I didn't realise I knew, waiting all the time for the next blow to land, bracing myself almost, seeing him come at me with the knife at the ready, and then in the midst of it all the back door is pushed open, causing him to halt with his arm held aloft, and Hector trots curiously into the kitchen to see what all the commotion is about.

Hector. My God. Hope's wouldn't-hurt-a-fly darling dog, who would lick an intruder to death sooner than show any aggression. I am filled suddenly with absolute terror at the thought of what Ryan might be capable of with a creature as gentle as him.

'Don't touch him.' The words are out before I've had a chance to engage my brain. In the cacophony of silence that follows the noise and confusion I suddenly realise that Ryan has frozen where he stands, and is regarding Hector with a look of utter terror in his eyes.

I can't believe it. He's just standing there, not daring to move, the frenzied attack brought to an abrupt halt by the appearance of the softest dog God ever gave breath to. I don't hesitate to take full advantage of this tiny sliver of hope. 'Keep absolutely still,' I instruct him. 'He won't hurt you if you do exactly what I say.'

If it occurs to Ryan to be suspicious about my saving him from my savage guard dog when he'd been about to do heaven alone knows what to me, he is too terrified to register the thought. I ease myself gingerly to my feet; every muscle in my body seems to cry out in protest. 'Come here, um, Satan.' (Well, I can hardly call him Hector, can I? I might as well stick a ruddy great notice on his back saying STAB HERE.)

Hector ignores me. I can't really blame him: he's never been big on instant obedience, having been bred from ancestors with the kind of independent thinking that would stop them from being driven by their ignorant owners to pull a heavily stacked sled across ice that they knew was too thin to support them. Hector's twenty-first century motives are less noble: he just prefers to weigh up what's in it for him if he does as he's told and, as far as he's concerned, I don't even have the manners to address him by his real name. After regarding each of us for a moment, and deciding that Ryan looks considerably more interesting than me, he trots across the kitchen to greet him. Ryan's eyes widen in panic. 'Call him off!' he threatens. 'Otherwise I'll kill him, swear down I will!' He waves the hand holding the knife around wildly. Sensing that his new acquaintance wants to play, Hector jumps up and places two massive paws against Ryan's rather puny chest, and the knife, to my utter heart-stopping relief, clatters noisily to the floor.

Ryan is beside himself. 'Get him off!' He pushes ineffectually at Hector, who seizes one of his hands in his great, gentle mouth. 'Aaaargh!' cries Ryan. 'Aaargh! Call him off! Aaaargh!' Hector is loving it; a low howl, somewhat muffled by the fist he is holding between his teeth, escapes from his mouth in response to Ryan's cries, a sure sign that he's having the time of his life.

By now Ryan is almost passing out with terror, and is aiming ineffectual kicks at the dog's massive chest. Hector can't believe his luck: nobody's played with him like this for months. Sam used to wrestle with him on the living-room floor, with Hope looking on and gurgling with laughter at the two of them romping together on the rug, but that hasn't happened since the old benchmark of the accident, along with a lot of other things. The next time Ryan raises his foot to try to fend off his assailant, Hector seizes the rather expensive-looking trainer in his mouth and begins worrying at it with Ryan's foot still anchored firmly inside it. He has his jaws tightly wrapped around the sole of the trainer and has begun tugging on it, his paws planted firmly on the floor and the whole of his not inconsiderable body weight thrusting backwards, while all the time he continues to emit low yowls of delight. Hope used to say he sounded like Scoobydoo talking when he started his howling, but I don't think Ryan spots the similarity. He is clutching hold of the kitchen worktop, white with fright and emitting small whimpering sounds as he tries to avoid being dragged clean off his feet by an enthusiastic Hector.

I limp across and retrieve the knife from where it's landed next to the sink, and hide it in the cupboard while Ryan's attention is otherwise engaged. Then when I've done that I go and open the door to the scullery and step out.

'Where're you going? Don't leave me!' Ryan's voice is shrill with panic.

I ignore him and cross to the cupboard where we store all of Hector's food and treats, and pick out a couple of the dried sausages he loves so much he'd do anything for them. In the kitchen Ryan, thinking I've abandoned him to one of the hounds of hell, bursts into noisy tears. I wait until he's really sobbing, and then I go back into the kitchen and stand regarding the pair of them for a moment. By now he has slipped onto the floor under the barrage of Hector's relentless tugging at his shoe, and is trying to shield his face with his arms, lest the vicious creature make a lunge for his throat. I put myself out of his line of vision, where Hector can see me plainly, and I show him the sausages. At the same time I say, very quietly, 'Satan. Come here.'

Wrong name or not, he doesn't hesitate, as I knew he wouldn't. In an instant Ryan is forgotten, the trainer and accompanying foot (still attached to the leg, luckily for Ryan) dropped. Ears pricked forwards, tail held high and tongue hanging out of his mouth expectantly, he trots eagerly to my side, coming in to heel and sitting without being asked, his face raised adoringly to mine. Ryan is shocked into immobility; he can't believe I have this kind of power over such a monster. When he's not looking, scrutinising his foot for signs of permanent damage (of which, of course, there's none: Hector is all bluff, though happily Ryan doesn't know that), I sneak Hector one of the sausages, making sure he knows there are more where that one came from. Then I cross to the table and pick up the chair that got knocked over earlier and sit myself down. Hector, never one to look a gift sausage in the mouth, lopes after me and curls himself meekly around my feet, his mouth open and his tongue lolling. He looks for all the world as though he's enjoying a bloody good laugh at someone else's expense. Which, of course, he is.

I keep him there beside me, where I know he'll stay for as long as it takes to try to levitate the remaining sausage out of my hand, and turn my attention to Ryan, who is still snivelling gratifyingly on the floor and nursing his mauled trainer (impressively undamaged apart from the liberal application of dog saliva) in his hands. 'Well,' I say after a moment, 'what do you suppose I should do now, Ryan? What would you do, if you were me?'

I'm treated by way of a response to a baleful look from Ryan. 'Fuck you,' he mutters under his breath, and Hector, sensing his newfound pal is rallying, ready for another bout of wrestling, jumps to his feet. Ryan visibly recoils, pressing himself right into the corner of the units as though if he tries hard enough he might be able to lose himself under the kick boards. 'Down, Satan,' I say to Hector, giving him a quick glimpse of the remaining sausage, and he drops like a stone. 'Now,' I say, turning back to Ryan, 'first of all, I'd like you to tell me how you got into my house.'

He mutters something again, and Hector pricks up his ears. 'Window,' he says hastily, nodding towards the small window on the wall next to the back door, the one I always keep open because it stops the kitchen steaming up when I'm cooking (not that I've been doing a terrific amount of that recently) – the one, I might add, that I've always felt safe leaving open, because it's so small you'd be hard-pushed to squeeze a cat through the gap.

I shake my head at him. 'No way. Not even with your puny bone structure.'

He looks at me with loathing. 'I didn't come right through t' window. Ah reached through and unlocked the back door.'

'Ah.' That possibility had never occurred to me. I make a mental note to remove the key from the back door in future if I leave the window ajar.

I look at him now, curled up like a cornered rat on the kitchen floor, snivelling still but trying to recover some shred of bravado to wrap his pride in. 'How did you find out where I live?' I ask him eventually.

'I said, didn't I? Con told me.'

I shake my head, sick to my stomach. 'I don't believe you.' I don't *want* to believe him, I should say.

I find myself feeling overwhelmingly tired all of a sudden, every muscle in my body complaining and my wrist throbbing angrily after the rough treatment it's just received. The picture of Hope and Sam is lying in pieces at my feet. I reach down and pick it up wearily, studying the somewhat battered faces of the two people I love most in the world, and realise I can't be bothered with Ryan any more – him or Con. Whether or not she was responsible for him tracking me down, I'm exhausted with all the hassle, all the aggression and violence that has invaded my life since I met the pair of them. I run my finger across the photograph to try to smooth out some of the creases, dismayed to find that the broken glass has torn a hole right in the middle of it, where Hope and Sam are leaning their heads together and grinning at the camera. This is all that matters to me – what's left to me of my daughter and my husband. Not some dropped-off-the-edge no-hopers whose lives have temporarily collided with mine. I fell into a world I don't much like that night when he tried to relieve me of my purse, partly through my own fault, I acknowledge silently. Somewhere inside my head, as though from a great distance, I can hear Con's voice telling me she's scum, warning me, maybe, of what I was getting involved in. I take another look at her snivelling boyfriend glowering at me truculently from the corner of my kitchen after chalking up yet another foiled attack, and a great wave of defeat washes over me. There's nothing to be done for either one of them. As far as Con's concerned, Ryan looks after her. Who am I to judge how well he does that? The two of them are probably perfectly happy without any outside interference from a screwed-up do-gooder like me. I should have left well alone, stayed away from Con instead of fixing her up with Esme. God knows how I'm going to be able to sort that mess out now. I close my eyes and tilt my head back wearily with a sigh.

'I'd like you to leave now,' I say.

He stares up at me with a mixture of hope and disgust on his face, as though he can't believe either his luck or my lily-liveredness. 'What?' He gives a snort of derision. 'Thought you were gonna ring t' police.'

'Don't push me, Ryan.' I don't know why I'm even bothering to talk to him any more. I just want him out of my house, out and away somewhere I don't have to look at his disgusting, snot-smeared, nasty face any more. 'Just get out. And I'm warning you: if I see so much as the back of your head anywhere around here, I'll let Satan here finish what he started.'

He scrambles hastily to his feet and, as he does so, Hector leaps up once again, eager to resume their rough-and-tumble game. I put my hand on his neck to restrain him. 'Go on,' I tell Ryan, nodding towards the back door. 'Get out.'

He's gone before I can change my mind, hurling himself out through the door into the garden as though escaping an inferno. As soon as he disappears Hector hurls himself off in pursuit, oblivious to my efforts to hold on to him, intent only on catching up with his new buddy for whatever new game he's dreamed up. I hurry as fast as my aching limbs will allow to the door, just in time to see Ryan vaulting onto the wall, a leg left dangling tantalisingly for just a second while his hands grapple to find a grip in the mortar along the top of the wall: just long enough, in fact, for Hector to seize upon the hapless trainer and give it one last tug. The final sight I have of Ryan is his white face, rigid with fright as he disappears over the far side of the wall, while Hector, realising the game's over, comes trotting back to see whether there's anything left of the sausages he's seen me with earlier, carrying a newly acquired trainer like a trophy proudly in his mouth.

Chapter 27

Somewhere from the depths of sleep, I can hear a bell ringing. On and on it goes, and I do my best to turn a deaf ear, but its persistent shrill sound just won't let up.

I drag myself to consciousness and sit up in bed, disorientated, picking up the alarm clock from the bedside table and scrutinising it through sleep-heavy eyes, stabbing ineffectually at the snooze button: 11.46, it reads. Quarter to twelve. When did I ever set such a late alarm? The ringing continues relentlessly, and eventually it dawns on me that it's not the clock that's making the noise. Downstairs, someone is leaning heavily on the doorbell and not going away.

Much as I would like it to be, I know it isn't Sam. He isn't due back from Nakuru for another fortnight at least. Long, long ago in a different life, Hope and I used to go to the airport in Leeds to meet him off his flights when he'd been away, though in those days they were short trips: a three-day hop across the Atlantic for a conference in Boston, an overnighter in Lyon for some convention or other. He couldn't get back to us fast enough in those days. The two of us would stand as close as we could get to the arrivals barrier, Hope hopping from one foot to the other in her impatience to see her daddy. 'When is he coming?' she would demand to know, as though I had X-ray vision and could see straight through the wall. 'Soon,' I would tell her. 'Any minute now.' And she would hop a bit more and crane her short body around those of the other people clustered around the arrivals gate, and suddenly there he would be, delivered up from the customs hall looking tired but infinitely sexy, his eyes scanning the crowd for the two of us, and my heart would give a skip of happiness. Hope would break free of my restraining hand and run down the bit you weren't supposed to go beyond, unstoppable, to get to him as quickly as she could. He would scoop her up in a hug, his eyes still searching me out, while she wrapped her legs around his waist like a baby chimp, turning his face with the palms of her hands so that she could pepper his cheek with kisses. Even at nine, when she'd started to worry about looking cool in front of other people, it would all go out of the window in the arrivals hall at Leeds Bradford Airport. Sam used to say it was the highlight of his trip, that moment when he caught sight of the two of us, that it was almost worth going away for.

Downstairs the ringing continues. I push back the duvet with a sigh. Frankly, after the events of yesterday, I just want to be left to pull the covers over my head and sleep for about a hundred years. I'm done with interfering in other people's lives, done with trying to sort out anyone else. If I can just get through one day at a time (suddenly all the well-meaning advice of friends after the funeral makes perfect sense), I figure it'll be enough of an achievement.

After Hector had seen Ryan off the premises, I'd sat for more than half an hour in the disarray left in the kitchen, staring at the broken chair and the shattered glass scattered across the floor, cradling my sprained wrist and wondering what had happened to my life. I couldn't quite take in the fact that just I'd been attacked in my own kitchen. Somewhere in the midst of my shock, the thought went through my head that maybe I should call the police, but I lacked the energy even for that. I don't know why: I suppose I just wanted to be done with the whole sorry episode. I didn't even have the energy to clean up the mess. Instead I went through to the living room with a brandy for myself and a bowl of dog food for Hector, and sat with the TV on mute, staring at the screen and not really taking in what I was watching. Around nine I took the pair of us off upstairs, where I climbed into bed, cradling a fresh brandy in my left hand, my right arm around Hector, who, in recognition of the part he'd played in ridding us of Ryan, had been allowed to sprawl out at the top end of the bed for once. I'd fallen asleep like that, lulled by the brandy, my arm still wrapped around the dog.

The bell is still ringing away – whoever's outside isn't giving up in a hurry. I ease myself to my feet with a groan. 'All right!' I grumble, shuffling across the carpet. 'I'm coming.' In his newfound role as hero, Hector pushes himself off the bed and follows hard on my heels.

Much to my surprise, it's Esme, looking harassed. 'Shouldn't you be at the shop?' I say, pulling the door open wide.

'I've just nipped out,' she tells me, stepping into the hall. 'Left a note on the door. It's almost lunch time, anyway.

I'm that worried, I cannae think straight.' She looks at me properly and her face drops. 'Oh my! Oh, dear, dear, dear. What happened to you?'

I turn to the mirror. The side of my face that Ryan hit when he knocked me off my chair is puffy and swollen, and the beginnings of a black eye are just starting to emerge. 'Oh, great,' I mutter under my breath. 'Worried about what?' I ask, turning back to Esme. 'Look, let's go through.' I stop abruptly on the threshold of the kitchen, and she almost runs into me. 'Oh sorry, it's a bit of a state in here.'

Her eyes widen as she takes in the broken glass and splintered chair. 'Oh, dear,' she says, her face falling even further. 'Oh, that's exactly what I was afraid about.' She shakes her head in despair at the mess.

'What d'you mean? Esme? What were you afraid about? Look, come through to the living room.' I close the door on the mess and point the way.

'I tried phoning,' she tells me as she sits down, 'but there was no answer, and your mailbox was full so I couldn't leave a message.'

I shoot a look at the answerphone. Maybe that's why I haven't heard from Sam. I have to resist the urge to go over and delete all the messages, so that I can concentrate on what Esme's saying. She launches into a rambling explanation that makes no sense at all to me.

'I thought she was reliable,' she starts. 'Did you not hear me calling her Constance? Not Con, even though she said to me that first day that everyone called her Con, said she didn't look like a Constance. I told her straight, I said, of course she looked like a Constance, because she looked the constant sort – the sort that wouldn't let you down. Didn't you think she had that look about her?'

'Um, I don't know.' I try to marshal my spiralling thoughts, to concentrate on what Esme's saying. I remember the fight we had, the fierce way she defended her relationship with Ryan. 'Yes, I suppose she is constant. In her own way.'

'Of course, that'll be one of the things that drew you to her in the first place, her name. Constance. So close to Hope. I expect you must have felt a connection there somehow. I certainly did, that day you brought her into the shop and introduced her to me. Put me in mind of one of Paul's letters, I cannae mind which one.'

'*Paul?*' I frown at her in confusion: the way she said his name, I'm obviously supposed to know who he is. 'Who's Paul?'

She gives her head a dismissive shake. 'Och, you know – Paul. The apostle. The one who was converted on the road to Damascus. He wrote about having constancy in hope. I think it was to the Thessalonians.' She lapses into a heavy silence, lost in thought.

I stare at her, dumbfounded. The correlation between the girls' names had never crossed my mind. But now Esme's pointed it out, I find myself wondering if that's what has lain behind the nagging feeling I've had ever since I met Con – that feeling that she was somehow connected to Hope. The prospect of such a mundane explanation is disappointing somehow. I try to focus back on Esme.

'Esme, is something wrong?'

She drags herself back to me. 'Well, obviously something's wrong. Look at the state of your face.' She tsks and shakes her head.

I shake my head impatiently. 'Never mind that. You were telling me about Con. Has something happened to her?'

'That's what I'm away to tell you. She didn't turn up for work today.' She pronounces this as though it has earth-shattering implications, and then sits back to see what effect it's had on me.

I can feel my face falling into a confused frown. 'Well, perhaps she's ill. Did she seem OK yesterday evening when she left? Weren't the two of you going to B & Q or something?'

'Yes, and that's just it. We never got there. About – oh – an hour after you'd left, some laddie turned up at the shop for her.'

'What laddie?'

She shakes her head slowly. 'Don't know who he was. Greasy hair. Bad skin. Constance went as white as a sheet when he came in.'

My stomach lurches. 'What did he want?'

'I've no idea. Soon as the door opened and he came into the shop, Constance was out from round the back of the counter like a shot and shooing him back outside onto the pavement. I could see them talking there from inside the shop. Couldn't hear what they were saying, mind, but he didn't look happy, put it that way, and neither did she. One time, he thumped on the shop window so hard I thought he was going to put it in. And then Constance came back in the shop and said she had to go – said her mum wasn't very well. I mind what you told me about her not having seen her mum in however long it's been, but I said nothing to her: I mean, it could have been true, couldn't it? You just never know, even though you have your doubts, so you've to mind what you say. You don't want to be putting your foot in it. So I said to her, "Well, not to worry, I'll see you in the morning, will I?" And she said she hoped so, yes. And then she went off to get her coat, her face tripping her, mind, and him still waiting outside the shop looking like he was chewing a wasp. I wrapped a bunch of those peony roses up while she was away fetching her coat, and I gave them to her and said to give them to her mum and say I hoped she felt better soon, and then when she'd gone I went outside and there were the peonies, just dropped on the pavement, like someone had thrown them away. And then she didn't turn up this morning. I couldn't help but think something was wrong, and then I come round here and find you looking like you've gone ten rounds with Mike Tyson, and there's something terribly wrong and I don't know what it is. Constance wouldn't just up and leave like that without a word. I know she's only been with me the week, but I could tell she was enjoying it.'

I sigh laboriously. 'Well, maybe she just isn't as . . . as *constant* . . . as you or I would like to believe. Not to you or me, anyway. Maybe she keeps all her constancy for Ryan. She certainly seems to have a bit of a blind spot as far as he's concerned. If he's turned up throwing his weight around and telling her he doesn't want her working there, she's quite likely to just jack the job in and go back to being the lookout for all his criminal activities.'

Esme's face falls. 'You don't really believe that, do you?'

'Oh, Esme, I don't know!' I throw my hands up in despair. 'All I know is, Ryan turned up here yesterday evening, in a major strop at me for what he called poking my nose into his business, and warning me off for the future.' I touch the side of my head gingerly. 'This was just him driving home his message.'

'Aye?' Esme leans over for a closer scrutiny of my eye and wrinkles her nose in sympathy. 'He must have given you quite a wallop for that to come up like that.' She hesitates. 'But how did he know where you live?'

My mouth twists. 'There's only one way he could know.' Her face crumples in confusion. 'Con must have told him.'

'Och, no.' Esme looks at me askance. 'No, no, no. Constance wouldn't do that, surely? I cannae believe that about her.'

I give a small shrug. 'Wouldn't she? You're the one that said she was constant. We don't get to pick where her loyalties lie. He told me she tells him everything. That figures, really, given that he knew exactly where to come to find her in the shop.'

Esme's not happy. 'You don't think he . . . well, he . . . forced her to tell him, do you?' Her face contorts with disgust at the idea.

I shrug my shoulders resignedly. 'I did moot that idea with him. He didn't take the suggestion too well – hence the mess in the kitchen. But even if he did, there's nothing you or I can do about it. If she chooses to stay with him, that's her decision. I mean, I know he's hit her before. She never upped and left him then. In fact, she went nuts at me when I told her he wasn't good for her, he didn't really love her. She just didn't want to hear it. And you can't help someone who won't be helped, Esme. Believe me, I've tried.' I gesture towards my face. 'This is where it got me.'

She is wringing her hands together. 'What should we do, then?'

I shake my head, dismissing both Con and Ryan from my thoughts, remembering my decision to stop trying to interfere in other people's lives and just to concentrate on taking one day at a time. 'I'm going to get my kitchen cleaned up. And then I'm going to make a cup of tea. I hope you'll stay and join me.'

Her face drops in disappointment. 'Aye, OK. I just don't like the thought of doing nothing. She's such a lovely girl: it's a crying shame. But you're right, I suppose: you can't help someone who won't be helped.'

I know I'm right, though I don't point this out to Esme as the two of us set about collecting up the bits and pieces of broken glass and splintered wood and restoring the kitchen to some sort of order. I know just exactly how intractable a person can be when they won't be helped, exactly how much havoc they can create for the poor fools who try to help them.

I've got the T-shirt.

Chapter 28

I'm just back from a short walk with Hector in the afternoon after Esme's left, sunglasses clamped firmly over my black eye to avoid frightening small children and animals while we're out, and I find the answerphone flashing away in the living room. I'd deleted all the old messages before we left, after Esme's comment about not being able to get hold of me because my mailbox was full. Sam, I immediately think, almost breaking a leg on the edge of the coffee table in my haste to get across to listen to it. He's probably been trying to call me for weeks, and hasn't been able to leave a message because the mailbox has been full.

'Marion, it's Charlie.' My sister's voice is like a balm, a symbol of something normal in my life, an anchor that's about a million miles from Ryan and Con and the sordid world they inhabit. 'Look, I've been calling you for bloody weeks now but you're never in. I've left you a gazillion messages but you obviously haven't picked any of them up because you haven't phoned me back, so this is just a last-ditch attempt to get hold of you. I have news. Exciting news. There: that's all you're getting. Call me as soon as you get this message. I mean straight away. You won't get me after about three, and it will be too late then, so hurry up.'

Intrigued, I check the clock. It's already after two. I pick up the receiver and dial Charlie's number in Michigan. She answers virtually before the phone has had a chance to ring.

'Marion! About bloody time. Where the hell have you been?'

'Um –' *Trying to kill myself.* The thought of that suicide attempt now, in the light of my sister's utter normality, sends a shiver through my body. 'Just – out and about. You know.'

'No, I don't bloody know. I've been worried sick.'

'Have you?'

'Of course I have. At least, until I got hold of Sam,' she amends.

I swallow. 'You spoke to Sam?'

'Well, I had no choice, did I? I've been trying to get hold of you for weeks. I even tried your mobile the other day, and I couldn't get through, number unobtainable, it said, and then I did start to panic a bit, and so I rang Sam's number. And you know how I hate ringing your mobiles. Costs a bloody fortune. But at least he answered. And he's out in darkest Peru or somewhere –'

'Africa,' I correct her. My throat has thickened.

'Well, whatever. I mean, what's he thinking about, running off to Africa like that?'

I hesitate before answering, wondering whether Sam has said anything to Charlie about leaving me. 'Didn't he tell you?' I eventually say, thinking I might prise a bit more information out of her that way.

'He said something about an exchange programme with the hospital. I wasn't really paying attention: I just wanted to know if you were OK.'

'And what did he say?' I hold my breath, waiting for her answer.

'He said you were finding things a bit tough at the moment. Which begs the question, quite frankly, as to why he's buggered off and left you.' My breath catches when she says that, but then she sweeps on, 'He says it's only for a few weeks, but all the same. I think it's a bit rich.'

'Yes, well.' An odd pang of loyalty towards Sam prods at my conscience. 'He needed a change of scene. Things haven't been . . . easy.' It's funny: Charlie's articulating all the thoughts that have gone through my head about Sam's leaving, and yet hearing her put them into words makes me feel defensive towards him. Of course he needed to get away. I'd just have felt a whole lot better about him going if I'd known he was planning to come back to me eventually.

'Well, that goes for you, too, I'm sure. You must feel like running away as well. Which is where I come into the equation.'

'Oh, Charlie –' She's going to invite me out to Michigan, I just know she is. And even the prospect of trying to undertake the journey is exhausting. 'I can't. I'm knackered. Plus there's Hector: I couldn't leave him.'

'Oh, I'm not suggesting you come out here.' She pauses dramatically. 'I'm coming over there. Well, not quite there. But to the UK. This evening. With Harry. That's why you had to call me straight away. Our flight leaves at six. We've got to go in half an hour. I was frantic, thinking I was going to have to leave without speaking to you.'

'But what are you coming over for? And who's Harry?'

'He's a colleague of mine. He's been offered a professor-ship at Edinburgh University, and he has to come over to talk to them. He wants to make a holiday of it, so he's booked us a cottage on one of the islands off the west coast of Scotland, and I want you to come and join us there for a few days. You can bring Hector. Harry loves dogs.'

'Oh – whoa! Hold on a minute.' My head is spinning. 'He's a colleague of yours, this Harry?'

'Yes.' Her tone is impatient: typical Charlie – she just wants to cut to the chase.

'And you're coming all the way back to the UK with him so that he can go for a job interview.'

'It's a bit more than an interview. He's already been offered the post. He just wants to go over and see what he thinks of the university, the city, all that jazz.'

'But you're going on holiday with him. To an island.' I sniff suspiciously, antennae at the ready. 'Sounds like he's a bit more than a colleague to me.'

She bursts out laughing. 'I'm not telling you any more, not until I see you. You *are* going to come, aren't you? You've got to, Marion. I really want you to meet him.'

I think about her invitation. It's such a breath of normality, talking to her. She's upbeat, sparky, bubbling with energy and excitement. It's such a far cry from anything I've had going on in my life recently, I can't resist it. Plus, I'm curious about Harry. My sister has been steadfastly single to my knowledge since she moved out to Michigan, despite her assertions about the male/female ratio when she'd been planning the move. I find myself desperate to see her all of a sudden.

'Which island is it?' I ask.

She gives a great whoop of delight. 'Yes! That means you're coming. Doesn't it? You are, aren't you?'

I give a sigh, though I'm smiling into the phone at the same time. 'Well I can't, can I, if you don't tell me where I'm coming?'

'Oh my God! This is brilliant. I really thought I was never going to get hold of you, that I'd have to wait until I got there and then it would be too late and you wouldn't be able to come. But I did and it isn't and you can. This is great. It's Mull. We're going to Mull. We're leaving tonight, flying overnight from Detroit to Gatwick, then up to Edinburgh, and picking up a car at the airport. We should be at the cottage by tea time, as long as we don't miss any of our connections. I mean, we'll be knackered, probably, but then we've got the next few days to be lazy and do nothing, and then Harry's got his meeting in Edinburgh on the Wednesday and he's got to go through on the Tuesday evening, so you and I can just chill out together and talk about him, and it'll be completely wicked. Harry's got all your directions worked out. So, how soon can you come? Tomorrow?'

My head is spinning by the time she pauses for an answer. 'Erm – I don't know! Won't you want a couple of days to get over your jet lag? What if I came after Harry gets back from Edinburgh?'

'No, that's no good at all.' Charlie's tone is dismissive. 'We'll only have a couple of days left by then, and I want you for much longer than that. Besides, if we're jet-lagged, you can take Hector out for a walk while we grab some zeds.'

'Well . . .' I must admit, the idea of just taking off with barely a moment's notice is tempting. 'I'll need to look up ferries and stuff.'

'No you don't. I told you, Harry's done all that stuff already. Have you got a pen?'

'No!' I can't help laughing at her enthusiasm. 'Just a minute.' As I put the receiver down to go on the hunt for a pen and a pad, I feel like I've just shed about a decade. 'Right,' I say once I've found the bits and pieces I need. 'Tell me what this Harry person has worked out.'

'OK. Well, you need to get the Corran ferry from Lochaber to Ardgour. That's about ten miles south of Fort William. You can look it up on Multimap if you like, but Harry says if you just point the car at Scotland and get yourself onto the A82 and keep going, you can't miss it. You get to drive right through Glencoe. It'll be magic. Then when you reach Ardgour, you head towards Lochaline, and pick up the ferry there for Fishnish.' She spells the names out for me. 'Aren't they the craziest names you ever heard? It's all signposted, apparently. After that it's about half an hour to Tobermory, which is where we're staying. Well, nearby, anyway. Sort of. Are you writing this all down?'

'Yes!' I am scribbling frantically. 'But what am I going to do with Hector on the ferry?'

'That's the best bit. He can just stay in the car. The crossings are really short. The Corran ferry only takes about five minutes – you can see the shoreline opposite when you board, apparently. The Fishnish one's a bit longer – that's about fifteen minutes. But even that's bearable – you can sit in the car with him. That's why Harry picked them. If you went up to Oban and got the ferry there, he'd be stuck in the car much longer and you wouldn't be able to stay with him, and I said to Harry he would probably eat the seat belts.'

'God, Charlie.' My head is still spinning. 'I'm going to have to be up with the birds.'

'Well, yes you are, but you can manage that, can't you? It's about a seven-hour drive door-to-door. Well, door-to-ferry, anyway. The Corran ferry is every half-hour, but the last one to Fishnish on a Sunday is at a quarter to six, and I do want you there tomorrow. I want to squeeze as much time with you as I can out of this trip. So the last possible Corran ferry you can get is the quarter past four one, but Harry says to aim for the quarter to four one just in case. Which means if you drive at your usual snail's pace, you will have to set off at about half-seven tomorrow morning. That includes a half-hour stop every couple of hours for Hector,' she says, a wheedling tone creeping into her voice. 'You *will* come, won't you, Marion?'

I sit back in the chair and reflect for a moment, looking around my once-lively living room, taking in the tidiness, the emptiness, the total suffocating quiet, and suddenly a great bubble of excitement at the prospect of running away from it all wells up inside me.

'Yes!' I say into the receiver, and across the Atlantic Charlie gives another whoop of delight. 'Yes, I'll come. I'll see you tomorrow for tea.'

I'm getting ready to hang up, when she gives an awkward cough. 'Erm, there's just one other thing.'

'You mean aside from dropping everything here –' I cast another look around the living room, '– not that there's much to drop – and getting up at the crack of dawn to drive halfway up the country with a large and drooling dog at my side?'

'Yeah, apart from that. Don't bring a suitcase.'

'Pardon?'

'Put all your stuff in a rucksack. The cottage isn't accessible by car, so when you get to Tobermory you'll have to find somewhere to park the car and walk the rest of the way. Take your phone and give us a call once you get to Fishnish, and Harry will come in to Tobermory and meet you. Look, I've got to run. I just heard the car horn. Oh my God, can't wait. Love you.'

'Charlie!' Just what kind of godforsaken place has she booked? 'I haven't got a phone. My mobile's broken.' An ominous silence comes back at me from the other end of the line. 'Hello? Are you still there?' There's no answer: somewhere thousands of miles across the Atlantic, Charlie is running out of her apartment to catch a flight home.

Chapter 29

Two other vehicles are already queuing at the tiny ferry terminal when I pull up shortly after three o'clock on Sunday afternoon. The first is a shiny red MG with the top down, its occupants basking in the warmth of what's turned out to be a spectacularly sunny day. The second is a battered light-blue Land Rover with a couple of sheep in the back, whose driver appears to be asleep behind the wheel.

We're early. I'd barely been able to sleep last night; I was too excited at the prospect of seeing my sister again, at the idea of taking off with scarcely a moment's notice. I managed a couple of broken hours between about midnight and five-thirty, and then I threw the towel in and got up, made a huge flask of coffee and some sandwiches, took Hector for a very quick early morning walk, grabbed the rucksack I'd stuffed with a variety of clothes the previous evening (an old one of Sam's that I don't think had seen the light of day since before our wedding), piled everything into the Passat and set off shortly before six-thirty. We stopped once south of the border, at a service station in Carlisle about two and a half hours into the journey, and then not again until we were well on our way into Scotland, after we'd skirted around Glasgow's industrialised fringes and the landscape had gradually given way to rolling hills and sparkling blue rivers and suddenly, amazingly, a great expanse of water that the signposts pronounced to be Loch Lomond. I found myself humming under my breath about its bonny bonny banks and then stopped, laughing at myself and feeling foolish and touristy. As we followed the shores of the loch, Hector sat up on the back seat, resting his head on my shoulder and thumping his tail. 'All right,' I told him, smiling at his laughing face in the mirror. 'I could do with stretching my legs as well.' I pulled over in a lay-by at a place called Luss, where the hills reached high into the sky, and the two of us abandoned the car for a quick foray along the shores of the loch.

It was spectacularly beautiful. Sunlight danced across the surface of the loch, and clusters of Sunday morning visitors were taking advantage of the good weather to swim and picnic around its shores. Further out, a water skier was cutting a graceful swath behind a motor boat whose engine droned like a persistent bee across the warm morning air, whilst a couple of jet-skiers dipped and lunged clumsily across the water. After all the rain we'd had in Yorkshire, I felt like I'd been beamed across to some balmy Italian mountain resort. I retraced my steps back to the car and brought out the sandwiches and the flask, and made my way back down to the shore again with Hector, where we commandeered a free bench and spent a lazy half-hour people-watching and eating the sandwiches. I closed my eyes and tilted my face to the sun, letting it warm my face, feeing the holiday atmosphere starting to soothe away the stresses of the last few weeks. Con and Ryan and all their problems seemed light years away.

Tempting as it was to loiter, I eventually gathered up the remains of our modest picnic and pushed on north. As the countryside became more sparsely populated and villages gave way to solitary stone-built houses that hugged the hillside, the tranquility of the landscape pulled me further and further into itself until Harrogate and all its heartache seemed a lifetime away. Ahead of me the hills climbed ever higher into an impossibly blue sky, and mountain streams spilled into broad rivers that tumbled and splashed their way across the rocky beds of the valleys. Then, just short of seven hours into our journey, the lush ground fell away into a craggy wilderness over which the mountains towered majestically, clad in rough heather and bracken and crowned with dark, brooding rock. There was an untamed feel to the land now that caught in my throat somehow and, alone with Hector in the car, I felt small and vulnerable. As the road swept around the fringes of another loch, I pulled over for the third time in my journey and, leaving Hector behind this time, I stepped from the car and took a moment to acclimatise myself to the sheer scale of the landscape surrounding me. In spite of all the exploring I'd ever done in the Yorkshire hills over the years, I'd never experienced anything like the sheer wildness of this lonely place before. It was raw, untrammelled: man and all his trappings had barely made a dent on it.

I felt like the land was reaching out and claiming me.

I sat there, leaning against the bonnet of the car, for ten minutes or more, and then pushed myself upright.

'Come on,' I told Hector as I climbed back behind the wheel. 'We've got a boat to catch.'

And now here we are, forty-five minutes ahead of schedule and third in the queue at what has to be the smallest ferry terminal I've ever encountered. I switch off the engine and reach for Hector's lead. 'OK, boy,' I tell him. 'Time for a walk before the boat comes in.'

There isn't, as it turns out. We've just made it down as far as the shoreline and Hector is sniffing curiously at the seaweed when I realise that the small vessel chugging its way across the narrow stretch of water is, in fact, the ferry, evidently an earlier one than I'd anticipated catching. We hurry back up to the car and no sooner are we back inside than we're boarding, bumping over the ramp and onto the back of the ferry – the MG, the farmer, a white transit van, a couple of foot passengers pushing bikes ahead of them and Hector and me.

The crossing is almost laughably short – five minutes chugging across the water and we're disembarking and driving the twenty-or-so miles to Lochaline, where I manage to track down some hot tea which I sip from a polystyrene cup while we wait for the next ferry to arrive. This second crossing, following so quickly on the heels of the first, gives me the impression that I'm escaping to another world, travelling much further than the 350 miles Multimap had worked out for me yesterday evening. As I bump off the ferry at Fishnish and follow the narrow road towards Tobermory, I really do feel as though I've run away at last, and that anyone tracking me wouldn't have a hope of finding me. The thought makes me giddy with excitement. 'Sixteen miles,' I tell Hector, reading it from a sign at the edge of the road and waving my thanks at a vehicle coming in the opposite direction that's pulled in at a narrow spot to let us through. 'But not as we know it.'

It takes us over forty-five minutes, twisting and turning along the little road, giving and receiving waves, until by the time we trundle down the hill towards the main street in Tobermory I feel as though I must know most of the locals on the island. I think about the months I've spent avoiding other people back home, and allow myself a wry smile.

By now it's just after half past five. We've been on the go eleven hours, including the breaks we've taken along the way, but I don't feel the slightest bit tired. As I pull the car into a parking space on the main street and step out, soaking up the early-evening light rippling across the surface of the water, admiring the way the late sun seems to soak into the coloured fronts of the buildings that line the waterfront, I feel exhilarated, full of energy. I could do the whole journey all over again without batting an eyelid.

Of course I may have to, if I can't find a way of tracking down Charlie and Harry.

Hector jumps gladly from the back of the car and stretches luxuriantly while I'm attaching his lead. 'Good boy,' I tell him, patting his ribcage. 'You've been a trooper. Now all we need is a phone box so that we can give Charlie a call.'

Along the waterfront, close to where I've parked the car, a long pier stretches out into the harbour. At the land end of the pier, behind a stone monument, a van is parked up dispensing fish and chips, the sharp smell of vinegar and salt on the air making my mouth water hungrily. I haven't eaten since our brief stop in Luss, I realise, and suddenly the need to call Charlie doesn't seem quite so urgent. We join the short queue at the side of the van and, a short while later, furnished with a portion of fish and chips for me and a sausage for Hector, we've settled ourselves on a stone seat at the bottom of the monument and are tucking in contentedly together. Halfway through my impromptu feast I shut my eyes again, like I'd done earlier, and tilt my face to the sun, breathing in the cries of the seagulls, the hubbub of the people around me, the sheer unfamiliarity of the place. I'm here, I've arrived, a stranger in a strange place, anonymous.

Free.

And then a man's voice suddenly speaks beside me, saying my name, jolting me upright.

'Marion? Sorry, I never meant to startle you. It *is* Marion, isn't it? And this, let me guess, is Hector, am I right?'

He's tall, I observe, and salt-and-pepper greying, with crinkly eyes that manage to look both shrewd and kind at the same time. Not so overtly handsome as Sam, he's compelling rather than good-looking in the traditional sense. He's wearing faded chinos and deck shoes, and a short-sleeved shirt with a sweater slung over his shoulders and, in spite of the fact that he has a couple of laden Co-op carrier bags dangling from his hands, for some reason his casual elegance makes him look like he's stepped straight from the pages of *The Great Gatsby*. And he's smiling down at me like I'm the person he most wants to see in the world.

Which, it turns out, I am. 'Charlie gave me a pretty good description,' he says, setting the carrier bags down and joining me on the seat. He leans across and looks closely at my face. 'Though I don't believe she mentioned anything about a black eye.'

'You're Harry,' I say, stating the obvious, returning the smile.

'Guilty as charged.' He holds out both of his hands in a gesture of submission. 'Actually, it was Hector I recognised. I guess there aren't too many wolves prowling the streets of Tobermory.'

'I'm glad you found me.' I give him another smile. 'I was on the lookout for a phone box to call Charlie, but we got waylaid.'

'Well, I can't say I blame you for that. Those fries sure smell good. I came in to buy supplies for supper, but maybe I'll just take some more of those back with me as well.'

His manner is ingenuous, completely lacking in any awkwardness, and I can't work out whether he's genuinely without curiosity about me or whether he's deliberately trying to put me at my ease. He gives no sign of weighing me up the way I'm trying to do to him. 'So, do we shake hands, or are we somewhere along the way towards a less formal relationship than that?' I ask him, probing, and he grins at me suddenly.

'I guess I'll let Charlie fill you in on that one,' he says, standing up and raising his eyebrows at me enigmatically. 'Be right back.'

He joins the ever-present queue at the fish van, hands in pockets, looking quietly composed and comfortable in his own skin, and not like someone who slept on a plane and just completed a jet-lag-inducing journey of 3,500 miles. My immediate impression is that I like him, and I find myself hoping he and Charlie might be more than just good friends. A few moments later he's back, yet another plastic carrier bag dangling from his fingers.

'What say we mosey back to the cottage while this is still hot? Did you bring any luggage?'

'In my car. It's just along there.'

We retrieve the rucksack, which he swings effortlessly onto his back despite my protests that I can manage, and the three of us set off along the main street, past the shops, which are beginning to close up for the night, and the restaurants, which are beginning to open. 'Charlie tells me the cottage isn't accessible by road,' I say. 'How far is it to walk?'

'About a mile.' He turns sharply left at the end of the street and heads past a pub and a building with a sign on the front that reads TOBERMORY HARBOUR ASSOCIATION, and then all of a sudden the road spills into a car park and we're standing at some railings looking out over the harbour. 'But we're not walking.'

I look around me in bafflement, and then realisation dawns.

Down on the pebbly beach, tied up at the end of a low pontoon, a small inflatable dinghy is bobbing up and down optimistically.

'You have got to be kidding me.'

'Gee, Marion, Charlie never mentioned you were a lame-ass.' He swings himself around the railings and drops onto the beach, turning to offer me a hand onto the pebbles. 'I thought all you Brits grew up on *Swallows and Amazons*.'

I freeze when we reach the end of the pontoon and Harry drops the shopping into the boat. He lowers himself inside and holds out a hand to help me aboard. 'Look –' I start to bluster. 'Maybe it would be better if we walked there and met you. I'm not sure Hector will manage this.' As soon as the words are out of my mouth, Hector pushes past me and lumbers aboard, treading confidently on the edge of the unstable dinghy as though he's been a salty old sea dog all his life.

Harry's grinning at me now. 'Looks like you're all out of excuses,' he says, still holding out his hand. 'Just step onto the side, like Hector here, and then sit straight down on the seat in the middle, OK?'

The hand that takes his is trembling so badly I almost fall, but he grips me steadily and almost lifts me aboard. Then he hands me a lifejacket and shrugs himself into a second one. 'I don't have one for Hector,' he apologises. 'But I guess he can swim ashore if we go over.'

'We're not likely to go over, are we?' I can't keep the note of panic from my voice.

'Not as long as you keep real still,' he says solemnly. Is he kidding? I can't tell.

I sit rigidly still anyway, just in case, clutching on to the sides of the seat, while Hector positions himself right at the front of the boat like a figurehead, his front paws up on the bow, his nose pointed into the wind. 'Attaboy,

Hector,' Harry tells him, approving. Then he settles himself in the back of the boat and tugs at the starter cord, and the engine roars into life.

We weave our way through the small craft that dip and bob at the end of mooring lines in the harbour, and then pick up speed as we round the edge of the bluff and Harry points the boat north. Across the Sound, the shores of the mainland loom like a distant country from another time. Even though we're only about twenty yards out, I cling diligently to the seat and pray the boat won't overturn, stealing an occasional surreptitious look at the man on the helm whose involvement in my sister's life is still unclear. He seems utterly at peace with himself, composed and relaxed, his eyes scanning the water ahead of us for obstacles. At one point he catches me looking at him and I'm granted another smile.

'Comfortable?' The wind snatches the word from his mouth and hurls it backwards across the water.

I'm not, but I manage a nod in return.

The boat takes another wide corner, and Harry points ahead of us.

'See the lighthouse up ahead? That's where we're headed.'

A moment later he's turning the boat towards the shore and cutting its speed. 'As we get close,' he tells me, 'I'm going to kill the engine and tip it forwards into the boat. Hopefully we'll drift onto the beach just behind the lighthouse.'

'Hopefully?' I bite my lip nervously. 'Don't you know?'

He shakes his head, unfazed. 'Never done it before. But it worked OK when I was coming in to Tobermory.'

It works this time too, much to my relief. Before I know it we're back on terra firma and Hector is bounding ashore. Harry steps carefully from the boat and holds out a hand again to help me out, then reaches in and gathers up the shopping and my rucksack in a single hand. He turns and nods behind me.

'Straight on. The only cottage for miles. You can't miss it.'

The walkway from the lighthouse leads straight to the gate of a low single storey whitewashed cottage that nestles into the hillside. I'm guessing it must once have housed the lighthouse keeper in the days before automation. 'How on earth did you find this place?' I ask him as we pick our way across the pebbly beach to the walkway.

'It belongs to a guy I knew at college. His father lived here for nineteen years before moving into the bustling metropolis that is Tobermory. He's hardly ever up here: said we could use it for the week as long as we didn't mind roughing it a bit.'

I laugh. 'Charlie was never big on roughing it. You must have some pretty powerful methods of persuasion if you've talked her into this.' I raise my eyebrows at him, trying to work out yet again just how big a part of her life is this enigmatic man walking beside me carrying my rucksack.

'Well, you can ask her that for yourself,' he says, swinging open the gate to the little garden and stepping aside for me to go ahead of him. A moment later the door swings open and Charlie appears, and as soon as I see her I realise exactly how big a part of her life he is.

She's grinning broadly as she takes in the look of astonishment on my face.

'Close your mouth, Marion,' she tells me, wrapping her arms around me in a tight hug. 'Anyone would think you'd never seen a pregnant woman before.'

Chapter 30

It's astonishingly good to see her. I fall into her arms, gasping and laughing, and then push her away so that I can check her out properly, taking in the utterly amazing sight of the swollen belly on her trim frame. I raise my eyes to hers and they're still full of laughter, with just a hint of apprehension while she waits for my verdict. 'Surprise!' she says, holding her hands in the air and giving a light shrug.

'Oh my God, Charlie.' I drop my gaze back to her stomach. 'Is that a new top you're wearing?'

'Stop it!' She punches my arm affectionately and then grabs my hands, placing the palms against her stomach. 'That's your nephew in there. Or maybe your niece,' she amends. 'Say hello nicely.'

I pull a face. 'Funny choice of name,' I tell her. 'I'd have preferred Andrew or Elizabeth, but hey, it's your choice. Hello, Nicely,' I say to her stomach.

She rolls her eyes at Harry. 'I forgot to tell you my sister has a weird sense of humour,' she tells him, shaking her head at me in mock-despair, and I think, My God, I do, don't I? I'd all but forgotten I'd any sense of humour at all. Being back with Charlie is so utterly normalising (even if she's pregnant and holed up in a miles-from-anywhere cottage on some tiny Scottish island), I'm suddenly rediscovering myself. As our eyes meet again and speak all the things neither of us can actually articulate, I feel a great vicelike clamp drop from around my heart.

'I brought supper.' Harry dangles the bag.

'Ooh, fish and chips! You clever, lovely man.' Charlie's eyes are sparkling, watching him as he disappears off in search of plates. 'Isn't he just –?' She sighs happily and doesn't wait for me to answer. 'I'm so in love. And we're having a baby. You know, there were times when I thought it was never going to happen, and suddenly I'd be too old, and then Harry came along and – bam!'

'Oh, Charlie. You're hardly old.'

'Believe me, thirty-five is geriatric in Michigan. There's a cartoon doing the rounds at the college at the moment, headed "Michigan Mom", and in it a little girl is standing watching her mum doing the dishes, and she's saying, "Mommy, why are your hands so soft?" and her mum replies, "Because I'm twelve."' She sobers suddenly and looks at me. 'You don't mind that I didn't tell you sooner?'

'About what? The baby, or the fact that you were in a relationship?'

'Well, both, I guess. I mean, I've known Harry for years. Well, three years anyway,' she amends. 'But we only started seeing each other about a year ago, and then after what happened to Hope there just didn't seem to be a good time to tell you. And then I got pregnant, which neither of us could quite believe, because for some reason I always assumed I would never have kids, and I knew I wouldn't be able to hide that from you for long. I mean, look at me!' She gestures at her swollen stomach.

'You look radiant,' I assure her.

'Ugh – I don't. I look like a walrus. But I feel great. You should have seen me for the first three months. My hair was greasy, my skin was a mess, I kept being sick all the time, and I was completely, utterly, *totally* knackered. And then one morning I woke up and thought, hey, I feel bloody fantastic.'

'How far on are you?'

'Twenty-five weeks and two days, but who's counting?'

'You are.' Harry, back with the food, drops a light kiss onto the top of her head. 'Between you and me, Marion, I think she's got it down to the nearest hour. Coming through?'

He leads the way into a tiny sitting room furnished with a lumpy sofa and a couple of sagging armchairs, all of which Charlie spurns for a rickety-looking dining-chair. 'I haven't quite plucked up the courage to try the easy chairs,' she explains. 'I'm terrified once I'm in I'll never be able to get back out again.'

She picks up a chip and nibbles on it, regarding me through lowered brows thoughtfully.

'What?' I ask.

She narrows her eyes at me. 'Why is Sam in Africa?'

'I thought you spoke to him. His hospital set up an exchange programme with a clinic out there.'

She puts the chip back down on her plate and doesn't shift her eyes from me. 'You were never very good at lying, Marion.'

'That's not true, actually,' I tell Harry. 'I can tell total whoppers and nobody suspects a thing.'

He doesn't answer, but regards me pretty much the same way Charlie's looking at me.

'What?' I say again, this time to the two of them, and neither of them answers me, they just go on looking at me. 'He's establishing an inoculation programme for the local children,' I offer, and they keep on looking. 'And setting up a prenatal class for pregnant women.' Their gazes don't flicker. 'And running a clinic for cervical cancer screening and health education.' I'm racking my brains, trying to remember all the things Sam had enthused about when the project was still in its infancy and he'd been hoping to be part of the team selected to go. Still the pair of them go on sitting there, waiting for me to get to the point. And I can't do it. I can't bring myself to tell them that he moved out because he couldn't live with me any more, couldn't breathe around me any more, and that after he'd gone I tried to kill myself. I can't watch myself destroy the happiness that's radiating from the two of them with the sordid details of my pathetic little life. 'Well, you know,' I eventually say, and I leave it at that. 'Hey, Harry, did I hear bottles clinking in one of those bags you brought in earlier?'

He takes the hint. 'I believe you did, Marion,' he says. He regards me thoughtfully for just a moment longer and then pushes himself to his feet.

I watch him leave the room and then I turn to face Charlie once again. 'Tomorrow,' I promise her. 'Let's just not spoil tonight.'

'He's moved out, hasn't he?' She shifts forwards in her seat, leaning towards me. 'After all you've already gone through, the bastard's moved out and left you on your own.'

I swallow and shake my head. 'I was already on my own, Charlie. I've made myself so unliveable-with, I've been on my own for months now. And I didn't really leave him any choice,' I add. 'I've spent the past seven months blaming him for what happened to Hope, and that wasn't fair of me.'

Her eyes sparkle, threatening tears, which she blinks away impatiently. 'None of what happened was fair.'

'No, it wasn't. You're right. I truly believed afterwards that I couldn't carry on without Hope. I didn't want to, to be honest. I wanted to just flick a switch and stop existing after she died. And then something happened that made me realise I was moving on from it in spite of not wanting to, and even though I've made a bit of a pig's ear of things in the meantime, that doesn't make me a bad person. I went just about as low as I could get, and, well, I guess I've probably reached bedrock now. But maybe it's a good thing that I'm on my own now.' I swallow, because I realise in my heart that I don't want to be on my own, trying to move on into a future without Sam. 'Maybe I need to be on my own so that I can find out who I am now that I'm not Hope's mummy any more.'

She slips from the seat and, taking a gamble on being able to vacate it at some point, comes to join me on the sofa. 'You aren't on your own any more,' she tells me softly. 'Harry's visit to Edinburgh – remember? I know it's not Yorkshire, but it's a hell of a lot closer than Michigan – a couple of hours on the train, tops.' She smiles at the puzzled frown on my face. 'Well, you didn't think I was going to leave him here and bugger off back to Michigan with his baby, did you? I can't have Nicely growing up with one of those hillbilly "I-moved-up-here-from-Lexington" twangs, can I? Not a chance.' She looks me in the eye, and tucks a rogue tendril of hair behind my ear, and suddenly I feel like I'm about six years old. 'You're not on your own any more, Marion. I'm coming home.'

Chapter 31

Later that evening, after Charlie has hit the hay and as I'm about to take Hector for a last walk along the beach before turning in myself, Harry appears in the doorway to the cottage.

'Mind if I join you? I could use the exercise. I guess my body clock's not switched to local time yet.' He slips into step beside me and together we pick our way across the rocks down towards the shore.

'Some place, huh?' He nods towards the dark stretch of water.

'I know. It's all so . . . empty. I feel like a pilgrim settler or something.'

He gives a laugh and shakes his head. 'This place wasn't settled by pilgrims. The first inhabitants were hunter-gatherers, probably Mesolithic, around 6000 BC. Give or take a couple of thousand years.'

'Well, I could do that,' I counter. 'Hunt and gather. I hunted down the chips earlier.'

'You sure did,' he agrees. 'But you should probably have killed the fish yourself, and used its skin for a water carrier or something, if you were gonna embrace the whole hunter-gatherer philosophy.'

I draw a deep lungful of air. 'This place is so peaceful.

I kind of envy your friend's father. Didn't you say he lived here for nineteen years or something?'

'That's right. Pretty quiet kinda life, huh? Though it wasn't always such a haven of tranquility.' He points ahead of us around the coastline. 'The bay just around that headland – they call it Bloody Bay. Saw one of the most vicious battles of its time between the Lord of the Isles and the earls of Huntley and Crawford, whose descendents went on to become big in the cracker industry.'

Ahead of us on the beach, Hector is busying himself with some washed-up treasure or other he's rooted out from among the stones. 'How come you know so much about this place?' I ask.

He looks at me, po-faced. 'I guess I'm just naturally brilliant.'

I give him a sceptical look. 'Sure you are.'

'What – you don't believe me?' He slumps in disappointment. 'You're right. I boned up on it before we came.' He pulls a face. 'Which makes me –'

'– a bit of a lame-ass,' I finish for him. 'I bet you were a right little teacher's pet when you were at school.'

He holds both his hands up. 'Guilty as charged, ma'am.'

We carry on along the beach. 'So –' I venture after a moment. 'You and Charlie . . . ?'

'Yup.' He nods solemnly. 'Me and Charlie. And Nicely, don't forget.'

I pull a face. 'You want to be careful. That name's going to stick.'

'Well, I'll sure know who to blame if it does.' He yawns

suddenly. 'Gee, I guess I must be more tired than I thought. Mind if we head back?'

And that, I think as we turn and begin to make our way back along the beach, is you put firmly in your place, Marion Bishop. If I'm going to find out anything further about the enigmatic Harry, I'm obviously probing the wrong person.

Chapter 32

Charlie is regarding me sternly across the top of a large panini, and after the chip incident yesterday evening I'm guessing I'm in for a grilling. She seems to have developed this way of using her food to interrogate me. It's quite remarkable, given that we've been talking inconsequentials since she joined me on my improvised picnic in the garden a short while ago. But now the brows are lowered, the eyes are narrowed and the lips pursed in consideration. Her whole face is arranging itself like a gathering storm. I can't help smiling.

'Spit it out,' I tell her, 'before you choke on your chicken tikka filling.'

I'm feeling remarkably at peace with the world. I woke around eight this morning, surfacing from a dream that I couldn't remember but that left me suffused with a feeling of well-being so profound I didn't want to let it go. I closed my eyes and reached back into the blackness to try to recapture the dream, but it was gone, slipping through my subconsciousness and away, tantalisingly out of reach. In its place, the day was pushing itself forwards, demanding acknowledgment, and I eventually gave in and sat up in the bed so that I could take in my surroundings.

The room I'd slept in was a bit of an enigma, rather like the rest of the cottage. High ceilinged, and framed

with a deep, ornate cornicing, it had a rather grand feel to
it that was more reminiscent of a boutique hotel than a
homely little lighthouse man's cottage. But there the
similarity ended: it had been furnished by a mishmash of
ill-assorted bits and pieces of furniture that seemed to have
come together by chance and decided to make the best of
things. Just about every conceivable bit of space that hadn't
been taken up by the old iron bedstead, a mahogany chest
of drawers and a spindle-backed chair was filled with books.
I'd had to clear a path through them to reach the bed the
previous evening. On the floor at my feet, Hector had
spent an enlightening night surrounded by an entire library
devoted to the marine life of the Outer Hebrides. I pushed
back the covers and picked a new path through the library
to the narrow window that looked out onto a strip of
garden at the rear of the cottage, bordered by a steep, rock-
strewn hill that clambered away out of sight. In every
direction the plants were in full bloom: bushes I didn't
recognise were top-heavy with fat white flowers that dipped
and nodded sagely in the morning sunlight, while an
unkempt rose scrambled unchecked along the top of the
wall that bordered the garden. There was even a palm
tree, stretching its branches incongruously into the sky
while gorse and heather crowded around its base. It was a
wilderness: a once-tended, carefully nurtured garden run
amok. All it needed was a handsome prince on a noble
steed to come cutting his way through the undergrowth.
'What d'you think, Hector?' I asked him. 'You could double
as a noble steed, couldn't you?' He thumped his tail on the
floor: of course he could. Noble is his middle name.

There was no sign of Charlie or Harry, so the steed and I slipped quietly from the cottage and down the path to the front gate. Ahead of us, the lighthouse stood sentinel against the blue sky, and we walked as far as we could towards it along a concrete jetty, until a locked iron gate prevented us from going any further. Turning back and surveying the cottage from our new vantage point, I drew a deep, cleansing breath of air so pure it almost made me light-headed. Above my head, seagulls swooped and called to each other, while fifty-or-so yards out from the shore a lone yacht was ghosting its way across the water, its sails filled by a wind so light it had died out before it came anywhere near our vantage point at the lighthouse.

We must have hung around on that little jetty for the best part of an hour, soaking up the unexpected warmth of the morning sun and letting the utter tranquility of the place work its magic on us. At least, I hung. Hector, growing bored, took to chasing seagulls across the rocky shore. And then, seeing as there was still no movement from inside the cottage, I went and retrieved my purse and the two of us set off to walk the mile or so along the cliff path to the little town, where we dawdled among the locals and the holidaymakers and picked up more supplies from an impressively stocked deli on the main street. The place was alive with activity: out on the water, the occupants of some of the boats moored in the harbour were calling greetings to each other, while all along the main street people dawdled and chatted in the sunshine. Nobody seemed to be in any kind of a hurry. Hector was treated like a minor celebrity, gathering a little crowd of admirers around the railings where I'd secured him while I was in the deli buying the food. By the time I returned to him, one of the shop-keepers had emerged from the hardware store and was feeding him dog biscuits and telling him what a beautiful boy he was. Hector lapped up the attention, and took his leave reluctantly from his new fan club. And then as we were making our way back along the cliff path towards the cottage, just as the noise and bustle of the town was dying away behind us, a heavy footfall behind me caused the two of us to stop and turn around.

The boy seemed to have materialised from nowhere, though looking through the dense undergrowth behind him I could see that there was another path twisting its way up the cliff. He'd obviously pushed his way through the bushes and jumped the last few feet to reach us and, as he straightened and took a step towards us, I was suddenly back in that dark stretch of Station Parade, the night that Ryan had put in his unexpected appearance, and in spite of the warmth of the sun and the balmy feel to the day, a cold chill swept across me and my heart set off at a gallop.

'Hey, missus,' he said, and I braced myself for the knife.

'Can ah stroke your dog?'

I blinked. 'What?'

'Your dog.' He made a move towards us and then hesi-tated as I retreated a step. 'Can ah stroke him?'

'Wh– Oh. Oh, yes! Of course you can!' I was almost gushing with relief. 'Yes, you can stroke him if you like.'

He stepped in closer and held out a hand, which Hector dutifully sniffed. 'He's one o' them malamutes, isn't he?'

I nodded, impressed at his knowledge. 'Most people mistake him for a husky.' My heart was beginning to settle back down.

He turned suddenly. 'Hey, Amber!' he called up the hill, and a moment later a couple of girls and another boy around the same age as him appeared on the path. 'This is one o' them malamutes ah was telling you about. This is the sort o' dog ah want.' He was tickling Hector behind the ears now. 'He's gorgeous, so he is. Dead strong, eh? They can pull, like, a bus behind them. Ah'll bet he's your best friend, eh?'

'Yes.' I looked at the boy, crouched in front of Hector scratching his neck, and suddenly felt a million miles away from all the heartbreak of the past few months. 'Yes, he is.'

'C'mon, Kyle,' one of the girls calls him. 'We're already late.'

He stood up reluctantly. 'Gotta go,' he told me. 'Thanks for letting me stroke him.'

And then in a few short strides he'd disappeared again, gathering up his friends along the way, and Hector and I were alone again in the sunshine, feeling our way out of the empty space his departure had left on the path. 'Hmm,' I said to him as we began to pick our way back to the cottage. 'If that wasn't enough to restore your faith in the youth of today, I don't know what would be.' Hector lolled his tongue, laughing at me, as though he'd never had any doubts about the youth of today.

By the time we returned to the cottage it was nearing eleven-thirty. I rummaged around and found an old blanket in a cupboard in the hall, and spread my purchases out for an impromptu picnic on the grass. Then, just as my mind started wandering back to a time not all that long ago when I was picnicking in my own garden with Con and I was in danger of starting to brood, Charlie finally put in an appearance, bleary-eyed and sleep-tousled, still in her pyjamas, and eased herself heavily onto the blanket alongside me. And now here she is, having finally thrown off the last tethers of sleep, doing that whole looking thing with the panini, and I brace myself for her to start interrogating me again about Sam.

She doesn't. 'I'm not going to marry Harry,' she says instead, taking me by surprise. 'I just thought I should clear that up. In case you were wondering.'

'Oh.' I blink. Having expected a grilling, I'm not too sure where this comment's come from. Not to mention where it might be leading.

'Don't get me wrong. It's not that I disapprove of marriage or anything. And it's got nothing to do with you and Sam and this whole —' She waves her sandwich around vaguely. 'I haven't suddenly become all cynical about marriage just because the two of you have separated or whatever it is you've done.' She takes a thoughtful nibble from a corner of the sandwich and chews on it for a moment before swallowing. 'And these days there's nothing unusual about parents not being married.' She places a hand protectively against her swollen belly and gives me that challenging look again, as though expecting me to argue with her.

'Well, that's your decision,' I manage. 'I mean, just because Sam and I ... What I mean is, marriage isn't for everyone,' I say lamely. 'You and Harry have to make your own decisions. It's not like Mum and Dad are still around to worry about. And if it's not what you and Harry want –'

'Harry was married before,' she interrupts me. 'About eight years ago.'

'Oh,' I say again, trying to figure out an appropriate facial expression, and settling for one that's meant to say *mildly curious* rather than *gagging for details*. 'So what? It was so awful he's been put off for life?' I hazard.

She wrinkles her nose. 'You could say that.' Her tone is giving nothing away.

Hmm. What's that supposed to mean? 'How long was he married?' I ask, thinking that's a relatively safe question.

'Oh –' She lifts her eyes to the sky as if she's doing the sums. 'About thirty-six hours.' Her eyes are back on me.

My mouth has dropped open. 'OK,' I say evenly. 'How –?'

'His wife was killed in a skiing accident at Lake Tahoe. They were on their honeymoon.'

I can't think of anything to say to her. All the time she's been telling me this, her eyes have been fixed in a challenge. And it's so awful, what she's saying, so utterly tragic, but that challenge is there all the same, like she's expecting me to disagree with her or something. I meet the look head on. 'Well, that . . . that must have been terrible for him,' I eventually say.

'Yes. Yes, it was. Of course, I didn't know him then. I just got to deal with the consequences after I met him. He was working at UCLA at the time. He only came to

Michigan three years ago. He was just . . . broken. So closed off. He'd go so far in terms of mixing with people, and then he'd just pull back and kind of retreat into himself. He'd built such a bloody great wall around himself, I practically had to use a wrecking ball to get through it. Took me almost two years to get him round to my place. Even then, I had to pretend it was an inter-departmental dinner to discuss proposed funding cuts. It was like trying to tease a hedgehog to uncurl.'

'Well, I expect that was just his way of dealing with what had happened,' I said, feeling defensive towards Harry all of a sudden. 'I can understand that.'

'I'm sure you can.' She's looking at me soberly. 'But that's my point, really. That's why I'm telling you all this.'

I can feel my face folding in confusion. 'I'm not sure I follow you.'

'Look at him now,' she says. 'I mean, not literally now. He's still fast asleep. But I mean generally. He's so happy. So excited about the baby. But he spent years in this bleak, barren wasteland, hiding away from people, only living a half life.' She gives her head a little shake. 'Such a waste, Marion. Such a terrible waste.'

'Well, but you can't say that! He was coming to terms with what happened to his wife. You don't know, Charlie. You don't know what it's like to lose someone.' The sense of panic I'd started to get used to not feeling comes sweeping over me, and I can feel sweat breaking out under my arms.

She puts a hand on my arm. 'I do know. Of course I do. D'you think I didn't feel it when Mum and Dad died? Or when Hope was killed? She was my niece, my only sister's only child. I know that doesn't come close to your anguish, but I still felt it. I still do. Every day, I feel it. But no one can fix what happened. No one gets out alive, Marion. That's the bugger of it all. No one gets out alive. Not you, not me. Not Harry. Not this baby. We have to find a way of getting our heads around that fact.'

'Yes, but –' I try to think about what she's saying, try to settle the feeling of panic. 'Some of us get longer than others.'

'And does that make a difference?'

'Of course it does!'

'Why?'

'Because . . . because it's fairer, that's why!'

She gives a short, sharp laugh. 'It's *fairer*? Some deaths are *fairer* than others?'

I feel like I've just regressed to somewhere around the age of five. 'Of course they are! Surely you can see that? Surely you agree that Mum and Dad had more of an innings than Hope? She was only nine, Charlie. Nine!' There's the panic, back again, threatening to overwhelm me.

'And Harry's wife was twenty-two,' she tells me. 'And on her honeymoon, with her whole life before her. And Mum and Dad hadn't even reached retirement. They were going to buy a house in France, remember? A place in the sun. Spend their twilight years doing the garden and drinking too much red wine.' She pulls a face. 'There's nothing *fair* about death, Marion. Nothing. It just *is*. That's all. The one inescapable, inalienable truth. Hope had a wonderful life. She had you and Sam for parents. No kid could have had better. She *basked* in your love. She was a beautiful, happy, funny, kind little girl who sucked the juice out of every day she had. Remember that time you all came out to see me and she spent so long trying not to smile, and then she couldn't help herself, and she cried for hours because she thought she was going to be sent home? God, she *loved* so much, that kid. Everyone that met her couldn't help but love her back. *Everyone*,' she emphasised, as though I'd contradicted her, and suddenly I remembered what Liam told me about the collage Hope's school had put together for her, the letters, the drawings, everyone wanting to have a say. 'If you were going to write an epitaph for her life, you could just say, "She loved, and was loved." What else is there, Marion?'

'There's *longer*,' I insist, tears springing to my eyes, spilling down my cheeks. 'I wanted her for longer, Charlie. Nine years wasn't enough.'

'It was a lifetime.'

Her words hang in the air after she's spoken them, so many truths bound up in them I can't breathe. I press my lips together, trying to suppress the anguish, thinking of Hope, wanting her back so much it hurts.

'I can't sit back and watch you do to yourself what Harry put himself through after Stacy died. Hope had nine years, Marion. Nine wonderful years. Her entire lifetime. What a privilege for you, who brought her into the world, to have had her with you every single day of her life. I know you would have wanted longer, of course you would. But we don't get to call the shots on death. The only way to take the sting out is to celebrate what we had, and to go on sucking the juice out of what we've got left.'

I fix my eyes at some distant point on the mainland, feeling my mouth wobble again, not wanting to acknowledge the truth of what she's saying, not wanting to just . . . let go.

'I can't just accept it,' I tell her after a moment, and another tear runs down my cheek. 'I'm terrified I'll lose her all over again if I do.'

She shakes her head at me. 'You'll never lose her, Marion. She'll live on in your heart for the rest of your life. This isn't just a platitude. I mean it. People who knew her – people like you, and me, and Sam – we're all connected to her. We're the ones who get to keep her memory alive. Right up until the point when our own time runs out, and after that – who knows?' She shrugs lightly.

'What – you think she's waiting up there somewhere for me to join her?' I give a short sardonic laugh. 'If I believed that, I'd have topped myself months ago.'

'Well, I don't know about the afterlife,' Charlie asserts. 'But I don't see an awful lot of point in wasting too much time fretting about life after death if you've lost the knack for life after birth.'

She moves up so that she's sitting right beside me, our shoulders touching, and follows my gaze across the Sound to the mainland. 'I can just imagine the kind of hell you and Sam must have been going through,' she continues. 'Trying to get your heads around it, to make sense of it, trying to find someone to blame.' I wince as she makes this last comment, thinking of how I've tried to blame Sam, knowing in my heart it was never his fault. 'No matter how it happened, Marion, you have to find it in your heart to forgive. Because a heart that can't forgive can't heal either. And you need your heart to heal, so that you can get on with loving life again.'

She pushes herself stiffly to her feet. 'I have to pee,' she says. 'That's all I seem to do these days: sleep and pee.' She drops her hand onto the top of my head as she passes, and then disappears back inside the cottage, leaving me alone on the picnic blanket with a multitude of thoughts crowding in my head, wondering where I start on the list of people I could do with forgiving, myself most of all, wondering whether I *can* forgive them just like that.

I've lived with the anger for so long, I'm scared I might have forgotten how.

Chapter 33

The rest of my time on Mull passes in a blink. Charlie studiously avoids any further discussion on Hope or Sam: maybe she feels that now she's made her point she can afford to back off. Whatever the reason, it's a welcome respite spending time with her, listening to her plans for the imminent move to Edinburgh, assuming all goes well during Harry's visit to the university. She's giddy with excitement when he returns on Wednesday evening, enthusing about the trip, waxing lyrical about the architecture, the history, the culture. There'd even been a piper, busking outside the railway station, when he'd arrived some time around eight the previous evening. 'You should've been there!' he told us. 'Unbelievable. Straight out of the movies.'

They're wonderful to be around; I can't help getting caught up in their enthusiasm, the way everything seems to be so uncomplicated for them. All the same, by the time Thursday evening arrives I announce my intention to return home the following morning. Charlie is loud in protest. 'But you were supposed to stay the full week!' she complains. 'I had it all worked out.'

'I'm sure you did,' I tell her, 'but you and Harry have a million things to talk over, and you should be making the most of spending some time alone together, not babysitting me. Once Nicely is born, you won't get a minute to yourselves. Besides, I'm fine. It's done me the world of good, coming away. I feel rejuvenated. And I really need to get back. There's stuff I need to be getting on with.'

Amidst her protests I pack up the few bits and pieces I'd brought with me: the sweater it had been too warm to contemplate wearing; the going-out-for-dinner dress that hadn't been out of the rucksack. She insists on accompanying us to Tobermory, the boat low in the water with its extra passenger. And then after I've transferred everything, Hector included, into the car, she hugs me tightly and makes me promise I'll come and see her as soon as the move is completed. 'We're looking for a big house,' she tells me. 'At least four bedrooms. I want you to be comfortable when you come up to help me look after Nicely.'

'Oh, I'm coming up, am I?'

'Of course you are. You have to come for at least a fortnight to do all my ironing and cook dinner and generally wait on me while I'm recuperating, like I did when you had Hope.'

My heart twists at the memory, but I give a laugh too. 'You came over for two days and spent the entire time cuddling her while *I* made dinner and did the ironing.'

'I meant to come for longer. I had it all planned. It wasn't my fault she decided to come early. I was running a summer school the following week. And anyway, I distinctly remember ironing something.'

I nod. 'Your travelling clothes for the flight home.'

'Well, I had to make the most of my niece, seeing as it was such a flying visit.'

'Charlie,' I tell her sternly, 'you are full of excuses.'

'I know.' She looks at me keenly. 'But you *will* come, won't you?'

I think about it for a moment, about the prospect of coming to take care of my sister and her new baby, about how it will feel now that I don't have my own child to factor in to the equation, and there's that twist again, mixed in with a fluttering of excitement, and I realise that that's the way it's going to be now, this agony-woven antici-pation. The fact that I can recognise there are things to look forward to is actually a pretty major step in the right direction. 'Of course I will,' I tell her lightly after a moment. 'Try and stop me.'

A light rain begins to fall as the Fishnish ferry pulls in to Lochaline, and stays with Hector and me for the rest of the drive home. By the time I pull in alongside the house around eight it has settled into a steady downpour, and I have to resist the urge to turn the car around and drive straight back to Mull.

The light on the answerphone is flashing itself into a frenzy as Hector, the rucksack and I spill into the hall. There are two messages from Heather, the first left last Sunday inviting me for lunch on Tuesday, which I've missed, and the second telling me she's presuming I've gone away for a few days and asking me to phone her when I get back. After that there are three messages from Esme, all left on the same day, all increasing in anxiety, wondering where I am, telling me things have 'moved on' since our talk last Saturday, that Con has returned to the shop, that she seems to have sorted things out with her boyfriend, that I should get in touch. Then there are another four messages where the caller didn't actually say anything but listened to my recorded greeting long enough for the answerphone to kick in anyway.

Shattered as I am, I pick up the phone and make a quick call to Heather, explaining that I'm just back from a short break on Mull. She's enthusiastic, telling me a holiday was just what I needed, and we make a tentative arrangement to get together for coffee some time on Saturday. Once I've cut the call I look up the number of Esme's shop, hoping to get away with leaving a message on the answerphone explaining my sudden absence, but to my dismay she picks up.

'Marion! Oh, I'm glad to hear from you. I won't say I've been worried, but I've maybe had the odd flutter of anxiety wondering if you were OK, after all that nasty business at the weekend.' I think of those three anxious messages and feel a guilty twinge. 'Aye, I'm still at the shop,' she says in response to my query. 'So is Con, as it happens. We're just finishing off, and then we're off upstairs to do a spot of painting on the flat. Well, I'll let her tell you all about it, shall I?'

Before I can object – I really don't have the energy or the inclination to talk to Con – Esme's handed the phone over and I can hear her voice on the other end of the line, tentative, unsure of the reaction she's going to get, none of the usual truculence anywhere in evidence.

'Marion? It's Con. Hi.'

'Hi,' I say in return, matching her tone.

'Um – we haven't seen you for a few days.'

'I've been away.'

'Oh. So, how've you been?'

'Fine.' I'm being unfair, I know: I just can't bring myself to engage with her any more.

'Well, we've missed seeing you.'

There's an awkward pause when neither of us says anything, and then she tries again.

'Esme and I are fixing up the flat, and I'm moving in at the weekend.' She waits to see if I'm going to pass any comment, and when I don't, she continues, tripping over her words in her anxiety to explain herself to me. 'You were right about Ryan. I didn't want to see it, didn't want to admit it, because I thought he was all I had, yeah? And then last week – well, I realised it was time to move on. And Esme said I could have the flat, so we've been fixing it up all week.'

'Well, that's handy for you,' I say. Even I can't quite believe what a bitch I'm being. 'Look, Con, I have to go. I'm only just in the door and I'm shattered.'

'Oh, right. Well, are you coming in to the shop?'

'I don't know. Probably. I'll see. Look –'

She cuts in. 'Yeah, I know, you have to go. Well – oh, hold on. Esme wants another word.'

I sigh heavily, and a moment later Esme's back on the line. 'Why don't you go on up,' I hear her say, 'and I'll be right behind you.' Then she pauses for a moment before continuing. 'He hit her, Marion. Mind how she never turned up for work on Saturday? I was that worried, after

I left you I called the hospital, but they hadn't had any admissions that matched Constance. And then she turned up on Monday at the shop. She was in a terrible mess; I had to take her to the hospital myself. She still is, to be honest. Asked if she could stay in the flat for a bit, said she'd left him.'

'Esme –'

'Och, I know all that stuff you said about not being able to help someone who disnae want to be helped,' she cuts in. 'But she does want to be helped, you see? Did I not say she wasn't called Constance for nothing?'

'Well, I'm glad you're helping her,' I say, a touch acerbically. 'Frankly, I've had enough of her and Ryan to last me a lifetime. After what he did when he broke in to my house, I'd be quite happy if I never clapped eyes on either one of them ever again.'

Esme draws in her breath sharply. 'Och, Marion. You cannae say something like that. That girl is just desperate to put things right with you. You think she doesn't know what he did?'

'She gave him my bloody address!'

'Oh, that's what you think, is it?' Esme's voice is heavy with irony. 'That girl took the beating of her life, Marion. You think she just whipped out a pad and a pen and wrote it down for him?'

'I could have been killed,' I counter.

'Two black eyes,' Esme continues relentlessly. 'A split lip. Three cracked ribs from where he kicked her repeatedly in the chest.'

I draw in my breath sharply. 'He kicked her in the chest?'

'And broke her hand,' Esme finishes. 'Stamped on it with his boots on. The ones that had just finished kicking her in the ribs. It's a miracle she wasn't killed.'

I swallow, my mouth suddenly dry. 'Well, then, I suppose it's no wonder –'

'– no wonder she told him?' Esme gives a sharp laugh. 'Constance never told him, Marion. She blacked out, which was probably just as well – probably saved her life. I don't know where he got your address from, but it certainly wasn't from that poor wee lassie upstairs. She wouldnae have betrayed you even if he'd killed her for it. Which he damn near did.' She stops at last. 'Anyway,' she says after a moment. 'She's making a good recovery. Cannae do much work in the shop for the moment, mind, not with her hand in the state it's in, but she's managed to master the paint roller one-handed. The lad's been in to see her once – turned up at the shop bold as brass. I was getting all set to call the police, but then Constance got wind he was here and let him in – said she had things she needed to get said. I was that worried she'd weaken, I went up to the flat with them, just in case he started anything. There was no way I was leaving her alone with him. He'd even brought her a present, crawling to her, begging her to come back, but she was having none of it. Threw the present right back at his head and told him she'd rather eat her own head than go back to him. Och, he wasn't happy. Went away in a right temper.'

'Oh, Esme.' My heart gives a lurch at the thought of the two of them trying to confront Ryan. 'You need to be careful. You've seen what he's capable of.'

'Oh, aye, I've seen it. And I'm not so daft as to think he wouldnae try something if he got the chance. Doesn't mean I'm going to turn the lassie away when she's needing my help, though, does it? Sometimes you have to stand up and be counted. Besides,' she adds, 'he's leaving, apparently. Taking off for London or some such. Constance gave him an ultimatum: told him she'd turn him in herself unless he was gone by the weekend. Said she had the goods on him, which she probably has, let's face it. God alone knows what she's witnessed while she's been hanging around with him. She can be quite fiery, can that girl. Especially when you consider the state she's in.'

I swallow, feeling guilt-ridden and miserable. 'What can I do?'

She's brisk and businesslike all of a sudden. 'Well, now, I think the best thing you could do is to come in and see us some time. Let her know you know she didn't betray you. She's tearing herself into pieces over what you must think of her.' She sniffs. 'The girl thinks the world of you, Marion.'

'OK.' I draw a deep breath. 'I'll come in first thing tomorrow morning.'

'Well . . . leave it until closer to lunch time: that way I can get through the morning orders and relax.'

'OK. But, Esme? Just be careful, won't you? He's a nasty piece of work.'

'Och, I know that. I'm taking nothing for granted.'

'Right, Well, I'll see you tomorrow, then.'

* * *

True to my word, in spite of the fact that my heart is heavy with misgivings, the following morning around eleven-thirty, Hector and I drop in at the shop. The rain has kept up a steady downpour overnight, and the sky is so dark it could be early evening. Still, at least the shop is cheerful: the lights are all on and Esme greets me warmly as I come through the door. 'Been raining non-stop since you left,' she tells me, dragging out a chair from the room at the back of the shop for me. 'Terrible weather. They say it's all down to this global warming, but I don't know about that. I mean, if it's global warming, why is it so cold?'

'It wasn't raining in Mull,' I tell her. 'It was warm and sunny the whole time I was there.'

'Aye? Well, they've the Gulf Stream, you see. Makes all the difference. And sometimes you just get lucky when you're up on the islands. It can be pouring with rain right across the country and they'll be out in their bikinis. Anyway –' I'm granted a bright smile, '– I'll give Constance a call,' she tells me. 'She's upstairs working on the flat. She'll be that happy to see you. Come on, Hector. You don't mind if I put him out in the back room with Amelia, do you? He'll probably want to say hello to Constance and she's still a bit sore.'

My heart drops when Con appears. A week on from the beating, her face doesn't look as bad as it must have done when Esme first saw it, but it's still a mess: her eyes are bruised, and there's a trace of the cut on her mouth. Her right hand is swathed in a thick bandage, and she's walking stiffly, like a very old person crippled with arthritis, but it's the expression in her eyes that really cuts me up.

She looks like a badly whipped puppy that thinks it's in for another thrashing.

'Oh, Con.' I stand up and put my hand to my mouth, and then reach out to hug her. She eases herself across to me. 'Mind you don't squeeze too tight,' she warns. 'Ah might snap in half.' She leans against me in an awkward embrace, and I have to content myself with stroking the back of her head.

'I'll put the kettle on, shall I?' Esme's doing her businesslike briskness again.

After she's left, Con lifts her head to look at me. 'Are you mad at me?'

I draw in my breath sharply and swallow, shaking my head, and her eyes fill with unexpected tears.

'Ah never told him,' she says. 'Swear to God ah never. Even after he jumped on my hand.'

I nod mutely. I can't trust myself to speak.

She drags another chair out from behind the counter and sets it next to mine, easing herself into it painfully. 'Matt followed you. That day when you went round. After you'd left, he sneaked out and followed you right back to your car, and got the registration number. After that it was easy. He's got friends, has Matt. Not nice ones. But useful, though.'

I shake my head at her. 'But if Ryan already knew where I lived –' I gesture to her injuries. 'Why?' I ask in bewilderment. 'Why do this to you?'

She wrinkles her nose and shrugs. 'To prove a point, ah suppose. See if I'd dob you in it. He were testing me, yeah?' She gives a wry smile. 'Ah think ah failed the test.'

'No, you didn't.' I take hold of her good hand in mine. 'You passed with flying colours.'

'Yeah, mostly black and blue,' she counters with a laugh, and then winces and clutches at her ribs. 'Oof – keep forgetting ah can't laugh yet.'

'You didn't want to go to the police, then?'

She shakes her head. 'What's the point? They're not interested in t' likes of me. Any road, Matt would swear he was with him when he was beating me up. Ah'd never prove it. Nah.' Another shake of the head. 'Better to use it to get rid of him. At least this way he'll be gone by the weekend and with a bit of luck ah'll never see him again.' She gives me an ironic look. 'Remember when I told you he were a knight on a white horse?'

I nod. 'But then I seem to recall you saying in the next breath that men could be right arseholes as well.'

She grins at me suddenly. 'Sounds worse when you say it,' she tells me. 'Much ruder.'

'Hmmph. I must need more practice,' I muse, and she laughs again.

'Well now, it's nice to hear the two of you laughing.' Esme's back with a tray, laden with tea and sandwiches. 'I thought we could have an early lunch, shut the shop up for half an hour and have a proper catch-up,' she tells us, balancing the edge of the tray against the counter. 'You can tell us all about your holiday, Marion.' She raises an eyebrow at Con. 'Apparently the sun's been cracking the flags up in Mull. Lovely spot.' She sighs reminiscently. 'Used to spend all my holidays there when I was a bairn.'

Con pushes herself upright. 'Ah'll lock the door. An' we

can take that lot upstairs if you like. The lounge is just about finished.'

The tiny living room is swathed in dust sheets, which Con is busy removing one-handed from the furniture as we come through the door. 'My first visitors,' she says gleefully. 'Marion, could you grab that coffee table? I can't do much lifting at the moment.'

I drop my bag on the floor and lift down the coffee table she's indicating from on top of the sofa and set it in the middle of the floor so that Esme can put the tray down. 'This is really great.' Con's like a little girl playing at tea parties. 'Bit parky, but the heating's on. It'll soon warm up.'

'I'll shut the door, will I?' I cross to close the door to help keep the heat in, but the bottom of it catches on a lump in the dust sheet, and I bend down to straighten it out. 'There's something in the way,' I say, pulling the dust sheet back from the wall so that I can remove whatever it is. 'I'll just –' I reach my hand under the sheet and close my fingers around the obstacle, which is cold and hard in my grasp. 'Got it.' I straighten up and uncurl my fist, and as I do so the world stops.

I lift my eyes to look from Con to Esme and then back to the object in my hand.

It takes a moment for them to realise anything is amiss. Esme is fussing around the tray, lifting the drinks and setting them on the table, and Con is dragging a chair up close to the sofa so that the three of us can eat our lunch in comfort. I'm watching them, and it's like seeing a scene from a film unfolding in slow motion. Then they turn to me, and I can see their mouths moving, but I can't hear what they're saying; my head is full of a loud buzzing noise that is drowning out their words. And then Con is beside me, probing at the object I've retrieved from under the dust sheet, tutting in dismissal and saying it's nothing, it's not important, just some stupid present Ryan brought round to try to bribe her into going back to him that she'd thrown right back at him. It must have landed behind the door, she's saying, and got lost under the dust sheet when she put it down before she started painting.

I can't get her words out of my head. They're buzzing around inside my brain like gnats, and I'm struggling to pin them down so that I can try to make sense of them.

Ryan brought it round.

She takes it from my hand and tosses it down onto the coffee table. *It's nothing*, she says again from a thousand miles away, and it lies there forlornly on the table, the ribbon still as bright as it always was, the heart, the horse and the hermit crab, the hockey stick and the helicopter with the rotating blades and the hyena that Sam rechristened Hector the dog, and all the other little charms, piled up in a heap of silver amid the sandwiches, and my heart is thumping so loudly it feels like it's about to explode right out of my chest, and suddenly I hear Hope's voice say *Mummy*, as clear as if she were standing right beside me.

'Hope,' I say to Esme and Con, though they don't seem to have a clue what I'm talking about. 'That's Hope's bracelet.' Then before I know what I'm doing I'm wheeling around and running, down the stairs and through the shop and out into a world where suddenly for the first time in months everything makes perfect sense and I know exactly where I'm going.

Chapter 34

The track leading to the cottage is a quagmire. About halfway along, a tree has come down in the deluge and is lying partially blocking the path. I try negotiating my way around it, but there's a deep drainage channel to my left, full of muddy flood water, on the rise and coursing through it at an alarming rate, and after the front passenger wheel tips heart-stoppingly towards it and spins in the mud I am forced to abandon the effort before the rest of the car decides to follow suit. Gingerly, I ease open the driver's door and cover the rest of the track on foot, arriving a few minutes later coatless and drenched at the door to the cottage.

Ryan's car is still in the same place I'd seen it the last time I was here, squatting incontinently among the weeds leaking oil into the ground. Like last time, my stomach lurches when I see it. No, not like last time. Worse than last time. This time I know it killed my daughter.

I bypass the cottage and cross straight over to the car and lean against the bonnet, which is cold and unyielding beneath my hands. And wet from the relentless rain. Cold and wet and unyielding, the way it must have been when it caught Hope's fragile body and catapulted her over a wall before driving off and leaving her there to die. The breath catches in my throat, and I kneel in the mud right there in front of the car and spread my arms across the bumper, as if by doing so I can take away some of the impact, somehow soften the blow. The car goes on sitting there, unmoving, oblivious to the crazy woman prostrating herself in front of it like a sacrificial offering, and all at once I hate its casual indifference, its utter intractability. It's not a car any more; there's nothing inanimate about it. It's a ruthless killer, cold and unfeeling and utterly without remorse, and I want to kill it right back.

Before I have time to think, before the rational part of my brain has a chance to kick in and say, *Marion, what the fuck are you doing?* I'm banging on the bonnet with a bloody great rock I don't remember picking up, raining blows down on the metal, another part of my brain watching in wonder as starlike dents appear in the paintwork like fireworks while my arms move with a will of their own, down and up and down again in an explosion of noise, a chorus of indignant protests ringing out from under the bonnet as the car screams for a mercy I've no intention of extending. If I'd had a car crusher, the thing would have been the size of an ashtray by the time I'd finished with it. With every blow I feel a surge of energy rush through me, and if it hadn't been for the fact that I was suddenly rudely interrupted in my orgy of vandalism I could probably have crushed it to an ashtray with my bare hands, car crusher or no car crusher.

Ryan.

He's hanging around my neck, trying physically to drag me away from the car, but I'm oblivious to his efforts. I can hear him shouting something, but it's just noise in my ear, the angry buzzing of an infuriated wasp. With no more effort than I'd use swatting a fly, I brush him aside and he lands awkwardly on the muddy track a few steps away. I turn and tower over him, the rock still held aloft in my hand, and with a rush of euphoria I see that terror back in his eyes, and I realise that I don't need Hector any more to put the fear of God into him. I can do it all on my own. He's holding both hands in front of his face in case I decide to use the rock to break his head open (the thought has, in fact, crossed my mind), gibbering incoherently, his eyes stretched so wide I swear his whole face is about to split wide open. I give him a look of disgust, then spin round and lob the rock straight at the windscreen of the car, shattering the glass into thousands of guilty little nuggets.

Even though I'm now disarmed, he doesn't move from his landing spot in the mud but goes on looking at me, wild-eyed, as though I might suddenly leap across and tear him limb from scrawny limb. 'I would have knocked,' I tell him, spitting out the words, 'but I wanted to make more of an impact. You know all about impact, don't you, Ryan? About the sound it makes when you hit a little girl with half a ton of solid metal, you piece of shit?'

My words scurry across his forehead as he tries to make sense of what I'm saying, and then his expression freezes as they settle into the pattern that brands him a killer. What's he thinking, right now, lying there in the mud, while the woman whose daughter he murdered towers over him, filled with a rage that the battered car beside her has done nothing to defuse?

'I saw the bracelet. The one you gave to Con. Except that it wasn't yours to give, was it? It was Hope's.' My voice breaks on her name, but I force myself to go on. 'You took it, didn't you? You took it off her when she lay there dying after you'd run her down. You bent down and unhooked it off her wrist and left her in the mud to die, didn't you? *Didn't you?*' I scream the last two words at him, lunging towards him as though I really am going to rip him apart, and he shrinks back in the mud. 'I swear to God, they'll throw away the key when they lock you up for what you did.'

'Ah didn't!' He inches away on his muddy backside. 'It were just lying on t' road. Ah never unhooked it.' His eyes are still wide with terror.

'You left her there. You got back in the car and drove away and just left her there.' The words are acrid, curdling in my mouth, spewing themselves into the mud.

'Ah didn't,' he says again, more sullen this time.

'What d'you mean, you didn't? I suppose you just happened along there after another car had run her down, did you? Stopped to see if you could help? Don't make me laugh.'

He doesn't, which isn't surprising really. Right now I can't imagine a time when I'll ever laugh again. He just goes on lying there in the mud like a rabbit pinioned in the headlights of my fury.

After a moment he licks his lips. 'You think you're so smart, don't you? Think you know it all.' His face convulses involuntarily and he looks at me with utter loathing. 'Come barging in to other people's lives and mess everything up.'

'I didn't mess up your life.' I spit the words at him. 'You did that all on your own. I saw what you did to Con – the mess you made with your fists. And your feet,' I add, my face twisting in disgust. 'That poor girl –'

He snorts. 'Oh, aye, that poor girl. Poor innocent little Con, lumbered wi' me, eh? You've been a right guardian angel, you have.' His face contorts again. 'Getting her off in t' supermarket that day, taking her under your wing, sorting out that job for her. Messed things up good and proper for her an' me, didn't you?'

'You messed things up for yourself. You didn't need my help. And Con deserves –'

'Deserves what? Deserves better than me? Deserves a chance in life?' His face pulls into a sneer. 'You know what? You're welcome to her. Bloody little leech, she is, always whining on in my ear. Does my head in. Christ almighty. That time she come back from your place, she were in a right state. Threatening to go to t' police all over again.'

'What?' I look at him in bewilderment.

'Said the kid hadn't been dead,' he continues. 'That she'd bled to death in t' road. Said if we'd gone for help, like she'd wanted, she might've lived.'

I stare at him, aghast. 'Con *knew*? All this time?'

''Course she knew. Why d'you think she kept coming round after? Kept saying we owed you.'

I draw in my breath sharply, thinking back to that first

time Con and I had talked properly in the kitchen, the way the atmosphere had changed when I was telling her about what had happened to Hope. *I've got to go,* she'd said, and I'd assumed it was because she was uncomfortable confronting my grief, that she was too young to handle what I was telling her. It hadn't been that at all, I realise now. It had been guilt. The whole of our relationship had been underpinned by her guilt over what she knew.

Suddenly everything's changed, like one of those magic eye pictures you look at, the sort that's just a series of dots until your eye refocuses and the real picture emerges. I don't like the look of the picture that's emerging now, and I press my hands to my eyes to try to come up with a different one. Con knowing what Ryan had done all this time, and saying nothing to me, returning to him night after night when we'd spent a good part of each day together in what I'd foolishly thought was the beginning of some kind of a friendship. Con, who'd become so much like Hope when I was first getting to know her, who'd brought my handbag back, who'd sat in Hope's bedroom playing with her bits and pieces of jewellery and hair ribbons waiting for me to wake up. Con, whom I'd taken for a decent kid who'd just lost her way and needed help getting back on track. I think back to that day in the kitchen, when I'd just finished cutting her hair and we'd had that awful fight. She'd not given any sign. Had she? *It were an accident,* she'd said. I remember her saying it. I just thought she'd been speaking generally. Hadn't she? Or had she guessed, at that point, that her boyfriend had been responsible for Hope's death? As she'd sat there in my kitchen, listening to me telling her the graphic details of that night, had she known the child I was describing was the one her boyfriend had mown down?

And then something else dawns on me, something Ryan said earlier. *Said if we'd gone for help, like she'd wanted, she would have lived.*

If we'd gone for help.

'Con was with you?' I finally manage, hoping somehow that I've misunderstood him, that he'll contradict what he's just told me and admit that she wasn't there at all.

Ryan gives a harsh laugh, looking at me – I'd say almost pityingly, but I doubt he's capable of anything approaching pity. "Course she were with me. Not so much of a little miss perfect now, is she? And, let's face it, she were just as capable of going for help as I were.'

Much as I don't want to believe him, somewhere deep inside me I know he's speaking the truth. *It weren't my fault.* Her voice is clear in my head, spitting the words at me like she loathed me. Bile rises in my throat, and I turn and vomit copiously onto the ground behind me, retching on the bitterness of what he's told me, choking on it. I'm like that poor schmuck of a woman in a film Sam and I watched years ago, the one who throws up all the cherry stones until she asphyxiates from the effort. At least I think she asphyxiates, though maybe she just dies. I spit the last of my stomach lining into the mud and don't die, much as I'd like to, and when I turn around to confront him again, Ryan has disappeared.

I suppose I can't blame him. I would have killed him.

What mother wouldn't, given the opportunity to avenge the killing of her child? What mother wouldn't have wrapped her unforgiving fingers around his throat and smothered the life out of him?

I lean against the battered car for a moment, getting my breath back and trying to adjust to the fact that, unlike the cherry-stone woman, I'm not dead but still very much alive. The news about Con has cut me off somewhere around the knees, and I have to stay like that, leaning against the bonnet of the car while I wait for my head to stop reeling, my heart to stop pounding, my legs to get some feeling back in them again. All that time there's no sign of Ryan, and I'm beyond caring where he's disappeared to. The pair of them have insinuated themselves into my life like a cancer, and I want to take a very sharp knife and cut them both out, digging the blade deep into my flesh to make sure I don't miss any bits. I squeeze my fingernails into the palms of my hands and imagine how it would feel, but I can't feel anything at all, not even when I press so hard I break the skin on my left hand. Maybe I've lost the capacity to feel any more. Maybe that's the bit of me that's died, and all that's left is a hollow shell that walks around and looks like a human being. If you took a mallet and smashed it over my head, I'd probably break into a thousand hollow pieces like Humpty Dumpty. With a bit of luck there'd be no putting me back together again, either.

Eventually, after what feels like an eternity, I push myself off the bonnet and begin picking my way tiredly through the mud and back along the track to where I left my own car. Every bone, every sinew in my body aches with a dull pain that has nothing to do with the battle I just underwent against the Corsa, and I have to fight the urge to just lie down right there in the mud and let the rain wash me away.

I'm about twenty yards away from the fallen tree when I hear a low droning noise behind me, ten by the time I manage to summon up the energy to turn around and locate its source. Incredibly, considering the battering I gave it, the Corsa is hurtling along the track towards me, the broken windscreen pushed out and Ryan's face bleak behind the wheel. He's driving far too fast; if he isn't careful he'll be straight into the tree before he knows it. Some instinct makes me step out to flag him down and warn him, and I raise my right hand towards the car as though by doing so I can stop it in its tracks. Don't ask me why: a heartbeat ago I wanted to strangle the life out of him.

He shows no sign of having noticed me. Grimly determined, he hurtles on down the track, and only when he's a few yards away and his eyes lock onto mine do I realise he's not aiming for the tree at all.

They'll throw away the key when they lock you up.

Maybe I should have kept that little snippet to myself.

With a sudden jerking motion he swings the wheel around and the nose of the car lunges towards me. The back of it swings round wildly and he almost loses it, but then it somehow finds a grip in the mud again and leaps forwards. Rain is coursing down my face, making it difficult to see properly, and my feet seem to have somehow lodged themselves in the gluey mud, pinning me there, and I realise that I'm beyond moving, that I'm not sure anyway that I want to move out of the way. After all these months when I've fumbled my way from one bleak moment to the next, wondering when it will ever stop, trying to precipitate the end myself, when I've swallowed pills and offered myself up to a mugger's knife and prayed so many nights as I fell into tormented sleep that I might not wake from it, there's a rich irony – a rightness, even – about the idea of meeting my end by the same instrument that took the life of my daughter.

I can't hear the rain any more. It's poured itself out, and in its place a bright sun is gleaming off a thousand rain-drenched branches, warming my face, dazzling me. The whole world is a blaze of light, and I think, I'm dead. About bloody time, too. The noise of the car has melted away, and in the silence that wraps itself around me like a shroud I hear her voice again, and feel her hand steal its way into mine right there on the muddy track. *Mummy*, she says, and I gasp and laugh at the same time, kneeling in front of her to straighten the little yellow Brownie neckerchief she's wearing, feasting my eyes upon her, exulting in the curve of her cheek, the fresh glow of her skin. *You're here*, I say, and she giggles. *You look good enough to eat*. She giggles again and squirms under my hands, in a hurry to be some-where else. *Hug*, I tell her, pulling her close and squeezing her hard, inhaling the soft freshness that is so much a part of her, marvelling at her solidity, holding on to her just a moment longer than she can tolerate, and she squirms again in my arms. *Mummy*, she repeats, *I've got to go now.*

I'll come with you, I suggest.

She shakes her head. *You're too big to be a Brownie. You have to stay here.* She pulls out of my arms and skips away, and I try to follow her but I can't: my legs just won't move. She scrambles up the embankment where the tree has come crashing down, stopping for a moment at the top to bestow a last wave, and then turns to run, the warm breeze snatching at her hair, the sunlight dissipating her, melting right through her. And suddenly she's gone, over the top; the world is empty again and I'm alone on the track in the downpour, blinking myopically like a sleepwalker who's woken unexpectedly in the middle of a somnambulistic wandering, trying to remember what the dream had been that sent me wandering in the first place.

It takes me a moment to focus on the spectacle before me. Deep tyre tracks have gouged the muddy path in front of me into a boggy mess, but there's no sign of the car. It's almost as if some cosmic hand has come down and lifted it off the face of the planet. Or maybe it was me that it lifted, out of the path of the oncoming vehicle. But then if it had, that still doesn't explain the car's disappearance – that, or the excruciating pain in my right hand, which for some odd reason I'm cradling in my left. And then I spot it – the underneath of it anyway – jutting awkwardly out of the drainage channel, the rear wheels spinning lazily in the air. It appears to have nose-dived right into the water. The front of it is just visible, a blur of green under the dirty flood water. As I pick my way through the mud towards it, I spot the body sprawled across the bonnet like a broken mannequin, the legs pinned by the steering wheel, the face half-submerged by the water.

With my left hand, I grab hold of a handful of hair and lift Ryan's face clear of the water, and he gasps and splutters, spitting flood water. 'Still alive, then,' I say, and he moans, trying to form words and failing.

'What?' I lean in towards him. 'I can't understand what you're saying.'

He gags on the water. '– me,' he manages.

'You,' I repeat back at him. 'What about you?'

He tries again, spitting more water from his mouth. 'Help me.'

I look at him properly then, at the weasel-like features, the puny frame, and in my mind's eye I see him standing over Hope, looking down at her broken body on the ground, her bracelet clutched in his grimy, nail-bitten hand. I see Con beside him, clutching on to his arm, pleading with him to get help. As if I'd been there, I watch as he forces her back into the car and drives away, while behind them Hope's lifeblood spills into the earth. I am so filled with revulsion it's all I can do not to throw up again right there in his face.

I don't know what's happened to it, but my right hand is beyond useless. Even if I'd been of a mind to pull Ryan from the car, I doubt I'd have got very far. I shake my head at him, though I don't suppose he notices. 'I can't help you,' I tell him, which he does notice, and his mouth moves again.

'What?' I say.

'– leave me,' he says.

'Leave you?' I say, deliberately misunderstanding. I give a shrug. 'Well, sure, OK.' I let go of his hair, and his head plunges back downwards again. With a struggle, he manages to lift it clear of the water. 'You can't leave me here!'

I stop and turn around, taking stock of the rapidly rising water, the fact that his legs are trapped good and proper by the steering wheel, and I look at him once again, disgust making my lip curl. 'No,' I say eventually. 'I don't suppose I can leave you here, can I, Ryan? I mean, you'd have to lie there, trapped, while the water rose around you and drowned you. Wouldn't be a very nice way to go, would it – watching your own death creeping upon you inch by inch? Almost as bad as watching yourself bleed to death, I imagine. And what kind of a person would do that – walk away and leave someone to die? Oh – of course!' I raise my eyes heavenwards as though illumination has just struck. 'You would.'

I feel euphoric, empowered by a callousness of which I never knew I was capable. 'Bitch!' he hurls at my retreating back as I scramble up the bank. 'Fucking bitch!' Then his voice cracks and he begins to beg. 'Come back! Ah'm sorry, all right? Ah'm sorry! Don't leave me!' He starts to cry then, terror turning him into a frightened child, and I gloat in his misery. By the time I reach my car he is sobbing properly, choking and spluttering on the dirty flood water, and every wretched snivel is a balm on my heart. I swear I can still hear his sobs as I turn the car with my one good hand and drive away down the muddy track. Somewhere deep inside me a slow smile starts to form, and I realise as I pull onto the main road that, for the first time since Hope died, I've found the beginnings of a fragile kind of peace.

Chapter 35

By the time I get back to the flower shop, Con has disappeared. 'Just took off,' Esme tells me. 'I thought she'd come after you, but you must have missed each other.'

It's Esme who drives me to the hospital, tutting over the state of my hand, the mess of my clothes. 'You look like you had a run-in with the Loch Ness Monster,' she chides, wrapping rugs around my knees and tucking me into the passenger side of the car like an invalid.

'Did she say anything?' I want to know. 'After I'd left, I mean. Did she –?'

Esme shakes her head. 'Never a word. She just picked up the bracelet and looked at it, and then she grabbed her coat and took off down the stairs.'

She is tactful enough to avoid voicing the questions that must be spinning around in her head, and I am too wiped out to volunteer any explanations, to relive the awful confrontation at the cottage; the few precious moments when Hope came back to me that I still can't make any sense of; the run-in with Ryan in the flooded ditch when I discovered I possessed a heartlessness that would make Stalin look like Mother Teresa; the few change-of-heart minutes at the petrol station on the main road when I discovered I didn't. Even as the attendant had been ringing for the ambulance, I was back in my car and driving away, desperate to put as much distance as I could between myself and what had just happened. By the time we reach the hospital, I can see she's desperate for me to fill her in. And, as unreasonable as I know I'm being, I just can't go there yet.

I'm sitting in one of the curtained triage areas after a brief visit to the X-ray department while Sam's colleague Bob consults with the A&E nurse, discussing the necessary treatment for the broken bones in my hand. I can see I've worried him. When he asked me what happened and I told him I'd no idea, but I thought perhaps I'd been hit by a car, his face dropped in dismay and he started looking into my eyes with a little torch. He's in the throes of organising a CT scan when the curtain is pulled aside and a fourth person joins us. He nods at the other two and doesn't meet my eye. 'Bob, Julie,' he says, taking the admission notes out of the nurse's hand without asking and scrutinising them for a moment.

'Sam.' Bob's face is performing all sorts of contortions as he tries to convey to him that his wife is deranged. 'A quick word?' He inclines his head towards the curtain, and the two of them disappear, leaving me alone with the nurse, who gives me an uncertain little smile. Behind the curtain, Sam and Bob discuss my mental state in muted tones, and after a moment the curtain jerks aside once more and Sam is back.

'It's OK,' he tells the nurse, dismissing her. 'I've got this covered.' I can see that she's about to say something, but he shakes his head very slightly, quelling her with a look.

His eyes are tired; that's the first thing I notice. There are small creases at the corners that I don't remember him having before he went to Africa. As he bends his head over the notes again, I can see flecks of grey in the chocolate-brown hair that I've never noticed before either. Maybe it's the sight of those grey hairs, the sudden recognition of his vulnerability, I don't know, but my eyes fill with unexpected tears.

'When did you get back?' I manage after a moment. Not what I was planning to say when I next saw him, but it's the best I can come up with given the awkwardness of the situation.

'About an hour ago.'

'And you're straight back to work?' I can't keep the incredulity out of my tone.

'No.' He hesitates. 'Bob called me and told me you were here.'

Our eyes meet briefly and he looks away and then back at me without speaking for a moment, his mouth moving as if he's weighing up what to say. 'Have you had anything for the pain?'

I shake my head, though he's not looking at me any more. 'It doesn't hurt now.'

'Hmm.' He scowls at the monitor that's got my X-rays displayed on its screen. 'You've got broken phalanges in two of the fingers. If that isn't hurting like hell, you're either extremely brave or extremely insensitive to pain.'

Especially other people's, I think but don't say as he tilts back my head to look into my eyes the way Bob had done with the torch. 'Did you knock your head?' he wants to know.

'No.'

He frowns at me then. 'Bob thinks perhaps you did. He said you couldn't tell him what happened.'

I saw Hope. Ryan tried to kill me, and I saw Hope. I think perhaps she saved me.

'No,' I tell him. 'That's right. I couldn't.'

He tilts my head to the side and looks into my ears. 'He said you mentioned something about a tree lying across the road. And a car.'

'I was trying to warn the driver. I think he must have skidded and hit my hand.'

'Only your hand?'

'Yes.' There's a pause while he looks at me in silence, waiting for more. 'The road was very muddy.' The prospect of reporting Ryan to the police now is too exhausting to contemplate.

'Does your head hurt at all?'

'My head's fine.'

'Any nausea? Vomiting?'

'Sam,' I tell him, 'I'm fine. No vomiting. No headaches. I never banged my head. Just my hand.'

He shakes his head at me. 'Bob thinks you're in shock.'

I ignore the diagnosis. "You must be tired.'

'I slept on the plane.' He drops his eyes to my hand and probes my palm gingerly. 'Does this hurt?'

I shake my head.

'This?' He's squeezing the sides of my fingers gently. Again I shake my head.

'Nothing at all?'

'Nothing.'

'Hmm,' he says again, letting go of my hand. I want to

tell him to take back hold of it, but the words don't get any further than a half-formed sentence that breaks apart inside my head.

'You're probably going to need surgery for the worst fractures,' he tells me. 'But we'll start with splinting and see how you go over the next couple of days.'

'OK.'

'Right.' He regards me for a moment longer and then disappears behind the curtain, and I'm reminded of that first time I met him, when I'd found him so rude and dismissive, only to discover later that he'd been shy, not rude; that what I'd taken for dismissiveness was him trying to find the courage to ask me on a date.

He's back a couple of minutes later with a tray of stuff, which he sets down on the bed beside me. He works in silence, bandaging the middle finger to the index, the ring finger to the little finger.

I clear my throat. 'I didn't think you were due back yet.'

He looks at me askance. 'I didn't think you cared when I was due back. After what happened that night –' He breaks off, and then ploughs on. 'I had to go. You do know that, don't you? When I saw you that evening, and you were looking so – so *together* – I felt –' He falters. 'I tried calling you. Day after day. I lost count of the times I tried. You were never in.'

'I was away.'

'I couldn't leave a message. The bloody phone kept telling me the mailbox was full.'

'I was away,' I repeat.

He hesitates. 'The moment the plane took off, I realised

I'd blown it. I couldn't figure out what I was doing there, all those miles away. And I was stuck out there. Couldn't even get hold of you to talk to you.'

I draw in my breath sharply; I don't know what to say to him. I can't work out whether he's trying for a reconciliation or telling me it's really over.

'Marion –' he begins, and my heart gives a lurch. He glances up at me briefly and then nods at my hand. 'Keep it elevated, rested and iced.'

'OK.'

I wait to see if he's going to say anything else, and when he doesn't I start gathering up my things, aware that he's still regarding me intently.

'I'm going back out there next month.'

I swear my heart stops beating in my chest. All of a sudden I wish Ryan hadn't missed when he came at me with the car.

'I only came back for something I'd forgotten.'

I swallow, and turn back to face him. 'What?'

He meets my gaze steadily, like he's trying to read what's going on inside my head. 'You,' he says simply.

He takes a tentative step towards me then. He reaches out and pulls me into his arms, tightening them around me and burying his face in my hair. Through the thin fabric of his shirt, I can feel his heart beating softly against my face, the warmth of his body warming mine, and I'm suddenly overwhelmed by his defencelessness. Somewhere amidst all the anguish of the past months, I'd missed that. The way he'd got on with his life after the funeral, I'd thought him indestructible. We cling to each other in the little consulting room, like the last two survivors of a ship-wreck whose only hope of reaching the safety of the shore will vanish if they let go of each other. A fat tear squeezes out and trickles down my cheek. 'Oh,' I tell him, and as I do so I feel my heart breaking in half and all the grief it's been harbouring since Hope died pouring out over our feet. 'Well, that's all right, then.'

Epilogue

The shop looks just as it always has. The same metal buckets cluster importantly on the pavement, the sunflowers and the delphiniums and the peony roses having given way to a more sober gathering of chrysanthemums, lilies and rowan berries, marking out the passing of the seasons as surely as any calendar. It's late autumn, fast tipping into winter, and the watery sun that is doing its best to break through the heavy October cloud is a far cry from the hot African sun that's warmed my face over the past fourteen months.

I reach up my hand to the door handle, and in that moment a host of memories comes rushing up to meet me. Steeling myself, I push open the door. These days I am done with ghosts.

Esme is in the same place she always was, poring over a ledger at the back of the shop, muttering away to herself. 'I'll be right with you,' she says without looking up.

'No hurry,' I tell her, and she drops the pen she's holding with a cry.

'Marion!' she comes hurrying around the counter to greet me. 'Oh, it's that good to see you! Let me look at you. My, you look wonderful. A bit thin, perhaps, but we'll soon sort that out.' She beams at me. 'Now, you'll have a cup of tea. Away you go upstairs and I'll just drop the latch on the shop.'

The flat is nothing like the last time I was here. My legs are trembling as I cross the threshold, but immediately I realise I'm a world away from all the dust sheets and the fresh smell of paint. Now it's a cosy book-lined haven with fat armchairs pulled up companionably around a gas wood-burner, which Esme lights as she joins me in the room. She had moved in a couple of weeks after we'd left. 'Con wasn't going to be needing it for a bit,' she'd said. 'And it seemed a shame to let it stand empty.'

I knew, because she'd come to see me while I was recuperating at home after the run-in with Ryan, what had happened in the aftermath of my discovering the bracelet. Con had, finally, gone to the police, and admitted to everything – the accident, the muggings, even the theft of the CD in the supermarket that day. Apparently they'd arrived at the cottage pretty much at the same time as the ambulance I'd called. I knew they'd all turned up at the hospital together, anyway: Frank had kept Sam up to speed with the drama. And I'd suspected, though I hadn't known for sure until Esme was round visiting, that their timely arrival was probably her doing.

Ryan had gone down for causing death by dangerous driving. Twelve years, he'd been given; the judge had apparently been in a bad mood when he was passing sentence. It meant nothing to me when I found out. I was done with Ryan when I left him in the ditch. Con had demanded she take her share of punishment, and had wound up being put on remand, back in a unit for six months. Esme had kept her job open for her, and once the remand period was up social services had helped her find a flat locally. I hadn't wanted to know where. Whilst I admired Esme's charitable nature, I didn't feel up to opening my heart back up to Con. Not yet, at any rate. I'd made it a condition of coming back to see Esme that she make sure I wouldn't run into her.

Esme knows that Sam and I are on our way up to Scotland. In the first soul-searching days and weeks after our reconciliation, recognising the need to take some time out together so that we could draw a line under everything that had happened, I'd thought over his suggestion that we return to Africa and finally taken the plunge, offering myself as a volunteer on the project he was working on. They'd fallen over themselves to accept. Sam had continued working with the clinic, educating the locals on health issues, while I'd spent my time helping at a newly opened nursery school for the orphaned children from a local mission. It had been heart-wrenching, emotionally charged work, a far cry from the half life we'd been living back in Yorkshire, and I knew within a week of arriving that it had been the right thing for us to do. Eleven months into the project, with the time for our return to the UK fast approaching, we'd instructed an estate agent to put the house on the market, knowing we wouldn't be returning to Harrogate. Sam had put out feelers and landed a twelve-month post as a locum consultant in emergency medicine for NHS Lothian, and Esme, who'd been keeping an eye on the house anyway, handled the practical side of the sale, clearing it out once a buyer had been found, arranging for its contents to be sent away to auction – all except a few photographs, which she'd hung on to for us to pick up from her when we were back.

'You must be excited about Scotland,' she says now. 'Found anywhere to stay yet?'

'Mmm-hmm. Well, Charlie found it for us. We're renting a place in Stockbridge. It's got a garden, which is a rarity in that part of town, so Hector won't feel too hemmed in.'

'Your sister'll miss him.'

'Yes, she will. She says it's been like having a four-legged nanny around. Apparently Harry Junior has been learning to walk by hauling himself up on Hector's coat. But they're getting a dog of their own.'

'You're sure it wouldn't be better just to leave him with them? I mean, there's no saying but you might want to take off back to Africa again.'

I shake my head at her. 'No. That's not going to happen. Africa was . . . well, it was an escape, I suppose. A chance for Sam and me to discover who we were when it was just the two of us again. And I'll always be grateful we had that time together. It helped draw a line under everything that had happened – close the chapter, if you like. Besides . . .' I hesitate fractionally. 'I need to be back in the UK. Charlie and I –' I place a protective hand over my stomach '– well, we've got this thing about having our babies on home soil.'

Esme gives a gasp, and I feel a great surge of emotion welling up inside me. I'd held off telling her over the phone for exactly this reason – I'd wanted to see her reaction for myself. 'You mean –? Oh, Marion.' Her eyes have filled with tears. 'I'm so happy for you.' She sniffs, pulling a tissue from her sleeve. 'Would you look at the state of me?' She regards me once again, tears running down her cheeks. 'I really am happy for you.' She's blubbering properly now, and I can't help joining in, laughing through my tears the way I'd done when I found out six weeks ago, incredulous that the miracle we'd stopped hoping for years ago had finally happened.

'It's like a miracle,' Esme echoes my own thoughts through her tears.

'I know.' I give a watery laugh. 'Of all the futures we glimpsed after Hope died, this wasn't in any of them.'

'Must be something special about the African water,' Esme surmises.

I think back to the water vendors who travel around Nakuru's outlying communities, making a living delivering water from the nearest water kiosk by bicycle. We were lucky at the orphanage, which boasted two new 10,000-litre water tanks and was relatively self-sufficient, though the water was still treated as a precious commodity, and not a drop of it was wasted. 'Very special,' I agree quietly.

'So.' She blows her nose vigorously on the tissue. 'A fresh start for you. I've those photographs you wanted in a box. I'll get them for you before you leave.'

'That would be great. Sam and I – we're so grateful to you for sorting everything out the way you did. The idea of coming back and sifting through all that . . . stuff . . . well, it wasn't something either of us fancied much.'

Esme's regarding me keenly. 'I've something else for you, too,' she says after a moment. She heaves herself to her feet and crosses to a small bureau in the corner, then fishes inside for a brown envelope, which she hands to me. It has my name scrawled on the outside in a hand I don't recognise. Mystified, I tear it open and upend it, and a flash of silver tumbles into my lap.

I sit transfixed, staring at the bracelet lying in my lap, and then I jump to my feet, knocking it to the floor.

'I don't want it.' My heart is hammering in my chest.

'Och, now, Marion.' Esme's on her feet in a flash. 'Come on, now, there's no need to go upsetting yourself. You've got that baby to be thinking of.'

She ushers me back into my seat, leaving the bracelet where it's landed between us on the carpet. Neither one of us makes a move to pick it up.

'I don't want it,' I say again. 'It's dirty,' I add after a moment, though the chain and the ribbon are as bright as they ever were.

'Well, that's all right.' Esme's voice is soothing. 'You don't have to have it. She just thought you might. You can just leave it there.'

My face twists. 'I can't bear to think of Ryan with his grubby little hands all over it,' I say. 'Picking it up off the ground and taking it, and then the two of them leaving her behind to –' I break off. A lump has come up in my throat, and I swallow. 'I don't want it,' I say for the third time.

Esme says nothing for a moment, and then she stands up quietly. 'I'll just take these tea things through and fetch that box,' she murmurs, collecting up our mugs and the plate of shortbread. She disappears back through to the kitchen, leaving me alone in the little sitting room with the bracelet still lying forlornly on the carpet at my feet.

Above my head on the mantelpiece, an old-fashioned clock is ticking away the afternoon. I hadn't noticed it earlier, when Esme and I had been talking. I lift my face to look at it: the hands are pointing at a quarter to two. I'm supposed to be meeting Sam in fifteen minutes.

I pick up the envelope again and discover a neatly folded note tucked inside it. I stare at it angrily for a moment, and then I pull it out.

Dear Marion, it begins. The handwriting is rounded and childish. Innocent, I suppose you could call it, though the thought makes my fingers curl. *I just wanted to say how sorry I am for everything that's happened.* I draw a deep breath. All of it – the bungled mugging, the odd friendship between Con and me – it all seems like a lifetime ago.

The letter continues:

I went to the police, Ryan got done for dangerous driving. I told them I'd been there, too, that I never said nothing at the time, and I got remanded, so it was back to another unit for a bit, which was OK, I suppose. I've got my own place now, though. Going to Manchester two days a week to do a floristry training course at the college, in between working for Esme. My social worker thinks I've got talent.

I don't know if you want the bracelet or not, but you might, so here it is. I think you should have it. If it hadn't of been for the bracelet, I suppose we might never of known the truth about what happened, not for sure, anyway. I wondered, all the time I knew you. Felt so guilty about it, but Ryan kept saying it could

*of been anyone, could of been a different kid. And
that's what I wanted, more than anything. I wanted
it to be a different kid. I didn't want to think I'd been
partly to blame for what happened to Hope. Then
when I saw your face that day in the flat, when you
picked up the bracelet, well, then I couldn't go on
pretending any more.*

   *Anyway. I'm done with all that these days. I'm done
with a lot of things, to tell you the truth. I'll always owe
you for what you did for me, and I never deserved a
second of it. Not a second. I'm not going to ask you to
forgive me because I know you can't, but I'm sorry.*

Swear down I am.
   Con

I look back at the bracelet, and eventually I reach down
and pick it up, holding it between my thumbs and my
forefingers so that I can look at each of the little charms
in turn, scrutinising them to see whether their adventures
over the past eighteen months or so have left any mark. I
start with the heart that had marked Hope's first birthday,
when she'd just learned to stand up and babble nonsense
at me, remembering the hours we'd spent with her fists
closed around my fingers, taking tentative steps across the
carpet as she was learning to walk. I move on to the hat
that had arrived on her second birthday, when she was
working on her running and her knees were permanently
scraped from all the tumbles she took in the garden. Next
to the hat came the horse, which arrived when she'd reached

the grand old age of three and had learned that she could undress herself, which she did with great enthusiasm and surprising speed, irrespective of where we happened to be at the time. By her fourth birthday, when she'd learned to skip and hop and ride her tricycle, Sam had stepped into his grandmother's shoes with the hyena/husky he'd rechristened Hector when she was five – the year of the hermit crab that marked the beginning of her school career. I remember that first day at school: she'd looked so grown-up in her uniform when we'd been leaving the house, and so small and apprehensive when she was queuing up with the other new pupils in the playground after the bell had rung. The little girl in front of her had been sobbing noisily, and Hope had taken her hand and said something to her – I never found out what, but it stopped the girl's tears and even produced a wonky smile. Just as they'd been disappearing inside, Hope had turned to seek out my face in the crowd of anxious mummies clustered at the school gate, and given me a determined wave. I sigh at the memory, and move on to the next charm – the hockey stick that had marked the year she'd learned to tie her own laces and had had her smiling crisis while we were out visiting Charlie in Michigan. Then followed the helicopter with the rotating blades that she got when she was seven and we'd gone out to buy her Brownie uniform together. I flick the blades, and they turn briefly. Next came the handbag Sam had chosen for her eighth birthday, when she had seemed to be so grown-up, and the hedgehog he'd found for her ninth, the year she sang a solo at the school Christmas concert and Sam and I had sat blubbering in the audience, our hearts overflowing with pride. I pick them over one by one, each little silver nugget marking a different milestone in her short life, and then I slide the bracelet into my pocket with a sigh.

'I'd better be off,' I tell Esme when she returns bearing a cardboard box, which she hands to me. She gives no sign of noticing the bracelet's disappearance.

'Well, it was grand seeing you.' Her tone is bright and brisk. 'Are you seeing your friends before you leave?'

'Heather and Martin?' She nods, and I shake my head. 'They're away on holiday. Italy, I think. They've promised to come up and visit us in Edinburgh.'

'Well, that'll be nice.'

I nod, agreeing with her. 'Yes, it will. If they come, that is.'

She looks at me, surprised. 'You don't think they will?'

I shrug. 'Who knows? If they do – great. And if they don't – well, that's fine too.' I give her a wry smile. 'That was then, you see. And this is now. A fresh start, like you said.'

'Aye, well.' She sighs. 'That's the way of things, I suppose. Some people just come into your life for a wee while, and then they're off again.' Then she nods at me. 'The trick is to remember all the good bits.'

I think of all the people that could apply to, besides Heather and Martin. Con. My parents. Hope. *Remember all the good bits*. I close my fingers around the bracelet in my pocket, and vow to try.

'You'll be up for Christmas?' I remind her of the invitation I'd issued while we'd still been in Nakuru, the day I rang her to say we were selling the house.

She nods and squeezes my arm. 'Try and stop me. Princes Street Gardens in December, all lit up like a Christmas card.' Her eyes are alive with excitement. 'I can't wait.'

Sam's still sitting in the same place I'd left him when I went to visit Esme, on the veranda of the tearoom in the park, watching out for me as I come walking up the path, his breath clouding in front of his face. 'You must be freezing,' I say, climbing the steps to greet him.

'Well, I have to admit it's a bit colder than Nakuru.' He stands and takes the cardboard box from me. 'All done?'

'Mmm-hmm.'

'Sure? There's nothing else you want to do before we head north?'

I slide my hand into my pocket and let the fingers close over the bracelet once again. 'Nothing,' I tell him, sliding my other hand into his.

We start to make our way back down the steps onto the path. 'You're quite sure?' he asks again. 'You don't want to stop off at the cemetery?'

I turn to check his face. 'Do you?'

He regards me thoughtfully for a moment, and then shakes his head. 'Not really,' he says. 'She isn't there, after all.'

'No,' I agree with him, tightening my grasp on the bracelet in my pocket. 'She was never there.'

As we reach the car I turn and take a final look around me. The autumn colours are breathtaking: a riot of crimson and gold leaves scattered untidily across the park and pavements. I've always loved this time of year, even though so much around me is coming to the end of its life. You always know, no matter how many leaves drop in that lazy freefall to the ground, that there'll be another crop of them next year.

And I, Marion Bishop, God willing, am planning to be around to see them.

*Turn the page for an exclusive interview
with Susy McPhee . . .*

EBURY
PRESS

What was the inspiration for The Runaway Wife?

This might sound a bit macabre of me, but I really enjoy putting my characters in a dark place and then sitting back and seeing how they cope! When I wrote *Husbands and Lies*, life for Fran was pretty sweet at the beginning, even though her best friend was terminally ill. She had a great job, a devoted husband, a gorgeous daughter – plenty to take comfort in. The real problems started for her when she began to suspect her husband of infidelity, and frankly she brought a lot of her problems on herself because she let her imagination run away with her and didn't tackle the problem head-on – a trait which, certainly from the feedback I've had, is something a lot of us can recognise! With *The Runaway Wife*, I put Marion in the darkest place she could be right at the start, and the novel became the story of her journey back into the light. Deciding what had brought her to that dark place was difficult: I had to spend some time just thinking about what would make her want to take her own life. The idea of losing a child must be every mother's worst nightmare, so I began with that premise and took things from there.

The Runaway Wife *starts with your heroine contemplating suicide after the loss of her daughter and the break-up of her marriage. Did you find it difficult to blend this tragedy with the lighter elements of the book?*

Really difficult! I didn't want to make light of Marion's situation, but at the same time the subject matter is so depressing! Getting the balance right between respecting the place Marion's in and not making the reader want to slash their own wrists was very tricky, particularly in the beginning. But then Marion herself is such a wonderful character, a real survivor: eventually she came to my rescue and just took over the story.

If you were only allowed to write one or the other, would it be comedy or tragedy?

I think you need both for the story to work, otherwise either one could become a bit relentless. Comedy itself often has a cruel side to it – someone's usually the fall guy in the jokes we tell, and it's that cringe-making I'm-glad-that's-not-me, or even the oh-that-could-be-me, that makes us laugh. I think my writing's more tragic than comic: the comedy is the light relief to help the characters get through it all.

Which book has made you laugh? Which book has made you cry?

My brother recently lent me Jeffery Archer's *A Prisoner of Birth*, and when I got to the last word I actually laughed aloud. I could see it coming a few sentences beforehand, but that only added to my anticipation. I wandered around the house afterwards with a big grin on my face and the feeling that all was right with the world.

As for crying, well, I hate to be a total sap, but I did bawl my eyes out at *Marley and Me*. I'd defy anybody who's even remotely doggy not to feel the tears prickling at this one. Mind you, I also laughed a lot along the way as well. I cried at places in *The Poisonwood Bible*, too, and in *A Thousand*

Splendid Suns. And I cry at some of the stuff I write myself, which is ridiculous really given that I made it all up! But maybe that's a symptom of general mental deterioration: the girls reckon it's only a matter of time before I'll be able to hide my own Easter Eggs . . .

Which book would you never have on your bookshelf?

Anything I've read that's disappointed me. I just put a stack of books out for the charity shop this weekend because they were such a let-down. I wouldn't mind, but a fair proportion of them had won or been shortlisted for awards. One of them – an international bestseller, apparently – had been longlisted for the Man Booker Prize. That made me laugh. Longlisted? How long's the list? I tell you, it must have stretched to Antarctica and back. The book was covered in quotes telling you it was spellbinding, vivid, brutal, exhilarating. I really, really wanted to like it. But I couldn't. It was awful. And then I felt as though there was something wrong with me for not liking it when all these other people had raved about it. So it made me feel guilty as well. Disappointing and guilt-inducing. It had to go.

Is there a particular book or author that inspired you to be a writer?

I hate to tell you, but I never really felt inspired to be a writer! I never got to the end of a book and thought, hey, I could do this! Writing is just something that's inside me and needs to get out, a bit like a dodgy appendix. That's not to say I don't find certain books or authors inspiring. I love John Steinbeck's *Of Mice and Men*. The idea of holding fast to your dream, however small or mundane that dream might be in other people's eyes, is really what I would call inspiring.

What is your favourite word?

I don't have one favourite word that stands out above all others, but some have caught my attention over the years and usually raise a smile. 'Moist'. That's a great word. I particularly like it because my daughter Carolyn can't stand it and will visibly recoil if you say it in her presence. I have a friend who was speaking recently about her time at boarding-school, and she mentioned the time they came back from somewhere and made a 'beezer' chili. I loved that – straight from Enid Blyton! I also like 'some' and 'chocolate' and 'have', particularly when they're ordered correctly. And I like 'yes'. It's just a much nicer word than 'no'.

Why do you write?

Well, I tried brain surgery, but I wasn't cut out for it. Also, dogs aren't allowed in the theatre, apparently, which is a mistake if you ask me. Dogs are known for their therapeutic value.

Which book are you reading at the moment?

The Rothbard-Rockwell Report. It's a collection of essays by the libertarian economist and historian Murray N. Rothbard, who died in 1995. They're witty, insightful, opinionated, and scathingly uncompromising.

Dream casting time: who in the movie of The Runaway Wife *would play Marian? What about Sam?*

I'd have someone like Emily Mortimer for Marion, with Emma Watson playing Con. I think they'd work well together. And Sam? Maybe Jeremy Northam or Greg Wise. Someone who looks good in a chunky sweater. Sam is definitely a chunky sweater kind of guy.

Hector plays a very important part in the story. Is Hector based on anyone? What's your dog-owning history?

Hector was named after a dog I met walking up the hill one day, but his personality is absolutely taken from my own dog, Mishka, although I think Hector is better-behaved: I can't imagine him ever stealing an entire tub of party rings or munching his way through a whole layer of Marks & Spencer chocolates while his owner was in the bath. I've had dogs all my life: at one point there were eleven flat-coated retrievers living in my house, nine of them under a month in age. The kitchen was a sea of black furry bodies in the morning. They would come sweeping towards you on a tide of piddle and attach themselves to the hem of your dressing-gown by their tiny but nonetheless sharp milk teeth, and not let go until you gave them their breakfast. My husband's as bad, to be honest, but I can usually beat him off with a spoon.

What are you working on at the moment?

Well, in between helping my daughter Helen and her husband Oliver renovate their very old and crumbling Victorian house, I'm on my next book, which is about an identical twin who steals her sister's life. More dark stuff: I think I'm getting a bit of a taste for it.

Turn the page for a taster of Susy McPhee's first novel, *Husbands and Lies*, also available from Ebury Press . . .

Chapter 1

My mother taught me to lie.

Don't get me wrong. She never sat me down and said, 'Okay, Francesca, today's lesson is all about the art of the tangled web' or any such thing. She was far subtler than that, although as a rule the use of the word *subtle* in conjunction with my mother would demand the immediate addition of the 'as a brick' qualification. My mother rode roughshod through life on a tougher-than-rhino saddle leaving a trail of debris the size of Africa in her wake.

She taught me other things, too, of course, like where to hide when she was in one of her rages and how to hold the tops of my hand-me-down socks in place with a rubber band – early lessons that were dismissed with ne'er a nostalgic glance backwards once I left home and had shaken off the shackles of my childhood. The lying, though: that was another matter altogether. That one I practised. By the time I hit twelve I had it off to a fine art.

Which was just as well, really. Lord knows what kind of adult I'd have made if I hadn't learned to differentiate between compulsive honesty and an occasional well-placed falsehood. Sometimes, during the long, interminable days and nights of Alison's illness, lying was the only thing that kept me going.

Not least, of course, the lying I did to myself.

Alison. My best friend since primary school, when she'd punched Billy Waterman after he made me cry during times tables practice by showing me his willy under the table. She'd waited until playtime and then collared him by the girls' toilets, where she'd split his lip with a right hook that Frank Bruno would have been proud of. When an unexpected promotion brought me south from Staffordshire seven years ago, one of the deal clinchers had been that my new office was fifteen minutes from where Alison was living.

And now she was shackled to a hospital bed by a tangle of tubes and could barely lift a hand from the covers, let alone throw a punch. I caught a glimpse of her through the corridor window as I approached the side room that had been her home for the past month and a half, and a thousand horrible truths rampaged through my head. *So this is what it does to you. What's happened to your hair? Is your skin supposed to be that colour?*

I ignored them and set my mouth in a determined line lest they try to break forth anyway. 'You look well.'

'Liar.' Alison gave me a weak smile. 'I look like shit.'

'No, really – I think you look – well, you don't look so tired today. Your eyes look brighter.'

Alison regarded me closely. 'More than I can say for you, then. You look like you haven't slept in a fortnight.'

'I'm fine.' I dropped my coat over the back of the chair and drew it up alongside the bed.

'Sure? Max and Lottie okay?'

'Mmn? Oh – yeah. They're fine.'

Alison eased herself forward in the bed. 'Hon? You sure you're okay? Only you don't look okay to me. You look – grey.'

I regarded her for a moment, and felt tears begin to threaten. Oh, God. I always vowed before I came in that I wouldn't go getting upset in front of her. But watching your best friend being taken from you by degrees, deteriorating with each visit as the cancer that had been diagnosed five months earlier ate her up from the inside, was never going to be easy. Her concern for my wellbeing was humbling.

I pulled myself together. 'Grey, you think?' I gave a mock sigh and folded my arms across my chest. 'Yeah, well, Max was saying much the same thing the other day.'

She raised her eyebrows at the suggestion of my paragon of a husband saying anything so maladroit. '*Max* was?'

'Mm-hmn.' I looked at her innocently. 'We've just bought this new full-length mirror for the bedroom. One of those – chevalier things, you know. In an antique pine frame, to go with the dressing-table. It's got this little design kind of carved into the top of the frame.' I gestured with my hand, and she nodded encouragingly. Then I sighed heavily again. 'Anyway, I was just out of the bath, and doing the whole *scrutinising* thing in front of it – *big* mistake, by the way – and I said to Max, "Look at me. I'm fat, I'm wrinkled, I'm old, and I'm grey." I was waiting for him to disagree, you see.' Alison nodded again. 'And he didn't, so eventually I said, "For goodness' sake, Max, say something nice to me."'

Alison waited expectantly. 'And did he?'

I lowered my eyes. 'He said – well, he said—' I hesitated. '"At least there's nothing wrong with your eyesight."'

Alison gave a shout of laughter, and a nurse who was busy at a desk across the corridor looked over at us and smiled. Then Alison sobered again.

'No, but seriously, Fran. I think you're overdoing things.'

'I'm not.'

'You *are*. How could you not be? Full-time job. Husband and kid to look after – admittedly both cute, adorable, blah blah, but still a handful. Useless best friend who's about as much help to you as a chocolate teapot.'

'Less,' I said.

'What?'

'Less use. At least I could comfort-eat my way through a chocolate teapot.'

She stuck out her tongue. 'Sod off. Though I suppose it might fatten you up, at least.' She reached out and plucked at the sleeve of my jumper. 'Look at you. You're all skin and bone. Fat, my ass. *I've* got more meat on me than you.'

'Yeah, well.' I gave her a sidelong look, and one of the earlier truths I'd been trying to suppress slipped out before I could help it. 'At least I still have my own hair.'

She bit her lip to stop herself from smiling, and I felt the tears welling up once again.

'Come here,' she ordered, and patted the side of the bed. I slid reluctantly onto the edge of the mattress beside her, and she wrapped her wasted arms around my shoulders and leant her head in against mine for a moment, so that I could smell the fresh perfume that was so quintessentially Alison, the fragrance she had never lost despite the prolonged stay in hospital and the punishing weeks of treatment she'd undergone, which made me want to cry all the harder and cling on to her and scream at the gods to leave her be and stop their relentless quest to take her from me. Then she pushed me away and studied me at arm's length, narrowing her dark-shadowed eyes at me intriguingly.

'I want you to help me with something.'

I sniffed unattractively, feeling around unsuccessfully for a handkerchief, and she passed me a tissue from a box that stood alongside a vase of white freesias on her bedside cabinet.

'Go on.' I blew vigorously into the tissue.

She gave me one of her wicked looks, her eyes gleaming. 'You're not allowed to say no.'

'Oh God.'

'I'm dying. Would you refuse the wishes of a dying woman?'

'Yes!' I blew again. 'No,' I admitted.

She grinned at me conspiratorially, then gestured towards the cabinet. 'Open it. Top shelf.'

I did as I was bidden.

'There's a notepad on top of my clean PJs. Got it?'

'Uh-huh.' I lifted it out, and she took it from me and rifled through the pages. Then she handed it back to me, and I began to read aloud what she had written in her clear, rounded hand.

'"Thirty-something, closer to my fourth decade than my third, alas; never done any online dating before."' I raised my eyes to Alison. 'You're joining a dating agency?'

She gave a tired laugh. 'Not me, you cheeky bugger. I'm nowhere near my fourth decade.' She nodded at the page. 'Keep reading.'

I cleared my throat. '"One careful previous owner (lady driver). Friends tell me I have a good sense of humour, that I'm trustworthy and fun, but then I pay them well to say all that stuff!"' I broke off and raised my eyebrows at her before continuing. '"I'm into good food, great wine and long lazy weekends in the country. Strengths: I can cook. And wash up afterwards. And iron my own shirts. Weaknesses: hopeless fashion sense. Besotted by my six-year-old daughter. Would love to meet lady with similar interests who isn't afraid of tackling someone with a wardrobe dating back to 1979, isn't repulsed by children, and enjoys at least the occasional glass of Cloudy Bay."'

'Well? What d'you think?'

I looked at her, confused. 'Um … he sounds divine. But – don't you think it's a bit optimistic to be looking at going out on dates, given the circumstances?' I gestured at the paraphernalia of equipment surrounding her bed. 'I mean, where will you hide the drip? Can you even remember how to put on anything that isn't a pair of pyjamas? Not to mention, won't Adam mind?' And do I care if he does, I asked myself, though I didn't voice this last, uncharitable thought. Adam, Alison's husband, worked as a producer for the BBC. The first time I'd met him, when Alison had brought him round for dinner and a checking-over after she'd been on a couple of dates with him, I'd been struck by his likeness to Max, and a bit dazzled on discovering that he routinely wined and dined some of Hollywood's finest. He was full of funny anecdotes about the lesser-known habits of the movers and shakers in the world of television, and I'd found myself seduced by his easy charm. Between the cashmere sweater and the fancy cufflinks he was wearing, he was like a glamorous version of Max, who wasn't wearing a sweater but who had rolled the sleeves of his shirt up above his elbows, and whose fingernails bore traces of the engine oil he'd been unable to scrub clean after he'd come in from work that evening. He had teased me after Alison and Adam had left at the end of the night, telling me I'd never be able to cope with a man who spent longer in front of the mirror than me. My admiration had been short-lived, however: the next time we were out together at a party, Adam had made a pass at me and had laughed in the face of my self-righteous indignation when I turned him down, calling me a prude. Since that time I'd harboured feelings of protectiveness towards both Alison and Max, neither of whom I'd ever told, and a desire to run a hot kebab skewer through one of Adam's eyes every time I saw him.

Alison looked hard at me now, her eyes glittering.

'What?'

'That *is* Adam.'

'What?' I felt stupid and slow all of a sudden.

'Adam and Erin.'

'What?' I said again.

'Fran!' She gave an exasperated sigh. 'I need you to say something other than just "What?" all the time.'

'But – I don't—'

'Yes, you do, Fran.'

I looked hard at her. My mouth felt suddenly dry. She continued to grill me with her eyes.

'You've written a dating CV for your husband,' I said eventually.

'Mm-hmn.'

'Because ...?'

She sighed. 'Please don't make me spell it out for you.'

'Spell it out for me.' I could feel a great surge of anger welling up inside me.

'Oh, Fran.' She reached out to take one of my hands, but I pulled away from her. She shrugged.

'Okay, then. I don't want Adam left moping on his own for the rest of his life. You should hear him when he's in visiting. Believe me, it's not like when you come in.' She broke off, and ran a hand distractedly across what was left of her ravaged hair. Then she rubbed her face with both hands for a moment, as though looking inside herself for the right words.

'I live for your visits,' she finally admitted, emerging from behind her hands. 'I love it when you come in: you make me laugh. You let me say things like "I'm dying", without giving me those great reproachful looks Adam's so good at. You poke fun at my hair, at the state I've become, without making me feel you're trying to protect me from some awful truth that everybody else already knows about but that I'm supposed to pretend I'm oblivious to. You tell me I'm less use than a chocolate teapot and make up stupid stories about looking at yourself in front of a mirror—'

'I do stuff like that to make you laugh!' I said, still angry. 'That doesn't mean I've become reconciled to losing you. It doesn't mean I haven't given up hope that they'll find some miracle cure. There are new advances in medicine every day now, and you've got to stay positive. You're not allowed to give up hope! You never know: the next treatment—'

'Stop it, Fran,' she admonished. 'Don't lie to me. Not you, too. There won't *be* any more treatments. You know that.' She reached out for my hand again, and again I refused her advances. She sighed patiently. 'Of all the people who surround me every minute of every day – the nurses, the oncologists, Adam, Erin, my mum – you're the only one who treats me any way that even approaches normal. When Adam comes in, I'm not allowed to mention the cancer. He doesn't know how to cope with it. He used to ask about the tests, the treatments, you know? But he stopped doing even that eventually. The answers were never what he wanted to hear. I feel as though I'm letting him and Erin down because I can't defeat this thing and I'm just going to up and – *disappear* one day, and the thought of them being left on their own terrifies me. You *know* how hard this is. You're a wife and a mother as well. Lottie's the same age as Erin. Adam and Max are so alike they could be twins – aren't we always saying that? And yet you treat me just the same as you always did, as though you're sucking the juice out of every visit and you're not going to let this foul thing that's eating me up steal what's left of our time together. I couldn't do this without you. I need you to stay honest for me.'

She was so calm. I envied her that, even if I didn't agree with whatever mad scheme she was cooking up. Frankly, I suspected that Adam would be more than capable of taking care of himself in the future.

I picked up the notepad once again.

'"One careful previous owner?"' I raised my eyebrows at her.

'Too much of a cliché?' She wrinkled her nose at me. 'I didn't want to put "widower". It makes him sound about a hundred. Plus, it seems a bit tasteless to mention it in a dating ad.'

'Whereas asking your best friend to collude with you in producing the ad whilst you lie dying in a hospital bed is the very height of good taste, I suppose.'

She smiled at me heartbreakingly. 'I love you, Fran.'

I sighed in exasperation, refusing to acknowledge the treacherous tears that were once again threatening. 'What do you want me to do?'

'Well.' She clasped her hands together in front of her excitedly. I had to admit, she hadn't looked this fired up in weeks. 'Nothing with the ad yet, obviously. Except – well, I'm not sure if I've hit the right tone. I thought perhaps you could go on to a couple of online dating sites and get a kind of feel for them – suss out what people normally say, that sort of thing. And then print a few out so that we can go over them together. I mean, mentioning Erin might be a huge no-no. I don't want to put people off before they've given him a chance.'

'Erin wouldn't put anybody off!' I said indignantly. 'The child is a doll.'

She laughed at my outraged tone. 'Of course she is,' she agreed. 'But there might be some *amazing* woman out there who is perfect for Adam and Erin, but doesn't even know how great she'll turn out to be with kids and would run a mile at the prospect, but once she meets Adam and realises how fantastic *he* is, she won't *want* to run. D'you see?'

'Not even remotely. But what the hell.' I looked at her eager face. 'Okay, okay: so − *if* I agree, you want me to suss out the lingo and report back. Is that it?'

'Well, no. Sorry. *Afterwards*−' She looked at me meaningfully. 'I want you to join him up without telling him.' I started to protest, but she held up a hand to stop me. 'This is important to me, Fran, so please hear me out. I mean, give it a decent period of time − six months, say. No longer than that. I don't want him brooding.'

I bit back a snort. The thought of Adam brooding was hard to swallow.

'And then go through any responses, and see if you can't find him a nice girl to look after him and Erin,' Alison continued. 'I mean, *I'm* not going to be around to filter out the fortune hunters from the singing nuns.'

'But − how on earth am I going to do that? I can hardly pretend to be him, can I, when all these would-be perfect women start phoning up to arrange dates with him?'

'Oh − you'll think of something,' Alison said dismissively. 'You can say you're his PA, or something. Didn't you tell me you worked with someone who met his partner through a dating agency? A really pretty girl who works in advertising?'

'Modelling,' I admitted reluctantly. 'Greg Patterson. He heads up the system architecture team. They're getting

married at the end of the month. Second time round.'
Greg's first wife had left him in the middle of a rainy
November day, hiring a van and clearing their carefully
constructed loft apartment of every stick of furniture while
he was at work. She hadn't left a note.

'Well, then,' Alison said, as if that solved everything.
'You can ask him for some hints and tips.'

'Alison,' I said, trying to sound patient, 'I am not going
to a colleague to ask for hints and tips on how to set up my
best friend's husband on a dating site. I mean, apart from
the fact that he would think me stark staring mad, it would
be completely unprofessional. Guys just don't talk about
that stuff in the office, plus I'm his *associate*—'

'So how come you know all about how he met his
fiancée?'

'He – I don't remember.' She raised her eyebrows at me.
'Okay, *okay*. He told me.'

'Well, there you are, then.' Alison looked smug. 'I'm
sure he'll be full of good advice.'

I shook my head at her. 'I'll start with stage one,' I said.
'I'm not agreeing to anything beyond that at this point.'

'Tonight?'

'What d'you mean, tonight?'

'I mean, will you go online and suss some agencies out
tonight?' She tore the page out of the notepad and folded
it in half before holding it out to me. 'Then you can report
back when you come in tomorrow.'

'I might not make it in tomorrow,' I said loftily,
gathering up my coat from the back of the chair. 'I do have
a life, you know.' I looked at the piece of paper, which she

was waggling at me, and eventually snatched it out of her hand and stuffed it into the pocket of my coat.

Alison grinned, unfazed, and with good reason. I hadn't missed a day since she was admitted six weeks earlier for intensive and apparently futile radiation treatment.

'Don't go anywhere,' I said, like I always did, dropping a light kiss on her cheek.

She winked at me, happy in spite of the tiredness that had begun to show in her features.

'I might,' she replied mischievously. 'I do have a life, you know.'